THE PILGRIM'S PROGRESS
Dangers, Toils & Snares

JOHN BUNYAN'S
TIMELESS CHRISTIAN ALLEGORY,
AS TOLD BY

Zachary Bartels

HIGH&
SILVER™

The Pilgrim's Progress: Dangers, Toils, and Snares
Zachary Bartels (based on, and containing some of, the prose of John Bunyan)

Requests for information may be sent via www.gutcheckpress.com

Published in association with KD Enterprises and Cardiff Giant.

This book contains content originally serialized on the podcast "High and Silver Presents: The Pilgrim's Progress" in 2022 and 2023.

ISBN 978-1-7337954-5-6 (pbk)
ISBN 978-1-7337954-6-3 (hrdcvr)

Also available in ebook and audiobook formats.

Publisher's Note: The following is a work of fiction. All characters appearing therein are fictitious. Any resemblance to real private persons, living, dead, or sunk to the bottom of the Slough of Despond, is purely coincidental.

Absolutely no AI was used in the creation of this text.

Scripture quotations are the author's original translation or are taken from the King James Version of the Bible or the ESV® Bible (The Holy Bible, English Standard Version®), © 2001 by Crossway, a publishing ministry of Good News Publishers. Used by permission. All rights reserved.

Cover design ©2024 Gut Check Press. Some poems contained herein were written by Erin Bartels.

Font "The Last Kingdom" © 2021 Jaime Rangel Castro, licensed for commercial use via Creative Fabrica. Font "Jim Nightshade" © 2011 Astigmatic fonts, licensed for commercial use under OFL. Fonts and graphics of collections New Victorian Printshop, Volumes 1, 2, and 3, licensed for commercial use from Walden Font. Font "Dominican" © 2006 Harold Lohner, licensed for commercial use vis FontBros.

Graphics contained herein are either in the public domain or licensed for use via Pond5.com, Shutterstock, or iStockPhoto.com.

For Alex, my Mister Sagacity,
a true friend and brother on the Pilgrim Road.

Halt, Pilgrim!

Before you begin your journey, be aware that this adaptation was initially an **enhanced audio presentation**. To enjoy it in its original format, scan the QR code in the gate below.

John Bunyan

Introduction

"Will This Be the Generation in Which *Pilgrim's Progress* Disappears?"

It was ten years ago when I read that headline. Actually, it was a blog post title (Justin Taylor's page on the Gospel Coalition website), and it turned out to mostly be a promo for a series Crossway was doing. All the same, it got my attention.

I've loved *The Pilgrim's Progress* since before I could actually read it. As a kindergartner, I got to be in not one but *two* productions of the kids' musical adaptation, *The Enchanted Journey* (both at my Baptist church and my Baptist school, although the school, being more Fundamentalist, changed the title to *The Amazing Journey* because it was the early '80s and the Satanic Panic was in full swing).

As corny as it must have been to the adults in the room, the depiction of Faithful being dragged away while calling back to his friend and brother, "Chris, I'll meet you at the Celestial City! Don't give up! I'll be waiting!" left a deep mark in my young soul. This road we're on is headed somewhere worth dying for.

Growing up, I read several versions of this great work: a children's edition, a "modern English" version, the original text. This story helped form how I thought about this Narrow Road we walk as Christians—how I thought about my very life! And then I sort of . . . *forgot about it.* Not entirely, of course; while reading the sermons of C.H. Spurgeon, I always loved his little cameo callbacks to Bunyan's characters. But with college and seminary came so much required reading that it was all I could do to stay on top of my devotional time in the Bible, let alone find time to re-enjoy Bunyan's timeless classic. Over the years, it fell to the bottom bookshelf and out of mind.

But then Justin Taylor's blog grabbed my attention. He told us of how great men like J.I. Packer were lamenting the lack of grounding in Bunyan's masterpiece, which had been a bedrock text for Christians in their discipleship and an ever-present touchpoint in preaching and discussing the faith for centuries.

In 2004, Packer wrote, "For two centuries *Pilgrim's Progress* was the best-read book, after the Bible, in all Christendom, but sadly it is not so today. When I ask my classes of young and youngish evangelicals, as I often do, who has read *Pilgrim's Progress*, not a quarter of the hands go up . . . Certainly, it would be great gain for modern Christians if Bunyan's masterpiece came back into its own in our day. Have you yourself, I wonder, read it yet?"[1]

There is no denying that, by the *aughties*, fewer and fewer were bothering with the Tinker of Bedford's epic tale. It is still the second-best-selling novel of all time (we're coming for you, *Don Quixote!*), but with the emergence of the Christian Fiction industry, there are endless titles to read, all of which seem (on the surface) more readable and more relevant than the dusty prose and awkward poetry of a late Seventeenth Century pastor. In this, I suppose I have been (a very small) part of the problem, in that I've contributed a handful of these "distractions."

And yet, not twenty years ago (as Packer), but 120 years ago, Spurgeon himself was mourning the waning interest in *The Pilgrim's Progress*. In his autobiography, he writes,

"Next to the Bible, the book that I value most is John Bunyan's *Pilgrim's Progress*. I believe I have read it through at least a hundred times. It is a volume of which I never seem to tire. The older I grow, the more I value it. But what is most remarkable is, that in proportion as I prize it, I notice that few people read it. It is sadly neglected; yet I would venture to say that if it

---

[1] Packer, J. I. *The Devoted Life: An Invitation to the Puritan Classics*, ed. Kapic and Gleason. Downers Grove, Ill.: InterVarsity Press, 2004, p. 198.

[2] Spurgeon, C.H. *Autobiography, Volume 2: The Full Harvest*. London: Passmore & Alabaster, 1899, p. 159.

were read in our schools, it would be of greater service to our youth than many of the books which now hold their attention."[2]

So perhaps the problem is that we have to keep rediscovering the good things. Maybe it's cyclical. This idea seems to have been borne out by the recent surge of *Pilgrim's Progress*-related media to hit the scene—much of it after that click-friendly post title, asking if we were witnessing a generation finally losing touch with it entirely. Apparently not.

There have been handsomely repackaged and re-illustrated deluxe versions, video games, comic books, and the spectacular 2019 CGI movie, which pulled in kids and adults (myself very much included) alike. If this is a resurgence or a renaissance, it is one of which I am glad to be a part.

We are surely not in danger of "losing" this classic. And yet, if the pastors of today's churches were to do a similar straw poll to Packer's among our congregations, I am sadly confident we would have similar—if not far worse—results.

"This work has been modified from its original version. It has been formatted to fit your attention span."

If you, like me, find that your haircuts no longer remove the gray from your temples, but reveal even more gray lurking beneath, you may remember those notices at the beginning of DVD and VHS movies, alerting you that, rather than show the film in letterbox (with black horizontal bars at the top and bottom), this presentation uses a technique called "pan and scan" to put the most important piece of each frame on your screen, filling it up from top to bottom. That meant, of course, that you were missing *a quarter* of the original picture, lopped off from the right and left of your squarish tube TV. It was a tradeoff.

Adaptations of large works of fiction face a similar quandary: do you stretch it out or cut it way down? If you've read

Bunyan's original work, you know that some of the stages of Christian's pilgrimage are rather pedantic. A majority of the pages are devoted to lengthy conversations between two or three people walking down a road together, punctuated only here and there with action, intrigue, and suspense. It is natural, then, in trying to instill a love of the work in modern readers, to want to cut some of the "fat. "

In addition, many forms of media, by their very nature, require massive cuts. It take 10-12 hours to read *The Pilgrim's Progress* out loud, and yet a film is usually only two hours in length (or, lately, only an hour and a half, much to my annoyance). In attempting to retell the story for modern eyes and ears, one might wind up "panning-and-scanning" in such a way as to only *keep* about 25% of the material. Even print versions have hacked away much of what makes Bunyan's work *Bunyan's work* in the interest of keeping the reader's attention.

But here's the thing: we live in a complex age, in which smartphones have allegedly devastated our attention spans to goldfish levels, and yet in which people *binge* entire seasons of streaming television shows in one sitting. This paradox became the core of my adaptation. I wanted to take this story (the *whole* story, leaving nothing out) and retell it—in its original setting, but with a more modern novel format, easier to read and harder to put down. And I was going to keep people engaged from beginning to end by releasing each chapter (enhanced with cinematic music and sound effects) to a bingeable podcast feed.

I knew from experience that people love to binge podcasts, usually with no regard for their length, and generally only complain when there is too *little* content available. Furthermore, *The Pilgrim's Progress* is written rather episodically; why not present it as actual episodes? The result was (or, rather, is) *High & Silver Presents: The Pilgrim's Progress.*

The book you have in your hands is sort of a reverse-adaptation of that podcast, back into an incredibly long novel. I know there has been some level of anticipation for its release, and I hope it will surpass your expectations.

"As I slept, I dreamed a dream."

Okay, so "leaving nothing out" is a lofty goal. And I admit, from the outset, I decided to ditch a couple of things—I think for the better, and having more to do with the storytelling convention than the actual content.

First, I slashed Bunyan's "apology" at the beginning. Pages and pages of hacky rhymed couplets, written in defense of allegory as an acceptable means of conveying spiritual truth. It seems monumentally unnecessary in our day, and is probably to blame for a good share of the people who started reading Bunyan on someone's recommendation, only to bail within a few pages.

The other main difference is that I have abandoned the "dream" framework altogether. Bunyan presents the entire story of *The Pilgrim's Progress* as a dream he once had. Or rather, a series of dreams, as there are instances of him waking up, only to go right back to sleep and resume the same dream. There are also *Inception*-esque dreams-within-a-dream. And in *Part Two* (which I am currently adapting as *The Pilgrim's Progress: Cloud of Witnesses*), our narrator bumps into a guy at the beginning of the dream, who fills him in on all the stuff that happened in the regularly scheduled dream (already in progress) *before Bunyan fell asleep!* Once this man has brought Bunyan up to speed, he heads off (to do . . . what? He only exists in Bunyan's dream, so how does he have other pressing stuff to do?) and leaves Bunyan to experience the rest of the story solo.

Yeah, it's weird.

And so, with the benefit of 350 years of allegorical storytelling behind us, I decided it was safe to axe both of those explanatory devices and just tell the story *as* a story.

A Note on the Illustrations

In my study, I have a large collection of antique copies of *The Pilgrim's Progress*. One thing they all seem to have in common is that they contain illustrations—usually impressive etchings, but also plates (printed on thicker, glossy paper and protected by a piece of tissue paper affixed above the art).

In my mind, no copy of this story (in any form) would be complete without some art. I have included in these pages a sampling of 18th-, 19th-, and very early-20th-Century illustrations by a variety of artists (William Blake, Gustave Doré, WJ Linton, Henry Courtney Selous, Frederick Barnard, George Cruikshank, John Tenniel, G. Woolliscroft Rhead, and others).

In most cases, I scanned these out of my own copies and painstakingly cleaned them up. Where no artist was cited, I had to use publication date, common sense, and feasible lifespans to determine that they are all now in the public domain.

Because these illustrations come from the minds of different artists, there is no continuity between the portrayals of these characters and events from image to image. (In fact, there is sometimes no continuity with the original text; e.g., where did Christian get the sword he has on his way *up* Hill Difficulty?) I include these depictions as a tether to the rich and wide-reaching legacy of *The Pilgrim's Progress* in capturing the imaginations and nourishing the souls of readers for centuries.

Because this adaptation does not perfectly comport to Bunyan's telling (and therefore to the illustrations of the original work), some images may be presented apart from the artist's intended subject and context. (i.e., one character may be presented as another). I have also supplemented these illustrations with other art of similar vintage and vibe.

For more *Pilgrim's Progress* illustrations, the audio presentation of this story, and resources for group study, please check back regularly at www.highandsilver.com.

Stay on the Narrow Road,

Rev. Zachary Bartels
October, 2024

Prologue

There's an old saying in the City of Destruction: "It's all about the journey, not the destination."

A certain Mr. Light-Mind was well known for repeating these words almost constantly, as if to justify everything he did by them. Even Christian himself had invoked the axiom here and there, mostly just to fill an empty space in the conversation, but also to keep his mind from drifting toward thoughts of his ultimate destiny.

In the earliest stage of his pilgrimage, the saying had come to mind again, and had immediately exploded into a thousand pieces—so violently that Christian almost thought he could hear it shatter. A pilgrimage *is* the journey, he realized, but it is *all about* the destination. That was why he must always keep to the Narrow Path—even now, as it twisted downward, all the deeper into the Valley of Humiliation.

Part of him wanted to turn back, of course, return home or chart a new, easier route through more pleasant places—enjoying the journey, as it were. But even while the temperature fell with unsettling speed and the distant desperate wails and whimpers seemed to close in all around him, Christian forced his feet to carry him forward toward the Destination.

The Narrow Path grew yet narrower and the ground beneath him rockier and more uneven. His new armor fit him well, but the leather doublet and leggings holding it to his body were still stiff and unyielding, digging into his joints. Every step seemed to bring a knife's dull blade again and again along the same raw lines in his flesh.

Christian was thinking of taking a breather, to sit and loosen his armor for a moment, when he saw an enormous, foul creature coming up from the misty distance to meet him. Fear banished all other thoughts and concerns from his mind and fixed his feet in place beneath him, even while it threatened to take his legs.

Turn back, he thought. *Run.* But he had no armor for his back. Only a breastplate to protect his organs from a frontal assault. Even if self-preservation were his only goal, retreat would be foolish here. And so he stood, fixed in place.

"Give me courage and strength to stand in the evil day," Christian said, aloud, to the King of this land.

With impressive speed for a creature its size, the beast covered the ground between them and drew up before him, hideous and horrifying. His yellow eyes bored into Christian's. He was clothed with scales, which clinked against each other like the sound of steel chains with each thick, noxious breath that chugged slowly in and out—ponderous like a steam turbine. Stretched behind and above him, blotting out the sky beyond, his black leathery wings spanned at least thirty feet. From his lion's mouth belched fire and smoke.

The yellow eyes traced Christian's form from head to foot and back again. The creature scoffed.

"You will now tell me," he said, "who you are, where you come from, and where you are going."

Christian looked down to his right hand, which a moment ago had been trembling, and placed it firmly upon the hilt of his sword. "I am Christian," he answered. "I come from the City of Destruction, the place of all evil. I am going to the City of Zion." He straightened to his full height and looked up directly into the monster's eyes. "And who are you?"

"I am Apollyon, the god and prince of your native land. Your prince who now finds you fleeing like a rat to the realm of another. If I did not think you might still be of some use to me, I would cut you to pieces where you stand."

"You are correct that I was born into your dominion," Christian said, "but your service was hard and no man could live on your wages. For the wages of sin is death. And so I've followed the footsteps of so many before me and abandoned your cursed kingdom ."

Apollyon laughed. "Easy enough to say. But there is no prince alive who would suffer his subjects defecting to another's dominion without severe consequences. But to show you that I am a kind and benevolent ruler, and because you have struggled to live on your wages, I promise this: come back with me and whatever our country can afford to pay you, I will pay it."

"It's too late. And far too little. I've already given myself fully to another King—the King of Princes."

Apollyon's lips curled back for a moment, revealing razor fangs glistening with viscous saliva. "Not to worry," he said, the words dripping with false comfort. "It is very common for pilgrims like yourself, who have sworn their allegiance to this 'king,' to lose heart or lose interest after a time and return again to me. If you do this now, all will be well."

"What you're describing is a traitor," Christian said. "And traitors are rightly hanged."

"You had no problem betraying your allegiance to me."

"I didn't know any better when I served you," Christian said. "I do now. Besides, the Prince under whose banner I now stand is the only One able to absolve and pardon all of my crimes—including those I committed under your kingship. And frankly, I like his service, his wages, his servants, his company, and his country better than yours. Move aside; I am following after him now."

The creature folded his wings up behind him and hunched in closer, looking smaller now. He pulled his tarrish lips back into a thin smile that concealed his fangs and said "Let's be logical. Consider what lies ahead—the trials and dangers and snares—and how you will face them all feeling far less bold and courageous than you feel even now, standing before me. Consider that most of this king's servants come to a brutal and painful end by my hand. And consider that I have come here, into his domain, in person, to bring you back home—something I have done for countless confused subjects, breaking them free of his grip by brute force or clever schemes. And so I will deliver you as well. Would your 'king of princes' do that for you? I think not."

Christian felt a surge of righteous anger, filling him up. "You're wasting your foul breath. And you're showing yourself to be a liar. You know that my Prince did go into your domain to save us. And now, while he calls us to come out of your damned land, he has a purpose in that as well: to test our love and prove whether we will be loyal to him to the end.

"And as for the shameful and painful deaths that so many pilgrims have suffered before me, they have cause to rejoice, knowing that they will be received into sudden and eternal glory. Pilgrims do not expect deliverance now, but are content to wait for future reward, when our King will ride down on your country on a white horse of war with all his holy angels, and us behind him."

Apollyon's pale talons clenched, and a stream of purple-gray smoke chugged up from his nose. "Do you really think you will escape his wrath on that day? You've already failed many times since you took to walking this road. My spies have been watching you closely and keeping detailed records of your many offenses."

"Indeed, I have fallen. Probably more than you know. But I have obtained pardon for each and every sin because my king is the King of Mercy."

The beast's massive wings shot open again with a concussive *whu-whump* that very nearly knocked Christian to the ground.

"I am an enemy to this Prince! I hate his person, his laws, and his people! And I am more than enough to keep you from going further along the Way. Consider well what you do next, pilgrim."

"Careful," Christian warned. "We are on the King's Highway—the way of holiness. You are the one who should watch his step."

Apollyon stretched his bear-like foot out to his left, straddling the entire breadth of the path. "I am void of fear," he growled, "and of further patience. Prepare to die, for I swear by my own fiery throne that I will spill your soul!"

And with that, he lit a short javelin with a blue flame from out of his mouth and hurled it at Christian, who brought up his shield just in time to glance the projectile off into the woods beyond.

Christian drew his sword and pounded his fist against his breastplate. "I will withstand you!" he cried out.

A wave of burning darts lit up the air around them. Christian dove, rolled, and came up to a tight crouch behind his shield. He almost cried out in pain, but then swallowed it back down. His foot had been pierced by a dart through a seam in his armor. He winced as he pulled it out and tossed it aside. Allowing himself a quick glance to survey the damage, he saw that the heat from the dart had cauterized the wound; no blood leaked from the blackened hole, although a whisp of steam was curling up from it.

Shaking off the paralysis of fear and the narcotic effect of the growing smoke, Christian raised his sword once again and lowered the shield to an inch beneath his eyes. Instantly, a dart struck his hand, knocking the sword from it and another connected with his helmet, rocking his senses and throwing him down to his back.

He looked up at the dull sky spinning slowly above him for just a moment before his field of vision was filled with the demonic creature's hulking form.

"You fall easy," Apollyon said, "like your pathetic Prince before you. Give him my regards." From behind his blackened wings, he drew a long and jagged sword, which he brought down onto Christian's prone body with all of his hellish might.

Destruction

Before he walked the Narrow Way as a pilgrim, Christian lived in the City of Destruction with his wife Christiana and their four boys. There, he often went by his legal name, Graceless. And there he was happy enough; or at least he told himself he was, plying his trade (which is of no real consequence to our story) and filling his days and his thoughts with the same sorts of things that filled his neighbors' days and thoughts.

That is, until he opened the Book and began to read. Then everything changed.

The Book's initial effect was to sort of mute everything in Christian's world. The taste of food, the warmth of the sun on his face, the satisfaction of earning, saving, and spending money—they all lost their luster. Not that food was less flavorful or colors less bright; rather, it was as if the very palettes these things had to explore now seemed so small and limited that they made Christian sad.

He could see the most beautiful sunset imaginable and the very fact that it was the most beautiful one imaginable would only serve to amplify his malaise. The momentary satisfactions that had previously propelled him through the stretches of tedious hours and days could no longer produce enough momentum.

After that, an even more disquieting realization: there was growing upon Christian's back a large and heavy burden. When Christiana first mentioned his hunched posture, Christian assumed he'd just slept on it poorly the night before, and said as much. But the weight and the presence grew each day, until one morning he looked into their glass and saw the burden, fastened to his back by cords which he was unable to cut, no matter how he tried. Squirming out from the burden's grasp, forcing it from his person, trying to burn through the ropes—nothing would release its grip on him.

It was clear that his wife and children could not see it and were beginning to think he was mad to begin with, but it was as real to him as his own hands in front of his face or the roof over his head. What's more, the cords holding the burden to his torso kept him from changing his garments and, before long, he appeared more like a beggar—dressed in rags, smelling badly, and bent toward the ground—than the pillar of his community he had once been.

No longer filled with the minutiae, worries, and niceties of everyday life, Christian's mind continually resounded with the same question over and over again: *What shall I do? What shall I do? What shall I do?*

To the degree that he was able, he kept all this from his wife and children as long as possible, until one day as they sat at dinner, she asked him pointedly, "What is the matter with you these last few months? Are you angry with us? Are you dying? What?"

"Oh my dear Christiana" Christian said, "my sweet boys ... I'm sorry I've been so distracted and dejected for so long. I'm afraid I am . . . undone."

"What do you mean, 'undone?'" Christiana asked, her frustration showing through the thin veneer of concern.

"It's this burden on my back, to be sure. But more than that, I have it on the highest of authorities that this city of ours will be destroyed by burning sulfur raining down from the heavens. And when that happens, we will, all of us, die."

"Ah, yes. I see. So now we've added to the burden talk *fire* . . . from heaven. Lovely."

"Haven't you ever found it odd that our hometown is called 'The City of Destruction'?"

Christiana bit down a smile. "We learned the story behind that as children. Remember? I can't recall exactly what it was, but I know it's not as on-the-nose as you seem to think. Besides, our city has been here for ages upon ages and it's always been called Destruction—and yet it has never been burned up by flames from the sky."

"That is no guarantee that it won't happen. And soon."

"I suppose not." Christiana sat back in her chair, folding her napkin meticulously. "Dear, would you mind telling me who exactly enlightened you with this information?"

"It is written in my Book."

Christiana's face fell. "And we're back to the book." She put a hand over his. "You're sick, my dear. You need rest. You need help. Should I call the doctor? I think some frenzy distemper has gotten into your head and you're not seeing things clearly."

"No," he said. "I wasn't seeing clearly before! As you're not seeing now. My eyes are open!"

"Then perhaps you should shut them for a while. Please?

"You're clearly not hungry; you haven't touched your food.

Get some sleep. You'll feel better in the morning. You'll see."

Christian opened his mouth to argue, but saw that his boys were all gaping at him, the youngest on the edge of tears. And so he agreed to go to bed.

Sleep eluded him, though. He tossed and turned. He sighed. He wept. More than once he was sure that his wife was also awake, but when he whispered her name, she would feign snoring to keep from being drawn into yet another conversation about the invisible burden, the pending destruction, and the Book that started all this unpleasantness.

As dawn drew near, Christian finally fell into a fitful sleep and dreamed of two ill-favored ones, skulking in the shadows of his house, watching the meal the family had shared that night as it unfolded, and whispering to one another.

"We're going to lose him," one of them said. "He's good as gone."

"Don't even say it," the other scolded. "He'll stay. We've got his wife, and so we have his children. What man would push forward on a pilgrimage without his family?"

The taller one laughed as he stepped from one shadow into another, unseen by those sitting around the table. "What he doesn't know is that by staying, he guarantees they will all burn together. The only hope they have is for him to blaze a trail for them."

"But look at him. He wouldn't know where to go even if he wanted to."

"And it's up to us to keep it that way." The figure stepped from the shadows, up beyond Christiana, and ran his fingers gently through her hair.

Christian woke with a start to find the sun already filling

the room and his wife bringing him a board of bread, cheese, and cornmeal, and a cup of tea.

"Thank you, darling. That's kind of you."

"You're welcome." She was chipper. "How did you sleep?"

"Horribly."

"Oh. And how do you feel?"

"Worse."

"Well . . . are you hungry?"

He looked at the food before him and answered, "No, not much."

"Fine," she said, yanking the board back from him and carrying it off. At the door to their bedchamber she paused without looking back and said, "We've indulged this long enough, Christian. Too long. For my sake . . . for your children's sake . . . it's time to get over it. Pull yourself together and get on with your life. I think you should start by throwing that book away." She looked back at him. "And I think you know it." She was gone before Christian could answer.

It was several more hours before he arose. Having again slept in his clothes, he stretched as high as he could, given the burden on his back, and felt his body complain. Christian was still a rather young man, but he felt as if he'd aged a decade or more in the past few months.

As he came out into the parlor, he found his four sons, all dressed in their Sunday best, sitting in a row on the floor, at their mother's feet. In an armchair next to her was the Rev. Mr. Smoothman, the parson of their local church.

"Oh, I'm sorry," Christian said. "I didn't realize we had company."

"Please, sit," the minister said, gesturing at the most uncomfortable chair Christian owned.

"What is this?"

"I've invited the parson here," Christiana said, "to try and relieve your troubled mind. He thinks he can help you understand your book far better than you presently do and lay your mind to rest at the same time."

Christian tried to sit, but the chair was too shallow and his burden had become too large. He slipped off the edge, stood again, and folded his arms. "I doubt that is true, but if you can relieve me of my burden, I would be eternally grateful."

"We shall certainly try," Mr. Smoothman said. "First of all, look at your children, sir. Think about the effect your sulking and carrying on is having on them. Boys, tell your father how sad he is making you."

Matthew, his oldest, piped up, "Bartholomew says his father thinks you're crazy as a loon. Muttering and walking around like this—" He stood and did a broad impression of Christian bent low under the weight of his burden. "Oh no, oh no, we're all gonna die. We're all gonna die." he mumbled.

Samuel laughed uproariously. "He's hit the nail on the head!" he shouted.

Christiana fought down a spiteful smile and chided the boys, "Children, the reverend is here. Behave yourselves."

Mr. Smoothman shifted in the armchair, as if to establish a new angle to come at things. "Tell me this: where in that book does it say that *our city* will be destroyed?"

Christian pulled the volume from his pocket and opened to a marked page. "For one, this passage here: 'For when the people are saying *peace and safety*, sudden destruction will come upon them.'"

"Is that what's got you all twisted up?" The minister laughed. "That's— *No*, don't take that at face value. That's not for us; it was written many, many centuries ago to other people in another land. Sure, we can learn from it, but don't let it frighten you. Besides, I know that book very well and there are many, far more uplifting passages that you could choose to focus on. Passages that will lift your spirits and make you a joy to be around."

"But what good are these if destruction is truly coming?"

The parson bit his lip for a few seconds, studying Christian.

He then turned to Christiana and asked, "Would you mind if I spoke with your husband privately, man to man?"

She threw up her hands. "Please. Lord knows I've had no luck with him."

"Come," Mr. Smoothman said, standing and beckoning. "Walk with me."

Christian followed him out the front door and about ten paces toward the road, where the minister's driver sat waiting on the board of his carriage.

"Listen, Graceless, I told your wife I'd do my best to get through to you," the minister said. "But I didn't think for a minute that I actually would. You know why? When someone gets as twisted up as you . . . when they become fanatical and lose themselves in that book and those confounded ideas, there's no coming back from it. You're lost, my friend. I will offer up a prayer for you now and again, but I doubt even the Almighty can bring you back to the land of the sane and the sensible."

"So you don't have any hope to offer me." Christian said.

The parson's face softened a bit. "I don't know. Maybe try to clear your head. Go for a nice long walk; see if things don't come back into focus for you." He suddenly leaned in and pushed a finger up to Christian's nose. "But I'll tell you this: it's your own concern how you comport yourself in your house with your own wife and children, but if I find you spreading your deep disquiet amongst my flock, I will denounce you from the pulpit as an heretic!"

He dropped his hand to the man's shoulder, which he gave a half-hearted squeeze before climbing into his carriage.

"There's no judgment coming," he called out the window as the coach pulled away.

Christian wandered out into some nearby fields and walked up and down the rows of barley, reading and praying in turn—technically following the parson's advice, but, truth be told, he had spent most of his afternoons this way since first opening the Book and learning the awful truth of coming judgment.

Over the next few hours, he found himself straying further from his home than usual, drawn to the far edge of their city.

And as he walked, the question that had been continually playing in his mind, "What shall I do?" became instead, "What must I do to be saved?"

And rather than spinning in his mind only, it began to spill out of his mouth.

He walked faster and yet faster, and said louder and louder, "What must I do to be saved? What must I do to be *saved?!*" until he came to the end of the field and stopped short. Stretched out before him was unknown land. Christian was in a quandary as to which way to go. At this point, he had only a general sense of how to head back toward his house. But he knew he couldn't go back there. At least, not now.

"Excuse me, sir."

Christian jumped and spun to see a man approaching him from behind. He was thin and wiry, with a rosy complexion, wearing a simple coat and breeches and no wig.

"I couldn't help but overhear you," the man said. "Why on earth are you shouting out into the wilderness?"

Christian held up his book and said, "Feel free to call me crazy, good stranger—everyone else has—but I know from the pages of this Book that I am condemned to die and after, to be judged. I cry out because I am not willing to do the former and not able to do the latter."

"I see," the man said, nodding. "My name is Evangelist, by the way." He reached out his hand and Christian gripped it by way of greeting.

"Christian."

"That's a good name. Do you mind if I ask you something? Why are you not willing to die, since you are so obviously overwhelmed by grief, anguish, and discontent, in addition to the natural evils that fill this world? Does it have something to do with that?" He poked his finger into the burden on Christian's back.

"It—it does. I fear that this burden will sink me far lower than the grave and drag me down into hell itself. And that is why you heard me crying out over and over again, *What must I do to be saved?* And look, I don't mean to be rude, good stranger, but if you don't have the answer to my question then I should probably—"

"But if this is all true" Evangelist said, "and death and judgment hang over your head, why are you just standing there?"

"Because I don't know what to do! Have you heard anything I've said? I've been asking—"

Evangelist plucked the book from his hand, quickly searched out a particular page and held it up to him, pointing at a particular line. "What it does it say there, good Christian?"

"'Fly from the wrath to come.' Yes, I've read that before, but fly. . . *where?*"

Evangelist pointed out beyond an expansive field and said, "Do you see the Wicket Gate, way off by the horizon?"

Christian squinted. "No. I see no gate."

"Hm. Do you see the shining light?"

"I . . . think so?"

"Good," Evangelist said. "Keep that light in your eye and head directly toward it. Don't veer to the left or the right. Go straight to the light. Understand?"

"Then what?"

"Well, that will bring you right up to the gate. When you get there, knock and you will be given instructions. This is all in answer to your question, *What must I do to be saved?*"

Christian looked back at him, slack-jawed. "Just like that?"

"Well, yes. If you persevere. But first, you have to leave."

"What—now?"

"Go!" Evangelist gave him a shove in the right direction and Christian began to run at a full sprint, surprised at how quickly he could move even with the heavy burden on his back. As he went, he began to hear the voices of his neighbors and his wife and his children, all echoing in his ears, calling him back, pleading with him not to go toward the light and the gate and whatever lay beyond. So he put his fingers in his ears and ran all the faster toward the middle of the plain, not looking back even once, and shouting, "Life! Life! Everlasting life!"

Obstinate & Pliable

Obstinate had been searching for nearly twenty minutes, with increasing nettlement, when he finally located his neighbor, Pliable, standing beyond the farthest edge of his field, his face turned out to the distance. He was leaning all his weight on a walking stick, which had been slowly sinking into the ground, as if to mark the duration of his idleness, as he stood, staring out—at nothing in particular, as far as Obstinate could tell.

"There you are," Obstinate barked, looking down with no little annoyance at his own shoes, which were also beginning to sink into the wet and heavy soil. "Is there some reason you've made yourself so impossible to find? I've been searching for more than an hour."

"Oh?" Pliable glanced back at him for only a moment before his gaze returned to the horizon. "So sorry. But you've found me now."

"You seem disinterested," Obstinate spat. "I suppose you don't really want your plow back after all."

Pliable perked up and swiveled around the stick, to face his friend. "You brought my plow?"

"Yes, it's in my waistcoat pocket."

Pliable laughed. "You're so funny, Obstinate." An awkward beat passed. "But you did bring it?"

"Actually," Obstinate said, "I came to let you know that I'll need it a bit longer."

"How much longer?"

"Indefinitely."

Pliable shifted his weight, still leaning heavily on the staff. "I don't know about that . . . "

"You said yourself that you don't need it."

"I . . . don't think I did say that."

Obstinate took a step toward his neighbor, face hard and unflinching. "Oh, Pliable. This is why so few of us enjoy your company. You're always reversing course. You said you were looking to buy a new one—one of those nice Dutch plows with a lighter blade. What do you need two plows for? You have no sons. No wife even. Will you stand astride them both at the same time?"

Pliable bit his lip in thought. "You do bring up a good point. I supposed it's about time I upgraded. It's just that . . . "

"What?"

"Well, it will take some time to acquire another one. Could I maybe borrow mine back? Just for a week or so?"

"I'm afraid that won't be possible. I don't have it at the moment."

"You— What?"

Obstinate sighed. "This is what's happening: *I do not have your plow*. I've rented it out to Mr. Lechery and it's not due back until early next week." He locked eyes with Pliable until the latter let his gaze drop to the ground.

"Is there a problem?" Obstinate pressed.

"Well, it seems a bit irregular for you to—"

"Isn't it right and fair," Obstinate demanded, "when a man is holding property, for him to do with it as he pleases? Whether to use it, leave it idle, or rent it out?"

"Well, yes, but . . . "

"Did you not actually intend to lend it to me? Or were there some strings attached to the deal, of which I was not aware?"

"No, of course not. I'm sorry."

"Apology accepted." Obstinate smiled. "I'll tell you what: come Monday next, I'll have the plow back and you may certainly use it. For the whole week."

"Oh, good. Thank you."

"No problem at all. Now, Mr. Lechery is paying two guilders per week. Three if I find signs of wear. Being an honest man, I'm sure you'd want to pay the going rate."

"Now, Neighbor Obstinate, that hardly seems fair."

"For two men to pay the same rate seems unfair to you?"

Pliable opened his mouth to answer, but came up empty.

"Look," Obstinate said, "you know I make it a rule to remain inflexible in matters of business. But since you and I are friends—"

"Friends since childhood," Pliable interjected.

"Well, don't make a big flap about it. I already admitted we're friends and that should count for something. Agreed?"

"Yes. Agreed. And thank you."

"Alright, then. Because we're friends—and only because we're friends—you may use the plow for one week at the cost of just one guilder. That's half off!"

"That seems a good price."

"Alright, then. And I'll need that up front. By tomorrow."

Pliable nodded happily. "You'll have it! And my thanks!"

"Don't mention it." He looked down at the muck creeping up around his feet. "I ought to have made you throw in some black for my shoes, dragging me all the way out to the edge of the earth to find you. By the way, what are you even doing here, staring out at that plain? Doesn't your field end a few furlongs back?"

"I was following a man."

"'Following a man?' Through your own field?"

"Yes. The oddest thing. It was that man, Christian. Do you know him? He lives closer to town. He was walking through my field, talking to himself, louder and louder. He stopped right where you and I are talking now and was shouting into the air."

"Really? Is he all right?"

"I couldn't say. He walked through my field and beyond, and met up with a stranger whom I've rarely seen before. The two of them spoke briefly, and then Christian began running off in that direction, hands over his ears, bellowing something like, *Life, life, life!* at the top of his lungs.

"Then he disappeared into the distance. I found it terribly fascinating. He had the sense of a man leaving on a great adventure. I had half a mind to go with him. In fact, I think I was building up the courage to try and catch up to him when you happened by. Just fascinating."

Obstinate crossed his arms over his chest. "'Fascinating?' Really?"

"Oh, very much so. Truth be told, I've never known what lies off in that direction. Perhaps we should both join him. Might be a welcome change of pace."

"Go *with* him? Tush! I know what he'll find traveling that way: trouble, hardship, and possibly death."

"You're right, of course," Pliable said. "A very foolish idea."

"We have to bring him back."

"Unquestionably. I fear for his life."

Obstinate rebuttoned his coat and said, "It's settled then. Let's go do our good deed for the day, Neighbor Pliable. Rescue this lamb from the pit as it were."

"Yes, let's."

"By the by, do you really need that walking stick?"

Pliable wavered. "I think I do. My hip has been tightening up on me of late."

"I'll tell you what—I'll use it on the way out and you can have it for the way back. Sound fair?"

"Oh, more than fair," Pliable said, handing it over. And the two of them began walking at a steady clip toward the middle of the plain.

Despond

Christian's initial burst of energy burned out quickly, as the light in the distance seemed to grow no closer during a full ten minutes of running at full speed. The straps on his burden were chafing and rubbing against his skin and a stitch in his side slowed him to a walk. Bent both crooked to the side and downward under the weight of the burden on his back, he pressed on in the same direction, but with a fraction of his initial zeal.

After another half hour of hobbling, he entered a clearing and heard the distant voices of two men behind him, calling out. At first, he thought it might be his ears playing tricks on him, but before long it became clear: they were shouting his name.

"Ho, Christian!"

"Christian, hold back for a moment!"

This idea struck Christian just fine and so he found a place to sit on a soft, moss-covered fallen tree. A moment later, the two men came clambering out of the woods.

"There you are," one of them said, stopping to kick his shoes against the walking stick he carried, knocking free a few clumps of dirt. "Had I known how much of this day I'd spend chasing my neighbors through uncharted lands, I'd never have left home this morning."

"Obstinate! And Pliable!" The sight of these men awakened

Christian to the stark sense of loneliness, which had been building since he left Evangelist's side. Or perhaps, he realized, long
before that. "I'm certainly glad to see you both. But what on
earth brings you out this way?"

"We're here to persuade you to come back with us," Pliable
said. "Don't you know you're headed for trouble, hardship,
and, uh, possibly death and destruction?"

"I think you're a bit confused." Christian laughed. "Destruction is what I'm leaving behind."

Obstinate mopped sweat from his neck with a handkerchief. "What you're leaving behind is your friends, your family,
and all the comforts of your life. Come, now. Enough silliness.
Let's go back."

"Back where? To the city of our birth? The City of Destruction? Mark my words, friends: wherever we go, we will one day
die. But if we die there, we will sink lower than the grave, into
a place that burns with fire and brimstone, and I mean to avoid
it. Be content, good neighbors, and go along with me."

Obstinate pulled out his watch and glanced impatiently at
the time. "I'm afraid the two of us are rather too grownup to
spend our days talking to ourselves, frolicking through fields,
and reading books full of fairytales with strange vagabonds.
We have lives, Christian. I have a wife and children just as you
do. And Pliable here is perhaps, what, the fifth most eligible
bachelor in our city."

"If not the fourth," Pliable said.

"Mmmm, I think the fifth."

"Fair enough."

"At any rate, he too has a house and fields and soon he'll
have a brand new Dutch plow with which to rotate his crops—
crops, which (I might add) have yielded more and more each
year for the better part of a decade. Why would we even consider leaving all that behind to follow you to who-knows-
where, all the while risking life and limb?"

"I'll tell you why," Christian said. "Because all that you

forsake is not even worthy to be compared with the smallest fraction of what I'll enjoy where I am headed. And if you go with me—and if you endure—you can fare as well as I do. Where I'm going, there is enough to spare! Come; you'll see!"

"You're being more than a little vague," Obstinate said. "What exactly are these things you expect to find, which are worth leaving everything behind?"

Christian absent-mindedly thumbed the pages of his book and said, "An inheritance, incorruptible, undefiled, that can never fade away. Pliable, your crops may be multiplying now, but next season, a drought or blight may bring them to nothing!

"The inheritance I am after is safe and  secure, laid up in heaven. And it will be bestowed at the appointed time on everyone who diligently seeks it." He extended the book toward his neighbors. "Have a look for yourselves."

"Tush," Obstinate spat. "Away with your book! Will you go back with us or not?"

"No. I've laid my hand to the plow, and I cannot so much as look back."

Obstinate slapped a mosquito, flattening it against his forearm. "Come then, Pliable. Let's head back. We tried, didn't we?

"What about you, Pliable?" Christian asked. "Will you join me on the Pilgrim Road?"

"Of course he won't join you. He has a life to live back in

our fair town." Obstinate looked from Christian to Pliable, shaking his head sullenly. "It seems that our friend Christian has joined the company of crazy-headed coxcombs. And you know what they say about crazy-headed coxcombs."

"Um, no," Pliable muttered. "What do they say?"

"When they've taken a fancy to a fool's errand, they become so wise in their own eyes that seven level-headed men couldn't show them the error of their ways."

"Don't mock him," Pliable said. "If even half of what good Christian says is true, what he's seeking after is far better than what you and I combined can hope to acquire in a lifetime. I'm inclined to go with him."

"What, more fools still? Listen to me, Pliable. Have I ever led you astray?"

"I mean . . ."

"You must be joking. *This* is the thanks I get for looking after your interests since we were children? Do you have any idea how many times I've saved you from being taken for a fool—looked out for you? I know what is best for you. Come back with me! Who knows where this brain-sick fellow will lead you? Be the wiser man!"

Christian put a hand on Pliable's shoulder. "Don't let him make this decision for you. For once in your life, set your own course. You can come with me. Everything I've promised is waiting for us and many more glories besides. If you won't take my word for it, read it here in my Book. It's all confirmed by the blood of Him who wrote it!"

Obstinate scoffed. "Blood? You have got to be kidding me."

Pliable's face twisted in painful, paralyzed indecision for what seemed like a full minute. Then he firmly set his face toward Obstinate and declared, "I intend to go along with this good man and to cast my lot in with him." Turning back toward Christian, he asked, "But tell me, do you know the way to this incredible place?"

"I do. The man I met at the edge of your field, Evangelist—

he told me to make haste to the Wicket Gate up ahead and there we will receive further instructions about the Way."

Pliable nodded, satisfied. "Well then, let's be on our way, Christian. Obstinate, you can keep the plow."

"I was going to keep it either way," he murmured, turning back and retracing his steps the way he'd come.

"But if you're going back . . . "

Obstinate stopped in his tracks. "Well, look who's found his nerve." He laughed derisively and tossed the walking stick toward the two travelers. It rolled along the ground and came to rest against Pliable's foot.

"Enjoy hitching your wagon to this fantastical fool," Obstinate called out. He then stomped off, muttering, "Fools leading fools into more and more foolishness."

When he'd disappeared again into the woods, Pliable reached out his hand and helped Christian up from the tree trunk.

"Thank you, Pliable. I don't mind telling you, I'm very glad you were persuaded to come with me. I do wish Obstinate had as well. And I'm sure he would not have rejected the idea so lightly if he'd felt even a fraction of what I've experienced: the powers and terrors of what remains unseen."

"Persuaded?" Pliable laughed. "I've never seen him persuaded to do anything. But there are two of us travelling now. And I am well-persuaded, and eager to learn about what lies ahead. Tell me more of what we'll enjoy where we're going." They began to walk together toward the distant light.

"It's easier to think of such things in my mind than to actually describe them. But, since you're curious, I will read to you from my book as we walk."

"And you're sure these words are true?"

"Without a doubt. They were written by Him who cannot lie."

"Well, then, tell me what waits for us!"

"There is an endless kingdom to be inhabited. And everlasting life to be enjoyed there."

"Well said, well said . . . And what else?"

"Crowns of glory will be given to us. And garments that will make us shine like the sun in the very firmament of heaven!"

"Nice, nice. And what else?"

"There will be no more crying or sorrow or pain. For the King of that land will wipe away every tear from our eyes."

"I love it. And what company shall we have there?"

"We'll be in the company of cherubim and seraphim—creatures that will dazzle your eyes and perplex your mind. We will also meet with thousands and tens of thousands who have gone before us, none of whom will hurt you or lie or mock you or take advantage of you, Pliable. Rather, they are all loving and holy, walking in the sight of God and standing in His presence forever. There will be elders with their golden crowns, holy virgins with golden harps, and men who were in this life cut to pieces, burned with flames, eaten alive by vicious beasts, or drowned in the sea for the love of their Lord and his Kingdom—there alive and well and clothed with immortality!"

Pliable grinned. "Just hearing about this is enough to ravish my heart. But how can we be partakers of these things? We're just ordinary men."

"The Governor of that country has decreed that these things be freely bestowed on all who are truly willing to have them."

"Amazing! Why are we inching along like this with all of that waiting for us? Let's pick up the pace!"

"I'm afraid I can't walk as fast as I'd like, because of this burden on my back. But I'll do my best to match you stride for stride. Come, Pliable, let us make some progress."

The two of them made good time for more than an hour. Pliable asked the occasional question, but due to his heavy burden,

Christian was short of breath and only able to give him the briefest of answers.

Finally, Christian stopped for a moment of rest. Doubled over, hands on his knees, he noticed that the ground was growing even wetter and his feet were sinking into it more with each step. What's more, the trees were closing in above them, which, with the growing clouds, seemed to turn mid-afternoon almost to dusk.

Pliable noticed the change as well. "My head is beginning to swim," he said. "I do not like this place, Christian."

"Nor do I. But I see no other option but to push ahead." He stood straight and resumed his former pace. "Are you coming?"

Pliable shrunk back. "I . . . don't know. This does not look like what you promised. At all."

"It's *beyond* this. Have you never taken a trip before? How often must one pass through a bad place to arrive at a good one? Come on!" He grabbed his companion by the wrist, took two steps forward, and suddenly found himself dropping into a miry swamp. His feet hit the muck at the bottom, which had both a slimy give and a suction take, pulling Christian down until he was up to his chest in mud and filth.

"You fool!" Pliable yelled, behind him. "You've pulled me into this slough! Oh, I should have listened to Obstinate. I don't think he ever did steer me wrong; you *are* a crazy-headed coxcomb. Oh, I don't feel good. I feel . . . dizzy."

Christian wasn't even listening. He'd noticed that what little daylight had endured was all but gone, although it couldn't have been later than three in the afternoon. Unable to see much of anything, it wasn't until he felt the surface of the swamp touch his chin that he realized the gravity of his situation. If he were completely sucked under, Christian could not see any way to recover and continue on with his pilgrimage. His burden would indeed sink him down lower than the grave.

An overwhelming sense of dread gripped him, mixing in with the dizziness and nausea. To perish here was perhaps worse than dying in the City of Destruction. At least there he would be together with his family and friends.

Time passed, but how much, he had no idea. The memory of falling into the swamp was as fresh as if it had happened a moment ago; and yet, to remember a time before this place was like remembering his childhood or recalling another place and time he'd only read about and never experienced. The stink of the place—rotting organic matter and the sulfurous stench of rotten eggs—so permeated everything that Christian couldn't believe the smell hadn't warned him off before he fell in.

All at once, he became aware of two things: first, that he had been unconsciously—and very tenuously—shuffling forward the entire time he'd been in the slough. And secondly, that the ground beneath his feet had less give here, where he stood, than it did near the edge of the swamp. He was able to go up on his toes and gain a few more inches, making it easier to breathe. This flicker of hope was immediately snuffed out by a third realization. Even if the ground beneath him were bedrock, his burden was now waterlogged with the filthy muck, heavier than it had been by a factor of three or four. Unless he could somehow release the burden from his person, he would not be able to climb out by his own strength.

"Christian!" Pliable called out, from a distance behind him. "Where are you now?"

"I don't know. Truly, I am so lost."

"I'm near the edge," Pliable said. "I think I can pull myself out. Can you make your way to me?"

"No. My burden is pulling me down. I can't go forward and certainly can't go back."

"I'm out! Christian, I'm out! Follow the sound of my voice. You can do it!"

"I'm stuck here, Pliable. I can't move. Besides, you are on the wrong side of the slough."

"The wrong side—? Are you really still entertaining these foolish ideas? Life everlasting and virgins with harps and all the rest? You've almost gotten us killed! Is this the happiness you've been going on about? This is the ecstatic journey's end— you sucked to the bottom of a swamp? A curse on you and your nonsense!"

"Pliable," Christian gasped. "Come back. Come—"Putrid swamp water began to fill his mouth.

Bouncing along the surface of the slough, he heard Pliable ranting as he made his way back toward the City of Destruction. "What a terrible day. Lost my plow and now my favorite walking stick. And of course these clothes are ruined. 'Garments that shine like the sun.' More like garments that stink like the dung." He repeated the last words, laughing contentedly at his own cleverness, before the distance swallowed up the sound of his voice.

Christian was now almost completely beneath the muck. Pulled backward and downward by the heavy burden, only his eyes, nose, and mouth remained above. He shuffled forward a few more steps toward the far side of the swamp, inches closer to the Wicket Gate, but even the thought of arriving there did nothing to lift his spirits. Everything seemed meaningless in this place. Hopeless! And not as though the presence of this filth was blotting out hope and the meaning of life. Rather, it was as if the muck was revealing a deeper truth that Christian had known all along. *All is vanity. Useless. Pointless. Nothing.*

Something slithered against Christian's left ankle, jarring

him from his stupor. He could feel scales sliding past him, then circling around and simultaneously rubbing against his right leg, at the knee, moving in the opposite direction. He sputtered frantically, trying to steal a breath but again tasting the filth and muck as it filled his mouth and slipped down his throat. He spit it out just as the creature beneath the surface began to tighten around him.

"Sir, take my hand!"

Desperately rolling his eyes in their sockets, Christian could barely make out the form of a man to his right, reaching toward him with an outstretched arm. Then suddenly a shaft of light broke through the clouds and trees and Christian could see him clearly. With every ounce of effort at his disposal he brought his right hand up slowly through the thick, mucousy muck to the surface of the swamp and out into the cool air.

The man gripped him tightly at the forearm, and despite the sliminess of the gunk, was able to pull him entirely free from the swamp's grip and the reach of the creature below. As he rolled onto his back, gasping for air, the light and warmth of the afternoon began to return. Christian ran his filthy hands through his filthier hair and, with much effort, sat up. It was then that he realized he'd been dragged out on the far side of the swamp—the side nearest the Wicket Gate.

"Thank you so much," Christian managed to say. "I am in your debt, Mister—?"

"My name is Help. And you're certainly welcome. But I

have to ask: what were you thinking going for a swim in the Slough of Despond?"

"Sir, I was told to go this way by a man called Evangelist."

"Evangelist told you to jump into the swamp? I find that hard to believe."

"He told me to head toward the shining light and the Wicket Gate, that I might escape the wrath to come. I was following his directions when I fell into the swamp. Or the Slough of Despond as you call it."

"But why didn't you look for the steps?"

"It came on me so fast I had no idea what was happening. But I have questions for you as well, sir. First of all, what is this slough filled with? It smells putrid and feels like death itself, sucking you down into the grave. And there's something . . . *alive* . . . in there."

"It's the low-point, where all the runoff of scum and filth that goes along with the conviction of sin gathers. Naturally, then, Apollyon sends some of his bottom feeders to look for easy targets."

"'Runoff?'"

"Whenever a sinner is awakened to his lost and hopeless condition, there's a byproduct in his soul: fears and doubts and deep anxiety. And this place is where all of that settles."

"But this swamp is directly between the City of Destruction and the Wicket Gate. Why isn't it filled in and made suitable for travelers?"

"Many have tried to do just that. And it's certainly not the pleasure of the King that this place remains as it is. Over the years, His royal surveyors have sent innumerable workers to come and fill it in with rocks and gravel. The project has been going on for nearly seventeen hundred years, and I myself have seen the royal records indicating that at least twenty thousand cartloads containing millions of sound instructions from all over the King's domain have been brought here to make this land more passable. Understand, these are absolutely the best materials to turn the slough into good ground, and yet it remains the Slough of Despond.

Christian pulled himself to his feet. "Almost seems like a cruel joke, though—to send a man down a road that disappears into a swamp."

"There were signs," Help said. "Signs you obviously missed. And, of course, there are the steps that would take you right through the midst of the slough." He gestured back at the burbling clay, now well lit by the sun.

"I see them now," Christian said, "although the bubbling filth seems to have covered them over in a sheet of slime. But I had no idea they were there before."

"It's a common thing," Help said. "The weather, a trick of the light, can hide them. I'm glad I found you when I did, and could help you. And be assured that the ground is good here. Godspeed, my friend."

Setting off from there, Christian was surprised at how quickly his burden dried out, and his clothes as well. Before long he was moving at a good pace once again and felt like the better part of the day's progress might still be ahead of him.

Just then, he spotted a man in the distance, walking toward him. As he drew closer, Christian could see that the man was incredibly fashionable and foppish, wearing a long coat, vest, baggy breeches gathered at the knee, cravat, and periwig.

Christian became newly aware of his own tattered rags, filthy burden, and mud-encrusted hair and he studied the ground as they were about to cross paths.

"Christian, I presume," the man said. "Is it you?"

Christian looked up at the man's face, which was altogether unfamiliar. "Do I know you, sir?"

"No, but I've heard of you. My entire town has been talking about how you set off on pilgrimage, leaving all behind!"

"Really. And what town might that be?"

"Just up the highway from Destruction: the town of Carnal Policy. Surely, you've heard of it. Oh, I'm being so rude. My name is Mr. Worldly Wiseman." He began to reach for Christian's hand, but glanced down and seemed to think better of it. "All of us in Carnal Policy," he said, "have been dying to know: where are you going in such a burdened manner?"

Christian leaned against an alder tree and looked down at himself.

"Burdened manner indeed," he said. "I'm headed to the Wicket Gate, ahead of me, where I shall no longer bear this burden. And I cannot get there too soon; I don't know how much longer I can bear it."

Mr. Wiseman furrowed his brow. "Do you have a wife? Children?"

"I do. A lovely wife. And four sweet boys. I love them so much. And yet, because of this burden, I can't even enjoy their company like I used to. It's as if I have no family at all."

Mr. Wiseman drew nearer, looking about conspiratorially and pulling a silk hanky over his nose and mouth, talking through it to Christian. "If I were to give you some advice— some wise counsel—would you consider it? I mean, really consider it?"

"I certainly would. I am need of good counsel."

"And what you want is to lose your burden, which has kept you from enjoying God's blessing in this life, correct?"

"Exactly."

"Well, I have to ask: who told you that this is the way to lose your burden?"

"A man named Evangelist; he opened my book and showed me where—"

"Evangelist? I know him!" He laughed uproariously. "What a wicked sense of humor that man has. You see, there is no more dangerous or troublesome way in the world than the way he sent you out! And, by the look and, uh, *smell* of you, I ascertain you've already discovered this!

"Listen, Christian, I'm older than you. I'm wiser than you. And I'm telling you if you keep on this path, you will meet with more of the same. Even worse! Hunger, peril, nakedness, sword, lions, dragons, darkness. In a word, *death* and whatnot. And you'll endure all this at the word of a stranger?"

"You don't understand," Christian said. "This burden on my back is far worse than all of those things combined. It grows heavier by the hour. The cords are even now digging deeper into my flesh. I don't care what I might come across between here and the gate. I'd go through anything to be rid of this thing once and for all."

"Sounds awful. How did you come by this burden?"

"By reading this book."

Worldly Wiseman nodded. "I thought as much. The same thing has happened to many weak men. They meddle in things beyond their grasp and suddenly fall into the same diversions. These men find themselves unmanned and chasing after desperate ventures to obtain they know-not-what."

"That doesn't describe me at all," Christian said. "I know exactly what I want to obtain."

"Yes, yes. But I can show you a far better way to obtain it, without the dangers and suffering. Instead, you'll find safety and friendship. And it's nearby."

"Are you serious?"

"As a plague of locusts."

"Well then, please, sir," Christian pleaded. "Open this secret to me."

"There is a village not far from here called Morality. There you will find, at the top of the hill, the house of a gentleman whose name is Legality. He is a very judicious man with much experience removing that sort of burden from the backs of people who are—how do I put this?—crazed in their wits because of them. This man will happily receive you, and his house is not quite a mile from where you stand now."

Christian felt a surge of hope. "This is incredible news. And you're sure he'll be home?"

"If he's not, his son will be."

Christian closed his eyes and recited. "Village of Morality, Mr. Legality. Or his son . . . "

"Civility. His son—very handsome young man and a fine dresser too. His name is Civility. Either of them can help you. And might I suggest that, rather than going back home to the City of Destruction . . . once that burden is removed (and, of course, you've bathed), you simply send for your family to join you there in the Village of Morality. There are many good houses for sale at very reasonable prices. There, you'll be happier than ever. Good neighbors. Good schools. Good soil if you plant crops. A good church; I myself go to church there."

"Alright," Christian said. "You've sold me. I'll go. Just point the way."

"Do you see the high hill, off to the southeast?"

"I see it. I'd almost call that a mountain."

"That's the one. Head toward it and the first house you will come to is his."

So Christian turned out of his way to go to Mr. Legality's house for help.

Upon turning back from the Slough of Despond, Pliable had quickly become disoriented. The darkness and dizziness of the place, followed immediately by the harsh light of the sun, caused him to venture deeper into the woods and before long he was all turned around. However, by noting the position of the setting sun in the sky and travelling toward a fixed point in the distance, he was able to make his way back to the City of Destruction, eager to find his friend Obstinate and fill him in on what had happened.

To that end, he made his way up High Street, toward The Crown, Obstinate's favorite pub. But he never got close. As he walked up the street, people began to point at him and whisper to one another. At first he assumed it was simply because he was covered in the remnants of the swamp.

But then a crowd began to form around him. "What are you doing here?" one man asked.

"Yeah," an old woman chimed in, "I thought you'd left us to perish in fire and brimstone. Now you're back?"

"Smart of him to come back," Mr. Light-Mind said. "I've known a few in my day who ventured out that way and were never heard from again. I'd never go, but I'm more sensible than most."

"If I *did* go," another shouted, "I wouldn't have given up after a few difficulties. He fell in some mud. So what?"

Pliable shrunk back and tried to slink away, but bumped into Obstinate, who regarded him with disdain and gave him a shove.

"First my shoes and now my coat? Are you determined to ruin every garment I own?"

"Sorry," Pliable said. "I just . . . I—"

"He was going to have everlasting life," Obstinate announced, "virgins feeding him grapes, and trifles growing on trees! An endless inheritance! Now what? You've come back here, with us unwashed masses?" He smirked, maliciously. "He doesn't even have a plow anymore; he gave it to me!"

"I was led astray," Pliable said quietly.

"Someone run and tell the *Gazetteer*; Pliable's been led astray!" They all laughed.

"It was that man Christian," Pliable continued. "He's crackers and . . . well, I guess for a short time I caught his frenzy. At least I came to myself quickly."

"Is Christian still on pilgrimage?" a young woman asked. The crowd had now grown to the point of nearly blocking the street.

"I guess so," Pliable said. "If he made it out of that slough. He refused to come back with me. Perhaps he has some Italian blood and loves soaking in the mud baths!"

Pliable noticed a woman standing just beyond the mob, watching him, surrounded by four boys. *Oh, no. Christiana.*

He broke from the gathered rabble and headed toward her. "Christiania, I'm sorry, I . . . " She turned and silently herded her children away.

Pliable kept going, trying to ignore the guilt and shame he felt for leaving Christian sinking in that swamp and then publicly mocking him to distract from his own teetering constitution.

He stopped to wait for a passing carriage and felt someone

staring at him from across the street. Looking up, he saw the town blacksmith. Or one of them. What was his name? The man stood at the edge of the street, in front of his shop, clad in his heavy leather apron, holding up a finger, beckoning Pliable. He wasn't mocking or laughing, but for some reason this increased Pliable's shame all the more. Pliable turned quickly away and skulked off, taking a roundabout route home via back streets.

The Blacksmith watched Pliable scurry away like a chastised dog. He shook his head in bemusement, and wandered back into the shop. There, he removed his apron and hung it on its peg. His partner, Revelry, was closing up for the night, placing each tool and instrument exactly where he liked it.

The sight of Revelry reminded him to double-check his apron. Yes, it was his. He'd been thinking perhaps they had unintentionally switched, as for at least two days it had seemed long on him. Or maybe the crick in his back was to blame. Several of their friends had commented on his hunched posture, joking that Revelry must be leaving him to do all the hard work, bent over the forge and anvil all day.

Placing a hand to the small of his back, he felt something unnerving. It wasn't flesh. It felt like *burlap*. Like a small burlap bag filled with sand and stones and concrete.

Revelry breezed by, his manner light as ever. "Let's get going! We're meeting up at the Crown—three men and seven women. So odds are good this night ends well for both of us. You coming?" He snapped his fingers an inch from his partner's face, to almost no response. "What, are you in a trance? Hey! If you don't want to buy a round for the house, don't say anything."

"Huh?"

"I said, if you don't not want to not buy a drink for every-one . . . say something."

"Wait—*what?*"

Revelry laughed and opened the door, shouting to the crowd milling in the street: "Everyone, head up to The Crown! The first round is on Faithful!"

Legality

Faithful had planned to start his morning by finishing a set of chisel blades for an old client. At nearly ten, though, he had made very little progress. His back ached like fury and his head was pounding, a little reminder of his drunken foolishness, like a mallet to the temples, with each beat of his heart.

Just as Revelry had promised, the night before was filled with all sorts of debauchery. In hindsight, Faithful knew this had mostly been an attempt to distract himself from the burden he'd discovered on his back. But when he awoke this morning, the thing had more than tripled in size, and there was no ignoring it now. He found himself unable to change his shirt, the cords of his burden now holding the ale-and-vomit-stained garment tightly to his body—a double reminder of his wickedness.

The burden also got in the way of his work, to put it mildly, pulling him ever downward, backward, forward—always toward the cake of purified coal, burning at 3,000 degrees. His concentration, which should have been focused solely on the skilled striking of his hammer upon the glowing metal and the anvil horn was instead divided, the better part going toward keeping his person clear of the disfiguring flames. His frustration was building to crescendo when the door swung open, and Evangelist walked in.

"Good 'morrow," he said, cheerily. "Oh. Only you don't look like it's going very well at all. Are you alright, Faithful?"

"I've been better. In fact, I've always been better." He struck the metal again with the peen of his hammer, flattening it a bit and drawing it out, but at the wrong angle. "Blast!"

"Hmm. I think I see what's throwing you off there. Your burden has grown quite a bit since yesterday noon. I can probably guess how you spent your evening."

"Not now, Evangelist."

"If not now . . . *when*?"

"I'm at work. Understand? Maybe we can talk again over dinner tonight." He hammered the metal back into square and hobbled over to the fire to reheat it, bracing himself to avoid tipping into the flames.

"I'm afraid I'm needed elsewhere this afternoon," Evangelist said, "and may not be back in the city for some time. At any rate, I think you already know what I would say to you. We've been round and round the same questions and read the same Scriptures again and again. All that remains is for you to flee the wrath to come."

Faithful returned to the anvil. "If you've said everything there is to say, good Evangelist, then why are you here?"

"The King of my country requires me not only to answer your questions, but to look for an answer from you as well."

"Well, that's annoying," Faithful said, bringing the hammer down again. The metal drew out uniformly. He struck it a second time, bringing a taper to the end of the blade. "That's more like it," he said. "Just one more little—" The hammer came down once more.

"No!" he threw the metal into a barrel of water, bringing up a loud, angry *tsssss.* "No! No! A curse on this burden!"

Revelry rushed up from the rear of the shop, drawing his sword. He regarded Evangelist with contempt. "Everything alright here?"

"All is well," Faithful said. "Put that away."

"Just think about it," Evangelist urged.

Revelry pointed at the door with the tip of his sword. "I think you should leave now, Mr. Prophet O' Doom. You're upsetting my partner, which means you're interfering with my business. *Our* business. And, frankly, you're just dragging down the whole spirit of the place."

Evangelist re-donned his simple hat. "As I said, I'm needed elsewhere." He put his hand on Faithful's shoulder. "Do think about it."

"Go!"

When he'd left, Revelry sheathed his sword and said, "Why do you consort with that man?"

"I am not going to have this conversation again."

"Do I need to point out the obvious?" Faithful turned back to his chisel blades. "Okay, I guess I do; before you met this *Evangelist*, you stood up straighter, you did far better work, and you were a whole lot more fun to be around."

"Alright then. You've stated the obvious. Now how about you finish those hinges for Mr. and Mrs. Discontent? You know they need to be perfect."

"When we were apprentices together, you were a true epicure. Living for the moment! In the moment! Women. Wine. Mischief."

Faithful groaned in pain and leaned his weight on the workbench. "Don't remind me. Please . . . "

"Old Faithful would have laughed in that man's face when he started yammering about the 'wrath to come.' Do you want to wind up like that farmer on the edge of town? The one who went out as a fanatic and tried to slink back in unnoticed? He's lost contracts over that. He may be ruined. Some used to say he was the seventh or eighth most eligible bachelor in the city, but I doubt any woman would have him now."

Through a building pain, Faithful gritted, "Is there a point to this, Rev?"

"My point is threefold. One: that man is now seven times worse than if he'd never gone out of the city. This brand of religious venture is nothing to fool around with. Two: you're obviously miserable and yet you refuse to cut yourself off from the one *making you miserable*. That's just insane. And three: you, my friend, used to be one of the greats. You were a real riot. And you—" He trailed off and stepped over to the window. "Speaking of riots, what's with all the shouting and carrying on outside our door?"

He peered through the glass and saw chaos unfolding in the streets. "What is going on out there?"

Christian's night had been the opposite of Faithful's in almost every way. He had arrived at the foot of the Hill Morality as the sun was beginning to set. He briefly considered waiting until first light to begin his ascent, but thought better of it. Once he stood at its base, it was not nearly as imposing a mount as it had appeared from a distance—at least from his vantage point, on the side closest to The Way. Besides, Worldly Wiseman had assured him that Mr. Legality lived only a mile away from where they'd spoken. If that were truly the case, Christian must have been practically on top of the house already.

But when he began to climb, things shifted quickly. The darkness roared in far faster than he had expected. His burden, heavier than ever, threw off his balance and threatened to drag him backwards at every moment. This was particularly alarming as the grade of the hill seemed to be changing, tilting, growing steeper and steeper with every little bit of upward progress he made. Likewise, his burden was growing heavier in direct correlation to his altitude.

His progress slowed further when the smell of smoke came wafting down from the top of the hill. Or rather, the peak of the mountain, for it was quite clearly a mountain now, craggy and massive and dizzyingly tall. How he'd ever thought this would be an easy climb, he had no idea.

The smoke was thickening now, both at the peak and, depending on the wind, all around him, like the smoke chugging from a great furnace. Thunder and lightning flashed above, lighting his world in a series of terrifying still images. Under his feet, the whole mountain trembled violently, and the sound of a deep, resonating trumpet vibrated his bones and joints.

The path up the mountain became yet steeper until it was truly vertical. Still, Christian ascended. For an hour and more he found footholds and handgrips, bracing himself against the shaking of the mountain and the crashing of thunder and lightning. An all-pervasive fear called him back to ground level, but still he moved upward. Christian began to hate Mr. Worldly Wiseman and his so-called "wise counsel," his promises of ease and comfort. Or, rather, he began to hate himself for falling so easily for whatever sort of ruse this was.

And that's when the vertical ascent became yet steeper, if that were possible. In fact, it was. Looking up, he saw the summit now hanging out over him, the entire mountain bent back toward him. Fire burned at the top, directly above his head—a consuming fire that he knew would never burn out. Reaching tenuously for the next handgrip, he felt the shift in his own weight just as his burden swung in the other direction, and he knew he was going to fall.

Christian seemed to hang in mid-air for the space of a breath, during which he twisted his body, putting the burden between himself and the ground.

Whether it softened the blow of his landing or not, he did not know. What he did know was pain, radiating out to all of his extremities. Rolling onto his side, the packed earth beneath him dug into his hip and shoulder—a dull, throbbing ache.

Lightning flashed again and Christian saw the mountain jutting out above him, hanging over him as if it meant to fall on him and bury him forever. He coughed a hollow, desperate laugh at what he saw: after all his work, all his sweat, all the fear he'd pushed against to try and reach the top . . . he'd fallen all of fifteen or twenty feet.

He could see the last handhold he'd gripped—the one that failed him, and a hundred more that he could have used, were he not exhausted, terrified, and dragging this burden with him. Another flash of lightning as the mountain again shook was all the warning Christian needed. One by one, the handholds he'd coveted began raining down: fistfuls of rock crashing against the ground all around him, larger and larger, slamming into the earth.

He rolled aside to avoid the first and then, covering his head, raced through the deadly downpour, praying for deliverance from the fire and lightning and crumbling mountain. Another flash of light brought an answer to his prayers. A few steps ahead, a small rocky recess opened up—an alcove in the earth. Christian took two more desperate, stumbling steps and threw himself into the mouth of the recess, which barely accommodated his entire body, burden and all.

Above him, he could hear rocks exploding against the earth. This continued for perhaps half an hour. Then, all at once, it stopped, as did the flashing lightning and quaking earth. The smell of smoke receded, and Christian was left in silent, inky darkness.

He dared not extract himself from his hole now. Nor did he have the strength. Best to stay here, ensconced in the earth and get a good night's sleep, he decided. He was, of course, monumentally uncomfortable, wedged into the rocky opening, lying on his stomach, unable to turn over. But at least he was safe, assuming no predatory beasts found him during the night. If that were to happen, he'd be a helpless victim and an easy meal.

Christian willed sleep to overtake him. He had no pillow and no blanket, only his burden, which he thought might at least offer some warmth, but which somehow seemed only to make him all the colder. Spent, hopeless, and full of regret, he began to weep, and he was still weeping when he fell asleep.

When he awakened, Christian could see fragments of daylight spilling in around him. Although he was awake, his limbs were very much not and it took quite some time and all of Christian's combined will and strength to worm his way awkwardly back out of the alcove.

As he stood, his body complaining all the way, he saw the sun already a good distance up from the horizon, nearly level with the top of the hill—which again looked like a hill, and a rather pleasant one at that. The only evidence of the previous night's terrors was the collection of rocks embedded in the earth all around him.

To his great relief, his burden had returned to its former weight as well. Christian smiled and took a moment to enjoy the sight of a beautiful English robin pulling a fat, pink worm from the ground for breakfast. A renewed sense of hope filled his heart and mind.

He stood for a moment in the contrast between this beautiful setting and the terrors of the night before. His mistake, Christian thought, had been trying to scale the hill in the dark. What a hasty fool he'd been. It was almost impossible to imagine all that fire and smoke and lightning manifesting now, in the pleasant light of morning.

A currant shrub a stone's throw away caught his eye. Stretching out his stiff arms and legs and cracking his weary back, he made a decision: he would eat some berries for break-fast and he would reach the top of that hill in time to have lunch with Mr. Legality.

Revelry slipped back into the shop and pushed the door shut, bracing it with his back.

"Everyone is going crazy!" he said. "It's like they've all been talking to your friend Evangelist, only they haven't. Which is odd."

"What do you mean?" Faithful asked.

"They're all saying that our city will, in a short time, be burned to the ground with fire from heaven. Sound familiar?"

"Really?"

"It is in everyone's mouth."

"Are they making plans to escape the danger? Perhaps I could join a party of—"

Revelry laughed. "Escape? Oh, Faithful, they don't *believe* it. Just as you don't believe it. It's just something to talk about. An excuse to blow off steam. A source of some excitement."

"How can you be so sure?"

"For one, they're all cursing and mocking that man Christian who set out from here as the cause of the crisis, rather than a worthy example to be followed. Oh, and that sad sack who came back as well. I hope for his sake they don't find him before their blood cools."

"You can't be sure, though. Any rational person would have to admit, it's not outside the realm of possibility that our city will burn."

Revelry stared out the window in thought. "You're right, Faithful." He walked to the back of the shop, retrieved a bulg-ing coin purse from beneath a loose floorboard, and tucked it into his belt. "If it all might end tonight," he said, solemnly, "there's something I must see to today." As he left the shop, he said, "Hold down the fort, would you, Faithful? Or close up shop. I care not."

Faithful stood at the window, watching his friend disappear into the madness, then stood a while longer, staring out into the unrest. But the sight seemed to inflame his burden, so he too stepped outside and locked the door.

He fought his way through the crowds, down High Street, not sure where he was even headed. More than once, he was jostled hard enough that he felt his burden almost lift away from his back for a moment, but never enough for any real relief.

Then he found himself shunted to the side of the street and looking up at the raised patio of The Red Horse Inn, his preferred public house. And there, seated at the very table where he and Evangelist had shared half a dozen meals while discussing the contents of that troubling Book, was Christiana, gazing down impassively at the uproar, sipping some tea. She seemed to Faithful like a jaded queen who, having given up on her people, made content to watch them destroy one another.

It suddenly occurred to Faithful that, of everyone in the City of Destruction, this woman may have some useful information about the burden on his back. After all, as everyone now knew, Christian's troubles had begun in the same way.

He mounted the stone steps and moved along the curved railing toward her table, unsure how to broach the subject.

"Parden me, ma'am," he said tentatively. "I have a question for you about . . . about your husband and his burden." He drew closer yet and added. "It's very important."

Christiana's eyes remained fixed on the street below. "I am a married woman," she said. "Sitting alone in a public house— which would itself undoubtedly raise many eyebrows, were the fabric of our society not unraveling before our eyes. Do you really think it proper to approach me like this, bending down so close? So familiar?"

"I'm sorry for that. It's not by choice." He lowered himself carefully onto a bench at the table next to hers, the last six inches in freefall. "You see, like good Christian, I—"

"I do not wish to discuss Christian. Not with you. Be gone." She waved her hand dismissively.

"What would you like?" A burly waiter hovered over Faithful. "Fish and Chips and shepherd's pie today. And of course, you know the drinks."

"I'm fine. No thank you."

"Mr. Faithful, if you're going to sit in here, you have to order something. Or take up a room."

"Fine. Whatever. Bring me an ale."

"And you, madam? Are you in need of anything else?"

Christiania glanced at Faithful and shook her head.

The waiter looked disapprovingly at the two of them and clomped off.

"Believe me, I would not normally bother you," Faithful pressed, "but it's a matter of . . ."

Christiana turned and locked eyes with him. Hers were bloodshot and glassy. "Please go away, blacksmith."

"I will. Just tell me one thing. When his burden began to grow, did your husband ever try—"

"I'll yell *murder*. On a day like today, perhaps no one would notice. But then again, perhaps they would."

The waiter returned with a pewter tankard, which he plopped down on the board. Faithful placed a coin in his waiting hand and stood.

"It seems I'm not welcome here," he said. "Someone else can enjoy this one, on me."

"You're not abandoning your drink, are you Faithful?" The Rev. Mr. Smoothman had appeared, seemingly out of nowhere, now eyeing the vessel on the table.

Faithful scoffed. "It's all yours, parson."

Smoothman flipped the lid and drained the drink in two long pulls, wiping foam from his pencil-thin moustache. Then, turning his attention toward Christiana, he asked, "Where are your children while you sit here, having tea?"

She rolled her eyes. "They're with Mercy, my maid, if you must know."

The reverend looked upon her with exaggerated pity for a few seconds before bellying up to the railing, overlooking the street, and bellowing the words, "People of Destruction . . . " His deep and resonating preacher's voice brought a hush from below.

"I know you are filled with fear, my children. Tares have been sown among you. Tares of terror. But remember the words of the Good Book: 'perfect love casts out fear.' My people, banish fear! I know many of you have heard it repeated by scoundrels and even by some good men that our good city will be destroyed by fire raining down. But remember the words of the Good Shepherd himself in the face of the storm: 'Peace, peace,' he said to the wind and the waves. And today he says to you, 'Peace, peace.' He bids you remember that God is a God of love, not a God of vengeance. And I bid you to set your minds on things that are more beneficial. Positive things. Happy thoughts."

Faithful descended the steps to the street. "Tell me this," the preacher's voice continued, "have you come to God's house on the Lord's Day? Then you are the Lord's. He would never cast you out. Be encouraged and do not worry . . . "

Two blocks down, Faithful found the entire roadway blocked by a frothing mass of hooligans who had a man cornered against the cobbler's shop, like a pack of hounds around a mink. As he drew closer, Faithful recognized their prey: it was Pliable, that poor little scapegoat who had followed Christian on pilgrimage before turning back. The crowd was pelting him with rotting produce and clods of dirt. For his part, Pliable alternated between begging and seemingly playing dead.

Righteous anger burned in Faithful's breast at the sight of this ruthless injustice. He pressed himself through the crowd, leveraging his burden to box out anyone who might challenge him. As he made his way toward the miserable victim, someone shouted. "Hang him! He's a turncoat!"

"Yeah! Hang all traitors! Against God *and* country!"

Obstinate emerged from the front of the crowd and turned back to address them, raising his hands for quiet.

"Friends," he said. "I was there when this man took a solemn oath to follow the Way of Pilgrimage, through fair skies or troubled, all the way to the Celestial City. He made it less than one day! He was not true to his profession! And now the Almighty threatens to pour out his anger on all of us unless we make of him an example and an expiation!"

Faithful squeezed between the last few shoulders and stumbled into Obstinate. Using the momentum, he shoved him hard away from his one-time friend and inserted firmly himself between Pliable and the mob.

"Stop a moment and think," Faithful warned. "You're all caught up in a frenzy. This man has been through enough. If you want to hurt him any more than you already have, you'll have to come through me."

For a moment, he thought he saw their faces soften. Then a voice from behind him—Pliable's voice—said, "If you're looking to hang someone, hang the blacksmith here! I saw him with that man Evangelist! A bunch of times! Christian only met him once, but the blacksmith has dinner with him every night at the Red Horse!"

"Look how he's standing!" someone called out. "Something on your back there, Faithful?"

"Hang 'em both!" Obstinate shouted. The palpable malice returned to the group as each man added a bit of heat to the pot, just waiting for it to boil over.

Just then, Revelry's voice rose up from beyond the mob. "Faithful! We're doing it! Every pub in town while the world still stands! Tomorrow we die? Tonight we drink!" He was leading a group of roving, staggering disciples through the city streets. "Faithful, join us!" he called out. "On to the Green Door Tavern!"

"I can't reach you!" Faithful replied. "Come get me and I'll buy the next round!"

At once, Revelry's carousing congregation shifted course, barreling into the midst of the lynch mob and bodily hauling Faithful up onto their shoulders, cheering all the while. They carried him with a sense of ceremony to the entrance of the Green Door, only to find it already mobbed and impassable.

Dropping to the street, Faithful made his way, as stealthily as possible, through the legs of the men all around him, between two buildings, over a fence, and down a circuitous route of backstreets and alleys until he was in open country, headed home.

Burned into his mind were the hateful faces of Obstinate and his other neighbors, glaring murder at him as he rode the crowd to safety. This would all blow over someday, but maybe not someday soon. Faithful felt a pressing need to get home and fortify his house.

Despite his best intentions and his resolution to the contrary, Christian remained at the foot of the hill for hours. It was the oddest thing. When he stood there, looking up at the rolling green grass and lush trees of the hill, he felt good inside. Safe. Content. When he *thought about* ascending the hill, he felt even better. The idea of it was a great comfort to him. But when the sole of his shoe touched that first inclining ground, he found all that displaced by a horrible, cold fear.

It was a problem of time, he realized. Of tense. Climbing the hill in the future tense meant comfort and security. In the present tense: trepidation, anxiety, and much worse. And so he hovered there in the sweet spot, looking up at the Hill Morality and thinking about how very doable a task it was and how, inevitably, he *would* climb to the top and plant his flag, like de Ville on the Mont Aiguille. Along with the warmth of the sun on his face, this brought a great sense of peace—at least as long as he thought of the hill in general, as a whole, and did not focus on any individual feature of it.

As noon came and went, his stomach began to rumble and complain, but hunger could not outweigh apprehension, and still he sat at the base of the hill, eyes fixed pleasantly upon it. But as the sun began its descent in the sky, warming his back now and not his face, Christian realized that if he tarried indefinitely, he would soon have to endure another frightful night in this place. And that was enough to bring him to his feet.

He set his face toward the summit and began to climb once again, one trepidatious step at a time, fighting the fear, trying to draw hope and comfort and courage from the afternoon sun. But the sun beat down on him, heating his burden and burning his neck, and he began to sweat into his already filthy clothes.

The daylight was no help at all, he realized. In fact, as the smell of smoke returned, along with the dizzying effect of the mountain tipping back toward him, the sun almost made things worse. He could see all the clearer the impossible task ahead of him.

"It's just an optical illusion," he said to himself, trying on common sense as a comforter. A travelling merchant had once told him about Francesco Borromini and his famous forced perspective sculptures that played havoc with the mind and the eyes. Perhaps Mr. Legality used a similar tactic to protect his house from thieves and marauders.

But Christian didn't believe his own thoughts. The now-familiar fear begins to grip him, even tighter than before. The fear he'd experienced in licks and whiffs this morning at the foot of the mountain, and had endured full-force the night before. It was unlike any fear he'd ever felt, in that it was far deeper. As thick and heavy as the dread had been in the Slough of Despond, this fear made that seem like water flowing gently down a stream. It was as if every anxiety and every nightmare he'd ever experienced in life up to this point had only touched the outside of his soul, as the muck from the slough still clung to the outside of his person. But this fear went all the way to his core.

It made him want to fall on his face and beg for mercy, but he knew he had to keep climbing—and so he did, out of simple necessity, passing beyond the point where he'd fallen the night before, climbing up the bottom of the exaggerated incline toward the top of the leaning mountain, one tentative grip at a time.

The clouds rolled in and the sun's light retreated. As he pushed upward, the rumbling resumed, and the lightning and the fire. The smoke choked him out and stung his eyes. Again, his burden sagged, digging into his shoulders, as though it contained the very mass of the mountain itself.

Another flash of lightning, and a flash of clarity with it: to climb this mountain was impossible. At least while wearing a burden on his back. This was all wasted effort. Wasted precious time. He'd lost a full day from his pilgrimage on this fool's errand. To waste more would be to multiply his sins.

But how to go back down? Climbing up was hard enough, but at least he was able to see what lay ahead of him, while he felt his way forward. He tried a step in reverse, reaching back, feeling about desperately, slipped, recovered . . . then fell.

A moment of freefall, interrupted by his burden connecting with the branches of a chestnut tree. He bounced downward from branch to branch like a billiard ball against the skittles. The last ten feet, he was unencumbered and the ground connected hard with his hands and chest, knocking the wind from him. He lay motionless for a few minutes before experimentally pulling himself to his feet, sore and battered, but seemingly unbroken. Looking up, he saw the peak of the mountain retreating from above his head and was filled with an inexplicable desire to try once again.

Feeling more than a little foolish for his fall, Christian looked this way and that, as if to make sure no one had been watching. And to his great dismay, he saw a familiar figure walking up the path toward him, his face severe.

"What are you doing here?" Evangelist asked. Christian studied his feet.

"I could be wrong, but I thought you were the man I found outside the City of Destruction, desperately shouting, 'What must I do to be saved?' Are you that man?"

"I am . . . that man."

"Did I not direct you to follow the shining light to the Wicket Gate? To go neither to the left nor to the right?"

"Yes, dear sir. You did."

"How then have you turned aside so quickly? You are *way* out of the Way."

Christian swallowed hard and looked up into Evangelist's face. "I met a man not far from the Slough of Despond who convinced me there was an easier way to take off my burden. In a town called Morality. I was to visit a man named Legality, or his son—"

"Yes, yes, Civility. I've heard this before. Stand still a little, Christian, that I might show you the Word of God."

So Christian stood, trembling.

"Hear the word of the Lord: 'See to it that you do not refuse him who speaks. If they did not escape when they refused him who warned them on earth, how much less will we, if we turn away from him who warns us from heaven?' Tell me, do you understand these words?"

"Yes."

"And these? 'The just shall live by faith. And if he shrinks back, I will not be pleased with him.'"

"I understand," Christian said. "And I am ashamed."

"You have rejected the counsel of the Most High and run back into this misery, back from the way of peace, into danger of damnation."

Christian fell at his feet and began to cry, "I am undone! I am lost forever, I know! I am—"

"Stand up," Evangelist said. "I'm a fellow pilgrim, not an angel."

Christian rose and stood again, still trembling, before Evangelist.

"This man who sent you here? What was his name?"

"Mr. Wiseman," Christian answered. "Worldly Wiseman."

"I gathered as much. This Mr. Worldly Wiseman who deluded you so easily along the Way is the same man I would have found picking the pockets of your corpse had I come along an hour later. He earned his name by loving only the wisdom of this world. He faithfully attends the First Church of Morality because the parson there, a Mr. Whitewash, preaches doctrine that saves, not by the cross, but *from* the cross! And when Mr. Wiseman sits in that cursed chapel and hears that preaching, he is filled with zeal to go out and pervert the ways of others."

"I see that now," Christian said. "So clearly."

"You 'see that now,' do you? Well, you listened carefully to his 'wise counsel'; do you think you can listen to mine?"

"I can. I will."

"Then remember these words: there are three things in Worldly Wiseman's counsel that you must hate with all your being."

"Believe me; I hate all of it!"

"No talking. Listen. Three things. Number one: his turning you out of the Way. The Lord himself told us to enter through the Narrow Gate, the very gate to which I sent you. 'For wide is the gate,' he tells us, 'and broad is the road that leads to destruction, and many enter through it. But small is the gate and narrow the road that leads to life, and only a few find it.'

"Secondly, you must *hate* his laboring to make the cross repugnant to you. This is how you know you are dealing with an agent of hell, no matter how well-dressed or polite or welcoming or friendly he may seem. Christian, you must cherish the cross more than all the treasures of Egypt. Remember what the King of Glory has told us: whoever saves his life will lose it. Without the cross you cannot have eternal life. If a man tries to convince you, instead, that the cross will be your death, you must hate his teaching and have nothing to do with him, except perhaps to rebuke him plainly and knock the dust from your shoes in his direction.

"And finally, you must *hate* that he sent you where he did. Consider how very unable that person was to deliver you from your burden. The man you sought after was named Legality and truly he does live on this hill. What the liar Wiseman did not tell you is that Legality is the son of a bondwoman who is even now in bondage, along with her children and grandchildren. The Scriptures tell us a mystery when they call this woman Mount Sinai, which you feared would fall upon your head and kill you. Tell me, if she and her children are in bondage, how could they possibly make you free?"

Christian could only shake his head.

"This man Legality is a swindler, a huckster. He has built for himself (with Worldly Wiseman's help) a great reputation for removing burdens, but I tell you he has never removed a single burden from a single back in all his days. In fact, he opens them up and adds many more heavy rocks to their load before sending his victims away. Therefore, this Mr. Wiseman is an alien and Mr. Legality a cheat. And as for his son, Civility, notwithstanding his simpering looks, he is a hypocrite. Together, these men offer nothing but a plot to trick you out of your salvation." He called out to the mountain, "Now, if what I have said is true, let heaven itself confirm it!"

From the top of the mountain came fire and smoke, more rumbling and quaking. Christian cowered. A voice rang out above all the noise of the mountain, saying, "These words are trustworthy and true: All who rely on observing the law are under a curse, for it is written, 'Cursed is everyone who does not continue to do everything written in the Book of the Law.'"

Christian gripped his head, fell to his knees, and began to shout in lament, cursing the moment he met Worldly Wiseman and calling himself a thousand fools for taking his advice. "I am so ashamed," he cried, "that this man's arguments, flowing from the flesh, should entice me to turn out of the Way."

Looking up to Evangelist, he asked, "Is there any hope? Can I turn back again? Will they still have me at the Wicket Gate?"

"Your sin is two-fold," Evangelist said, his voice hard. "You have forsaken what is good and tread on forbidden paths."

The fire burned louder and the thunder crashed and the ground shook. Christian squeezed his eyes shut, sending a torrent of tears cascading down his cheeks.

"Be comforted, Christian," Evangelist said, taking a knee and putting a hand on Christian's shoulder. "All manner of sin and blasphemy will be forgiven. Do not doubt, but believe. You have repented of your sin. Far be it from me to condemn you."

The sound of the great fire subsided. And the thunder ceased. And the earth became still, as a still, small voice spoke in barely a whisper, directly to Christian's soul, saying, "Neither do I condemn you. Now go, and sin no more."

Faithful lived in a small cottage, a good distance out from the City itself, which he'd inherited from his father. By the time he arrived there, it was already twilight.

Only when he had locked and barred the door, and checked every inch of his home for concealed intruders, could he finally stop and think about what to do next. Every man in that crowd today knew where to find Faithful. Many of them had been inside his home. How far would this frenzy go? Would they come all the way out here to string him up? Perhaps they had already put poor Pliable to death and satiated their bloodlust. Or perhaps not.

Then, of course, there was the matter of fire and brimstone raining down from heaven to consume the city. In the back of his mind, Faithful had been thinking that his house may be far enough out in the country to avoid any direct hits from above. Yes, that was a good bet—a bet he would take. He would not be pressured to set out like Christian on a pilgrimage—a life-long promise made based on a moment's misgivings. He would wait out this madness here in his home, comfortable and secure.

He had enough supplies: wood for the fire, a cellar full of root vegetables and canned fruit. Water was plentiful. And the house itself was rather secure. Faithful looked down at his sword—one of the finest in the city. He was adept enough with it, assuming he would not be overrun. This called to mind another source of security.

He ran to his bed chamber and dropped to his knees, reaching under the bureau and coming out with an ornate oak case, which he opened to reveal a velvet lining, cradling a flint-lock pistol, six lead balls, powder flask, and rod.

The weapon had been payment in full for a rather extensive job he'd done two years earlier for a retired naval commander. Since then, Faithful had only pulled it out once. And now he re-moved it a second time, pouring a measure of powder down the muzzle, followed by wadding, and the deadly ball itself. With the rod, he pushed it all down to the breach.

He lit no lamps and, in the dark, pulled a chair out from his table and sat in it, facing the front door. He would not sleep tonight. He would be vigilant. Faithful to his own cause. He himself would be his own security. For an hour or so, he sat there, nodding off in the chair twice, but coming quickly back to himself both times.

It was in the deadest, darkest hour of the night when he heard someone approaching his door. He dropped to the floor and crawled quickly to his front window, peering out into the darkness. There he saw a man's face glowing in the light a lantern, approaching the door. How many more might be following behind him he could not tell.

Three quick, hard raps at his door brought a spear of alarm into his heart, his lungs, his mind.

Faithful had always been a man to look danger in the eye, not slink away from it. He figured his best approach to the sort of rogues who slink in under cover of darkness was to meet them face to face.

He stood, quickly lit two of his own lamps, filling the house with a dappled light, and opened the door. There he stood tall, framed in the doorway, his broad shoulders drawn up, the pistol pointed downward, toward the man's feet.

He was an old man with a long white beard and piercing

brown eyes. Faithful's courage faltered for a moment as he realized that this man carried no lantern after all. Rather, his face glowed by its own light.

Squinting into the darkness beyond him, Faithful saw no one else.

"Who are you?" he demanded. "And what do you want?"

"I am here for your house," the old man said.

Faithful chuckled. "I'm sorry. It's not for sale."

"I am not here to buy it, but to burn it to the ground."

"Look, I'm sure this was a hilarious joke when you conceived of it, but believe me, you've picked the absolute worst night and the worst house on which to carry it out. I want you off my land as fast as those tired old legs can carry you, or things are going to take a turn you won't like."

"I have every right to burn this house," the old man said, reaching into his coat and producing a folded document, which he held up with a flick of his wrist. "All legal and in order. Always legal and in order."

The document was dense, written in a tight script. Faithful could see an official seal and several signatures, although could not make them out. Something about this man's presence—even apart from the glowing face—evaded Faithful's courage. He felt oddly like a small child caught in a lie.

"It's late," he said, "and this conversation is over. Leave. This is your last warning."

"No. You need to leave. Heed your own warning."

Faithful raised the gun, pointing the muzzle six inches from the man's face. "I'm going to count to three. One . . . "

With unexpected speed, the man grabbed the pistol and slammed it against the ground, breaking the frizzen loose and rendering the weapon useless.

"Enough of this." Faithful drew his sword and made to swing it at this intruder, but his burden threw him off balance. The old man needed only take a leisurely step back and watch Faithful fall unceremoniously to the ground. The sword spilled from his hand and the old man kicked it away by the hilt, out into the darkness. Stooping down, he casually scooped up a large rock and hefted it over his head.

"Are you quite finished?" he asked. "Or shall I finish you?"

"No. Don't. I give up."

"Then do as I say and leave this place, never to return. I'll give you an hour to gather your belongings."

Faithful stood, his knees smarting, but his pride all the more. "And if I'm still here?"

"Then I will burn it down over your head."

Spoil-Five in Fair Speech

Each night, the pews were moved off to the sides of the Pleasant Chapel in the town of Fair Speech, and a long oak table brought in. There a group of men wiled away the hours playing cards well into the night. Considering this to be a form of religious fellowship, the parson, a Mr. Two-Tongues, provided refreshments purchased with funds from the offering box.

Play was by invitation only.

Tonight, seven men were gathered for their favorite game, Spoil-Five.

"Ace of Hearts," Mr. Money-Love announced, flipping the card triumphantly atop the others. "And I take the trick. The third in a row."

Lord Fair Speech (from whose ancestors the town took its name) clapped half-heartedly and said, "Good game. Take your winnings, Money-Love. That is, unless you want to, uh…"

"I'm thinking," said Mr. Money-Love.

"Of what? Going for five?" Lord Time-Server sneered. "Seems foolish."

"Foolish how?"

"After four spoiled rounds, you've got 28 coins in that pot. Yours for the taking. Why risk it all for another six coppers?"

The Rev. Mr. Two-Tongues laughed. "Have you met this man? He'd sell his mother for six coppers."

Lord Fair Speech clucked and fairly sang the words, "That doesn't sound like fair speech."

The parson laughed again. "I meant nothing of it. I admire your single-mindedness, Mr. Money-Love. I think you know that."

"I do," he said. "And I've decided; I'll be jinking indeed. Keep your cards and loosen your purses, gentlemen. Two more tricks and I'll be that much richer, my dear mamma still safe in her bed." He giggled and added, "Lord Fair Speech, if you would?"

"My pleasure, but I'm all out of trump." He dropped a five of clubs onto the table. "Say, Reverend, where is your nephew tonight? Mr. By-Ends?"

"Yes," Lord Turn-About said, following suit with a two of clubs. "I wouldn't expect him to miss his last game for who-knows-how-long."

The parson took his turn and answered, "I believe he's collecting some debts. He'll join us later, I'm sure. Just preparing for his big trip. They leave tomorrow after service."

Play came around again to Mr. Money-Love, who tossed a four of clubs contemptuously onto the table, drained his drink, and bit down his ire with a frosty, "Well-played, Lord Turn-About. You've spoiled the round, haven't you?"

"Turn-About is fair play," the other man laughed. "Fair play in Fair Speech." He adjusted his wig and anted another copper into the pot. The others did the same and Lord Fair Speech gathered the cards and dealt five to each man in pairs and triplets.

The door opened and a young man breezed in, several bags of coins jingling in his hand. Mr. Money-Love looked with longing at the heavy purses.

"Mr. By-Ends!" Lord Turn-About called. "Glad you could join us!"

"That's not my name," the young man replied, doffing his hat and approaching the game. "Oh, it seems the pot is fat. I suppose I'll have to wait until someone wins this sum before you deal me in?"

"You may have my spot," Lord Time-Server said. "Need to be in church in the morning. As you know, I attend three services."

"Not sure why," Mr. By-Ends said, assuming the man's seat and examining his cards. "If you really want to take five tricks for five—spiritually speaking—you should do what Money-Love and I are doing. It's the ultimate trump card for Judgment Day."

"No thank you," Lord Time-Server said. "I enjoy my own bed, my own cook, and my upholstered chairs. Three churches will have to be enough. Fairwell, gentlemen." And with that, he left.

Lord Fair Speech flipped the top card of the deck to reveal a queen of hearts, drawing cheers and groans from around the table.

Mr. Two-Tongues led with a ten of hearts.

Mr. Facing-Both-Ways studied his hand and mused, "Hm. I have privilege to renege. I think I will. No. No. I won't." He began to play a jack of hearts, then drew it back. "Or maybe I will, or—"

"Make up your mind," Mr. By-Ends commanded, and the little man released the card.

"So, By-Ends," Mr. Anything said, "will you be back for church tomorrow morning? Oh, look! I've taken the trick! What a nice surprise."

"That's not my name. And I haven't decided."

The parson shot him a sharp look and said, "Don't think I won't report you on account of your being my nephew. Twelve pence fine for missing church."

"Aye, but I won't be here to pay, will I? At any rate, aren't I attending church right now? Lord Time-Server travels to three towns to attend three churches, but I'm here almost every night. Church is church as I see it." He played another card, absent-mindedly.

Lord Fair Speech collected the trick and said, "It's not quite a proper church service, I suppose, but I do appreciate these games. Our last parson wouldn't hear of it. You two men are too young to remember, but Mr. Holy Desire despised our wasting every night playing cards and drinking to excess, much less doing it here in the chapel."

"And keeping a mistress," Lord Turn-About said. "He wouldn't shut up about that."

"Not to speak ill of anyone," the reverend put in, "but that may be why your Mr. Holy Desire was run out of town. Live and let live, I say. If you don't miss church, the magistrate won't fine you. Why should the good Lord? I am, of course, expected to condemn it all from the pulpit, but at this table we can be more realistic. Oh, and another trick for Lord Fair Speech!"

"Speaking of mistresses," Mr. Anything said, "By-Ends, my good man, how are you going to manage on your journey without the beautiful Lady Folly?"

"I'll take care of her for you," Lord Turn-About said with a laugh.

"What is this journey everyone keeps talking about?" Mr. Facing-Both-Ways asked. "I've missed something."

The parson answered, "By-Ends and Money-Love are leaving on a religious pilgrimage tomorrow, along with some other young men: Mr. Save-All and Mr. Hold-the-World. Headed to the Celestial City. I'm quite proud of them for undertaking such an important rite at such a young age. In fact, I might even fail to notice if you miss the service tomorrow. Get some extra sleep; you'll need it."

"A Pilgrimage?" Facing-Both-Ways scoffed. "Why would you go and do a thing like that? I'd never do it! Or maybe I would. But it doesn't sound like the Mr. By-Ends I know…"

"Call me Mr. By-Ends one more time and see what happens!"

Lord Fair Speech clucked again and chided, "That doesn't sound like fair *speeee-eeeech*."

"Indeed. I'll just say this: my pilgrimage is my own affair. Besides, there's plenty in it for us."

"There had better be," Mr. Money-Love grumbled. He then brightened, announcing, "Well look at that—I've won the trick! Another round spoiled . . . "

Danger at the Gate

Faithful stood frozen in the doorway for perhaps a quarter of an hour—or, more accurately, a quarter of *the* hour he'd been granted. Behind him, the warm glow of his familiar home (the only home he'd ever known) called to him with empty promises of peace and safety. However, he knew the blackness of the night, foreboding as it was, offered a far better hope of survival. With one weapon broken and the other now lost in the tall grass and total darkness, Faithful would be all the less able to protect himself if the old man came back. When he came back. Clearly, he needed to leave.

Breaking himself from the trance, he withdrew a few steps into the house and surveyed his meager possessions. When setting off on an odyssey over difficult and unfamiliar ground, toward parts unknown, it was only wise to bring provisions. Of course, Faithful would have loved to fill a pack with food and supplies. But he already carried on his back the burden, larger and heavier than ever. There was no room for more, nor did have the strength to carry it.

But he ought to at least take a few minutes to find his sword, he decided. After all, who knew what kind of dangers lurked the way he was going? A few minutes of crawling through the grass on hands and knees, in the light of a single lantern, proved fruitless, however. And the grass seemed to be growing dryer by the moment, causing Faithful to fear he might accidentally burn his own house to the ground—and perhaps himself along with it—if he kept this up.

In the end, as Faithful set out from his home in the purple pre-dawn glow, he was weighed down by nothing but his burden, carrying no staff, no bag, no bread, no money, no sword, and no extra clothing. And yet, as the sun broke out above the horizon, he felt a sense of peace and promise.

For the first time in a long time, Faithful felt like he would lack nothing.

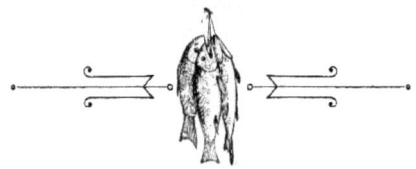

Christian awoke refreshed. The evening before, he and Evangelist had hiked back to the Way and made a little progress toward the Wicket Gate, before the sun began to set. Then they built a fire, ate some smoked fish and bread from Evangelist's pack, and talked well into the night about the road ahead—its trials and dangers, as well as the blessings and comforts set in place by the King for pilgrims to enjoy along the Way. They fell asleep under the stars while the fire slowly waned.

Sitting up now, and rubbing his eyes, Christian called the world back into focus. The coals were yet red and glowing, but Evangelist was nowhere to be seen. At first, Christian thought he may have ducked out as quickly and unexpectedly as he'd appeared. But then he saw his friend come strolling out of the woods, carrying three fish on a line.

"Where on earth did you catch those?" Christian asked.

"I haven't always been an Evangelist." He pulled a curved knife from his pack and began cleaning the haddock with quick efficiency. "Let's just say I've fished every creek, stream, and pond in these woods—some of them I've just about fished dry."

Christian rubbed his stiff shoulders, and asked, "Do you think I might make it to the gate today?"

"If you persevere, I don't see why not. It's not far at all. In fact . . . Well, never mind."

"No, tell me."

"If one walks briskly and takes no side trips nor stops to rest, it's less than a day's journey from the City of Destruction to the Wicket Gate."

"Oh . . ."

Evangelist set two sticks parallel over the coals and began laying the fish across them to cook. He regarded Christian's downcast face. "You wasted a day and a half on that side trip," he said. "Correct?"

"Yes."

"Tell me this: does it make sense to waste the very best part of this beautiful day pouting about it?" He flashed Christian a crooked smile.

"I suppose not."

"Will it somehow bring glory to our King for you to replay your missteps again and again in your mind?"

"You're right. I'm done."

"That's good. We only do Beelzebub's work when we let our past failures halt our present progress. You know, I think I saw some chanterelles growing in a cluster just beyond those trees there. That would go nicely with this fish."

"I'll go have a look."

Christian had walked all of thirty feet from their campsite when he saw the fine white mushrooms growing in abundance. He poked through them, looking for the best specimens.

"Tell me something, Christian," Evangelist called from the fire. "Do you think I've ever strayed from the path?"

Christian followed the sprawling troop of mushrooms further down into a shady hollow, where they grew darker and thicker yet. "I don't know," he called back. "I can't really imagine you going astray."

"You don't have to imagine it, good Christian. If we remain friends long enough, you'll see it with your own eyes. All like sheep have gone astray. Each of us has turned to his own way. But God has laid on our Savior the iniquities of us all."

Looking down, Christian suddenly felt his stomach turn. The mushrooms growing here in full shade looked slimy and smelled musty. He could almost see the poison spores floating up from beneath their caps, causing his head to swim. A dark feeling—a shadow of what he'd felt in the slough and on the mountain—began to creep over him.

"Your little side-excursion may have been borne of wickedness, Christian, but God uses all things for his good. And in your going astray, you've seen that there is grace upon grace flowing from the hands, the feet, the side—the very heart of our Savior. If anyone says he has no sin, he's lying—even lying to himself. But when we confess our sins, he is faithful and just to forgive us and cleanse us. And if we walk in the light, as he is in the light we have fellowship with one another and with Jesus himself. Keep that light in your eye, dear pilgrim, and do not turn aside again, to the right or to the left."

Christian looked up in Evangelist's direction and saw the rising sun shining out on an inviting cluster. Stepping back into the light, he felt the oppressive weight lift from his spirit.

"You're taking long enough with the fungus, my friend," Evangelist laughed. "Have you found anything yet?"

Scooping up a handful of picture-perfect mushrooms, he answered, "Aye, some real beauties. On my way."

As he approached the fire, the smell of baking fish brought Christian's appetite to life with a vengeance and the sight of his friend sitting there, tending the meal warmed his heart.

"Let me see what you've got," Evangelist said, examining the fruits of Christian's hunt. "Can't be too careful. Some false chanterelles grow deeper in these woods. Very similar in appearance but very deadly if eaten. But these are good." He smiled widely. "Come and have breakfast."

They sat across from one another, returned thanks to the King, and broke their fast. For several minutes, they enjoyed the sights and sounds of the fresh morning while they ate.

"You know," Evangelist said, breaking the silence, "it was over a breakfast of fish that the Lord Jesus restored his disciple Peter after his fall into sin. Three times the Lord asked Him, 'Do you love me?' and three times Peter answered, 'Lord, you know I love you.'"

"Yes, I've shed a tear more than once while reading that passage."

"As have I, my friend. Because it shows us his heart—the fact that our Lord did not respond, 'Then why did you deny me?' Or, 'You have an odd way of showing your love.' Or even, 'I don't believe you.' No, he said, 'Feed my lambs.'" Wiping his hands and standing, Evangelist said, "He uses broken people, Christian. People like me. Like you."

"Will you walk with me a little further?" Christian asked, swallowing down the last bite of fish. "Maybe up to the gate?"

"I'd love to, but I'm afraid I'm needed nearer the city today. I will be praying for you, though, as I travel." Evangelist tucked two of the mushrooms into his pack and embraced Christian heartily. Then, smiling, he bid him Godspeed to the Wicket Gate.

Christian girded up his loins, and resumed his trip.

As the morning wore on, the Way grew rather busy. Several times, a stranger offered a greeting, tried to engage him in conversation, or asked a question about how to get to this place or that. But having already been duped by a slick-talking cheat (and knowing that he was not fully safe on this side of the gate), Christian offered only the curtest of nods by way of response.

He encountered children playing and a number of men and women walking toward the gate—some with their own burdens (big or small) and some without. A few of these pilgrims Christian passed along the side of the road, where it was wide enough to accommodate two, and a few passed him, moving with a speed Christian could only dream of, considering his enormous, ponderous burden and general sense of fatigue. He also met with a number of people headed back toward the City of Destruction, most of them walking slowly with an air of defeat.

More than once, the blisters on his feet and the stiffness of his back almost convinced Christian to take a brief rest, but then he thought of the precious day he'd wasted, and how close he must be and instead, he pushed himself all the harder.

The sun was nearing the top of the sky when Christian realized he hadn't seen any fellow travelers for some time. Here, the Narrow Path passed through a beautiful arbor and alongside a very long and intricate trellis, interwoven with vines of downy clematis. The sweet scent of almonds filled the air, and he could not help but take this as a good sign. The gate must be close.

As he neared the end of the lattice, Christian was taken aback by a woman emerging from behind it. She walked slowly, her hips swaying sensually. Her dress was long, but the fabric thin, clinging to her form and rendered translucent by the sunlight. Moving to the middle of the path, she looked up at him with painted eyes and said, "I've been waiting for you, Christian."

"I don't know you," he said , walking toward her quickly, unabated, letting his eyes fall to his feet.

"But you can," she purred. "My name is Wanton and I have prepared my bed with flower pedals, perfumes, and fine linens of Egypt. Come and lie with me a while. Rest your weary body before you reach the gate. There's nothing but more drudgery beyond it." She piled her hair atop of her head, then let it fall, cascading down so as to partially obscure her face.

A series of thoughts passed through Christian's mind and spirit in the space of a second. The first was of his own wretched, filthy appearance (and, as Mr. Wiseman had so kindly pointed out, smell) and how this woman could certainly not be truly charmed by his present state, regardless of what she said. The second was of his wife, Christiana. He loved her more than words could adequately convey, and he felt sick at the very suggestion of betrayal. Then he thought of the Lord who had already so graciously restored him after his bold and willful infidelity.

He turned sideways and slipped around Wanton, supplanting her from the center of the Way with the burden on his back. "That should have gone the other way around," he said.

"What are you talking about, you vile man?" she called out, spitefully.

Christian didn't look back. "I should have thought first of my Lord, then of my wife, then of myself."

It took hours for Faithful to reach the outskirts of Pliable's field. It was not so far, but he was unwilling to pass through the city itself, staying instead to the borders, moving through the tallest crops, the loneliest places. At one point, he found himself on Obstinate's land and was nearly overcome with fear, darting stealthily from one hiding place to the next.

Man to man, Obstinate was no threat at all to Faithful. He was nothing. Bluster. Hot air. But a mere day after trying to fetch Christian back by words alone, he had easily commanded a crowd of murderous men. Faithful had no desire to find out how this bloodlust might escalate on a third day, nor did he wish to find himself the subject of an ad hoc posse comitatus with the single-minded, unyielding, and self-assured Obstinate as its leader.

As luck or providence would have it, though, he made his way, safe and unseen, to the far edge of Pliable's land. He took a moment to wonder whether the little man was yet alive to work it, and whispered a prayer for him, if he was.

Faithful looked out at the plain beyond and simultaneously felt a surge of triumph at having finally arrived and a sinking sense of deflation as he realized he had no earthly idea which way to go from here. Out, further from the city, to be sure—but in which direction?

The uncertainty weighed heavy, as if it resided inside his burden. But even deeper than that was a growing *certainty* that the old man with the glowing face was closing in on him, tracking him, preparing to overtake him. The bright outlook of the morning had proven fleeting. Faithful did not know why, but he was sure he hadn't seen the last of that frightful man.

Feeling quite exposed, standing here in the open, Faithful did his best to put the center of the City directly at his back and set out in the opposite direction. He hadn't quite reached the middle of the plain when a man came into view ahead, moving quickly toward him. Faithful reflexively reached for his sword, but found only the empty scabbard. His heart began clanging the alarm, but then let off as the man drew close enough to identify.

"Evangelist?"

"Good day, my friend! I'm so pleased that you decided to—*ooph!*" Faithful grabbed him up in a bear hug, taking his feet six inches off the ground.

"You have no idea how glad I am to see a friendly face." He set the smaller man down and glanced back toward Pliable's land. "Are you headed back there? To the city?"

"Well, I came in part to check on you, my friend. And so, in a sense, *you* are my destination. Let us walk together a while."

"But you just came from that direction. You don't mind covering the same ground again?"

"I can't imagine I'll ever tire of accompanying pilgrims down this road."

"Let's go." Faithful picked up his pace, again glancing behind him.

"Why do you keep looking back toward the town of your birth? Have you not set your hand to the plow and your face to the Celestial City?"

"Without a doubt I have. I look back, not out of longing for that doomed place, but out of concern that an enigmatic enemy of mine could at any moment overtake me."

"You're not talking about Obstinate?"

"No. With or without my sword, I worry not about Obstinate—unless he has a rowdy mob at his back. I am speaking of a man who came to my home last night and threatened to burn it down over my head. "

"Ahh. Had you ever met this man before?"

"At first, I thought him a stranger. But the more I think about it, the more I'm inclined to believe that I've seen him and his glowing face skulking in the shadows my entire life. I've seen him and feared him. And, while I did acquiesce to his demands last night, I still feel him on my tail now."

"This may be hard to hear, Faithful, but that man was doing the will of the King. Our King. Can I assume that, when he knocked on your door, you had determined to stay in the City, come what may?"

Faithful hesitated. "I—I had."

"And this man's approach, as unpleasant as it might have been, finally brought you to the Pilgrim Road?"

"In that case, I guess I'm worrying in vain."

"Perhaps not. Having hounded you your entire life and having chased you out from your home, this man may now consider you his own. If you see him again, be on alert, even beyond the Wicket Gate."

"The 'Wicket Gate?'"

Evangelist came to a stop. "Oh, that's right; I've yet to set you on your course." He laid a hand on Faithful's shoulder and pointed off into the distance. "Tell me, Faithful, do you see yonder Wicket Gate?"

Faithful squinted toward the horizon. "I think so? Or . . .

No. I don't believe I do."

"Do you see the shining light?"

Between the woman Wanton and the gate itself, Christian encountered no one. He kept his eyes fixed on the ground, three feet ahead of him, unwilling so much as to glance off to either side, until he nearly walked right into the gate itself. Coming to a sudden stop, and to his senses, he took a dozen steps back to get his bearings.

Before him, an enormous stone wall as tall as ten men stretched out in either direction, as far as he could see. To his right, it seemed to disappear into infinity. Off to the left, perhaps a mile away, the wall curved back a bit toward the forest. And there, taller by half than the wall itself, an enormous fortress surrounded a massive gateway, yawning wide open. Two round towers flanked the fortress and a turret rose up from the one closest to Christian. Hanging above the gate and billowing above the towers were dozens of large, brightly colored flags. Even from this distance, he could make out dozens of men moving about behind the battlements of the towers, three men up in the turret, and scores of people pouring in through the gate.

In stark contrast to all this, directly in front of Christian was a simple wooden gate, wide enough only to admit one person at a time. Along its rounded top edge were carved the words, "Knock and it shall be opened unto you."

Christian took a deep breath, stepped up to the entrance, and knocked twice.

At first there was no response. And so Christian called out, "Please open up! I come not as a worthy guest of the King—rather as an undeserving rebel. But if you will let me in, I will never stop singing his praise or serving his cause!"

After another uncertain moment, the gate creaked open

about a foot and a very grave looking man peered out at him.

"Who are you?" the man asked. "And where do you come from and what do you want?"

"My name is Christian. I am a poor, burdened sinner. I come from the City of Destruction and am on pilgrimage to Mount Zion in order to escape the wrath to come and to love and serve the King of that place all of my days—to glorify him and enjoy him forever. A good man who also serves the King sent me to this very gate and assured me it is the only way in. So, if you are willing . . . "

The man's face broke into a wide smile that seemed to erase twenty years. "I am willing with all my heart." He opened the gate the rest of the way.

But before Christian could enter, the gatekeeper lunged at him, swinging a large, curved wooden shield from behind the gate. He knocked Christian to the ground and crouched beside him as two flaming arrows came roaring down from the turret in the distance and thudded into the shield.

Standing quickly, the man grabbed Christian by his burden and bodily hauled him through the gate as another volley of four arrows narrowly missed them.

Christian stood, trying to gather his nerves.

"I apologize for the rough handling," the gatekeeper said, drawing a short sword from his belt and knocking the now-smoldering arrows from the shield. "The strong castle in the distance belongs to Beelzebub, and his forces often fire arrows at pilgrims who approach this gate, hoping to kill them before they enter."

He hung the shield on the wall and extended his hand. "My name is Goodwill."

Christian gripped the proffered hand and said, "I am in your debt, sir, for your protection and for letting me in. I rejoice and tremble. There was a moment when I feared that no one would answer."

"For you, Christian, an open door is set, which no man can shut. I gather that you are travelling alone? Not the wisest way to walk this road if it can be helped . . . "

"I am alone indeed. I tried to persuade my wife and children to join me. And there was another—Pliable was his name—who traveled with me for a very short time before turning back. But I am alone now."

"Already? What caused him to abandon the pilgrimage, before it had really begun?"

"We both fell into the Slough of Despond. It was . . . too much for him."

Goodwill shook his head, sadly. "This man Pliable holds the celestial glory in such low esteem that a few momentary troubles are not worth enduring?"

"If I'm being honest," said Christian, "the only real difference between Pliable and myself is that he turned off in the direction of his own house, while I turned away, just a short time later, toward the Hill Morality, persuaded by the carnal arguments of a Mr. Worldly Wiseman. And if Evangelist had not happened upon me there, I might have wound up even worse off than Pliable. It seems I'm more fit to be buried under that mountain than to enter through this gate."

"And yet, here you are," Goodwill said. "And here we do not weigh the past mistakes of those who knock. In fact, those who come here will never be cast out. Now, come with me and I will give you your instructions." He handed Christian a skin of water, which the pilgrim slurped down with no regard for his manners, and led him a few dozen paces beyond the gate. "You see the Narrow Way, of course." he asked.

"Yes. And much more clearly defined than the way leading up to the gate."

"This is the way you must go. It was paved by the patriarchs, the prophets, by Christ himself, and his apostles. To deviate from it would be the height of foolishness. But beware: there are many wide and crooked roads that butt up to this one. Stay on the Strait and Narrow Way."

Christian noticed that, while the gate was now behind him, the shining light was still far beyond, in the distance. "What is that light?" he asked.

Goodwill chuckled. "It's the Celestial City itself. You can see it from most stretches of the Way, but there will be times when you find it obscured by something or other. Do not be discouraged; keep moving along the Narrow Way."

"I will," Christian said. "But before I leave, I wonder if . . . "

"Yes?"

"Well, I've just been carrying this burden for so long and it grows heavier and bulkier and I know I could make better time along this road if you could just remove it for me."

"I'm afraid that's beyond my abilities. Be content to bear your burden a while longer, until you come to the place of deliverance. There it will simply fall from your back. But first, you have one more stop to make. The Interpreter's House is less than an hour's walk from here, situated on the right hand side of the path. When you arrive there, once again you need only knock, and you will be shown some wonders."

Christian's spirit felt lighter, having passed the first milestone in his journey, and he made good time to the front gate of a pleasant Tudor style country house, where he followed Goodwill's instructions and clacked the knocker a few times. When no one answered, he knocked again and yet again before someone finally called, from behind the door, "Who's there?"

"I am a traveler who was instructed by a friend of yours—or a friend of the master of the house—to call on you."

The door swung open and an old man with long, salt-and-pepper hair stood between the lintels. His pants were a bit too short and his jacket threadbare. He looked long and hard at Christian before saying, "I suppose you're hear to see the wonders."

"That's what I'm told."

"Come in then," the old man said. "I am the Interpreter. And I will show you things mysterious and things profitable." He beckoned Christian further in and said, "Deacon, would you be so kind as to light some candles?"

Only then did Christian notice an even thinner, very pale young man standing off to the side of the foyer. "This is my man, Deacon. My servant, but also my dearest friend. I love him like a son. Oh, thank you, Deacon."

When they each had a light in hand, the Interpreter led the way through a doorway, down a narrow hall, and into an expansive parlor. Around the room, inviting upholstered chairs and an ornate gate-leg table painted a picture of some wealth and sophistication, as did the oak wainscoting on the walls.

But the floor was absolutely covered with dust. Not a sheet of dust. Not even a thick layer of dust. Rather, piles and piles of it—hiding their feet entirely as they walked into the room. Christian felt his mouth drying up and his throat growing scratchy.

The Interpreter asked, "When do you suppose this room was last swept?"

"I can't imagine," Christian said.

"It has been many, many years."

Christian laughed. "Good thing your servant is like a son to you or he'd be out on his ear . . . no?" Both Deacon and the Interpreter blankly stared back at him.

Christian chuckled nervously. "Um . . . sorry."

"You may have the right idea," the Interpreter said. "Dea-

con, fetch the broom." The young man left the room for a moment and returned with a whisk-broom. He shut the door behind him, and began to sweep vigorously.

Christian's eyes clamped shut as the air in the room filled with swirling particles. He began to choke and cough. He felt a pressing need to leave this place, but the air was so thick with dust that he could not find his way back to the door. Putting a hand to the wall, he began moving in what he thought to be the right direction, only to find himself in a corner, where he doubled over, hacking violently, and fell to his knees.

The air was unbreathable here. Christian tried to pull his shirt up over his nose and mouth, to at least filter some of the particles out, but the cords of his burden, even tighter now than when he'd arrived, made that impossible. Involuntary tears streaked his cheeks and spittle gathered on his chin as he continued to cough and hack.

Somehow, he managed in the midst of his gagging to shout the words, "Stop! Please, stop it!" The churning dust began to thin immediately, settling slowly to the floor. It took a few minutes before Christian, rubbing his encrusted eyes, could see the two men standing against the far wall, again just staring at him. Their clothes and faces were covered in dust.

Christian stood and tried to wipe his clothes clean, but the dust ground into the other grime, mud, and dirt, leaving them all the filthier.

The Interpreter and Deacon gave themselves a quick shake and all the dust seem to sluff off of them, falling back to the floor, where the sum of it was even taller now, having been unsettled by the sweeping.

The older man opened another door, behind him, and called out, "It's time to fetch the water."

A few minutes later, a young woman entered, carrying a bucket. Starting in the far corner of the room, she began sprinkling water on the dust until she had wet down all of it. Taking the broom from Deacon, she swept the floor clean and, with the help of her two companions, gathered up the wetted dust into the bucket, where it seemed almost impossibly small, considering that it had filled the entire room a short time before.

He then looked at Christian expectantly and asked, "Do you understand?"

"I— Do I—? Am I even in the right *place*?"

The Interpreter rolled his eyes. "You are indeed, good Christian. Now seeing, understand. This parlor is the heart of a man never sanctified by the sweet grace of the Gospel. The dust is his original sin and all his inward corruptions, which have entirely defiled him. As Deacon began to sweep, he was for us a perfect picture of the Law. He could not cleanse the room. And the more he tried, the more we were choked by all the sin stirred up. In fact, it revived and strengthened the sin. Although the law uncovers and forbids sin, it has no power in itself to remove it. This young damsel is the Gospel. She immediately subdued the sin, vanquished it, and removed it, leaving the soul clean through faith, and as a result, leaving the room fit for the King of Glory to inhabit."

Christian digested this for a minute. "Yes, I do understand," he said. And his burden loosened a bit.

Faithful noticed the sign right away. *Slough Ahead: Mind the Steps*, it warned.

When they'd parted, a half an hour earlier, Evangelist had cautioned him to keep alert and sober-minded as there were potential pitfalls and many hidden dangers ahead. This one seemed rather obvious, though. There was the prominent warning sign, as well as the sensation of his feet beginning to sink a bit with each step.

Next to the swamp itself was a faded marker, identifying it as "The Slough of Despond." Faithful gazed into the bubbling muck and noticed the steps placed every two or three feet, from this side to the other. The sun shined straight down into the slough, even cutting into the thick, murky gunk, and Faithful could see that that the stone steps went all the way down, ostensibly to the bedrock beneath.

He placed his foot carefully on the first step and immediately felt it slip along a thin layer of slime. He did a panicked, flailing dance to regain his balance, somehow remaining upright. He stood there awkwardly on the first step, his burden seemingly working against him, always pulling in the worst direction in any given moment.

Another step sent Faithful sprawling forward. He stumbled to the next step, then the next, using his forward momentum, and before he knew it, he was closer to the far side of the slough, his eyes fixed on the shining light in the distance.

Then he looked down and saw the silhouettes of three long, eel-like creatures swimming in the muck beneath him, slowly circling the step on which he stood. His heart began to pound and he turned his attention to the next step, which seemed further away than the last one had been. The downward pull of his burden seemed to be moving in a circular pattern, now drawn to one of the creatures below.

Faithful stood immobilized by fear and indecision for a moment. Then he remembered Evangelist's parting words: "There's a lovely group of widows I must check in on today, but remember this, Faithful: keep the light in your eye. Do not look to the left or the right and, whatever you do, don't fix your eyes on things below. Godspeed, my friend."

Focusing again on the point of light in the distance, he took a blind step forward and felt solid rock beneath his feet. This he did a dozen more times, until he felt the squish of wet soil underfoot. He was beyond the slough, and a few more steps brought him to far dryer ground. There, the path resumed and Faithful pushed ahead.

The Interpreter led Christian into a small antechamber, containing only two benches and a large oil painting: a portrait of a very grim looking man. His eyes were looking up to heaven. In his hands, he held the best of books, and the law of truth was written upon his lips. He stood like one pleading with men.

He stepped closer and saw that, unlike any painting he'd seen before, this picture had depth. A third dimension. Behind the man, he could see the world at his back, and by tipping his head back and forth, he could see new angles, further in either direction. He began walking back and forth before the portrait, his eyes fixed upon it, then came to an abrupt stop, noticing a golden crown hanging above the man's head, only visible from one particular vantage. He continued to study the painting, from every angle, for the space of a quarter-hour.

Finally, still gazing at the portrait, he asked the Interpreter, "What is the meaning of this?"

"This man is able to unfold dark things to sinners. The world is behind him and his eyes are fixed on things above, for, compared to the love of his master's service, he despises carnal and earthly things. As a result, the crown of reward hangs over his head, to be received in the world that is to come.

"But who is he?"

"He is the only man the Lord of the place you are headed has authorized to be your guide in hard and difficult places. As you go, you will encounter—indeed, have already encountered—pretenders who claim to lead you in the right way, but it is only right in their eyes, and will lead you to death."

Christian meant to answer him, but had nothing to say.

"Come, then," the Interpreter said, "to the bedchamber of two very different siblings. There is more for you to understand."

Faithful wasted not a step that afternoon and he was soon rewarded with a break from the sun, as he passed beneath an arbor and was able to hug tight against a long, beautiful trellis, covered entirely with fragrant flowers. His eyes were still fixed on the light and, to his great excitement, he noticed the top of a tall stone wall at the horizon. This must be where he would find the Wicket Gate, he decided, pushing aside the soreness and creeping exhaustion and pressing ahead.

Then, all at once, a woman stood blocking the path. She was very beautiful, voluptuous, and casting her eyes at Faithful with a smoldering desire.

"I've been waiting for you, Faithful," she said.

"You have?" Faithful took a few staggering steps toward her before his knees locked up. There was something amiss here.

"Yes. My name is Wanton and I have prepared my bed with flower pedals, perfumes, and fine linens of Egypt. Come and lie with me a while. Rest your weary body before you reach the gate. She closed the space between them.

"Are you not married?" Faithful asked, intoxicated by her perfume and the softness of her every feature and movement.

"My husband is away," she said. "And he may never return. Besides, he is weak and delicate. I've been so lonely waiting for you, my strong, handsome blacksmith."

Faithful's eyes traced her form from head to toe and back up again. Suddenly, for the first time in many days, the weight of his burden was entirely lifted.

Deacon led the way up a staircase and, using a taper, lit a few small leaded lights affixed to the wall of the landing.

"Through here," the Interpreter commanded, pointing to an ornate door. Entering in, Christian found himself in a small bedroom, where two little children sat in wooden chairs.

Christian was immediately reminded of his own children and felt a renewed stab of longing to have his family with him on this journey. Forcing his thoughts back to the matter at hand, he asked, "Who are these?"

"The eldest," he said, "is Passion. And the other, Patience."

Passion sat fidgeting, frustrated, his face turning red with discontent until he let out an angry yell and kicked his heels back against the chair. Patience was very quiet, sitting still, hands in her lap, happy and content.

"Why is Passion so upset?" Christian asked.

"The governor of these children is making them wait until the first of the year for his best things. But Passion wants them now."

The boy suddenly gripped the armrests of his chair, threw his head back, and shrieked at the top of his lungs. Christian covered his ears in pain.

Between the two children, a man materialized, holding a cloth bag, which he handed to Passion. The impudent child emptied its contents on the floor: treasures of all kinds. He laughed and laughed, mocking poor Patience and inspecting each jewel and coin. As he continued to scoff and mock, Christian saw him growing up into a young man, wasting his inheritance on parties, clothes, wine, women, and companions who only suffered Passion's unpleasant disposition because of the treasure at his disposal. But soon, he had spent it all and was left with nothing but rags on his back.

Christian said, "I think I understand. One of these children was willing to wait for next year—that is, the world to come—for her treasure, while the other insisted on having all the good things now, in this life. He thinks a bird in the hand is worth two in the bush."

"Indeed," the Interpreter said. "In his mind, that old proverb has more authority than all the divine testimonies of the world to come."

"Patience has the best wisdom," Christian said.

"Yes, for three reasons. First, she waits for the better portion. Secondly, she will have glory while her brother has only rags. And finally, the glory of the next world will never wear out or be fully spent, as Passion's treasures have been. And yet he laughed to scorn at his sibling. But by and by, he came to understand that he did not have so much reason to laugh. Perhaps another proverb would be more appropriate for young Passion—the one about he who laughs last. In our Lord's kingdom, the first will be last and the last will be first."

"So the lesson here," Christian said, "is not to covet the things that are now, but to wait for things to come."

"Well said. The things that are now seen are temporary, but the things to come are eternal. And yet, because our fleshly appetites are such near neighbors to the things of this world, even while they are such strangers to the eternal things to come, they tend to fall in love with the former and remain cold and distant to the latter."

"I have experienced this," Christian said. "Your warning is well received."

"I am happy to hear it. Now, follow me. The greatest wonders are yet ahead of us."

Something inside Faithful broke him from the spell and he took a few more steps toward the Wicket Gate. But something else inside him was yet bewitched by the sight and scent of Wanton, and so he reached an internal accord—a compromise—and said, "Walk with me, good lady." After all, what harm could there be in that?

She stuck close by his side as they went along, continually dropping hints (which grew less and less subtle) about her intentions with him and how she would have them spend the afternoon, the evening, and all of the night.

They'd been travelling together for ten minutes when she wrapped her hand around his bicep and tugged him aside, saying, "My house is this way. Come with me now."

Faithful could now see the Wicket Gate at the base of the wall, no more than a hundred yards away.

"Come," she said again, more insistently. "You will not regret it."

"Her feet go down to death," Faithful said. "Her steps take hold on hell."

"What?"

"I just remembered those words—ancient words that I heard again and again as a boy." He yanked his arm free, his feet anchored to the Narrow Path. "I will not defile myself with you."

She pressed herself against his chest and purred, "This road will be here tomorrow. The gate will be there tomorrow. I am here right now. Think of the journey, not the destination. Live in this moment. Don't be a fool."

"A fool is exactly what you'd have me be. Leave me," he commanded. The words were strong, but there was no conviction in them. Faithful clamped his eyes shut to avoid being further enchanted by her beauty, and felt her lips against his neck.

"It's not as if you've never done this before," she whispered. "Just once more before you walk through that gate. Get it out of your system."

He lashed out at her in desperation, meaning to shove her away and make his escape. But when he opened his eyes, he found his hands on her bare shoulders. She was gazing now into his soul with her heavily painted eyes, worming deeper and deeper into his desires.

Faithful felt his resolve breaking. He was too weak to resist her. Pulling his hands to his sides, he took two long steps back and again closed his eyes, praying for deliverance. The gate was so close.

"No," he said again—this time with conviction and constancy.

That's when Wanton began to beat him with a strength he would never have anticipated. He went down to his knees as she rained blows upon him, avoiding his burden, instead striking at his ribs, his neck, his arms, which he'd wrapped around his head to protect it.

"Who are you to reject me?" she yelled. "You foul, wicked man! You will not deny your carnality. You cannot stand for long in the face of temptation. I will have you, one way or the other!"

Faithful was praying for strength to resist, knowing that he could not endure this beating indefinitely. He was too weak. Too feeble, too fallen.

As he realized this, he was filled with a holy resolve, and stood, eyes open, hands ready for battle. But Wanton was gone.

Only the faint remnant of her smell hung in the air. What had a few minutes ago been the aroma of life itself now stunk worse than sulfur in Faithful's nostrils.

Shaking off the pain and panic of the attack, Faithful ran with all his remaining strength until he found himself pounding his fist against the Wicket Gate.

The Sad Case of Little-Faith
-of the Town Sincere-

They were three brothers: Faint-Heart, Guilt, and Deep-Doubt, and they had a habit of following one of those winding roads down from the Broadway Gate to where it abutted the Narrow Way. These wicked men made it a practice—along with many others of the Wide Road—to come down under cover of darkness and attack unsuspecting pilgrims. These three brothers tended only to rob the travelers they found, for gain and for sport, but so many had been killed at this place that it was commonly called Dead-Man's Lane.

It was in the wee hours of the morning that they travelled this road once again and came upon a pilgrim, foolishly sleeping, just off the path—exactly where Dead-Man's Lane met the Narrow Way. Furthermore, they were pleased to find that he was alone.

Guilt hefted his club and made to rush straight for the prone figure, but Faint-Heart held him back. "Hold, brother. Does this not seem too easy to you? In all the years we've worked this place, have we ever come across a pilgrim sleeping just where we tend to enter the Way? What's more, a pilgrim sleeping all alone, with no one to stand watch or to help him defend himself against attack? Doesn't this seem odd?"

"No, it doesn't," said Deep-Doubt, "and I look not a gift-horse in the mouth."

"Agreed," said Guilt. "Pick apples long enough and a plump one is bound to fall right into your basket eventually."

"But . . . what if it's a trap?" Faint-Heart asked.

"Stay back if you want to. But don't think you'll share in the spoils if you do."

"No, no, I'm coming. Just . . . take care."

The three of them rushed in at the pilgrim, trying to move with stealth, but still rousing the man so that, by the time they surrounded him, he was standing, shocked and speechless, gaping at each of the brothers in turn.

"Do you want to die tonight?" asked Deep-Doubt.

The pilgrim shook his head and raised his hands, white as a sheet. He clearly lacked the power to fight or fly.

Faint-Heart growled, "Then give us your purse to save your life."

The man glanced down at the money bag on his belt, but made no move to retrieve it. Rather, he looked out beyond the robbers, as if he expected someone to ride in and rescue him.

Never a patient man, Guilt reared back with his club and bludgeoned the pilgrim along the side of the head, right above his ear, sending him down, hard, to the earth, where he lay half-conscious and bleeding profusely.

Deep-Doubt reached into the purse and pulled out a bag of silver coins, much to the delight of his brothers.

"Thieves," the pilgrim groaned. Then, suddenly arching his back, he shrieked into the darkness, "Thieves! Thieves!"

Guilt silenced him with a kick to the side, but the three robbers were spooked now.

"Did you hear that?" Faint-Heart said, his eyes wide in fear.

Guilt scoffed. "You're such a nervous little—"

"Shh!" Deep-Doubt held up his hand. "I hear it too."

"So what? Let another pilgrim bring us another purse. We can carry a lot more."

"But what if it's him?" Faint-Heart said, the words catching in his throat. "What if it's Mr. Great-Grace? We've all heard the tales: Mr. Great-Grace of the town of Good-Confidence. He makes short work of our kind."

Deep-Doubt jingled the bag of coins and said, "We got what we came for. Let's away, and divide it up."

That poor bleeding pilgrim's name was Little-Faith and he had come on pilgrimage from the town Sincere. He lay there for several more hours, not sure whether he would bleed to death on the side of the road or whether some sympathetic traveler would come upon him and nurse his wounds. Neither thing happened, though, and as the sun brought the mercies of a new day, Little-Faith was able to sit up, though his vision was blurred and his head throbbed.

He first took stock of his person, gingerly touching the flesh near his gash and realizing that the blood had coagulated over a nasty goose egg—nothing to sneeze at, but certainly not a mortal wound. Then he inventoried his possessions. The bag of silver had contained almost all of his spending money, which was a terrible loss to Little-Faith. However, in the dark, they had apparently missed the other purse tucked into his belt at the hip, and the scroll, which he had received from the Shining Ones at the Place of Deliverance. And when the brigand clubbed him on the head, by good providence, he had fallen down on top of both the jewels and the scroll, and the rogues had skittered off before discovering them.

He looked around to ensure that no other bandits skulked about, and then dumped out his remaining possessions on the ground before him. The ransacked bag still contained three silver coins. He also had all of the precious jewels entrusted to him and, again, the scroll which he was to present at the Celestial Gate.

Certainly, it could have been much worse, he thought, but no measure of comfort came forth from this truth. In fact, he could not be comforted, because any thought of what had happened—what he'd endured, or even what he'd been spared—only made him fume at the wrong these rogues had wrought. How he had been so well prepared for this trip, but now would have to struggle to make it to the end. How there would doubtless be no justice in this case, as he was quite sure he'd be unable to identify these men in the light of day, even if they were apprehended.

After washing and bandaging his wound, and resting for several days, Little-Faith resumed his pilgrimage, but with a fraction of his former speed and an even smaller part of his former zeal. Although he had only a little odd money left, he was not wise in how he spent it and, before long, it was all gone, and he was reduced to begging (for he knew he could not sell his jewels), and he went on with many a hungry belly for the rest of his pilgrimage.

But even apart from this, the remainder of his journey—from Dead-Man's Lane on—was singularly marked by that one unfortunate event. Little-Faith became rather paranoid and sewed both his scroll and his jewels into the lining of his jacket so that no thieves would spot them and set upon him.

Without easy access to his scroll, he could not read it for

comfort, and even when he occasionally felt moved to touch it (through his coat) or simply call it to mind, this would dredge up fresh thoughts of his loss and these thoughts would swallow up all.

His journey continued to be a solitary one, not because he came upon no other pilgrims, but because he continually spewed doleful and bitter complaints. If anyone would come alongside and make conversation with him, he would immediately begin to relate how he had been robbed and where and when—who it was that did it, and what he had lost. He would show them his scar and describe the pain and how he hardly escaped with his life. Like a bird tweeting the same irksome song over and over, he eventually drove away any fellow travelers, save for those who tended toward similarly bitter dispositions.

And when he finally came to the Celestial Gate, he entered only by the skin of his teeth. For when the gatekeeper there asked for his scroll and jewels, he forgot what he had done with them, for he had not laid eyes on them in many years.

Only when one of the Shining Ones came and removed his coat and cut a slit in the lining with his sword did he remember and, all at once, was filled with shame for having buried this Great Treasure in his own person under a pile of anger, regret, and cynicism . . . for having been beaten and robbed by Faint-Heart, Guilt, and Deep-Doubt, only to become them.

Deliverance

Faithful only slowed a bit as he approached the Wicket Gate, throwing himself into it, causing it to shudder—but not quite buckle—against his weight. He only noticed the instructions engraved in the wood when he had already begun to obey them, pounding his fist against the little gate.

The door opened a bit and a very grave man asked, "Who are you? And where do you come from? And what do you want?"

"Who am I? Who are *you*?" Faithful demanded.

"Why, I am Goodwill, and—"

"Sir, if you've any good will, you will let me in now, for even one more moment on this side of the gate might mean my death."

The gatekeeper smiled widely and stepped back, pulling the gate open behind him.

"I was watching you," he said, closing and bolting

the gate, "through a peep in the wall. I saw the enemy's attack and was considering how I might lend you aid when suddenly—victory was yours."

Faithful nodded sharply, his eyes glazed over and fixed on the backside of the little gate.

"Are you alright, sir?" Goodwill asked. "Don't worry; the gate is secure."

Faithful enveloped him in a rough embrace that quite nearly crushed him. Then he began to weep.

"Oh, take heart," Goodwill croaked. "It's all over now. She's gone."

Faithful let him go and wiped his face against his sleeve. "It is not the woman Wanton that has me so shaken. It was not she who almost brought me down to the grave. It was something inside of myself—something deep in me that truly wanted to follow her down to hell, even knowing that's where she would lead me. I fear I've slipped in through this gate under the guise of a true pilgrim, when I actually don't deserve to be here at all."

"I know you, Faithful, and you are true to your name. No pilgrim 'deserves' to enter through the Wicket Gate or to journey to the Celestial City, but our King is full of mercy and grace and will look upon your faith and count it as righteousness. Why, it was by his grace that you even withstood the enemy at the gate. For it is written, *The abhorred of the Lord fall into her pit.* But you escaped her."

Faithful slumped against a dogwood tree and slid down the trunk until he sat in its shade, eyes closed. "Goodwill, my friend, I know not whether I did wholly escape her."

"Don't be so dramatic. And don't go to sleep just yet, Faithful. You have more to do while it is still day."

"Just a few minutes . . . "

"Maybe you just need a drink," Goodwill said, sloshing his water skin onto Faithful.

"Whoa! I'm up! I'm up! Good grief . . . "

"What is it about today?" Goodwill mused. "Two pilgrims in a row, travelling all alone. Our Lord sent his apostles out two by two for a reason."

Faithful shrugged. "I am unmarried, my partner in business would sooner trample holy things underfoot than accept them, and my neighbors tried to string me up just yesterday. How would I arrive, if not alone?"

"Mm hmm. You know, you say that you're 'up,' and yet there you still sit under that tree."

Faithful stood, groaning under his burden. "There; happy? Save a little water for drinking. And tell me: where would you have me go before nightfall?"

"An hour's walk from here, you will find the house of the Interpreter, who will reveal great wonders to you. And beyond that is the Holy of Holies, where you will be delivered."

The weariness faded from the pilgrim's face, replaced by a hint of hope. "Delivered," he repeated.

"By the grace of God. Now make haste," Goodwill commanded, tossing him the half-full waterskin. "You may yet catch him today."

"Catch . . . who?"

"Two are better than one. They can help each other up. Keep each other warm. Watch each other's backs."

"The pilgrim who just passed through here before me. You think I can catch him."

"I do. If you mend your pace and make some real progress."

The Interpreter led Christian back down the stairs, through the parlor, and into a small kitchen, where a table of ash and a fireside chair filled most of the room.

A roaring fire burned in the brick fireplace, hot and high. Before it stood a sallow, hunched man, fixed in place, continually dowsing the fire with water. Bucket after bucket he sloshed into the flames, trying to extinguish them, and no sooner did he run out than a ghoulish boy would drag in yet more water, carrying six buckets at a time on a long staff balanced over his shoulders.

The result was that water gushed continually into the fire, and yet, rather than being quenched, the flames blazed all the hotter, edged with a pyrotechnic blue. Still, if the man tired of his task or grew impatient or frustrated, he hid it well.

Christian studied the man, as he mechanically emptied unending containers of water into the fireplace. Then the man turned his head and met Christian's gaze, and the pilgrim took an involuntary step back. His eyes were yellow, their elliptical pupils nothing more than horizontal slits. He glared at Christian as he poured out another bucket, then turned his attention back to the flames.

"What means this?" Christian asked.

"This fire is the work of grace, wrought in the heart of a saint. This man is the devil himself, ever endeavoring to extinguish the flame, with the help of his servant, the world. He tires not, nor is he distracted from his work. And yet, as you can see, the fire waxes hotter and brighter and higher yet."

"But how? The fire itself is supernatural?"

"It is indeed," the Interpreter said. "In days of old, our King sent fire down from heaven, upon the altar of Elias, which burned up not only the bullock upon the altar, but the water in the trench and the stones themselves. But even holy fire can languish and die over time."

"And how long has this fire been burning?"

"Many, many yeears."

"I confess," Christian said, "that I do not fully grasp the meaning of this vision."

"Ah, but you will. Follow me."

He led Christian out a servant's entrance, to the outside of the same wall, where another man stood, holding a vessel in his hand, from which he continually poured oil into a channel, constantly feeding the fire.

"Does he not run out of oil?"

"Never. Do you recall another tale of Elias the prophet? He and the widow of Zarephath?"

"Yes. Her oil was miraculously replenished until the dire draught had ended. Is this man . . . that prophet?"

"By no means. All the prophets of old bow down and worship at this man's feet. This is Christ himself. With the oil of his grace, he maintains the work already begun in the heart. His grace is never exhausted and, whatever wiles the enemy may concoct to snuff out that fire, he feeds the flames with his grace, ever sufficient to keep the souls of his people burning bright. And yet, he works here in secret, his ways mysterious and often unseen."

"I understand," Christian said. "When tempted and tried, a pilgrim may not see how this work of grace is maintained in the soul."

The Interpreter nodded. "And yet, he can rest assured that God is applying his grace, feeding the fire, which he himself kindled."

Christian thought that he would be content to gaze upon this vision of Christ, feeding the fire with his unending oil forever, although he could only see his back, but the Interpreter took him by the hand and began leading him away from the house.

"Come," he said. "I will show you a stately palace where more wonders await."

They walked for a few minutes along a pleasant path, over rolling hills, until a beautiful, majestic palace came into view. Christian turned around twice, surveying the land and trying to get his bearings.

"Which way is the gate?" he asked.

"Worry not about that," the Interpreter said. "Tell me what you see."

"A fortress as delightful as it is secure. I see men and women walking on top of it, clothed entirely in gold. I see turrets and towers and battlements all of pure gold as well! In all my life, I have never seen anything as lovely or magnificent as this and I have never wanted to enter any place as badly as I want to enter through that gate. Please tell me that's where we are headed next."

"Keep watching, good Christian," the Interpreter said, leading him closer. About fifty yards from the door stood a great company of men, all gazing upon the palace with the same longing that Christian felt, but none of them dared to go in.

"What do you suppose is holding them back?" the Interpreter asked. Only then did Christian notice the detachment of troops guarding the entrance—frightful, battle-hardened men, heavy-laden with armor and brandishing swords, maces, and battle axes. Beside them, a clerk sat at a small table with a book and inkhorn before him, pen poised in his hand, to take the names of any who would dare try to enter.

One by one, the gathered rabble approached the clerk, only to lose heart at the sight of the armed guards, and shrink back. Just when Christian thought that none would find his courage and gird his loins for battle, a stout and determined man drew up to the table and loudly declared, "Write my name down, sir." He wore a leather breastplate, tassets, and grieves. When the clerk had obliged him, he pulled a helmet onto his head, drew his sword, and rushed into the midst of the guard.

As one man, they descended upon the warrior, swarming down from the gate and striking blows upon him with their weapons, their fists, the heels of their boots. Undeterred, he slipped their attacks and countered, cutting and hacking with deadly precision. In the space of a minute, he had gained a good deal of ground and left half a dozen bleeding bodies behind him.

Christian gasped as one of the guards managed to circle behind the brave warrior and pierce his flesh, sending him down to one knee. But as quickly as he went down, the valiant warrior rose, spun, and, with a single blow removed the man's head from his body. Turning again to face his foes, he saw them shrink back, no longer in tight formation.

Pushing his advantage, the warrior rushed forward once again, cutting the legs out from beneath one, pushing through  a painful wound to his temple and dispatching two more enemies with savage, piercing strikes.

Regrouping, the remaining men made to surround him, but the warrior advanced too quickly, parrying a lunge, feinting a strike, and then ramming his sword through the belly of the nearest man. Releasing the hilt, he grabbed up the axe from his vanquished foe and charged at the last few men, crushing skulls and felling them all in a vicious advance, which brought him finally through the gate.

When he had disappeared into the palace, one of the men watching from atop called out in a pleasant voice, "Come in, come in. Eternal glory shall you win."

A moment later, the warrior himself appeared with the men above, who clothed him head-to-toe in the same golden garments they wore.

Smiling, Christian said, "I think I know the meaning of this one. Please, may I go in now?"

"We will go in," the Interpreter said, "but not to the heights. Follow me."

Leading him around the back of the palace, the Interpreter pointed to a set of rock-hewn stairs, leading down beneath the ground and said, "The next wonder awaits you through that door."

Christian balked. Something about this descent into darkness brought to life a sense of blind fear the likes of which he had not known since childhood. "Could I at least see the inside of the palace first?" he asked.

The Interpreter simply pointed again, down into the belly of the earth. Pushing against his fear, Christian descended into a dank dungeon, which stunk of filth and despair. There, in the middle of the room, an iron cage was suspended from the ceiling. In it, an emaciated man sat, gripping the bars. His eyes, filled with sorrow and devoid of hope, met Christian's for a moment before his gaze fell back to floor of his cage.

"Who is this?" Christian asked.

"Why don't you ask him?" the Interpreter said.

"Who are you?"

"I am what I once was not."

"Well then, what were you?"

The man sighed heavily, like the sound of a breaking heart. "I was a professing Christian, determined to walk the Narrow

Way. Or at least that's what I told my friends and my family. And even myself. If you had asked anyone back then what I wanted—what I lived for—they would have told you the Celestial City was my aim. And if you asked me, I would have told you with true joy in my breast that I would enter in there at the last."

Christian stepped closer. "So . . . what are you now?"

The man lurched forward in the cage, eyes wild. "I am a man of despair! I am shut up in this iron cage and I cannot get out!" He slumped again against himself and studied his hands, folded in his lap. "Oh, how I cannot."

"But how did you go from one to the other?"

"I slept when I should have watched. I left off being sober and alert. I laid the reins upon the neck of my lusts and sinned against the very light of the world and all the goodness of God. I have grieved the Spirit and now . . . he is gone! I tempted the devil and now—he is here, with me! Always with me. It's one thing to be tempted by the evil one, but to tempt him is far more dangerous. And now here I sit in this cage with God's wrath kindled against me and a heart so hardened that it cannot repent."

Christian wanted to offer some consolation, but was at a loss. Turning to the Interpreter, he asked, "Is there no hope for this man?" The old sage simply gestured at the man in the cage.

"Is there truly no hope for you, sir? Nothing but to remain locked in this iron cage of despair?"

"Nothing at all."

"But that can't be. The son of the Most High is merciful and kind."

"This is true. And yet, I have crucified him anew to myself and put him to open shame. I have despised his person, despised his righteousness, despised his mercy. I have counted his blood an unholy thing and made a mockery of it. I have trampled the spirit of grace underfoot. And in doing so, I have shut myself out of all the promises so that nothing remains for me but threats—dreadful threats, faithful threats of certain judgment. Wrath and fire. The fruit of the curse."

"What could have been worth all that?"

The man laughed a desperate, hollow laugh and said, "Worth it? Nothing! I traded the promises of life eternal for the lusts, pleasures, and profits of this world. They promised me great delight and satisfaction, but they never intended to deliver. And now they just gnaw at me, biting my flesh, feeding on me like a burning worm while I remain locked in this cage."

"The answer is plain to me," Christian said. "Repent. Turn from your lusts and passions and throw yourself at the mercy of the Prince of Mercy!"

"You aren't listening. Repentance is out of my reach! My heart is hardened, my conscience seared. God has handed me over to my own shameful desires and now I cannot even bear the thought of parting with them—even while they consume me! In this state, His Word gives me no encouragement, no hope. In fact, it was your *God* himself who locked me in this iron cage so that all the men in the world cannot let me out." He threw his head back against the bars and shouted, "Oh, eternity! How can I grapple with this misery through all eternity?"

Christian reached through the bars to comfort the man, but his hand was cold upon the prisoner's flesh and he pulled it back immediately.

The Interpreter said, "Remember this man's misery, that it might be a perpetual warning to you, Christian."

"I am sure I will never forget it. God help me to watch and be sober and alert, to pray that I would never walk in the way of this man's desolation." Christian turned his back to the man in the cage and said, "I can take no more. I think it is time for me to go now. My burden is so heavy. I cannot bear it even another hour. Just send me on my way, good Interpreter."

"Your deliverance is at hand. But before you go, allow me to show you just one more thing."

The Interpreter led him deeper into the dungeon, through a grotto, and down a narrow hall, where, even stooping down, Christian had a hard time squeezing through with the burden on his back. Then they came to a door, which the Interpreter opened and bid the pilgrim to enter.

Passing through it, Christian found himself back on the landing in the Interpreter's house. The old man shuffled past him and opened the door to the same bedchamber where they had previously encountered Passion and Patience. Only the room was entirely different. There a man was rising out of bed, white as a sheet, shaking and trembling as he got dressed.

"Sir," Christian said, entering the room, "Why are you shaking like that?"

The man fell back onto the mattress and ran his fingers through thick black hair. "Last night, I had the most intense and vivid and terrifying dream. I dreamt that the sky grew exceedingly black, blotting out the moon and every star. Thunder began to rumble in from the East, and flashes of lightning all but blinded me. In each new flash I saw new terrors: four men on horses, riding over the land, bringing with them plague and war and famine. The angel of death, emptying vials of pestilence all over the land.

"In due time, the sky suddenly burned bright with a prime, pure white light, as if the last flash of lightning had been drawn out indefinitely, and I saw a Man sitting on a cloud, arrayed in gold and shining like the sun. He was surrounded by creatures I cannot begin to describe—all blinking eyes and beating wings and awesome terror. And around them, thousands and thousands of celestial warriors, clothed in shining garments, their swords drawn and ready for war. And I heard the sound of a trumpet and a voice saying, "Arise, ye dead, and come to judgment!" And with that, the rocks began to shake and crack and crumble and the graves of the dead were opened, and they came forth—some exceedingly glad, looking upward, and some scurrying hideously about, like scattering insects exposed to the light, trying to hide themselves even beneath the broken rocks.

"Then I saw the One who sat upon the cloud open a Book and gather all the world to himself, drawing them in, many against their will. But they were kept at a distance, as the accused in a courtroom is kept back from the magistrate, for a wall of fire held them back. And the Man who came on the Clouds of Heaven said to his host, 'Gather the tares, the chaff, the stubble, and cast them into the lake of fire.' And I saw the bottomless pit opened up, right where I stood. And I was overcome by the smoke and flames that issued forth from it and paralyzed with fear by the hideous noises from beneath.

"And the One on the cloud spoke again, saying, 'Now bring the wheat into the granary,' and I saw many gathered and caught up into the clouds with him. But I was left below. I tried to hide myself, but the Man who sat upon the clouds kept his eyes fixed upon me. And my sins—all my sins—came into my mind all at once and my own conscience accused me on every side." He looked up at Christian. "And that's when I awoke."

"You dreamt that the Day of Judgment had come, and you were not ready."

The man nodded. "But what frightened me most was not the bottomless pit or the shrieks from the Lake of Fire—rather, the Judge whose eyes were ever upon me."

The Interpreter took Christian by the arm and led him back out to the landing. "Have you considered all these things?"

"Yes. They have given me hope. And fear."

"Keep them in your mind, to press you forward in the way that you must go and to keep you from veering off to either side. And take solace in this—that the Comforter will always be with you, to guide you along the way. And now it is time to go."

"Thank you, good Interpreter," Christian said. "I don't believe I've ever met anyone like you."

"I hear that a lot." From downstairs came the sound of

someone knocking at the door.

"Deacon," the Interpreter called, "could you answer the door? I am showing good Christian out." He led the pilgrim down the stairs, through the kitchen, and out the servants' entrance. Before him, Christian saw the Narrow Way, starting right there in the doorway and headed straight out toward the Shining Light.

Christian travelled for less than half an hour before the highway became fenced in by a wall on either side. A brass plate bearing the word "Salvation" gave the name of the wall. At this point, the road began to incline—slightly at first, but, before long, it was so steep that Christian struggled to ascend with the burden on his back.

He hated his burden with a renewed loathing. It had become intolerable, cutting off circulation so that his hands tingled and tremored, compressing his spine so that every move ached and creaked. Walking along level ground was hard enough, and yet Christian pushed ever upward, even as the walls on both sides closed inward and the road became so narrow that it barely accommodated the breadth of his shoulders.

And yet, despite his pain and lethargy, Christian felt a renewed sense of hope for what lie ahead, as well as a rekindled fear of the destruction at his back. And so he began to run. And the faster he ran, the more power he felt coursing through him.

Soon, he came to a brief leveling, where the road curved a bit, so as to take him around a large, rocky outcropping. Only when he had reached the other side did he see it for what it was: a tomb. This was confirmed for Christian when he leaned down to peer in the entrance (for the stone that would have sealed the tomb had been rolled back). Upon the rock-hewn shelf where the body should have lain was a burial cloth, blood-stained and bearing the faintest image of a man. Closer to the entrance, apart from the sheet, was a smaller cloth, folded up and absolutely caked in dried blood.

Studying these unclean graveclothes, it occurred to Christian that these were pure and spotless compared to his own filthy rags. For the first time in many days, he truly looked down at himself and assessed his condition. His shirt, which had once been a pleasant beige, was no longer any particular color. It was tattered and threadbare, nasty and putrid-smelling. Having slowly grown accustomed to it long ago, Christian could suddenly smell his own foul odor anew and see his own disgusting condition as if taking himself in from another's point of view. The burden itself was foul, he now realized, in a way that it had never been to him before. It had been a source of pain, worry, and alarm; a weight to slow him down and hold him back. But now he was aware of its contents—the horrific rotting filth he'd carried with him everywhere he'd gone. The filth he was even now carrying with him toward the Celestial City. It was clear as could be. And it was *this place* that made the difference. Christian was sure of it.

Turning again toward the uphill path, he could now see the summit, not far ahead, and there, a cross of wood stood silhouetted against the orange sky. Christian began to run once again, faster than he ever had, racing up the mount toward the cross. The walls at his sides seemed to be propelling him forward, as did every hope and desire within him. The cross itself was drawing him upward and he moved now as if he wore no burden at all, feeling lighter than he'd ever felt before.

And then he heard it: something behind him. He stopped for a moment and looked back, only to see his burden, having fallen away, tumbling down the hill, end over end, faster and faster, until it disappeared into the mouth of the tomb.

Resuming his climb, he practically floated the last few feet and fell down at the foot of the cross. There, he felt as if his heart would burst with joy and holy sorrow. Hope enveloped him— the kind of hope he'd never dared even hope for. Words came to his lips and he praised the Prince whose cross and empty tomb had won his salvation, saying, "He has given me rest by his sorrow and life by his death! To him be glory and honor and wisdom and thanks and all power and might forever and ever!"

When he had tarried a while, on his face before the cross, he stood and gazed up at it, amazed that, simply by his looking upon it, his burden should fall from his back. As he studied the

blessed sight of his Savior's passion, the floodgates broke, and tears streamed down his cheeks—tears of repentance and joy and relief and awe.

He was still weeping when three Shining Ones came to him, greeting him with the words, "Peace be with you."

Christian could only nod back at them.

The first approached him and touched him on the back, where his burden had been— where he'd felt nothing but chafing and stiffness and pain for such a long time. "Your sins have been forgiven you," he said.

The second came forth and stripped him of his filthy rags, washed him clean, and clothed him with all new raiment. including a beautiful coat the likes of which Christian had never seen before. "You are now clothed in the righteousness of the Savior," he said.

The third approached and placed a mark on his forehead and a scroll in his hand with a seal upon it. "Keep this close to you at all times," he instructed. "Look upon it for comfort as you travel, and present it at the Celestial Gate."

Christian again began to weep, saying, "Forgive me for my tears. I just never thought I would arrive. And now . . . I'm finally here."

"Your tears are good and right," said the Shining One, "but do not be misled. Here you receive forgiveness and here you are relieved of your burden. But this is not the end; this is only the beginning."

Difficulty

Faithful watched the valiant warrior defeat his last few foes with savage blows from his sword, and enter triumphantly into the palace.

"Do you understand?" the Interpreter asked.

"Well," Faithful answered. "This beautiful palace is obviously a picture of the magnificence of the Celestial City. Many wish to enter, but only a few dare to truly commit; the others are scared off by trials or charmed away by this world's riches and pleasures—by the fear of men or the praise of men. And to truly obtain the rewards and be clothed in glory as this man is now being clothed, we must approach our lives as a battle. Putting to death the deeds and appetites of the flesh and taking every captive thought. Is that about the size of it?"

"Well put. That is, indeed, the approximate 'size of it.' This man does not shrink back or stand at a distance, simply waiting to enter the kingdom. Rather, he takes it by force, whatever the cost, whatever wounds he might sustain. They that will have heaven must not be held back by any difficulties they meet with, but rather press, crowd, and thrust through all that may stand between their souls and their Great Reward.

"Now, follow me, good Faithful. I have one last wonder to show you." The Interpreter led him away from the palace, out toward the wilderness. Faithful noticed a very faint trail beneath their feet, as though it had been walked by only a few, or perhaps none at all for quite some time. The forest grew thicker around them and, more than once, the Interpreter raised his cane to chop at a vine or sapling that stood in their way.

They walked for such a long time, over such a great distance that Faithful began to wonder if the old man was lost.

They'd reached the top of a hill and were now descending when Faithful joked, "If you're planning to lead me out into the wilderness and leap upon and leave me for dead, I have to warn you, it won't be as easy as you might, um . . . oh."

They'd arrived at a clearing, looking down into a wide, stark valley, which was absolutely covered in human bones. Skulls, ribcages, femurs, all picked clean by the birds and bleached white by the sun.

"Please tell me this is another one of your wonders."

For Christian, simply to walk along the path—the most monotonous of tasks—was pure delight. Only now, with his burden gone, did he realize just how heavy and ponderous it had become. Without it, he now sometimes felt like he might actually float away. And only now, stripped of the rags and cleansed of the patina of grime he'd carried about, did he recognize just how needful this all had been. Apparently, he'd been itching continuously for long enough to develop a habit of absentmindedly scratching his arms, chest, and neck as he walked. He kept catching himself raising a hand to address this, only to find that the old itch was no longer there.

Christian had tarried there, at the Place of Deliverance, even after the three Shining Ones had departed. There he began writing a verse about his deliverance, and now, as he walked, he continued composing it in his mind:

> *I came to this point, my sin on my back,*
> *Not daring to hope I'd be free*
> *My knuckles were white, my soul was pitch-black*
> *I felt the weight of it all crushing me*
>
> *But here at the cross at the end of the line*
> *The chains started falling away*
> *My burden fell off and I straightened my spine*
> *Now my heart cries out just to say*
>
> *Blessed cross! Blessed grave! Both empty today!*
> *How can this miracle be?*
> *I owe everything to the Son of the King*
> *Who was there put to shame for me*
> *He was there put to shame for me*

He hesitated over the words, "Here at the cross, at the end of the line," as the Shining One had emphasized that this was not the end, but the beginning. And yet it was *an end*: an end for the man born Graceless and the beginning of a New Creation.

When he'd finally departed that holy place, Christian had been certain he'd spent hours and hours there and his immediate impulse upon leaving was to find someplace to make camp for the night. But then he noticed the sun still hanging at mid-afternoon and felt a great joy at the prospect of making new progress beyond the gate—now unfettered by his burden, and walking downhill to boot.

He'd covered perhaps five miles when he came upon a very peculiar sight: right where the ground leveled out, not even a stone's throw from the path, were three men, sleeping on the ground, their ankles shackled with leg irons.

Drawing near to them, Christian's first thought was of the poisonous mushrooms that Evangelist had warned him about. Could those also grow on this side of the gate? Lifting his gaze beyond the three men, he saw the wall separating this land from the other—Beelzebub's land, he supposed—and he saw a number of vines and plants spilling over. It was certainly possible.

But then, these men did not seem drugged. He approached the nearest man, and, with his thumb, he gently pushed up one of his eyelids. The pupil looked normal. Perhaps they'd just been drinking the day away. He thought of the words of his precious Book, whose pages were now mysteriously gilt with gold since his encounter with the Shining Ones. In that book, a wise man had written, "They that tarry long at the wine; they that go to seek mixed wine. Look not upon it when it is red and sparkles and flows easily. In the end it bites like a serpent, and stings like a cobra. Your eyes shall behold strange women, and your heart shall utter perverse things. Indeed, you shall be like one who lies down in the middle of the sea, or falls asleep at the top of a mast."

Wise words, but could these men be so drunk in the daytime, along the Narrow Way? And why on earth were their feet shackled? Shaking him by the shoulder, Christian called out, "Wake up, sir. Are you all right?"

The man's eyes fluttered open, struggling to focus on any one thing. He smacked his mouth, frowning, and eventually found Christian's face. "What is it?" he asked.

"Sir, you were sleeping."

"Yes. I *was* sleeping. The question is: why am I *no longer* sleeping?"

"Your legs are shackled together. As are theirs. What is going on with you?"

"My legs . . . ?" He struggled to lift his lolling head enough to peer down toward his feet. "Oh, I suppose they are." He chuckled. "Ah, well. That's something that happens, I suppose."

"No, it isn't something that— Who are you?"

"My name is Sloth, and these are my mates. That's Simple, and over there—snoring away—is Presumption."

"Did you know that they also have leg irons fastened to their ankles?"

Sloth laughed again. "What do you know?" He peered out at his friends for a moment then shrugged at Christian and said, "The journey of life, right? Crazy . . . "

Christian kicked at the chains binding the man's legs, rattling them, and said, loudly, "You need to get up, Sloth. I can help you remove these irons, I think. Where I used to live I was rather good friends with a blacksmith and I—"

"What is going on?" Presumption moaned. "I was having a dream about a trifle that never ended. The more I ate, the more there was. And now—" he looked at Christian, "—you. Sloth, who is this fellow?"

"My name is Christian. Sir, did *you* realize your legs were bound? And what's more, why are you sleeping during the day?"

"Why not?"

"For one thing, it's not safe. It's as if the Dead Sea were under you—a gulf that has no bottom. Don't you know that your enemy stalks about like a roaring lion, deciding whom he should devour? If you awakened to see him, how would you even attempt to run away, chained as you are? You would immediately become prey for his teeth. Arise, all three of you! Let's remove those irons. You, over there—wake up!"

"I'm already awake," Simple snipped. "Thanks to all this infernal racket. Nice coat, by the way." The others snickered.

"Are you not hearing me? You're not safe right now!"

Simple flopped his head from one side to the other and announced, "I see no danger."

Sloth nodded. "Nor do I. Just a little more sleep."

Presumption draped an arm over his eyes and said, "Yes, yes, every tub must stand on its own bottom."

"What does that even mean?" Christian asked.

Sloth waved a hand, dismissively. "It's an old saying."

"Okay . . . ? But, again, what does it—"

"It means," Presumption said, clearly annoyed, "that we all must be self-sufficient."

"I don't see how that applies here. You men are obviously not self-suff— and they're all asleep. Wow. Rest well, I guess. I hope you have more sense in the morning."

Christian returned to the path and kept on his way, thinking how disconcerting it was to encounter men in such danger who cared nothing about the kindness he'd so freely offered them: awakening them, counseling them, even offering to remove their irons.

After a while, he consciously put those men out of mind and instead began to thank the King for his own deliverance, for the removal of his burden, for dressing him now in these fine, clean garments, and for how quickly he had been able to cover so very much ground immediately upon setting off from the cross.

Then, at the very thought of the cross, he found his pace quickening yet more, and glancing behind him, noticed that the sun seemed to be no further down in the sky than when he'd first encountered those three slumbering fools.

When the Interpreter did not answer him, Faithful looked back, only to see that he was nowhere to be found.

"Well, that's not what you want," he said to himself. "But I can see the Narrow Way crossing through the midst of these, uh . . . mortal remains. I will simply follow it."

He'd reached the very bottom of the valley, the place thickest with bones, when he noticed the armor and weapons mixed in with them. This was clearly the site of a great and terrible battle, fought quite some time ago.

Faithful looked closer at the sword nearest him. It was finer even than the one he'd left behind—the finest craftsmanship he'd ever seen. Then he thought of the empty sheath still hanging from his belt and found himself rather conflicted. Was it possible to steal from a dead man? What's more, a man who had been dead so long that his children and grandchildren were undoubtedly dead as well? Were the abandoned weapons of an ancient war the property of whoever came upon them? He glanced around, looking for the Interpreter, suddenly thinking this may be some sort of test. He did not see him, but he did feel quite silly. If this was indeed a vision—a wonder, as the Interpreter called them—was this sword even real? Then again—

Faithful drew back, the breath sucked from his lungs. While he'd been focused on the abandoned weapon, the bones had begun to quiver and rattle, then they were sliding along the sandy soil, making a hideous clacking sound as joints came back together, spine reattaching to skull and ribcage. Long, white arms and legs flopped and clacked together as the pile of bones became a gathering of skeletons—each one grinning, as skeletons seem to do—their empty eye sockets all staring directly at Faithful.

His hand went again toward his sword-hip and found only the cord of his burden. The blade he'd been coveting was now in the closing hand of a dead warrior. Or was he dead? Sinew and muscle and veins were forming now on his hand and arm. A heart—still and unbeating—was visible in his chest cavity until fluid and flesh began filling in around it. Forcing himself to turn and look around, Faithful confirmed his fear: he was surrounded by such men, their flesh now generating a gray, paperish skin, spreading out to their arms, legs, and heads— where thousands of unseeing, unblinking dead eyes still stared up at him. Hair and beards grew, half-rotten clothing and rusty bits of armor were restored onto these corpses.

Turning his attention back to the man at his feet, Faithful let out a gasp. The dead man's face was his own face, looking up at him in a lifeless, silent scream.

"I know!" Faithful called out. "I already knew that! I already knew I was dead! I already knew that the city of my birth was full of walking corpses, marking time until their own burials." His hands shook and sweat stung his eyes. He'd been around his share of death and carnage, and the sense of sheer terror—something Faithful had almost never felt—confused him. "I knew all this! Show me something else!" The only response was his own voice echoing back to him.

Christian was composing more songs of praise in his heart, walking briskly along the Narrow Path, when he noticed movement at the wall. He came to a stop and looked over, to see two men come tumbling over from the other side. They landed none too gracefully, stood, brushed themselves clean, redonned their hats, and began to approach Christian.

"Good day," they called out in unison.

"Good . . . day," Christian echoed, bewildered.

"I see we are going the same way," one of them said. "If you are looking for company along the way, we are known as very adept conversationalists."

"I am anyway," the other said, and the two shared a brief, fastuous laugh. "My name is Formalist," he said.

"Hypocrisy," said the other, tipping his hat.

"I am Christian." They shook hands and began to walk together toward the shining light.

"What a beautiful day," Hypocrisy said. "I do not think we could have chosen a better one for this journey."

"It is the most beautiful day I have ever experienced," Christian agreed, thinking again of the cross and all the accompanied it. "Do you mind if I ask where you men come from and where you're headed?"

"Not at all," Formalist replied. "We were both born in the land of Vain-Glory and we are going for praise at Mount Zion."

"'For praise,' you say? To give it or receive it?"

"Either one," said Formalist.

"A bit of both, I suppose," said Hypocrisy.

"I see. And why didn't you come in at the gate at the beginning of the Way? After all, it is written, 'He that comes in not by the door, but climbs in some other way, the same is a thief and a robber.'"

Hypocrisy laughed. "Do you have any idea how far it is from Vain-Glory all the way back to that gate? It is very much the consensus of our countrymen that it's just too much trouble. Our practice is and always has been to pop over the wall right back there where we entered; there are even some steps built up on the other side for just that purpose."

"And you don't fear that the Lord of the City where you are going will count this a trespass?"

"If taking a little shortcut is a crime," Formalist said, "then lock me up!" At that they both descended into more pompous laughter.

"It's just, it seems to me that by climbing in as you have, not only do you violate our Lord's revealed will, but you rob yourselves of the very benefits of pilgrimage. Don't you fear that you might become rather like a painting of fire, devoid of warmth, or like painted flowers, with no sweet smell? Or better yet, like painted trees, which bear no fruit?"

Formalist rolled his eyes. "I see our friend Christian is the master of the simile. Don't you worry your pious little head about it. We have our customs and you have yours. And I'll have you know that we could easily produce testimony that would bear witness to our ways going back a thousand years."

"Witnesses are good indeed," Christian said, "but would they stand in a court of law? If you were in fact charged with trespassing?"

Hypocrite gave a bumptious, disdainful snort and said, "I'm quite sure that any magistrate worth his salt would admit such a long-standing precedent. I say again: *a thousand years.*"

"To you and I, that is a very ancient practice. But to the Lord of that City it is as a day."

"You bore me, Christian," Hypocrisy said. "I'm bored. What is the point of arguing the law when no offence has been committed? Just look at the result: you came in your way and we came in ours. But we're all three in, aren't we? If a fourth were to join us now, would he perceive that you were in a better condition than us? Sure, we tumbled in over the wall, but from childhood all of us in Vain-Glory master the old tuck-and-roll so that we may land without so much as soiling our clothing."

"Speaking of Clothing," Formalist said, "I suppose they would see the difference in that. We are dressed like gentlemen, after all, while you appear a bit more gauche, wearing that peculiar coat, which I have to assume was given to you by some of your more sympathetic neighbors to hide the shame of your nakedness." At that, the two men laughed again, more boorishly than before.

"You are correct about one thing: this coat on my back was indeed given me to cover my shame and nakedness. And I take it as a token of my master's kindness to me, for I had nothing but rags before."

"Christian, old boy, I think it may have been a lateral move."

"Feel free to mock me, gentlemen," Christian said. "But by the coat on my back, the mark on my forehead, and the scroll in my hand, the Lord will know me when I arrive. Perhaps you didn't notice these other emblems, busy as you were climbing over the wall like sneak-thieves. I walk by the rule of my Master and you two by the rude working of your fancies. Make no mistake, you *are* counted thieves by the Lord of the Way. You have come in without his direction and you will go out without his mercy."

At this, the two men made no real answer, other than to chuckle nervously, and the three walked along the way in silence for some time, until the two men of Vain-Glory dallied and fell back, leaving Christian to pull ahead, traveling once again on his own, reading from the scroll given him by the Shining Ones—a practice which greatly refreshed his spirit.

Faithful stood still amongst the corpses for a long time, doing his best not to make eye contact with the one at his feet. The eyes were dead, of course, but they were all too familiar. He half expected the Interpreter to reappear and open some new aspect of these truths to him. It did seem a bit odd that he hadn't even said goodbye. Then again, he was rather odd himself, in an intriguing sort of way.

But he did not appear. Looking ahead, Faithful saw the Narrow Way stretching out into the distance and the shining light beyond, hovering at the top of a hill. Faithful shuddered. Even the hill resembled a skull, he thought. It occurred to him that he might just continue on his way, but for some reason, he could not walk away from all these felled warriors who had gone to the not-insignificant trouble of reassembling from a pile of bare bones—apparently just for him.

And so he prayed, aloud, "Lord, show me something hopeful in this bleak and haunting place. You are the Giver of life and I doubt you would bring me here to show me only death. Breathe your Life where death reigns. Give me hope for my lifeless soul."

A breeze began to blow—from where he could not tell—picking up more and more, blowing against Faithful's face and through his hair, and filling the valley, whirling about. All at once, every dead man took a sudden, gasping breath and stood. They were clothed in battle array, hands on their swords, faces pointed to the East, toward the Celestial City shining on the hill. Then they all drew their swords at once and in unison saluted an approaching figure, coming this way, down the Narrow Road.

Faithful followed their gaze and saw the Interpreter drawing near. "I was going to ask you if you understand, but I see that you do."

Only then did Faithful realize that his cheeks were streaked with tears. "Yes," he said. "The Lord, who breathed life into Adam and every one of us, will breathe new life into all who believe in him, all who truly want it."

"Do you want it, good Faithful?"

"More than anything."

"I know you speak the truth. Now look into the distance. What do you see?"

Faithful looked again toward the light at the top of the hill and could see something directly in front of it. "I see . . . a cross?" And he realized that these men were not saluting the Interpreter at all, but every one of them pointing Faithful to that blessed emblem.

"Go to it now," the Interpreter said. "Delay no longer. At the cross your burden will fall away and you will know the breath of life—that which you have lately felt upon your face will fill your very soul! Life eternal is within your grasp. God-speed, pilgrim."

He stepped aside and Faithful nodded goodbye to his teacher, then ran toward the cross, without looking back.

Christian came to a stop at the foot of a very high hill. Not unlike with the Hill Legality, he thought it might more properly be called a mountain, but a tattered old sign, erected at its base identified it as The Hill Difficulty. There he stood, looking up, wondering if he still had the strength within him to make it to the top today. Then he remembered the last time he'd made camp to put off ascending a hill, for a similar reason—how he had wasted so much precious time. It was early enough—not even quite the dinner hour. No, he would not put off so great a task; he would climb this one tonight.

Evangelist had told him about the comforts and provisions the King had furnished for pilgrims along the way, and how he could always expect to find some place to lay his head at the top of a hill or at the end of a particularly difficult stretch of road. He took these words to heart now.

"What have we here?" It was Formalist, addressing his fellow as the two came up behind Christian.

"Mmm. The Hill Difficulty," Hypocrisy read. "This looks rather arduous."

"Oh, you know I don't do *arduous*."

"That I do. I mean, I know you don't. And, of course, neither do I . . . you know."

Still gazing up at the grueling climb ahead, Christian asked, "What other choice do you have, but to turn back?"

"There are other options here; why, look!" Formalist announced, clearing away some overgrown grass from the base of the sign. Christian saw two directional arrows affixed to the same stake and, from there, he saw two paths diverging, one to either side of the hill, seemingly leading  around it. The one pointing to the right identified the road as "Danger," and the one to the left was called "Destruction."

"You can't seriously be entertaining one of these other routes." Christian said.

"Why not?" Formalist said. "They go along level ground. Think about it mathematically: it's a matter of half the circumference of the base of the hill versus its entire height, twice. I submit that either of these alternate roads should be shorter, maybe by a third, in addition to being far easier travelling."

"But our options here are Danger, Destruction, or Difficulty. If you know anything of the pilgrim road, you know that difficulty is to be expected. Destruction is the land I'm fleeing. And Danger, well . . . if I can avoid it, I will."

Hypocrisy raised an eyebrow. "You take things quite literally, then, don't you?" He laughed derisively and added, "It's an actual mountain as opposed to a couple of winding roads. If I go this way 'round—the road called Destruction (for whatever reason—perhaps a Mr. Johannes Destruction named it after himself; I don't know)—I would bet you a shilling I'll make it to the other side before you."

"I have no interest in bet—"

"Oh, count me in," Formalist interjected. "I'll take this road to the right and I'll beat both of you!"

"You're on." Hypocrisy waved back at them as he set off on the Road Destruction, calling out, "Have my money ready, you two. Oh, and Christian—enjoy your mountain!" His irritating falsetto laugh seemed to echo behind him long after both men had disappeared from sight.

Without the noise of those two yammering, Christian could now hear the sound of a babbling brook. Having had no drink since the gate, he now realized how parched he was. He followed the sound and discovered a cold, crisp, clear spring of water, from which he drank deeply, reviving himself all the more and filling the pilgrim with a determination to climb the Hill Difficulty.

He took off running, once again reminded of his shed burden. The hill was steep and high, though, and after he'd made a good deal of progress, he fell—with no intermediate stage between—to clambering up on hands and knees, fighting hard ground and gravity for every foot of progress. As he was about midway up the hill, the sun was more than halfway down to the horizon, and he thought of how he might be the one in Danger or facing Destruction if he did not reach the top before dark. There was no way to stop and rest here, steep and rocky as it was; a good deal of effort was required simply to hold on, and so he continued pushing upward, as fast as he could manage, asking all the while for help.

Although it made the act of climbing a bit more comp-licated, he pulled the scroll from his breast and gripped it in his hand. This comforted him and seemed to give him the final push he needed to reach the halfway point, where he crawled up one last rocky ascent and found himself looking at a pleasant Arbor—a love-ly garden alcove, well-tended and inviting.

"Surely this is one of those places Evangelist told me about," Christian thought. "A place constructed by the Lord of the Hill for the refreshment of weary pilgrims." Sitting in a soft place, Christian took a moment to admire the coat he'd been given at the cross. It was a fine garment, regardless of what Formalist and Hypocrisy had said, and he was quite proud to wear it. Then, to relax, Christian opened his scroll and read for a while. But soon, his eyes grew heavy, and he re-rolled it, leaning back in the soft grass.

"I won't sleep while it's still daytime," he thought. "Not like those three lethargic men I encountered. Just a moment to rest my eyes. I'll set off again in just a few min . . . " And Christian slept in that place until it was nearly night. And as he slept, the scroll slipped out of his hand.

Losing Light

Faithful came within six feet of the spring at the foot of the Hill Difficulty, but never saw it, never heard it, never drank of it. Because, as he stood, assessing the climb ahead of him, a very old man hobbled up to him. He was bony, cleanshaven, and moved with the sort of rickety steps that make bystanders constantly anticipate a fall.

He approached Faithful purposefully, making eye contact from a good distance away, and holding it awkwardly through many short, halting steps. Faithful guessed that this man had spent his life toiling outdoors as his skin was tanned like a hide, like the skin of a sailor.

When he was a few feet away, he asked, "What is your name, pilgrim?"

"I am called Faithful."

"Oh I like that. You look like an honest fellow, and smart. Wise enough to spot a good deal when you one presents itself! I have a proposition for you. Will you hear it?"

"So long as it will not interfere with my pilgrimage to the Celestial City."

"It may, but hear me all the same. I've been around a very long time and I'll tell you this: you can try your luck with that hill and a thousand more after it. Probably seems quite doable now. You're undoubtedly feeling relieved having come from the hill behind you. I see that mark upon your head, and I have one too, as you can see."

Faithful squinted at the man's forehead, but he waggled it so much as he talked that it was hard to make out what exactly was engraved there "I'm in favor of all of it, to be sure," the old man said. "But believe me, it's a lot of toil for a man to undertake, with no guarantee he'll reach the end. And when you remember that you'll only get your wages if and when you reach the end . . . well, would you rather not be content to dwell with me, for wages provided each and every week? You work, and you get paid. Then you work some more and get paid again. Imagine that."

"This is a most unusual proposition. Who are you, sir? And where would I be 'dwelling with you?'"

"My name is Adam the First and my home is in the town of Deceit."

"What sort of work are we talking about?"

"Not trudging drudgery like you see laid out ahead of you. My work has many delights and my wages are sufficient. More than sufficient! Not to mention that you would be my heir when I shuffle off."

Glancing back up at the Hill Difficulty, Faithful thought it was at least worth considering this man's offer. After all, he'd already entered through the gate and been delivered at the cross and that had to count for something. Perhaps he could work for this man a few years and save some kind of security for himself and then set out for the Celestial City, all the more prepared.

"Tell me about your house," Faithful said. "And how many others work for you. Give me a sense of the place."

"Oh, you will love my house. It is maintained with all the dainties of the world. And I have a good number of servants, all my own descendants."

"And yet, you offer it to me to be your heir. How is that?"

"It's a long, long story. But we will carry it out all proper and above-board. You will give me grandchildren—big and strong like yourself—and then, by leaving my estate to you, I will leave it to them. See?"

"Grandchildren? You may have missed a step there, my friend."

"Oh! Did I not mention? I have three daughters. Beautiful and far younger than you would think. Their names are Lust of the Flesh (she's a handful), Lust of the Eyes (the prettiest one), and Pride of Life (my pride and joy). You may have your pick. Marry them all if you like! I can tell by your build and your obvious intelligence that you would give me many strong, handsome, clever grandsons to carry on the work."

"Oddly enough, this is rather tempting. I would love to marry and have a family. But, as you have gathered, I am on pilgrimage. I can't be tied down forever. How long would you have me live with you?"

"As long as I live myself. But look at me. I've been on this earth quite a long time."

Faithful nodded in thought. And the old man finally stopped wagging his head, his face frozen in hopeful anticipation. Faithful grabbed him by his meager white hair and pulled him in for a closer look. There, on his forehead, were engraved the words, "Put off the old man with his deeds."

Faithful released him and took a step back. "No," he muttered. "No, I won't go with you."

"Oh, but think again. Your reward will be—"

"Shut your lying mouth. If I followed you to your house, you would sell me as a slave, all your flattering words notwithstanding. Tell me I'm wrong, you rotten old cheat."

A wicked grin spread slowly over the man's face. "You are not wrong. But you will come all the same!" He grabbed hold of Faithful and commended pulling at him. Faithful tugged his arm back but the wiry old man held on, like a tick to its host.

"You're coming home, like it or not! That's right! I said coming *home*! You are already my son!"

Desperately, Faithful slammed his elbow into Adam's chest, throwing him to the ground, where he fairly bounced back up with all the spryness of youth, still grinning, his wild eyes fixed on Faithful. "A little fight in you, I see."

"More than a little, you wicked old snake. Now leave me. I'm warning you: follow me one step up this hill and I will kill you. I'll throttle you to death and leave your flesh for the birds of the air and the scavengers."

"Oooh. A big fellow—threatening an old man like me."

"My Lord has commanded me to mortify the flesh and put to death the old man."

"A lot of big promises there. But I see you have no sword."

"I aim to rectify that soon. In the meantime, try your luck if you will. But mark my words, I may not be able to cut off your head, but I will wrap my hands around your throat and cut off your air. I make no provision for the old man, and that includes the breath of life."

"Fair enough," Adam the First said, turning his back and scrambling away. "Have it your way."

"O wretched man," Faithful said aloud, not knowing if he was talking about Adam or himself, of even if there was a difference. Then he set his face toward the hill and began his ascent.

As he slept in the pleasant arbor, Christian dreamed. He saw himself lying there while the sun went down, until even the twilight had all-but-faded. And in that moment when the darkness began to overtake the light, from the trees around him came the two ill-favored ones, crawling like bears upon their hands and feet, circling closer and closer.

As they moved, the sound of dragging chains alarmed Christian so that he tried to rouse himself, but he could not. Both of these men, carried shackles with them and they set about affixing them, first to his ankles and then to his wrists.

"No," he thought. "I will be worse off now than Simple, Sloth, and Presumption, for thy were only chained at the legs." The cold metal pinched and squeezed at his flesh as the ill-favored ones went about their dark work.

Suddenly a flash of light came from the East and the three Shining Ones rushed to his aid, swords flashing. They sent the wicked creatures fleeing and dashed the chains from Christian. The one who had clothed him in his new garments bent close and spoke softly, saying, "Go to the ant, ye sluggard. Consider her ways, and be wise."

Christian woke with a start, sitting upright and immediately rising to his feet. It was not yet dark, but he had no time to waste.

Faithful was about a third of the way up the hill, pacing himself and making good time, when he sensed it: someone was following him. That old wretch, Adam the First, he thought, and he determined to make good on his threats. But when he looked back it was another old man: that haunting specter with the glowing face who had threatened to burn Faithful's house to the ground.

He was climbing up now behind the pilgrim, slowly gaining on him. Faithful felt a heavy, oppressive fear pushing down on him, threating to crush his courage and steal his clarity of thought. Then he remembered what Evangelist had told him: this man was doing the King's will. Yes, he'd said that, but also that if he should see the old man again, he should be on his guard.

Having hounded you for your entire life, and having chased you out from your home, this man may now consider you his own.

Faithful began to climb faster. Surely he could outrun an old man. Or, failing that, he would turn and fight.

Christian made such good time to the top of the hill that he almost thought he'd made up for his ill-advised nap. He was in sight of the summit, when he saw two figures running down toward him, flying from the top, back toward the gate.

They rushed past him without saying a word, but then one of them came to a skidding halt and turned back. "Christian? Is that you, my friend?"

"Mr. Timorous?" Christian offered his hand and the two shook heartily. "Are you on pilgrimage too?"

"I was," he said. "Or, we were. This is my friend, Mistrust."

Christian offered his hand to this stranger, who only studied it skeptically.

Timorous chuckled. "Don't worry; I know Christian from back home in the City of Destruction. In fact, our wives are rather good friends. I shall tell good Christiana that I saw you here and that you looked well. But, truly, I must go. It was good to see you, neighbor."

"Timorous, wait! I'm happy to see you as well, but what are you men doing running the wrong way? The City of Zion is behind you. Having climbed this difficult slope do you now turn around and go down the same way and, thus, waste your efforts?"

Mistrust shook his head. "We *were* going to the City of Zion, but the further up this mountain we went (and make no mistake about it—this is a mountain and not a hill), the more danger we met with. And the last feather that breaks the horse's back was this: we saw before us two lions. They may have been awake or asleep—we did not stay to find out—but we knew for a fact that if we got within their reach, they would pull us to pieces!"

"Is this true?" Christian asked Mr. Timorous.

"I'm afraid so. And they were monstrous! When I've read of lions, I thought of them as massive beasts, but never dreamed they would be as large and frightening as these were. Why, one of them was as long from head to rump as Mistrust and I lying head-to-foot. I'm not ashamed to say that this frightened us both enough to send us back the way we came. And if you've any sense, it will do the same for you."

"This report does indeed frighten me," Christian said. "But where can I fly to be safe? Do you head back to our own country, which is prepared for fire and brimstone? I fear burning there far more than any sleeping lions."

"They might have been awake," Mistrust repeated. "As I said, we did not stay to investigate the matter."

"At any rate, if I go back to the City of Destruction, I am sure to perish there. If I can get to the Celestial City, I am sure to be safe there. I must put fear behind me and venture forth. To go back is nothing but death. To go forward is fear of death, yes, but life everlasting beyond it. Come with me, friends. We will face these lions together."

Mistrust sniffed at him and resumed running down the hill. Timorous only shrugged and followed after him.

The bearded old man continued to gain, having nearly closed the distance between himself and Faithful, who, seeing the way this would eventually fall, decided to turn and face his pursuer.

Faithful squared his shoulders and stood his ground, shouting, "You told me to leave my home and I left. Are you not appeased?"

"Once you enter my debt, I am never appeased."

"Sorry to hear it. But you'll notice that, unlike the last time we met, I am unencumbered. If it's combat you want, it will be a fair fight this this time. Why don't we just part as friends, yes?"

The old man smiled, doubled his fists, and rushed at Faithful, who made to grab him in a bear hug and throw him onto the ground. But even in his powerful grip, the old man wriggled his arms free and crushed a fist into Faithful's temple, stunning him. The pilgrim dropped the old man, took two steps back, and gave his head a painful shake.

Then he went on the offensive, throwing all of his earthly strength into tackling this man to the ground. But his opponent simply stepped aside and watched Faithful bounce and tumble twenty feet down the hill, until his back connected with a tree, bringing his fall to a sudden stop.

"You're all the same," the old man said, following him down the hill. "You think your strength will be my match. But it's never quite enough. I use your feeble strength against you."

Faithful planted his hands on the earth and tried to push

himself to his feet, but the sandy soil gave way and he fell back to his hands and knees.

"I saw you with Adam the First. In league with the man of works are we? The first man to break the Law and pay the price. And I know of your secret inclining toward that man. He is mine and, now, so are you."

Faithful threw a handful of sand in the old man's eyes, knocked him onto his back, and ran again up the hill, like a gazelle with a lion on his heels.

The warning of Timorous and Mistrust played over again and again in Christian's mind, and he found himself dreading the top of the hill more with each upward step. To calm his nerves and comfort his soul, he did what had become automatic since encountering the cross. Where formerly he would absentmindedly pick at the cords of his burden when worry racked his mind, now he reached to his bosom to find the sealed scroll given him by the Shining Ones.

Christian froze. Where was it? He checked the pockets of his coat, his boots, and anywhere it might have fallen on his person. But it was gone. Christian fell to his knees in distress and despair. Somehow, he had dropped his most precious possession along the way. That thing which brought him relief in his fear and heaviness of heart, that holy charm which should have been his entrance to the Celestial City. And now, as evening was already upon him, he had to backtrack, hoping against hope to locate it while there was still some light by which to see.

He rose and made his way again down the steep hill, finding it scarcely easier than climbing up had been. As he walked, his eyes crossed back and forth over the Way, searching on either side for the precious scroll, and begging God's forgiveness for foolishly losing it. What little hope he' held soon began to ebb away. At this rate, it would take three times longer to go down the hill than it had to ascend, and he had very little time left before night would be upon him.

Again he prayed for help and direction and insight.

Suddenly, it burned hot in his mind that he had been clutching the scroll when he fell asleep in the arbor. And that was the last he'd seen it. He needed not to inch along searching for his lost scroll; he would run to that place of rest and, God willing, have it in hand before the sun set.

Faithful's lungs burned as he reached the halfway point up the Hill Difficulty—a beautiful garden alcove set aside as a place for pilgrims to stop and rest. But Faithful could not rest. He could almost feel the hot breath of his pursuer on his back. Glancing behind him, he saw that it was hopeless and, in the same moment, felt his ankle twist against a tree root, bringing him down hard to the ground.

Before he could even roll over, he felt an explosion of pain in his abdomen, as the old man kicked him. In a surreal moment, Faithful thought about how embarrassed he'd be at taking a beating from such a man if he were not overwhelmed with pain and fear for his life. If Revelry could see him now, he'd laugh to scorn at his old friend and call him a milksop.

The old man plopped down onto Faithful's chest, his bony knees bringing explosions of pain in the shoulders. He then gave him a thrashing, bringing his fists down like hammers upon the pilgrim's face and chest. The sound of packing flesh and cracking bones thundered in the backs of his ears.

"Mercy!" Faithful cried. "Have mercy!"

"I know not how to show mercy."

Christian arrived at the arbor just as the sun kissed the horizon. He felt some comfort at the prospect of reuniting with his scroll and a sense of gratitude at having arrived in the daylight. But more than that, he was filled with sorrow and self-loathing, rebuking himself over and again for foolishly falling asleep in that place, which had been so graciously erected to offer a little refreshment for the weary. "O wretched man that I am," he thought, "that I should sleep in the daytime, even in the midst of Difficulty."

He searched for the soft patch of ground where he'd slept, but he could not identify one place from the other as he walked among the trees just this side of the garden.

And then he saw something that caused him to stop short. An old man, whose face shone like the setting sun, straddling another, giving him the type of drubbing that might kill a man. Christian again reached for his scroll by instinct and again chided himself for having lost it. Without thinking, he drew back behind the trunk of an ancient olive tree.

Peering out, he saw that the attacker was now hefting a rock over his head, preparing to crush the skull of his victim. Christian opened his mouth to cry out, but produced no noise. He willed himself to come out from behind the tree and rush to the man's aid, but remained locked in place. He had no sword, after all, or weapon of any kind. He did not even have his scroll. What if he intervened only to have his own head caved in? Without his scroll in hand could he hope to enter the Celestial City?

"It's not my business, it's not my business" he said to himself, hating the words as he thought them. "For all I know, the old man was put upon by a thief and is just now getting the upper hand." His fear increased and he shrunk back all the more.

Then he heard a voice, both powerful and serene, calling out, "Peace! Be still." A young man was emerging from the woods, not far away, his back to Christian. The man wore a long robe and held his hands up as he spoke.

At the word "peace," the aggressor tossed the rock aside, scrambled to his feet, and bowed low before the robed man.

"He is not yours," the robed man said. "He is mine. He is not in your debt, for I bought him with a great price. Now leave him be."

The old man bowed deeper yet and something seemed to catch his eye—something lying in the woods.

"That's not yours either."

"But it's been abandoned, so little esteemed as to be tossed aside like so much trash."

"Peace," the man said again, and only then did Christian notice the holes in the backs of the man's hands. He covered his mouth as he wept at the sight of his Prince. He wanted to run to him, but how could he, when the evidence of his treachery lay right there, discarded on the ground, in the words of the white-bearded man, like so much trash?

And then the most dreadful thought yet filled Christian's mind. The warning of the man in the Iron Cage. He had been a pilgrim before losing all hope, locked forever in his own misery. When Christian had asked him how he'd gone from the former state to the latter, he had said, *I slept when I should have watched. I left off being sober and alert and sinned against the very light of the world, and all the goodness of God.*

Had Christian followed in this man's footsteps? Was repentance beyond his reach? Would his Lord condemn him? He pulled back further into the shadows and gathering darkness, still watching and listening.

"There is more work for you to do in the City," the Lord was saying to the old man, whose face shone now brighter and brighter. "The woman I told you about, and her children. They need your heavy hand right now. This man does not. Leave him with my burden—easy and light."

The old man drew up to the Lord, kissed his pierced feet, and turned away, moving quickly down the hill, the way he'd come.

The Lord looked down with compassion at the poor victim, whose face was battered and bruised beyond recognition.

"Oh, my child," the Prince of Mercy said. "When will you learn? He can only assail you if you forget the Truth you received at the place of Deliverance. Come with me and I will help you." Reaching down, he draped the poor man's arm around his shoulders and, bearing his weight, helped him stand and walked him into the woods on the far side of the arbor.

When they were out of sight, Christian scrambled to his scroll and snatched it up to himself, examining it for damage, finding none, and kissing it again and again. He placed it in the inner pocket of his coat, next to his heart, vowing to never again let it leave his sight.

The sky was orange now, prelude to true darkness, but Christian could not bear the thought of sleeping again in this place. Turning back toward the top of the hill, he ran, fleet-footed as Asahel, toward the top.

The Prince brought Faithful down into a ravine, where a pleasant pool sparkled with the waning light of the sun. The battered pilgrim was so stunned by the ordeal that it did not even occur to him how odd it was to find these features halfway up a hill. His Lord led him to the edge of the pool and helped him sit.

"I'm so sorry," Faithful croaked.

"I know. And I forgive you. Be cleansed now of all your unrighteousness." Pulling the sash from his own robe, the Lord dipped it into the water and washed Faithful's wounds. "Old Adam the First will call to you again, but do not listen to him. And do not give heed to false gospels: whether they come from that women Jezebel or from those who change grace for works. Look at my hands, my feet, my side. I was pierced for your transgressions and my grace is sufficient for you."

Faithful began to weep and the Prince wrapped his arms around the broken pilgrim.

"Rest your head upon my breast," he said, "for you yourself are the pilgrim whom I love. And I am with you always, whatever you face, whatever you do, and whatever you fail to do."

"In the city of my birth," Faithful sniffed, "they think of me as the strongest, the bravest. But I am so weak."

"You must learn to boast in your weakness and to find your strength in me. And mark my words, when the time comes, you will have more courage than you ever thought possible and in exercising it, you will bring great glory to my name."

Faithful rested upon his Lord until the sun had set and only the last faltering purple light remained in the western sky.

Taking him by the hand, the Prince led him along the edge of the pool and pointed to a boat moored there.

"Night has fallen," he said to Faithful. "Get some rest. I find it particularly pleasant to sleep below-deck."

Faithful nodded, kissed the Prince, and climbed into the boat. As he snuggled down into the darkness, he found a soft blanket and pillow waiting for him there. Touching his face tentatively, he found no wounds and felt no pain.

As Christian ran, continually holding his hand over the scroll, his guilt, fear, and sorrow melted away. In their place, a deep and enduring joy filled his heart. While replaying those moments of cowardice and double-mindedness, he had remembered something else. He was sure of it: the Prince of Mercy had looked back at him, looked him right in the eye, and smiled.

And now Christian smiled as well, running toward the top of the hill in the fading twilight. He was loved by his Master still.

Yes, he had been a sluggard and had failed to keep alert. Yes, that meant he must now cover the same ground three times which he might have trod only once. And yes, he now had to run in the dark, without the sun, hearing the noise of doleful creatures all around him, knowing that even lions had been spotted skulking nearby. But if he had been kept through all of this so far, he did not doubt that he would live to see the morning.

Full darkness was minutes away when Christian looked up to see, just shy of the apex, a sprawling, beautiful palace—not the equal of the place the Interpreter had shown him, but of the same sort. Hope flamed up all the brighter as he mended his pace toward the well-lit edifice.

But as he drew near, he saw the lions his neighbor had described, one on either side of the path. Only, Timorous had perhaps understated their size. And now there was no question: they were indeed awake.

One of them spotted Christian as he shrunk back, fixed its eyes upon the frightened pilgrim, and roared, so deep and loud that he felt reverberating it in his bones. Christian gripped his scroll and took another step forward, bringing the other lion to its feet to snarl and roar as well.

Christian looked down at his own feet, frozen in place, and thought for a moment of turning back. Then the Porter of the lodge called out to him, "Is your strength so small, pilgrim?"

"Too small, I think, to fight two lions a once," Christian answered.

"Fear them not," the porter said, "for they are chained, placed there only as a trial of faith, to discover those who have none. Stay on the path and they cannot hurt you."

Christian fixed his eyes on the door of the great palace and pushed ahead, through the midst of the roaring beasts, until he stood at the gate, before the porter.

"My name is Watchful," he said, "and I surmise that you have had a trying day and could perhaps use a place to rest."

Christian let out an exhausted laugh. "You have no idea."

Setting off on the road to his right, Formalist was wishing he'd bet not a mere shilling but a pound sterling that he would arrive first at the other side of Hill Difficulty. Despite his never having been particularly athletic, he was beyond confident in his prospects. Obviously, the foolish man Christian would be the last to see the other side, intent as he was on scaling what could easily be circumvented.

But his old friend Hypocrisy was likewise ill-suited to win this race, primarily because there was no way to circumvent the hill but to actually circumnavigate it, and Hypocrisy was not known for undertaking even such relatively easy work as this.

As youths, the two of them had once entered, with their classmates, Boastful and Swagger, in a race from one end of town to another—not only for bragging rights but for a considerable sum put up by each boy, to be kept by the winner (considerable, at least, to such young boys). The rules stated that one could not ride a horse, mule, or donkey, but had not specified the exact route or any other aspect of the race.

Formalist had arrived at the finish line last, where he was informed that Boastful and Swagger had been neck-and-neck to the end, only to come upon Hypocrisy already sitting comfortably on the fence, waiting for them. When pressed, he swore on his honor and the cornerstone of their local church that he had not broken the rules.

It later came out that he'd hired a carriage to take him to the designated endpoint—something that would never cross the mind of the average boy to do. Swagger had doubled up his fists and demanded his money returned, but the other boys held him back from violence, even while Hypocrisy happily explained that he had broken no rules—only found a loophole.

By hiring a carriage for twice his entrance fee, he had guaranteed that he would be reimbursed twice over by his winnings, all while never sitting astride any animal at all. He related this with such obvious satisfaction that Boastful and Swagger never spoke to him again, even as all four of them grew up into men.

Formalist, however, admired his fellow's pluck and his creative gaming of the system, and so the two became closer friends than ever. But now, in this contest, that same foible would prove Hypocrisy's undoing, as there were certainly no carriages for hire on these narrow roads. And, while it was a paltry sum for a grown man to win, Formalist took a secret satisfaction in the fact that winning a shilling from his old friend would mean winning back the ill-gotten gains of that boyhood race.

Coming to a fork in the road, Formalist thought back to his training as a boy. "Always go right," he'd been taught, which is why he'd taken the road on the right to begin with. "Always go right" had been a rule among his people for many generations. He smiled to himself as he continued on his way. The ground beneath him was just soft enough to cushion his feet without impeding his steps, the road was flat and growing ever wider as he went, and even the scenery was beautiful—flanked as he was on both sides by gorgeous topiaries, taking the forms of birds, fish, shells, and other pleasant shapes.

It wasn't until three or four hours later when he began to worry that he may yet lose the bet. He'd come to two more forks and taken the right branch each time, but those had been a while ago. The road now twisted and turned, but never split. The topiaries continued to delight him, but it was as if he were caught in a hedge maze, leading him along a complex path, which continually turned this way and that and sometimes even doubled back.

Before he knew it, darkness was upon him. Given the beautiful, serene setting, Formalist was not frightened, only annoyed at the thought of how smugly his friend would greet him if he won the bet, and the even more odious thought that Christian himself might beat him to the other side of the hill. Hating to do it (for he loved a good botanical sculpture), Formalist broke off some soft branches until he had a nice, comfortable place to lie down, and there he slept through the night.

In the morning, he continued on his way. By noon, he was increasingly sure that he was passing over the same ground for the second time. And by early evening, he was certain of it, for he now came upon the place where he had made his bed the night before.

Still, Formalist felt no sense of alarm. He remembered an old Vain-Glorian proverb: *All who wander are not lost*, and this comforted his heart. But as he continued on his way, the reality sunk in that, to follow this path would mean coming again and again to this same place. And he remembered that his father had given him a map to consult, should he get lost on his way to Zion—a map which his father had procured from a pilgrim long since dead and gone.

Retrieving and unrolling the document, he was less-than-sure how to read it. There was a key, but Formalist didn't really think to take it at face value. These were symbols, after all, and likely open to wide interpretation. There were also indicators by which he might return to the mouth of the maze and retrace his steps to the foot of the hill. But that seemed stupid to him. He looked around at the pleasant, sculpted shrubbery, then thought of the starkness and steepness of the hill, and made up his mind that he would not go back that way.

At the bottom of the map, in large, bold letters, read the words, "If you find yourself lost, turn back. Turn back immediately and return to the Narrow Way." That was all well and good, Formalist thought, but obviously not meant for him. His stomach rumbled and he ate some more of the red berries growing on the bushes. They were sweet and, while they never truly satisfied his appetite, they would sustain him enough to carry on.

Formalist stuffed the map back in his bag and resumed wandering through the labyrinth, all thought of receiving his prize—either from Hypocrisy or at the Celestial City—now far from his mind.

Respite

Faithful awakened in the Pleasant Arbor, feeling the first rays of sun warming his face. His night had been so restful and the morning was so lovely that it wasn't until he'd sat up and rubbed the sand from his eyes that it dawned on him: he'd fallen asleep in a boat. How had he gotten back here?

He thought again of the old man who had attacked and bludgeoned him, of the Prince who had rescued him, tended his wounds, and forgiven his sins once again. Faithful stood and stretched, his body unbroken by the savage attack, and thanked his God for the miraculous rescue and the mysterious respite.

Today he would make great progress on the pilgrim road, he determined. If he met the old man again, he would stand his ground, holding fast to the Truth he'd received at the place of deliverance. If he met Adam the First again, well . . . he cracked his knuckles.

Or perhaps he would see neither of these rogues, nor any other enemy along the road today. Maybe this would be the day he would catch up to that other pilgrim Goodwill had spoken of—the one who had passed through the Wicket Gate just a little before him. The thought pleased him. Not only would that be safer, enabling a system of watches through the night and better defense against attack, but it would also provide him with companionship along the road. As much as it pained him to admit it, Faithful was a bit lonely.

And so, he ate the last of his food—half a stale biscuit and a bit of turnip—and set off at a determined pace.

When the pilgrim had cleared the arbor and begun to climb Hill Difficulty once again, a thin, pale fellow emerged from the stand of trees beside the garden. His name was Shame and, as he watched the pilgrim disappear up the hill, a wicked smile spread slowly across his ghoulish face.

The night before, Watchful had invited Christian to follow him along a flagstone path that wound its way up toward the front of the towering edifice.

As they walked, the Porter asked, "Have you no baggage?"

"None to speak of, no."

"That is good to hear."

"If you don't mind my asking, sir, whose house is this?"

"It is called the Palace Beautiful to those who know it. It was built by the Lord of the hill ages ago, for the relief and security of pilgrims, if indeed you are one."

"I am indeed."

"That is what I aim to find out," Watchful said. He gestured to a rough-cut wooden bench a stone's throw from the door of the palace and invited Christian to sit.

Despite the hard edges, Christian was greatly relieved to put his whole weight on the seat and lean back. He'd been on his feet almost continuously since leaving the Place of Deliverance, walking, running, climbing, hiding, scrambling. He was exhausted, and secretly resented the prospect of enduring a round of questions from this odd stranger.

"Tell me, then," Watchful said, "where have you come from and what is your destination?"

"I am on my way from my hometown—a city called Destruction—to the Celestial City."

The Porter nodded, approvingly. "And your name?"

"My name is now Christian. But I was born Graceless."

"Graceless? Truly? Who are your people?"

"I come from the race of Japheth, whom God will persuade to dwell in the tents of Shem."

"I will be honest, Good Christian: all that you have said is pleasing to me and to all those who dwell in this house, but I can't help but wonder, why you are arriving so late? The sun is set and darkness has fallen."

Christian studied his feet. "I would have been here sooner, but—wretched man that I am!—I slept in the arbor that stands on the hillside, halfway up the hill. In fact, I slept a good portion of the day away. And what's worse, as I arose, I left my evidence behind, a foolish mistake which I did not realize until I'd reached the brow of the hill, at which point I had no choice but to go back for it, my heart broken and mind reeling. And yet, here I am. I may have arrived late in the day, but it's only by the grace of God that I arrive at all."

Watchful put a hand on the pilgrim's shoulder and gently squeezed. "All like sheep have gone astray," he said, "but God has laid on our Prince the iniquity of us all. I will call for one of the virgins of the house, who will come down and talk with you and, if she is satisfied with your testimony, she will bring you in to the rest of the family, according to the rules of the house."

So Watchful the Porter rang a bell. A moment later, the door opened, and a solemn-looking young woman came down to meet them. Christian scrambled to his feet.

"Why have you called?" she asked.

Watchful gestured at the visitor and said, "My lady, this is Christian. He is on a journey from the City of Destruction to Mount Zion; but being weary and benighted, he asked if he might lodge here tonight."

The woman introduced herself as Discretion and, after repeating the porter's questions and posing a few of her own, she finally asked, "Why do you wish to lodge with us?"

"My lady," Christian said, "I am very weary. When this day began, I had not yet reached the Wicket Gate, and now I am depleted, longing for any place to lay my head. But I desire to rest here, particularly, all the more now that I know this house was built by the Lord of the hill for the aid of his pilgrims."

Discretion smiled and said, "Come with me and I will introduce you to the others who dwell here."

As they neared the door, Christian saw three more women waiting at the threshold.

"These are my sisters," said Discretion, "Prudence, Piety, and Charity."

Christian bowed his head and said, "Grace and peace to you all." In the lamplight, he could see that all four of these women were not only beautiful—with a beauty that went far deeper than the outward appearance—but also had a purity and innocence about them. Not naivety, thought Christian, but the sort of innocence toward evil, for which all pilgrims should strive.

"Come in, you blessed of the Lord," Charity said, leading Christian into an expansive parlor. "I hope you're hungry."

The smell of cooking meat and bread brought an audible roar from his stomach, but Christian said, "I am hungry indeed, but please do not trouble yourselves preparing anything on my account. Not at this hour. I would be content with a crust of bread if you have it."

"Nonsense," Charity said. "Supper is nearly ready. But for now, let us sit and talk."

"Supper? Do you always eat so late in the day?"

"Not always," Discernment said. "We've been waiting. For you."

Christian sank into a comfortable chair near the fire, next to an oval gate-leg table, where a young man set a cup of tea and saucer. "To warm your bones, good pilgrim," he said.

Christian took a sip and marveled at the heavenly flavor,

realizing that this was his first tea in recent memory.

"Well, tell us about your journey so far," Piety said, leaning forward in her seat.

"I don't even know where to begin."

Prudence laughed. "How about at the beginning? What first motivated you to set out on the Pilgrim Road?"

"Oh, yes," Piety agreed, "and leave nothing out. It is good for the souls of pilgrims to share such stories, and good for all of us to hear them."

Christian thought for a moment and answered, "I was driven out of my native land by a dreadful sound that was continually in my ears and a crushing weight on my soul: a sense of unavoidable destruction that would follow me and drag me down to hell if I did not set out from that place.

"For some time, I had no idea where I should go to avoid it, but then by chance—or rather, by providence—I came upon a man as I was weeping and wandering. This man, Evangelist, directed me to the Wicket Gate, which I am sure I would never have found on my own. From there, I followed the Narrow Way all the way here."

Charity nodded. "We have known that man for a very long time. He is a friend to all in this house. I trust that he has been a great help to you, even after you set out on pilgrimage?"

"Indeed he was. And not only him. But a man who called himself Help—which, now that I say it, seems a bit on the nose, but he could not have been more aptly named, for he pulled me out of the Slough of Despond. Then there was, of course, Mr. Goodwill at the Gate, with whom I would have loved to spend more time in fellowship, but he kind of hurried me along. And of course, the Interpreter, who helped prepared me for this trip—I suspect, in ways that I have yet to comprehend.

"Oh, do tell us some of the wonders you saw in his house," Piety said.

"There were many. The two that have been most on my mind were the dreadful vision of a man in an iron cage who had sinned himself quite out of hope of God's mercy, the sight of which filled me with great caution and even fear. Then there was the sight of a great fire, a hopeful reminder that all the enemy's toil and mischief can never douse the work of Christ in a true pilgrim's heart.

"Beyond this, I saw many other things and encountered other people, but all of them combined are less than a shadow compared to the man I saw at the place of Deliverance. I have been thinking of him continually, ever since I left that place. It's as if the sight of him landed upon my eyes at the top of the hill, but has been slowly impressing itself on my heart ever since."

"Who did you see there?"

"A man hanging upon a tree, bleeding. It was the very sight of him that made my burden fall from my back." He gazed into the fire. "I never saw such a thing before, and while I was gazing upon him, three Shining Ones appeared to me, pronounced my sins forgiven, stripped me of my filthy rags, and clothed me in this embroidered coat. One of them set this mark upon my forehead and another gave me this." He retrieved the scroll from within his coat and held it up.

"May I see it?" Piety asked. Christian hesitated only a moment before handing it to her. Piety examined it and passed it around to the others. Each held it gingerly and beheld it with reverence before returning it to the pilgrim.

"And since being delivered," Discretion said, "what have you experienced?"

He told them of Simple Sloth and Presumption, of Formalist and Hypocrisy, of Timorous and Mistrust.

"You have done well," Prudence said. "But do you not sometimes think of the country you left behind?"

"Yes, but with shame and loathing. I would have expected to feel homesick by now, and sometimes I do. But not for the land I left—rather I am homesick for the place I am going."

"You never think back to the things you enjoyed in that city?"

"I do, but always against my will. I think of the carnal delights that preoccupied us in that place. But those thoughts inevitably bring me around to grief and sorrow. And if I possessed absolute self-control, I would never think of these things again. I would vanquish them and banish them entirely. But, God help me, there are still within me vestiges of my old self—thoughts, words, and deeds of the flesh."

Piety nodded. "Some pilgrims find that there are seasons in which you have that victory."

"I can surely relate to that! There are certain golden hours when I am free of these former things. But they are few and far between."

"Think," Piety said. "Can you recall what prompts these 'golden hours?'"

Christian rubbed his chin in thought. "I suppose it's when I think of the man I saw on the cross. That will do it. And when I look upon my new coat. That will do it as well. Or when I look at the scroll I carry next to my heart and think of where I am headed."

"And why is it that you long to reach Mount Zion?" Prudence asked.

Christian laughed. "For a hundred reasons! It is in that City that I hope to see the man who hung dead on the cross, whom I have seen in mere glimpses in the Pleasant Arbor and along the road—only there at length, alive and reigning on a golden throne, surrounded by an emerald rainbow, before which are the seven torches of fire and the twenty-four elders, ever bowing down and worshiping him.

"There I hope to be rid of all the carnal thoughts and selfish desires that plague me. I am weary of this inward sickness and long to be rid of it! In that City, there is no death and there I will gather with ten thousand times ten thousand, myriads upon myriads—saints who have gone before me and who will came after me. But mostly, it is the first thing: to see my Lord. I love him because he first loved me. I loved him at first because he relieved me of my burden. But I love him more every hour simply because he is worthy of all love and honor and glory and power, and I long for the day when I join the company singing his praises, eternally crying, 'Holy! Holy! Holy!'"

Charity dabbed her eyes with a lace handkerchief and asked, "But Christian, don't you have a family?"

"I do. A wife and four small boys."

Piety asked, "Why did you not bring them?"

Christian fought back the tears crowding his eyes and creeping up his throat. "You have no idea how badly I wanted to—how earnestly I tried! But as much as I sought to convince them to come with me, they sought just as hard to persuade me to stay back."

"You must have told them of the grave danger of remaining behind."

"I did little else for a very long time. I warned them of the coming destruction of our city. I showed them in my Book. I wept. I pled with them. But my wife was afraid of losing this world, and my children, of course, were preoccupied with the foolish delights of youth. They would not believe me. Even the youngest of them mocked me."

Charity's face was heavy with sympathy. "I trust you prayed that God would bless your words to them."

"Of course. Zealously! My wife and children are beyond precious to me."

Prudence alone remained dispassionate. "I suppose it was your own vain life that dampened the power of your words to persuade them."

"Really, sister," Charity scolded, "show some grace and kindness to our guest."

"No, she is right," Christian said. "I cannot commend my life. I am well aware of my failings, although I was incredibly careful not to give my family, by my conduct, any reason to reject my words. But even when they saw this, they would tell me I was *too precise*, foolishly denying myself things for their sakes, which they thought were good and well. Even my great tenderness in sinning against my God somehow put them off pilgrimage all the more."

Charity nodded. "Cain hated his brother because his own deeds were evil, while his brother's were righteous."

An older man wearing a fine livery entered the parlor, announced that supper was ready, and directed Christian to a room containing a water basin, pitcher, and towel, where he was able to wash up before the meal. While conversing with these likeminded people, his fatigue had lifted, along with his spirits, and hunger now dwarfed his desire to sleep.

As he entered the dining room, Christian's jaw dropped. The feast laid out was like nothing he'd ever seen. He doubted that the highest nobles of his homeland had ever even laid eyes on such a meal, let alone partaken of it. The smell of roasted meat, the finest of wine, and savory sauces mingled in the air. The servant directed Christian to a seat of honor and asked him to say grace.

"Gladly," he replied. "Most gracious God, and merciful Father, we beseech thee, sanctify these your gifts to our use, make them healthful for our nourishment, and make us thankful for all thy blessings, through Christ, our Lord and only Savior. Amen."

Then they sat down to eat—Christian, the women he'd already met, and a dozen more members of their family, all happy to see Christian and receive him into their house. The food was rich and delicious, seeming to blend in with the conversation, which was the same. They all spoke on one topic: the Lord of the Hill. What he had done and where and why. How he had built this very house with his own hands.

As they continued to recount his exploits, it became clear to Christian that this Lord had been a great warrior, that he had entered into deadly combat with the greatest Enemy of these people, and had slain him. As they spoke of the wounds their Lord had endured and the blood he shed, their love for him became almost palpable. In fact, it seemed that the more they spoke of him, the more they loved him.

An old man named Steadfast, his face crisscrossed with battle scars and one eye covered over with a patch, raised his glass and declared, "To the Lord of the Hill, who put the glory of grace into all he did and did it all out of pure love for his people!" "

"Have any of you actually seen this Lord?" Christian asked.

A hush befell the room for a moment and then a boy of about fourteen said, "I have. I spoke with him even after his death on the cross."

"As have I."

"Me too."

"Well?" Christian demanded. "What did he say to you?"

"That he is a lover of poor pilgrims such as you will find nowhere else on the face of the earth."

"Aye," Steadfast said. "He said so, with his own lips. And he'd have to be to have stripped himself of his own glory as he did, in order to rescue the poor and wretched. And then to make us princes, though by nature and birth we were beggars. To build us this house even while we chose to live on the dunghill!"

They all looked at each other in silence for a long time, tears standing in their eyes. And then Christian raised his glass again and said, "To the Lord of the Hill—the one who died and behold he is alive forevermore!"

When the meal was finished, a group of them invited Christian to retire to the drawing room with them. There they continued to talk about their Lord and about each one's calls to follow him.

At one point, a sweet old widow named Gladness said to Christian, "Well, young man, are you just going to keep *talking* about that book of yours? Or are you going to read it for us?"

Christian took the jab happily, opened his book, and began to read:

The earth is the LORD's and the fullness thereof,
*   the world and those who dwell therein,*
for he has founded it upon the seas
*   and established it upon the rivers.*
Who shall ascend the hill of the LORD?
*   And who shall stand in his holy place?*
He who has clean hands and a pure heart,
*   who does not lift up his soul to what is false*
*   and does not swear deceitfully.*
He will receive blessing from the LORD
*   and righteousness from the God of his salvation.*
Such is the generation of those who seek him,
*   who seek the face of the God of Jacob.*
Lift up your heads, O gates! And be lifted up, O ancient doors,
*   that the King of glory may come in.*
Who is this King of glory?
The LORD, strong and mighty, the LORD, mighty in battle!
Lift up your heads, O gates! And lift them up, O ancient doors,
*   that the King of glory may come in.*
Who is this King of glory?
The LORD of hosts, he is the King of glory!

Christian closed the Book, and they sat in silence for a few minutes. Finally, Discretion said, "It's very late and I believe our guest arrived here already quite tired. I suggest we commit ourselves to the Lord for protection through the night, and retire to our beds until morning.

When they had prayed, a young man led Christian up a series of winding stairways, lit by burning candles in wall sconces, and finally to a spacious upper chamber, whose windows opened toward the east. The servant told him the name of the chamber was Peace and bid him good night.

Christin lay down on the soft featherbed, sinking slowly into it and reflecting on the goodness of his Lord. To think, the night before, he'd slept all alone in the earth itself, burrowing down into it like a lesser beast to avoid the judgment raining down from above. And now he lay his head on the softest pillow he'd ever known, thanking God for the many other kind pilgrims finding rest in this house.

He fell asleep with a smile upon his face and woke to the sight of the most breathtaking sunrise he had ever seen. Rays of light shone up into the sky in all directions, cutting through the clouds. Shades of orange and pink and purple and gold all vied for the honor of announcing the new day's arrival.

After praying and reading again from his scroll, Christian ventured back down to the dining room, where he found happy pilgrims filling their plates with eggs, bread, and cornmeal mush. Christian got in line and filled his own plate. His cup was filled with coffee—the great soberer, recently arrived in their land from the exotic East. It was delicious, invigorating, and gave him all the more occasion to thank and praise his God.

As he began to express his great gratitude and bid his new friends goodbye, they all began to object.

"You must not depart just yet," Piety said. "You have only seen this house in the darkness. We would show you all the rarities of this place. I promise you, these will be a blessing and a boon to your travels."

Christian laughed, "Well, what can I say but *lead the way*?"

Charity, Piety, and a very quiet man named Teacher led him first into the study—or at least that's what they called it. To Christian it appeared to be no less than the greatest library he had ever seen. The teacher found his tongue quickly when the documents and artifacts came out, and he showed Christian many records of the greatest antiquity. These proved the pedigree of the Lord of the Hill, showing him to be the only Son of the Ancient of Days, having never been born, but rather eternally begotten.

Christian sat in rapt attention as the annuls of the Lord's great acts came out, one beautifully illuminated page at a time. Then there was the logbook, filled with the names of many thousands he had taken into his service and placed in mansions that were impervious to the passing of time and the laws of entropy.

Just as Christian was beginning to feel a bit tired and hungry, some members of the household brought in tea and a few delicacies, which they enjoyed together while discussing the exploits of some of the King's great servants—how they had subdued kingdoms, wrought righteousness, obtained promises, stopped the mouths of lions, quenched the consuming fire, escaped the edge of the sword, and were in all other ways made strong out of weakness and valiant out of fear, even turning to flight entire armies.

Christian looked down at the butter sandwich in his hand. It would only just hold him over to supper, but these tales of the Lord and his people would feed him for the rest of his pilgrimage.

Faithful made it from the Pleasant Arbor to the top of the hill by noon. The blood was pumping and his desire grew to quicken his pace all the more and make this day more productive than any three days he'd ever known before. All the same, as he crested the hill, he had to stop and take in the sight of a palace sparkling in the noonday sun.

He decided to take just a moment to have a look and renew his strength. He fixed his eyes on the highest spire and walked toward the place, gawking. Then he froze in his tracks, gripped by an yielding panic. Faithful stood perfectly still and looked down to his right and his left. He was standing between two massive lions—the sort of creatures he had only read about in books or spoken of in grave and frightful tones around the campfire.

Both cats were massive, stretched out in the grass. But they were also asleep. The fear ebbed away as one of the cats rubbed at its eyes and rolled over, snoring loudly in the warm sun.

Faithful chuckled to himself and carried on along the path, to the place where a stone walk diverged from the Narrow Way, leading up to the door of the palace. Near that intersection, a man stood, regarding Faithful with admiration.

"Sir, I have never seen any pilgrim walk between those lions with the calmness and courage that you have shown just now. Could I have your name?"

Faithful grinned. "I am called Faithful. And it may be that I am just better at hiding my fear than those other pilgrims."

"I think you're being modest. Which is another thing to commend. Sir, please do me the favor of joining us tonight for supper."

"I couldn't impose," Faithful said. "But thank you very much for the invitation."

"It's no imposition at all," the porter said. "This house exists for the relief and security of pilgrims."

Faithful glanced up at the sun, as if to check whether it was still above his head. "Again, sir, you are very kind. But I still have much of the day before me and I've sort of a challenged myself to cover as much ground as possible before the sun sets. I think I will carry on. But certainly, a blessing upon yourself and this house for your kind offer."

He made to leave, but Watchful caught him by the shoulder and said, "Good pilgrim, you would be wise to stop even for an hour before you descend this hill and, after it, descend further yet, into the Valley of Humiliation."

"It's just—I just have too much to do," Faithful said. "You understand."

The porter sighed. Then, reaching into the bag he carried across his shoulder, he pulled out a slice of bread and a hunk of cheese, which he wrapped in a loose cloth and handed to Faithful, along with a skin of wine. "At least take my lunch," he said.

"Oh, I . . . I couldn't."

"I insist," Watchful said, then added with a wink, "Take it or fight me."

Faithful chuckled and accepted these gifts with his thanks. He took a few steps, then turned back. "The 'Valley of Humiliation,' you say?"

The porter nodded.

"Is there some secret to surviving it that may only be obtained in that palace?"

"No, that's not quite it. Keep your head up and your heart fixed on our Lord and you should get through the valley without too much trouble, good Faithful. Godspeed."

It was nearly dark by the time Christian and his new friends finished in the study. At the pilgrim's insistence, they had skipped nothing and skimmed nothing related to the Lord's great deeds on their behalf. They read about how willing he had been to receive into favor even those who had previously insulted him with slurs and blasphemies.

They then dove into several other histories, both ancient and modern, together with prophecies and predictions of things sure to come, both to the dread and amazement of the

Lord's enemies and to the comfort and solace of pilgrims.

When they had come to the end of these, the teacher stood upon a stool and gazed out the small window. "Well," he said, "I had hoped we could take you to the heights today and show you the Delectable Mountains. But they are shrouded in darkness now."

"Perhaps tomorrow before I leave," Christian said.

"Certainly. For now, l suggest we all take some time to contemplate all that we've read before supper is served."

Faithful continued his slow descent into the Valley of Humiliation as the sun set behind him. His one recurring thought was that he should have accepted that kind man's offer and gone inside—to be fed, strengthened, and equipped for this leg of the journey. As it was, despite his best-laid plans, Faithful had made very little progress during the remaining daylight. In fact, he could look back over his shoulder and see the place where he'd rested two hours ago.

Upon entering the Valley of Humiliation, he'd found that every step required an intense act of the will—namely an act of submitting his own will to the Lord's—and this caused him to make slow and indirect progress. He was also plagued with a sense that someone was following him, stalking him like a predator, biding his time.

Faithful thought of Goodwill's consternation at the sight of a pilgrim approaching the gate all alone, rather than two-by-two or three-by-three, and he understood it all the more. Perhaps he would have found in that beautiful palace some other pilgrim or even a band of pilgrims to which he could have joined himself.

Two are better than one. They have a better reward for their toil. If one falls, the other can lift him. If two lie together, they keep warm, but how can one keep warm alone?

Faithful's mind was suddenly filled with the image of the woman Wanton—tugging at his wrist, inviting him into her warm bed. She was all lace and soft skin and sultry words. A deep sense of shame welled up within him, and Faithful cried out for help against enemies, seen and unseen.

The image of Wanton dissolved and, in her place, stood another woman—modest and kind and good. Faithful had never met her, but somehow he knew her. Piety was her name. When she spoke, her voice was strong and sincere, free of any duplicity: "Two are indeed better than one," she said. "Though a man might prevail against one who is alone, two will withstand him—and a threefold cord is not quickly broken."

A threefold cord. Faithful thought of the Father, the Son, and the Holy Spirit; of God's omniscience, omnipotence, and omnipresence; of the living creatures around the throne declaring him thrice holy.

"The words of him who has the sharp, two-edged sword," the woman was saying. "'Just as Jonas was three days in the belly of the great fish, so I will be three days in the belly of the earth. Then . . . will I rise.'" The woman faded into the falling night.

"What shall I say to these things," Faithful said. "If God is for me, who can be against me?" And with that, he spread his cloak on the ground and lay down upon it, falling into a shallow sleep.

It was in the deadest part of the night that Faithful awoke with a start. The sense that he was being watched was reinforced by every pounding beat of his heart. He could hear the sound of something out there, breathing deeply, a roar building in its throat. The clink of scales working against one another echoed up through the valley.

Faithful thought of the words of the kind porter at the palace. *Just keep your head up and your heart fixed on the Lord, and you should pass through without too much trouble.*

Faithful stood up, shook the drowsiness from his head, and cracked his neck, his eyes tracing the moon-tinged darkness around him and ultimately falling upon a good-sized rock a few paces away. He picked it up and hefted it. One side was round and fit perfectly within his palm; the other came to a point like an axe head. Faithful resolved to stand guard through the rest of the night. He may be only one pilgrim, but would keep watch. And he wasn't exactly alone.

Only fifty yards away, concealed in the thicket, the creature Apollyon watched and waited. He knitted his dragon's brow in thought. Physically, this pilgrim was an impressive specimen, which usually meant that he would be soft, spiritually— trusting in flesh and bone. For that reason, Apollyon had intended to let him sleep on the cold earth for an hour or so and then set upon him and tear him to pieces.

But when he had extended his wings, intent on doing just that, the sound of his scales had awakened the pilgrim, and it was now clear that this man was more than he seemed. True, a single rock—a crude makeshift weapon—would be nothing against Apollyon the Great Destroyer. Less than nothing. But this man reminded him of someone else. Someone he'd underestimated and attacked long ago, only to be defeated and humiliated. It had taken him decades to fully recover from that defeat.

And so Apollyon decided to wait this pilgrim out. Eventually, he would grow bored, grow tired . . . lie down and drift off again. From here, a few fiery darts could be launched to stun and injure him in his sleep, softening him for the final snuffing out. He smiled to himself.

Then, with lightning speed, he thrust his talon out into the darkness and wrapped it around the throat of a gaunt, gray man, lifting him off the ground. The man kicked and sputtered, struggling for breath, the yellow glow of Apollyon's eyes illuminating the man's desperate, sputtering face.

The massive demon laughed. "Shame? Is that you? Are you truly foolish enough to sneak up on me in the darkness?"

Shame tried to answer but only succeeded in choking on his own words and spittle. Apollyon dumped him to the ground.

"Speak," he spat.

"My lord, I was just coming to inquire: are you planning to set upon this man tonight?"

"Why do you ask?" He sneered. "Do I report to you now?"

"No, no. Of course not. It's just . . . I figured that if you were going to, you would have already done so, and—"

"I will not attack while he is awake. This man has no real weapon, true, but he is formidable. He reminds me of young David who felled a champion of hell with one small stone. And if you'll notice, this man hefts a heavy rock."

"I came to tell you, master, that—" he swallowed hard—"I can take him for you." The last words came out as a question.

Apollyon laughed, louder than he intended, and said, "You?"

"Yes, lord. I will let him go down just a bit deeper into the Valley of Humiliation and will use the setting to my advantage while I spring my trap! You remember how that same David fell himself, don't you? He was a great man, far stronger than this neophyte, and favored of the King—a king himself! And yet, after he sinned, *I* pulled him down into an undertow of shame, sucking him further and further into the mirey pit. Sin. Shame. Sin. Shame. Let me have a crack at this one. I will send my associate, Discontent, to soften him up and then I will go in for the kill."

"You have misread this one, Shame. He does not tend toward hiding his sins. My spies tell me that he makes them known, even with blubbering tears, and then he gives glory to the God who forgives them."

"Just so. There are different types of Shame, Lord Apollyon. I have been watching this pilgrim too and I know precisely how to trap him. Besides, if I am not mistaken, another pilgrim comes this way in the morning—one who will be armed to the teeth and anxious to meet you in battle."

"*Chrisssstian*," Apollyon hissed.

"Yes."

"Very well. I will rest for battle. As for you: do not let this man out of your sight for one moment. Should he escape your grasp, you will pay—in shrieks and agony."

In the morning, Christian arose to another spectacular sunrise. He thanked the Lord for this place and these people as he gathered his things and prepared to depart.

The members of the household seemed to be fasting this

day, but knowing that Christian had a hard journey ahead of him, they brought him some bread and fruit preserves and more of that delicious brown beverage.

Then Piety, Charity, and Steadfast led him up, almost to the top of the highest spire of the palace, where a watchtower was set. Pointing out to the East, Charity said, "Do you see that ridge there? Those are the Delectable Mountains." The mountain range was barely visible from here, the tops of the tallest peaks shrouded in mist, but they were beautiful to behold. Spread out before them was a colorful tapestry that Christian assumed to be vineyards, flowers, fruit of all sorts, springs, and fountains.

"Magnificent," he said, unable to tear his eyes from the glorious sight.

"They certainly are," said Piety, "but we show these to you, not just to enthrall you, but to encourage you. You see, those mountains are closer to the Celestial City than they are to where you stand right now."

Christian thought on this. "What is the name of that land?"

"It is Immanuel's land," Charity said. "And when you arrive there, you will be able to see the gate of the Celestial City from its heights, as the shepherds who live there make it visible to you."

"I have to go," Christian said. "I will make great progress today." He was feeling restless now, longing to think with each step how every footfall in the right direction would take him measurably closer to those mountains and, thus, to the Celestial Gate."

"Aye," Steadfast said, "you should be going. But first, one more, very important, stop."

"Where?" Christian asked.

"The armory."

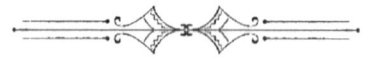

Faithful had dozed only a bit in the first purple light of day and he now rose to his feet as the sun burst forth above the canopy of trees, bringing with it new mercies and fresh perspective.

Despite his dearth of sleep, he felt all the more prepared to pass through the Valley of Humiliation and onto whatever lay beyond. As he set out, his feet were steady and his pace quick. He thanked his Lord for protection during the night and asked him for guidance, courage, and wisdom for this day.

They entered the armory from the south side of the palace, wishing the Peace of Christ upon the armorer, who unlocked the gate and helped the ladies down the rock-hewn steps into a vast subterranean keep.

Christian had been intent on spending as little time here as possible before resuming his travel, but such thoughts fled his mind as soon as he laid eyes on the collection of weapons and engines exhibited along the ornate near wall.

One by one, the armorer showed him Moses' rod, which had become a serpent, drawn water forth from the rock, and parted the Read Sea; the tent peg which mighty Jael had driven through Sisera's skull and the mallet with which she struck it; trumpets, lamps, and fragments of the jars that had obscured them on the night that Gideon's tiny force wiped out a massive army of Midianites; the ox-goad with which Shamgar slew six-hundred Philistines, and the jawbone with which Samson killed a thousand. As they neared the corner, Christian saw the sling with which David killed Goliath and the giant's sword, which King David had carried with him into battle. But even that huge weapon looked modest compared to the last one there on display: an enormous sword, embedded into the earth itself at the far corner of the armory.

"What is that?" Christian asked.

The armorer smiled. "That is the sword with which our Lord will kill the Man of Sin on the day that he shall rise up to the prey. But we are not here just to look, are we?" He motioned for Christian to turn around. And when he did, he saw enough armor and weapons to outfit tens of thousands of soldiers for battle, all lined up and perfectly organized by piece and size.

The armorer stood back and studied Christian's frame for a moment before issuing orders to the others to bring him particular pieces. When it was all piled at his feet, he began by helping Christian gird his loins with a thick leather belt.

"This is the belt of Truth," the armorer said. "It will hold you fast and protect your vitals in battle. From it will hang your sword and any other weapons you carry."

Next, they affixed a hard leather-and-metal shell over his chest. "This is the breastplate of righteousness," Charity said. "It will guard your heart and give you courage in facing the Enemy. But look here." She pointed to a metallic emblem over the heart, in the shape of a key. "This is Promise. It will help you never to forget the promises of God, and may indeed save your life one day."

Christian's shins were then fitted with grieves, followed by leather footwear. "These shoes will never wear out," Steadfast said, indicating his own pair of the same. "Never. They will bring you forward as you herald the Gospel of peace."

The armorer handed Christian a tall, rectangular shield, curved in at the sides, and said, "The shield of faith will extinguish the flaming darts of the Evil One."

Steadfast pushed a helmet down onto the pilgrim's head, a bit roughly. "The helmet of salvation. Let it guard your mind from threats, both without *and* within."

"And now for your weapons," the armorer said. "First and foremost, the Sword of the Spirit." He handed a sheathed sword to Steadfast, who affixed it to Christian's belt. "And, of course, All-Prayer." He handed Piety the short javelin, which she attached to the pilgrim's back.

"That should do it," the armorer said. "Be strong in the Lord and in the power of his might. Steadfast. Immovable."

Christian nodded and followed his new friends back out into the late morning sun, where he saw Prudence and Watchful waiting for him.

"Now *that's* a man ready for pilgrimage!" the porter called out, drawing near. "Look at you! Do you need any help, my friend?"

"Not unless you want to accompany me the rest of the way?" Christian laughed.

"I'd better not leave my post," Watchful said. "But there are many others on the Pilgrim Road. And your instinct is good; you should not be alone. In fact, a man passed by here less than a day ago. A man of great faith and good cheer. Perhaps you might catch up to him."

"Did he mention his name?" Christian asked.

"He did. It was, uh, Faithful. It was Faithful. I wished he'd stayed with us for a time."

Christian laughed. "Faithful? I know him! He was my near neighbor in Destruction! In fact, until a year or two ago, we had been rather close friends. And you say he has just a one-day head start?"

"I'm sure he's reached the bottom of the hill by now, but the Valley of Humiliation can be slow-going for those who have no armor. I should think you can catch him if you set your mind to it. But be careful; as it was difficult coming up, it is dangerous going down."

"Well, good Porter," said Christian, "the Lord be with you, and multiply your blessings for the kindness that you have shown me." He gestured at the others and the palace itself.

"And that goes for all of you."

"May we accompany you to the foot of the hill?" Charity asked.

"You'll get no argument from me."

As they walked, they spoke of all Christian had seen and

experienced at the Palace Beautiful. And when they reached the bottom of the hill, they all bid him Godspeed with a holy kiss.

Prudence left him with a warning: "Going into this valley, you are liable to lose your footing and slip. Do not tarry, but do not rush either." Then she handed Christian a loaf of bread. And Charity gave him a bottle of wine. And Piety, a cluster of raisins. And after a prayer together, they turned back and began to climb the hill toward the Palace Beautiful.

Christian put the food into his bag and tied it shut again. As he fastened it to his back, he looked down at his new armor and weapons.

He had no doubt that there were many potential dangers, snares, and pitfalls ahead—but as long as he wore this armor, he felt sure that no one would dare set upon him.

Hypocrisy grinned as the wide, level path curved ever so slightly to the left, alongside a beautiful orchard of heavy, ripe apples. He plucked one from a low-hanging branch and bit into it, thinking of his old friend Formalist, always following his silly rules and proverbs. He laughed out loud and took another bite.

Those proverbs had sent Formalist in the other direction, and the sign designating this the Road to Destruction had kept Christian from an easy journey. But Hypocrisy knew better. Such a label was the perfect way to protect a pleasant path like this from being overrun by travelers, its fruit picked clean and its ground packed hard. Those who dared defy this warning would be rewarded with leisurely travel and all sorts of comforts. If anyone knew the value of presenting things in a particular way for one's own advantage, it was Hypocrisy. He'd practically invented the practice.

After two hours of walking, the road led him into a wide open field, full of dark mountains, and doubt began to cloud his good humor. But Hypocrisy pushed on and soon found himself walking alongside a high stone wall. It looked similar enough to the one he and Formalist had tumbled over, but he could not be certain whether it was the same one.

He followed the road, along the high wall, until darkness was falling, and made camp beneath a pleasant willow tree, where he not only found a good night's sleep, but woke to find several silver coins scattered about, shining in the morning sun. He laughed as he gathered them, and could not wait to show these to Christian and Formalist. Why, even if he lost their little bet, he would come out ahead. This delighted, but did not surprise the man. Things generally worked out for Hypocrisy

He resumed the road, which he walked for several days, until he came upon a large earthwork, rising up to the top of the wall itself. There the road terminated, with a sign that warned, "No Re-Entry." Hypocrisy thought for a moment and decided he'd had enough of this pilgrimage. And he'd seen enough—enough to convince the other residents of Vain-Glory that he had seen it through to the end. A combination of stories he'd heard, his own meager experiences on the road, and his ever-reliable imagination would prove sufficient. Besides, his supply of food was nearing its end; he had to arrive *somewhere*, and soon.

Looking down to the ground beneath, on the other side of the wall, he realized it was not much higher than the free-fall he and Formalist had undertaken a few days earlier. Going limp, he dropped nearly 20 feet, perfectly executing the tuck-

and-roll as he landed. He sat, dazed, for a few minutes before gathering himself up, shaking off the dust, and carrying on along the path.

Within a few hours, Hypocrisy found himself at a fork in the road. A sign pointing to the left indicated 50 miles to the City of Destruction. Another sign, pointing the other way, promised to take him home to Vain-Glory. He thought again of Formalist and all of his rules and chuckled to himself as he turned right. *Always go right*, they'd been taught as children. And Hypocrisy happily obliged—when it served his purpose.

It was the dinner hour when he arrived back in his hometown and he went right to his favorite tavern, where a crowd quickly formed around him, excitedly taking in his tales of the Narrow Way, the beauty and majesty of the Celestial City, and—for good measure—the story of Formalist giving up and turning aside when things got hard.

His boyhood chum Swagger challenged him a bit, questioning how such an epic journey could be accomplished in less than a fortnight. But Hypocrisy had prepared himself for this, and related the shortcuts he'd taken, the wisdom and cunning with which he had outsmarted giants and hobgoblins, and finally, how he had traded his father's prized amulet for the fastest horse he'd ever seen, which brought him with unbelievable speed to the shining holy city.

They all ate it up. Hypocrisy's cup was never empty that night, as his admirers jostled for the honor of buying him a drink. Even Boastful and Swagger clapped him on the back and raised glass after glass to his health and good fortune—and those men hadn't spoken to him since they were lads.

It was very late, when the crowd had thinned considerably, that the local parson—The Rev. Mr. License of the United Church of Ease—invited Hypocrisy to join him at a corner table.

"That's quite a story," he said, eyes gleaming.

Stomach full and head swimming, Hypocrisy nodded and emptied yet another tankard.

"Have you considered what you will do with this new-found fame and wisdom?"

Hypocrisy shrugged.

The reverend leaned closer and asked, "Have you considered church work?" When his companion balked, he added, "For men like us, it's far more lucrative than you might think."

Black Smoke

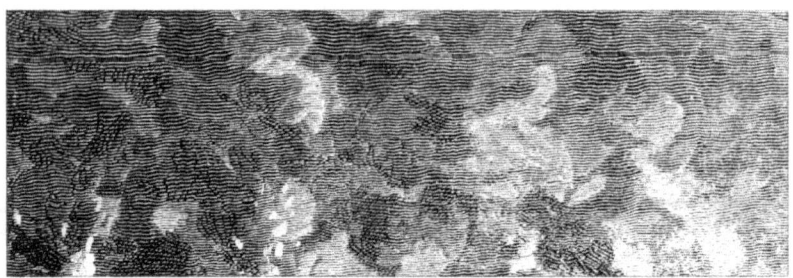

Watchful sat on his bench, a small fire in an iron kettle warming his body as the heavenly sound of singing saints, filtering out through the windows of the chapel, warmed his soul. Watchful had a terrible singing voice and hated to sully the music of his brothers and sisters, even out here, so he sat in silence and sang in his heart. He wished he could close his eyes and focus entirely on the song of worship, but he had to keep watch, even this morning.

His eyes drifted along the soft distant canopy of trees and the three highest peaks of the Delectable Mountains rising up above it, as the beautiful words permeate his soul:

> *All glory be to Thee, Most High,*
> *   to Thee all adoration;*
> *In grace and truth Thou drawest nigh*
> *   to offer us salvation;*
> *Thou showest Thy good-will to men,*
> *   and peace shall reign on earth again;*
> *We praise Thy name forever.*

As he listened, he fished a clay pipe from his pocket, carefully packed the night before. He pushed a strip of cedar into the fire and, when it began to burn, used it to light the pipe, drawing in the sweet smoke and rolling it over his tongue, then releasing it in a thin stream so that it curled upward, like the visible manifestation of earnest praise going up to heaven—a burnt offering of old.

The door at the corner of the house opened and Steadfast came out, a large cup gripped in his massive hand.

"I've brought you something," he said, extending the cup. Watchful accepted the warm vessel and inhaled its aroma deeply. "I figured you could use it."

"Have I told you I love you, brother?" Watchful laughed.

"I can't drink it without breakfast," Steadfast said, sitting next to the porter. "Comes back up my throat."

"I prefer it this way. It quickens me all the quicker on an empty stomach."

They sat in silence, listening to the beautiful hymn and watching the last of the morning mist slowly burn off the mountains. Watchful took another sip and another pull on his pipe.

"My lady will have a fit if she sees you smoking that thing."

"Piety? Nah, she's come around. Says she loves the smell now."

"Aye. It's Prudence who will have your head."

"I'll take my chances." Another wisp of white smoke came up from his mouth and Watchful waited for it to disappear into the air above them. But it didn't. Rather, it seemed to turn black, chugging upward all the thicker, blotting out the sky behind it like a swarm of locusts coming up from the abyss.

The pipe fell from Watchful's mouth and shattered against the ground, ejecting red-hot embers of tobacco onto his feet.

Watchful stood and pointed out to the distance. "Look!"

Steadfast stood as well, his eyes fixed on the point in the distance, from which the smoke was rising.

"Apollyon." He stood there, hand on his sword, frozen in a moment of helpless indecision. "Christian! We have to—"

"He's way down in the valley by now," Watchful said. "We'd never reach him in time. But we can still help."

Steadfast nodded and rushed back into the palace, down the narrow hall, and into the chapel, slamming the door against the wall in the process. "Black smoke!" he cried.

The singing came to a stop and Expositor, who had been leading the song, asked, "What is it, brother?"

"The Destroyer. He is moving in the Valley of Humiliation, up the Pilgrim Road."

Expositor nodded his understanding. "Then let us leave off singing and return to our prayers for Good Christian."

Christian followed the Narrow Way deeper and deeper into the valley. Like the terrain, the temperature was falling with unsettling speed, and the distant sound of desperate shrieks and whimpers seemed to be closing in all around him. But Christian pushed ahead all the same.

The Narrow Path narrowed further, and the ground grew rockier and more uneven. Christian's confidence in his new armor—absolute just two hours ago—was flagging. It fit him quite snugly, yes, but the leather doublet and leggings holding it to his body were still stiff and unyielding, digging into his joints. Every step seemed to bring a knife's dull blade along the same raw lines in his flesh.

Christian was thinking of stopping for a moment, to sit and loosen his armor, when he saw an enormous, foul creature coming up from the misty distance to meet him. Fear banished all other thoughts and impulses from his mind and fixed his feet in place beneath him, even while it threatened to take his legs.

"Turn back," was his first thought, to his shame. "Run." But he had no armor for his back. The only thing to do was stand and fight.

"Give me courage and strength to stand firm in the evil

day," the pilgrim said, aloud, to the King of this land.

With impossible speed for a creature its size, the beast closed the gap between them and drew up before him, towering over the pilgrim.

The monster was hideous to behold. Long, curved horns like those of a ram crowned his devilish head. His body was clothed with scales like a fish; they clinked against each—the sound of steel chains—as thick, noxious breaths chugged slowly in and out like a steam turbine. Stretched behind and above him were black leathery wings, spanning at least twenty feet. From his lion's mouth belched fire and smoke.

Glowing yellow eyes traced Christian's form from head to foot, and back again. The creature scoffed. "You will now tell me," he said, "who you are, where you have come from, and where you are going."

Christian looked down to his right hand, which a moment ago had been trembling, and placed it firmly upon the hilt of his sword. "I am Christian," he answered. "I come from the City of Destruction, the place of all evil. I am going to the City of Zion. And who are you?"

"I am Apollyon, the god and prince of your native land—your prince, who now finds you fleeing to the realm of another. If I did not think you might yet be useful to me, I would cut you to pieces where you stand. What do you have to say for yourself, 'Christian?'"

"You are correct that I was born into your dominion. But your service was hard and no man could live on your wages. For the wages of sin is death. And so I've followed the footprints of so many before me and left your kingdom behind."

Apollyon laughed. "Easy enough to say. But there is no prince alive who would let his subjects defect to another kingdom without severe consequences. But to show you that I am a kind and benevolent ruler, and because you have struggled to live on your wages, I promise: come back with me, and whatever our country can afford to pay you—I will pay it."

"It's too late. And far too little. I've given myself fully to another King. The King of Princes. How could I possibly go back to you?"

Apollyon's lip curled back for a moment, revealing razor fangs glistening with viscous saliva. "Not to worry," he said. "It's very common for pilgrims like you who have sworn their allegiance to this king to lose heart or lose interest after a time and then return again to me. If you do this, all will be well."

"What you're describing is a traitor," Christian said. "And traitors are rightly hanged."

"You had no problem betraying your allegiance to me. Even so, all will be forgiven if you simply recant and come back home."

"Look, I didn't know any better when I served you," Christian said. "Now I do. Besides, the Prince under whose banner I now stand is the only One able to absolve and pardon all my crimes—including those I committed under your kingship. And frankly, I like his service, his wages, his servants, his company, and his country better than yours. Now move aside; I am following after him now."

The creature folded his wings behind him, looking smaller now. He pulled his tarrish lips into a thin smile that concealed his fangs and said, "Let's be logical. Consider what lies ahead: the trials and dangers and snares and how you will face them all feeling far less courageous than you feel even now, standing before me. Consider that most of this king's servants come to a brutal and painful end, at my hand. And consider that I came here, into his domain, in person, to bring you back home—something I have done for countless confused subjects, breaking them free of his grip by brute force or clever schemes. And so I will deliver you as well. Would your 'king of princes' do that for you? I think not."

"You're wasting your foul breath and revealing yourself as a liar. For my Prince did go into your domain to save us. And now, while he calls us to come out of your damned land, he has a purpose in that as well: to test our love and prove whether we will be loyal to the end. And as for the shameful and painful deaths that so many have suffered before me, these have cause to rejoice, knowing that they will be received into sudden and eternal glory. Pilgrims do not expect deliverance now, but our content to wait for future glory, when our King will ride down on your country on a white horse of war with all his holy angels, and us behind him!"

Apollyon's pale talons clenched and unclenched and a ribbon of purplish smoke streamed from his nose. "Do you really think you will escape on that day? You've already failed so many times since you took to walking this road."

"Indeed I have fallen, probably more than you know. But I have obtained pardon for each and every sin because my king is the King of Mercy."

The massive wings shot open again with a concussive *whu-whump* that almost knocked Christian onto his back. "I am an enemy of this Prince! I hate his person, his laws, and his people. And I am more than enough to keep you from going further along the Way. Consider well what you do next, pilgrim."

"Careful," Christian warned. "We are on the King's Highway—the way of holiness. You are the one who should watch his step."

Apollyon stretched his bear-like foot out to his left, straddling the entire breadth of the path. "I am void of fear," he growled, "and of further patience. Now prepare to die, for I swear by my own fiery throne that I will spill your soul!"

And with that, he lit a javelin with a blue flame from out of his mouth and hurled it at Christian, who brought up his shield just in time to glance the projectile off into the woods beyond.

Christian drew his sword and pounded his fist against his breastplate. "I will withstand you!" he cried out.

A wave of burning darts lit up the darkness around him. Christian dove, rolled, and came up to a tight crouch behind his shield. He almost cried out, then swallowed down the pain. His foot had been pierced by a dart, through a seam in the armor. He pulled it out and tossed it aside. Allowing himself a glance at the damage, he saw that the heat from the dart had cauterized the wound; no blood leaked from the blackened hole, although a whisp of steam was curling up from it.

Shaking off the paralysis of fear and the narcotic effect of the growing black smoke, Christian raised his sword once again and lowered his shield an inch beneath his eyes. Instantly, a dart struck his hand, knocking the sword from it, and another connected with his helmet, rocking his senses and throwing him down onto his back.

He looked up at the dull, gray sky, spinning slowly above him for just a moment before his field of vision was filled with the demonic creature's form. "You fall easy, like your Prince before you. Give him my regards." From behind his blackened wings, he drew a long and jagged sword, which he brought down onto Christian's prone body with all his hellish might.

Christian brought the shield up to meet the blow, which glanced off to the side, grazing the pilgrim's left arm in the process. He gaped at his shield, which was now half the size it had been a moment earlier. Then he saw his sword lying there, within reach. Grasping desperately for the weapon, he swung his shield at the beast, followed by a blind flailing blow with the blade. He did no damage to the enemy, but managed to roll to his feet once again.

As he righted his helmet, thanks and remorse intermingled in his mind. By God's grace he was alive to fight on, but he'd missed a great opening. When the beast was rearing back, Christian's own sword had been within reach. God had granted him a clear way of victory. And he'd missed it. Wasted it.

"Alright," Christian said. "This is your last chance; lay down your weapon and surrender or die at the edge of my blade."

Faithful had no sense of the hour. He would have guessed it was mid-morning, but the sky was growing darker with each downward step that he took.

For quite some time, it had seemed almost on the verge of total darkness—and yet it never quite arrived. To keep his spirits from falling, he repeated Scriptures to himself. "If we walk in the light, as he is in the light," he said, "we have fellowship with one another and the blood of Jesus, his son, cleanses us from all sin."

He'd hoped these words would make the darkness wane. Instead, they brought his solitude to mind once again. "Fellowship one with another" sounded incredible. But it, of course, required *another*.

Just then, as if in answer to a prayer not yet offered, a man overtook him along the road and fell in step alongside him. He looked a bit familiar to Faithful, although his name would not come to mind.

"Hello," the man said.

"Good day to you," Faithful replied. The man's eyes were unhappy and his tone as well, but Faithful told himself this traveler may be feeling the same lack of fellowship that plagued him. Perhaps they could cheer each other up.

"Do I know you?" Faithful asked.

"I think you might," the man answered. "My name is Discontent of Grumbleton."

"I'm Faithful. Born and raised in the City of Destruction, but now on my way to the Celestial City."

"Well, that answers it," Discontent said, perking up a bit. "I have family in your hometown, and I've visited many times. In fact, I believe you and I have tipped back more than a few pints over the years. The Red Horse, right? You're friends with that wild man, Revelry!"

"Friends, yes! And he was my business partner for years."

"Huh," the man said, thoughtfully. "What on earth did he think of your going on a religious quest to the Celestial City?"

"If I'm honest, not much."

"I wouldn't think so."

They walked in silence for a minute or two before Faithful asked, "What do you think of it?"

"Of pilgrimage?"

"Aye."

"The pilgrimage that has you here in this valley?"

"The same. Yes."

"Well, I'll tell you, this valley is altogether without honor. I sure wouldn't want my friends to know I'd been here."

"Then . . . why *are* you here?"

He leaned in and spoke softly. "I am looking for a treasure. It's an odd story; I won a treasure map in a game of cards in the town of Fair Speech. I doubt there's anything to it, but I have to check—for my own satisfaction. The spot is just up ahead here. I'll have a look and head back—as it happens, to the City of Destruction. Why don't you come with me? I'll even cut you in on the treasure . . . if there is one."

"Go back? I wouldn't think of it! That place is doomed and its people in utter denial—perhaps none more than Revelry."

Discontent shook his head with disdain. "Are you really so taken in? How can you not see that this whole enterprise of yours is a great offense to all your friends and family back home? All of those young, carefree men and women you used to spend your evenings with—Pride, Arrogance, Self-Conceit, Worldly Good? If they saw you making such an ass of yourself, they'd disown you!"

"These people were indeed my friends at one time. And in fact, two of them were my family according to the flesh. But the last time I saw them, every one of them—to a man—had joined an angry mob intent on stringing me up. So you see, there is no danger of them disowning me now, for they did that the moment I became a pilgrim. And I have also rejected them."

Discontent frowned even deeper. "All the same, you can't deny that walking willfully into humiliation is a foolish and shameful thing."

"Sir, I'm afraid you've quite missed the point. Before honor is humility, whereas a haughty spirit comes before a fall. I would rather pass *through* this valley to the honor that lies beyond—counted such by the wisest—than try to impress the likes of Revelry or Arrogance, or you for that matter, and find myself falling to my death."

Discontent shrugged and slinked his shoulders low.

"Maybe you ought to check that map of yours," Faithful said. "We wouldn't want you to miss your great treasure, would we?"

The pilgrim Christian and the creature Apollyon had been locked in combat for more than an hour when the beast drew back a few massive steps and leaned upon his sword, breathing heavily. Christian also seized the opportunity to rest, sitting back against a felled tree.

"You cannot possibly think yourself more powerful than my Lord," Christian said. "He created the world and everything in it. What have you done?"

"I concede that your Lord has done some mighty deeds. And that he is holy. And that it is a fearful thing to fall into his hands. And for that reason, I again urge you to renounce him and join me, for my spies have been filling my ears with tales of your betrayal against this Lord. You must realized that, even if you do arrive at the City you seek, you will only be ushering yourself into judgment."

Christian knew it was fruitless to engage with this lying beast, but he coveted a bit more time to replenish his strength and so he asked, "In what have I been unfaithful to him?"

"Where to even begin? Why, upon first setting out, you were almost choked to death in the gulf of Despond. My spies saw you seeking after wicked ways to be rid of your burden and nearly paying the ultimate price at the foot of Hill Legality. My agents took note as you sinfully slept and lost your choice things. You were almost persuaded to go back at the sight of the lions. And even when you talk of your journey on the Narrow Road—of what you have seen and heard and done—you inwardly desire vainglory in all you say. Need I go on?"

"But you speak of debts paid, stains washed clean. As I have said, my Lord has pardoned me for all these transgressions."

"There is no pardon for sins like yours," the creature roared. "Willful! Wicked! Profane! Abandon hope, Graceless, for it is an illusion."

Christian stood again. "Your lies are empty and powerless to one who knows the truth."

"Then let us leave off words and come again to blows."

Apollyon rushed forward, swinging his massive sword. Christian brought his own blade up to meet it. He was pushed back the space of three steps, his feet sliding in the dirt—but his arms did not fail and his sword did not break.

Shame watched Faithful draw near the bottom of the valley. He hid, shrouded back in total darkness and prepared himself.

He had to time this just right. The report from Discontent had been so disappointing that Shame lashed out at his associate, turning some of his unique ammunition upon Discontent, burying him in self-loathing until he fell to the earth, crippled by weaponized humiliation. On any other ground, Shame and Discontent might been evenly matched, but here in this valley, it was an easy victory.

In the last moments before emerging from his hiding place, Shame closed his eyes and thought of Faithful. And as he thought, his appearance began to change. His body, thin and willowy in build, began to grow, up and out. His jaw squared down, his chin stretched out, and his chest puffed up. He cleared his throat and his voice grew deeper as he said, "Okay, Mr. Faithful, let's see how you handle a real trial."

Just as Faithful put his foot down on the lowest point of the valley, where heavy black smoke was pooled up to his knees, Shame emerged from the wood and approached him casually.

"Well," he said, "I did not think I'd find a fellow traveler here. What on earth are you doing?"

"I'm on pilgrimage. And you?"

"Pilgrimage? You mean like *pilgrimage*-pilgrimage? A religious journey? Superstition and the like? Devils and angels, the Holy Trinity and life everlasting?"

Faithful narrowed his eyes. "What of it?"

"I'm surprised is all. You look like a real man. But there is no more pitiful, low, sneaking business for a man than religion."

"Why do you say that?"

The man scoffed. "I will tell you—but first, you tell me this: are there true and false religions?"

"To be certain."

"And what makes the difference between them?"

Faithful thought for a moment. "Well, for one thing, true religion is marked by a tender conscience before the Lord."

The man laughed. "There, you see? Is there anything less manly than a tender conscience?"

"You are wrong there, my friend. In fact—"

"Or for a so-called 'man' to watch over his words and his ways and tie himself up and hold himself back from the true liberty of brave spirits—well, such a man would deserve to be the ridicule of this age!"

Faithful folded his arms over his chest. "You say that religion is unmanly. I say it's quite the opposite. And since I have no idea who you are or what gives you the right to make such pronouncements, I really don't care what you think."

"Then forget about me! Think bigger! Consider how many of the mighty, rich, or wise ever agreed with you on the subject? And even if you can name one or two, I'll show you how they were persuaded to be fools and lost all that they had by chasing such nonsense. Or just look around at your fellow pilgrims and see their lowly condition, their ignorance, their lack of knowledge and education. Rubes, all of them. Absolute rubes."

Perhaps it was the combination of the Valley of Humiliation and these two antagonistic companions, but Faithful was having no more of this and said, "Clearly, the opinions of others are far important to you than they are to me. I do not need the prating praise of men to find worth in my creed or my conduct."

"I suppose that's one way to look at it. But consider—"

"What is your name, sir?"

"I am called Shame."

"Hm. I believe you are misnamed. For you are a bold villain indeed. Perhaps they should call you Shameless."

"Perhaps. After all, while I bear the name, you are the one so wrapped up in religious delusions, all of which are a very shame. It is a shame to sit whining and mourning under a sermon. It is a shame to come sighing and groaning home. It is a shame to beg your neighbor to 'forgive you' for petty faults or to make restitution for things you have taken. A real man takes what he can get and then takes some more. A real man demands his liberty no matter what, in every situation. And what's more, Faithful, when I look into your eyes, I see such a real man. Tell me I'm wrong."

"Shame, you've got it all backwards. These libertines you describe are weak. They are cowards. It requires no courage for a man to let the lust of his flesh drag him around by the nose."

"On the contrary, those libertines are brave. Stunningly brave! And if you intend to continue on this Narrow Road, you had better man up yourself. For, when you've come up out of this valley, another waits just beyond it: the Valley of the Shadow of Death. And it makes this place look like a picnic at the seashore. Do yourself a favor and put this sentimental foolishness behind you. It's a bunch of trouble and danger and the only reward is to be thought a halfwit and a milksop by your fellows!"

Faithful looked this man in the eye and asked, "Have you heard of a man named Adam the First?"

"Yes! That old man is a dear friend of mine. In fact, he taught me everything I know."

"Yeah, that figures. Shame, I see you for what you are. You are no fellow traveler at all, but a servant of the enemy sent to arrest my progress. Or worse. So I'm going to tell you what I told your friend Adam. I'm heading up out of this valley. If you follow me one step, I will throttle you. Feel free to test me in this, if you really want to find out who's more of a man."

Christian slammed his shoulder into Apollyon's hip, hoping to knock his legs out from underneath him. Instead, he bounced off and fell to the ground, rolling over quickly and rising again to his feet. The weary pilgrim wondered how long he had been fighting. In the thick of the black smoke, it seemed as though struggling against this beast was all he'd ever done. The darkness of the sky overhead compounded the sensation. Although, as the two combatants again withdrew a few paces from each other to rest, Christian noticed that the slight distant glow, which had shone in the eastern sky when they had first engaged, had now moved to the west.

"We've been fighting more than half the day," Christian realized. Then, looking up at his enemy, another realization followed: "This creature is not recovering out of necessity like I am. He has been taking advantage of these interludes to weaken my spirit with his words."

"I know your mind, feeble pilgrim," Apollyon said. "Your thoughts return to that man on the tree. That twisted, bleeding, defeated man. Perhaps you have more in common with him than you even thought, bleeding and defeated as you are."

"Don't you speak of him. Don't you dare."

The beast laughed. "'Do not speak' of that penniless, pathetic coward, who died humiliated, as the most repugnant of criminals? I supposed, then, that I should not talk of his illegitimate birth, his ignoble boyhood, or the bands of outcasts, whores, drunkards, and rabble that he called his closest friends—rabble that left him to bleed and die alone. Fitting, though. No less than he deserved."

Righteous rage flashed up Christian's spine and he rushed the monster, swinging his sword with all his might, intent on decapitating his foe. But at the last moment, the creature spreads his wings and shot up into the shrouded sky, hovering there, twenty feet above the earth, laughing uproariously.

From there, he launched still more flaming darts down upon Christian, proclaiming, "I am the Prince of the Power of the Air. I am not suspended here by nails, but am enthroned in might, to be worshipped by you mortal fools. Now—bow down before me!"

Fear, wrath, and confusion swirled in Christian's breast as he crouched beneath his shield.

Then a bird lighted on his forearm—a soft, white dove, tilting its head as if to look Christian right in the eye. A deep and abiding peace came over him.

Peering out from behind the shield, Christian smiled at his adversary and said, "I see that you are afraid to face me on level ground, Apollyon. I can't say that I blame you."

The enemy's only response was to pull his wings back and roar down into the pilgrim, slamming him to the ground and pressing hard into him, crushing him against the earth. Feeling his bones bending, threatening to collapse in on all his vitals, Christian called out to the King—in his mind for his lungs were failing him. He struggled to free himself, but it was hopeless.

His left arm was trapped between himself and Apollyon, inert and useless. His right hand was free, but no longer holding the sword, which had flown from his hand on impact—off into the distance, where it now glinted in the veiled light, some fifteen feet away. And while Christian could not see his shield, he was sure that it was somewhere behind him, also out of reach and useless in this moment.

Out of sheer panic, he grabbed one of Apollyon's horns, jerking it hard to the side with a burst of strength, hoping to snap the creature's neck. But the beast just chuckled darkly and over-powered the pilgrim, the sinewy muscles of his neck sliding visibly beneath his hide as he turned his head, bringing the horrifying image of Apollyon's face within inches of Christian's.

"I am sure of thee now," Apollyon rasped, his breath stinking of sulfur. His glowing eyes seemed to hypnotize the pilgrim and steal what little courage remained.

Christian felt the last vestiges of fight ebbing away even as the monster pushed down all the harder, the blade of his glowing sword now burning against the pilgrim's neck and his serpent's tongue sliding up over Christian's face, leaving a trail of slime.

"*Yessssss*, I am sure of thee now."

Just as Christian was on the verge of giving in to his fate, the dove returned, lighting upon Apollyon's head, right between the horns, distracting him for a moment. A glint of light from beside them revealed a sudden hope to Christian: his sword lay to his right, just five feet away. Whether their wrestling had brought them closer to it or whether the Lord himself had brought it near by miraculous means, Christian did not know. Nor did he care at the moment.

Lurching for the weapon, he found its handle and struck with a frantic half-swing, half-stab, which managed to open the beast beneath his left arm. Apollyon cried out in pain and rage, and Christian rolled out from beneath him.

He stood and shouted the words, "Rejoice not against me, you foul beast. For when I fall, I shall rise again!"

The demon straightened up as well, but wincing and groaning all the while. Christian rushed his enemy, chopping with all his might, like a woodsman with an axe, upon the monster's left arm. The blade embedded itself so deep that the pilgrim had to pivot on his hip to dislodge it.

Apollyon's arm went limp, his sword hanging impotently at his side, still locked in the leathery talon. He looked down at it in bewilderment for a moment before coming to himself and drawing another dart from beneath his wings. He held it up to his mouth to light it, but only a pathetic orange spark came forth and, in that moment, Christian took a long stride forward and buried the two-edged sword in the monster's belly, sliding it up between two scales—all the way to the hilt.

Feeling the demon's shallow, ragged breath on his face, Christian looked up into those yellow eyes and said, "No, in all these things we are more than conquerors through him who loved us."

Then he withdrew his sword slowly, slicing downward as he pulled, feeling dense, sticky entrails splitting open within the beast. When the tip of the blade emerged, the angry wound belched forth thick, red tar, which seeped down Apollyon's body.

Christian took two long steps back and stomped the curved

edge of the shield, launching it up into his waiting hand. Raising sword and shield before him, he smirked at his bleeding foe and said, "Tell me then, you vile son of hell: are you 'sure of me' now?"

The yellow glow of the beast's eyes flickered out twice, then returned, far dimmer than before. He looked down at his bleed-

ing torso, and then back up at the pilgrim, in utter shock and disbelief. Then he opened his dragon's wings, turned away, and tried to take flight.

But before he'd risen far into the sky, he began to spin back down in a wide arc, tumbling against the ground and then scampering away in an uneven, faltering gait, toward the distant tree line.

During Faithful's ascent out of the Valley of Humiliation, he was no longer wishing for a companion. Having done away with two wicked fools who would have gladly pulled him down to hell with them, he was quite content to travel on his own for now. And he was sure he would emerge from the valley quite soon, at which point he planned to build a fire and eat the rest of the food Watchful had given him.

But then he had a sudden sense that he was not alone. It began with a voice in his ear. "This is foolishness. You are being foolish. Were you raised to be foolish? Your father would be quite ashamed to see how far his son has fallen."

Faithful stopped and spun around. He saw no one. The words were very much like those of Shame, but the voice was not. He resumed his climb and again heard that voice, right in his ear. "You know shame better than most, don't you? You've already fallen. You're compromised. Do you really think you escaped that woman Wanton?" Faithful tried to block the noise out by singing a hymn at the top of his lungs, but still he heard it. "She pulled you away and you very nearly followed. And speaking of pulling, we both know what happened at the foot of Hill Difficulty, when Adam the First pulled on you. You haven't spoken of it, but that doesn't mean it's not real."

The pilgrim stopped again, but this time closed his eyes and prayed for discernment. For eyes to see and a sober mind to judge. When he opened them, he saw Shame, now scrawny and fey, but clearly the same man he'd met, dressed in the same clothes. His mouth twisted into a wicked smile as he spoke again, clearly believing himself to be hidden from sight.

"You know it's true: stop trying to be what you're nev—" The word died in a sick, choking gurgle, as Faithful gripped him around the neck and marched him backwards five steps into the trunk of a tree, where he pinned the pitiful man.

"You are going to shut up," Faithful said, "and I'm going to say something. Agreed?"

Shame nodded as much as the meat of Faithful's hand permitted.

"Good. You see, you seem to be under the impression that I want to be highly thought of by the world. I don't. That which is highly esteemed among men is an abomination to the Lord. And I noticed something about you: while you've been running your oily little mouth, you've told me an awful lot about what men are. But you've said nothing about who God is or what his Word is. On the great and terrible Day of the Lord, I will not be cast into hell or welcomed into heaven according to the spirits of this world, but according to the wisdom and law of the Most High. If I am ashamed of my Lord now, he will be ashamed of me at his coming. And so it is clear that what God says is best, even if the whole world is against it. This includes a tender conscience, a heart that seeks forgiveness and the wisdom of God, which is the foolishness of men. The things you most disdain are the things in which I see the most glory.

"You, Shame, are an enemy of my salvation. You will try in vain to attempt further business with me. I will spare you just this once. Return now to whatever corner of hell you've come from. For if I find you haunting me along the Way, whispering in my ear as you were just now, I will make a spectacle of you that will—well, it will put you to shame."

He released his grip on Shame's throat and the thin figure stumbled a few steps before looking up into the sky, deeper in the valley. As soon as his eyes fell upon a broken plume of black smoke drifting up into the sky, he turned his back to it and ran in the opposite direction.

When he'd gone, the clouds parted, and the late afternoon sun warmed Faithful the rest of the way out of the Valley of Humiliation.

Christian watched Apollyon disappear into the trees.

He thought for a moment about giving chase, but decided against it—primarily because he was too exhausted to take another step.

Instead, he yelled out after him, "The Lord rebuke you, Apollyon, you destroyer, destined to be destroyed by his might!" Then turning his head toward the twisting tower that jutted into the sky beyond the high wall, he cried out, "Great Beelzebub, your captain is defeated! Do you hear me, you vile serpent? Beelzebub, you need not fear me, for I am frail, feeble, and fallible. But *fear the one who goes beside me, before me, and behind me!* For greater is he who is in me than he that is in the world!"

Then he turned his voice to heaven and began to praise his King. "Oh, God of this Road, of this country, of the blessed City that lies beyond the delectable mountains—you are my salvation in every trial, every day, every moment! The Enemy sent this hellish fiend, to bring me low, but you sent your captain too. Blessed Michael helped me! Your strong hand upheld me! And by your might, my meager strength sent him flying. And so I say: to you be everlasting praise! To you be thanks and honor! May I always bless your holy name! For ever and ever, world without end!"

Christian's legs almost buckled beneath him and he hunched over, hands on his knees, to assess his condition. He had not come through unscathed. His head was pounding. His hand ached where the sword had been knocked from it, so that it was now difficult to open and close. His ankle was burned where he had pulled the dart free. Drawing back the grieve, he examined the flesh—which resembled an animal carcass turning on a spit—and winced. But worst of all, he was suddenly aware of a gash in his side, behind the breastplate, where Apollyon had reached around him with his claws and ripped the flesh, right down to the bone.

Christian slumped to the ground and wondered if he had perhaps celebrated too soon. The thrill of the fight now subsiding, a wall of pain came up behind it. And with every move, every breath, it welled up higher.

The sound of footsteps to his right brought a flash of alarm—a mere formality, as there was no way the pilgrim could act on it. Had Apollyon circled around to come and finish him off? Christian tried to sit up, but found it impossible for the pain in his side.

"Rest easy, pilgrim," came a soothing voice. Christian rolled his head to see one of the Shining Ones approaching. In his hand, he held a bunch of lush green leaves.

"These are from the Tree of Life," he said, pushing them to Christian's side. The wounded pilgrim could feel the blood stop leaking from the opening, and then the wound itself closing up. Still, it ached, and Christian had a sense that this pain would be with him for some time to come.

"Thank you," he said to the Shining One. "I am glad it was you and not the enemy. For I am without strength."

"Did your sisters give you nothing to eat or drink?"

Christian remembered the food in his bag and, with some difficulty, made his way to it and withdrew the bread, which he wolfed down, followed by some of the wine. He felt his strength beginning to return.

"Rest for a time, good pilgrim," the Shining One said, "but do not sleep; not here. When you have come up out of this valley, there is another. The Valley of the Shadow of Death."

"I'd just as soon skip that one," Christian said.

"Perhaps you would, but you must pass through it, for the way to the Celestial City lies through its midst."

Darkest Night

Christian emerged from the Valley of Humiliation and gazed up into the black sky. Neither star nor moon was visible, and Christian could not say whether it was truly night or just a property of this place to be always dark, as it had seemed to be in the valley itself. Off to his left a hundred feet or so, he saw the glowing coals of a fire and what looked to be a person sleeping near it. Christian was considering whether he too should get some sleep when two men approached him from the east, moving quickly and holding lamps out before them.

"Ho there!" one of them called. "Stow your weapon; we travel in peace!"

Christian looked down at the sword locked in his hand. He'd carried it with him since the battle with Apollyon, unsure of what other enemies he might encounter. He had met no further opposition in that valley, though, and now he slid the sword back into its scabbard.

"Where are you men going at this hour?" he asked.

"'At this hour,' you say? I supposed it is quite early in the day. But not too early to flee from danger and head back home to safety! And that is where we are going. Back! Back! And you should as well if either life or peace is prized by you."

"What's the matter?"

"Well, we were headed the way you are headed and in fact

we pushed on as far as we dared go—almost past coming back! I've no doubt that, had we gone even a hundred feet further, we would not have been able to bring you this warning, for we would be very much . . . dead." The man's silent companion nodded his agreement, eyes wide and frantic.

"What warning? What have you met with? And where?"

"Where? Why, at most two or three furlongs from here. Just ahead, in the darkness. We almost followed the road down into the Valley of the Shadow of Death, but we happened to spot the danger and avoid it."

"The danger? Be specific, man!"

"Why, the valley itself! It is darker than pitch and yet, in flashes of light, we saw goblins, satyrs, and dragons moving about! We also heard a continual howling and shrieking—the sounds of unutterable misery. And over that whole valley hangs the discouraging cloud of confusion."

His companion whispered something in his ear and the man added, "Oh, and death too! Death always spreads his wings over it. In a word, it is formless and void: dreadful and chaotic. I suppose that's several words, but you get the point. And even if you make it through the valley, you will find the ground on the other side soaked with blood and littered with bones and human remains! For there, two giants—Pontiff and Pagan—live in a cave, just off the way, and have from antiquity. These giants have slaughtered many in the cruelest ways imaginable and they have a particular taste for the blood of pilgrims."

Christian was unmoved. "I have already met with similar warnings from others. My townsman, Mr. Timorous and another, Mistrust. They told me to turn back as I neared the top of Hill Difficulty. There were lions in the streets, they said, and the only sane course of action was to flee back down the hill to the town of my birth. But I ignored their foolish, wicked counsel and, as you can see, I still stand and still make progress, day by day, hour by hour, along this pilgrim road."

"We, sir, are not your townsmen or some other rabble. We are descendants of famous men. In fact, I would bet a pound to a shilling that you now carry on your person the record of their exploits."

"I'll admit," Christian said, "that you have piqued my interest. Whose line are you descended from?"

"From those who spied out the land of Milk and Honey while the people of God wandered in the wilderness."

"You two men are descended form Caleb? Or Joshua?"

Clearing his throat uncomfortably, the man said, "No, our ancestors were among the . . . other spies."

Christian smirked. "That sounds about right. 'Let us turn back, for there are giants in the land?' Did not this sort of cowardice cost an entire generation their inheritance? How dare you?" He drew his sword again. "I do not wish to hear any more of your warnings. If you are intent on fleeing, then get on with it. I am headed to the Celestial City, through whatever this road might take me."

"Fine, then. Be it your way. We will not choose it for ours." And the two men continued back toward the Valley of Humiliation.

"Well," Christian said to himself, "let's see how bad it is. I've now defeated a devil; I doubt there's anything to top that down below."

But in that valley, Christian found himself far more frightened, felt far more alone, and faced such terrors that he would have gladly traded them for a dozen Apollyons.

Faithful pulled in a chestful of fresh, cool air, tinged with the smell of lavender and vanilla, and thanked God for this beautiful, sunny day and for this oddly named place. The Valley of the Shadow of Death was bright and breezy this morning. Birds lighted on branches overhead, singing happily. Butterflies flitted about. This, of course, was not what he'd expected. Indeed, Faithful might have assumed that Shame was lying about the valley's name had there not also been a sign identifying the place as such, right where the Narrow Way entered into it.

The pilgrim had come up out of the Valley of Humiliation just as the sun was setting and made good on his intention to enjoy a fire and a good meal. Then he'd slept deeply for just a few hours, while the fire slowly died, awakening a bit before dawn. He felt so refreshed and full of energy that he'd begun his descent immediately, expecting to face great trials and difficulties.

But, apart from a narrowing of the path, he'd encountered nothing frightening or even all that challenging. Still, he'd seen these things turn quickly in his time as a pilgrim, so he kept his head up and prepared for the worst.

Christian pressed on, downward into the dark and solitary valley. He recognized the place from the words of the prophet Jeremiah: *a wilderness, a land of deserts and pits, a land of drought and deep darkness and of the Shadow of Death, a land through which none passes and in which none dwells.*

The pilgrim could feel the effects of the dark cloud of confusion pressing down on him, impressing words and pictures upon his heart, pushing them in so firmly that Christian began to think he'd always known them—like déjà vu of the soul. Flashes of truth and lies mixed together, searing themselves into his mind.

In the near-total darkness, Christian struggled to stay on the narrowing road, knowing that he was always one step from ruin. To his right was a deep ditch, and he could see, in the occasional flash of lightning, bleach-white bones and yawning skulls scattered along its bottom—and he *knew* that these were the remains of the blind from all ages, having been led by their fellow blind until they miserably perished together. To his left was a dangerous quag, which seemed to be without bottom, and Christian knew he would not survive the fall should he stumble into it.

He felt the oppressive cloud pushing down again and he saw King David, the man after God's own heart, falling into the quag, smothered in the putrid slime. Hope began to drip away from the pilgrim's heart, as if displaced from above by the cloud pressing in, filling him up with doubt and despair. If mighty David could not stay clear of the quag, how could he hope to?

Then he remembered his Book. David had not stayed in the pit. Had he? It was too dark here to read any passages, but he had hidden much of it in his heart. Christian called to mind David's own words, from while he was in the pit: *Deliver me from sinking in the mire; let me be delivered from my enemies and from the deep waters.* Had that prayer of the king been answered? No. No, surely not. He saw the image of David, face-down in the filth, slowly sinking, disappearing into the quag beneath him.

No. No, no, that wasn't right. He searched his heart again, sifting through the deception and sin within, looking only for the eternal Word. Yes, this was it: *He drew me up from the pit of destruction, out of the miry bog, and set my feet upon a rock. He put a new song in my mouth, a song of praise to our God. Many will see and fear, and put their trust in the LORD.* David was rising up now, carried out of the pit, washed clean once again, set on his throne by the grace of the King of Kings.

Christian found his courage and began moving along the Narrow Path. It was difficult and he was prone to overcorrect; when he tried to give the ditch a wide berth, he was in danger of falling into the mire. And when he turned away from the mire, the ditch was there, waiting to swallow him down. He remembered the feeling of being sucked down into the Slough of Despond and took a moment to thank his King that he was no longer carrying that awkward, heavy burden on his back; for if he was, he would have doubtless gone head-long into a muck-filled grave a dozen times already.

As he moved through the valley, it became commonplace for Christian to take a step, unable to see where his foot would land. This caused him to sigh bitterly, resenting this stretch of the road, trying with all his being not to resent the King who had called him to walk it. By and by, though, the path widened just a bit, and the darkness gave way to a diffused glow that served more to elongate and distort every shadow than to actually illuminate the path.

At first, *any* light seemed like an improvement to Christian. But the orange glow had an indefinable malice in it. And by it, Christian could now see scurrying goblins to match the skittering sounds of wicked webbed feet as they dashed from shadow to shadow, circling ever closer. He kept the sword clasped in his hand — ready at any moment to lunge, to strike, to lop off a goblin's head or stab through another dragon's belly.

Any sense of time continued to elude Christian, even as the light increased. The further he descended, the more of that troubling orange light seeped in, revealing glimpses of hideous creatures all around.

At about the middle of the valley, Christian came upon the source of the light, and he again knew just what it was, as if he'd been here before: it was the mouth of hell itself. The flames and smoke poured up continually, amidst sparks and hideous noises. As the pilgrim gazed into the raging flames, a creature dashed past his back so closely that he felt his coat ripple in the wind of its wake. He spun but saw nothing behind him.

"With this sword, I bested Apollyon!" Christian shouted, first into the flames, and then into the darkness behind him. "Goblins, satyrs, demons, and dragons beware, for I will slay you as well!" Through the flames, an impish little winged goblin flew right at Christian's head. Rearing back with his sword, he had no time to swing it, and instead threw himself to the ground, dangerously near the flames.

"They do not fear my sword," Christian realized, and put it up. He then drew All-Prayer from his back and cried out, "O Lord, deliver my soul!"

The goblin came through the flames again, wings beating, mouth open wide, fangs bared. Christian thrust the lance upward, impaling the grotesque creature through the chest and driving it to the ground. With a flick of his wrists, he cast the goblin into the fiery pit.

The sound of many more beating wings was growing ever louder, and Christian decided to move on from here as quickly as he could. Putting the fire at his back he resumed the Narrow Road. And yet, for the space of several miles, the fingers of flame seemed to continually reach for him, bearing in their vapors the sounds of doleful creatures, screaming and moaning. Two more flying monsters swooped in on him and paid the price with their miserable lives.

Christian pushed ahead all the more, struggling to divide his attention between the enemies above, the flames behind, and the sound of monsters rushing to and fro—until he felt sure that he would be torn to pieces. More than once it occurred to him that he should go back rather than face further terrors. But then he reminded himself that he was certainly more than halfway through, and had already faced so many dangers that going back might be far worse than pushing ahead.

A wretched, chalk-white creature rushed in on Christian from the shadows to his right and grabbed hold of his weapon, tugging with surprising might for its size. It glared at him and shrieked. Christian called out, "Lord, give me victory against my enemies!" and jerked the handle of the lance along the ground, sweeping the creature's legs out from beneath it. In one fluid motion, he brought the head of the spear down, through its hideous face and into the earth beneath. The creature's body spasmed for a moment, went still, and then burst into flames.

"I will walk in the strength of the Lord God," Christian said, picking up his pace yet more, "and in the light of his Truth." Then he heard the creatures begin to shrink back, the skittering sounds of their feet and the foul flapping of their wings barely audible.

But something worse took their place.

For at this point, Christian was so confounded by the cloud of confusion above and so disoriented by the many attacks form all around him, that he no longer knew his own voice. And as he walked, he heard in his head many wicked blasphemies, the likes of which would never have crossed his mind, even before he was a pilgrim.

They came relentlessly, one on top of another. And of all the things that Christian had faced in either valley, this came the closest to breaking him.

Faithful had now been several hours in the Valley of the Shadow of Death and still he'd seen no sign of the terrors and dangers that Shame had promised him. The day was growing brighter, although deep in the valley as he was, he could not yet see the sun. Still, it was a lovely walk along the pilgrim road. Perhaps the name of the valley was meant ironically, he thought.

If anything, this place made him want to dawdle. A hot spring beside the path had drawn his interest a short time ago, about midway through the valley, and he'd watched it bubble until the sulfurous smell made him a bit light-headed. He'd seen gorgeous flowering plants the likes of which he'd never encountered before and many colorful birds, each with its own song.

As the road began to incline in earnest, it took him past a peculiar tree—so peculiar that it briefly arrested his progress. It came up from its roots as a solid, singular trunk, which then split into three at about waist level. These three smaller trunks grew up parallel to each other for another twenty or thirty feet before coming back together in a beautiful braid. Pleasant white flowers—each with three petals—bloomed from its branches, smelling sweet and heavy. The tree and everything about it called to mind the Blessed Trinity.

Looking down, he saw a bird's nest sitting right where the trunk divided into three, and in it, three perfect blue eggs: the promises of new life.

Faithful laughed. How could this place bear such an ominous name? He said aloud, "Yea, though I walk through the Valley of the Shadow of Death, I will fear no evil, for you are with me."

Then Faithful saw a man, hunched over, either in fear or pain or both, just a few feet beyond the tree, his face buried in his hands. Now and then, the man would swipe at the air, as if to repel some insect or perhaps something larger.

Compassion welled up in Faithful's breast, but then he thought of the last two men he'd met along this path. Both had laid a trap for him, hoping to play on his loneliness and desire for a companion. And neither of them was quite the spectacle that this man was. Nor had they been armed to the teeth, as this man was. If Faithful drew near, a single blow might overcome him. Yes, it was probably best to err on the side of caution here and continue on his way. Still, he should offer some words of encouragement.

"Take heart, friend," Faithful said as he stepped away from the tree and returned to the path. "It could be so much worse. You could be unarmed, like me. Or you could live here instead of just passing through. On your feet and on your way."

The flames had finally stopped licking at Christian's heels. But before he could even give thanks for this grace, the renewed darkness dropped a heavy blanket of apathy over his heart. He shuffled forward, driven more by habit than anything else. The thought of the Celestial City—which had been continually before him since leaving his home—did nothing whatsoever for him now. Slowly he walked, making progress, but not really caring if he reached his destination.

The light of day—thin and strained as it was—came upon him so slowly that he barely noticed it until he found himself standing before a hideous, twisted tree, the sight of which brought him to a stop and made him long for the darkness to return.

Beneath Christian's feet and spreading out through the entire valley floor, as far as he could see, gnarled roots snaked this way and that like varicose veins. Where they came together, the trunk of the tree split upward into three smaller, dark and twisting trunks, entwined together grotesquely. The shape of it reminded Christian of Apollyon's vicious talon, reaching out to flay the flesh from his back, and his wound—though healed—flared up in pain again.

A subtle movement beneath him caught Christian's eye. There, nestled in the midst of the tree was a nest made of ink-black thorns and filled with three fat, purple eggs, pulsing and quivering, ready to hatch. Christian stepped back, wondering what manner of abomination might be about to burst forth. His apathy grew heavier until it dragged him quite literally to the ground and there matured into hopelessness, even as the darkness again rolled in and yet more blasphemous words filled his heart.

Christian shuddered, crying without tears. He could feel the creatures closing back in on him. The goblins and demons circling above like vultures. He would not reach the Celestial City. That much was clear. He'd been beyond foolish to think he ever could. For him to leave on pilgrimage was the equivalent of a young boy playing at being a soldier. What nonsense.

"Yea, though I walk through the Valley of the Shadow of Death, I will fear no evil, for you are with me."

Christian stopped his crying for a moment. That voice had not been his own. It had not been in his head. And hearing it broke him free from the spell he was under. He began to fight against the weight on his spirit and the fear in his heart, wanting to stand. Willing himself to rise up.

"Take heart, friend," came the same voice. "It could be so much worse. You could be unarmed, like me. Or you could live here instead of just passing through. On your feet and on your way."

Who was speaking these words? He did not bother to lift

his head and peer into the darkness, as it was pointless, and for fear of seeing that frightful tree again. Still, a spark of gladness flared up in his soul and the joy he felt began to burn away the fear. Then the hopelessness. Then the apathy.

Christian began to number his blessings by way of banishing the darkness.

Blessing #1: there was someone else in this valley who feared the Lord. That alone was something.

Blessing #2: these familiar words from a beloved psalm, spoken by he-knew-not-whom, reminded him of a bedrock truth: God was with him through this dark and dismal place. "I may not see him," Christian thought, "but that has only to do with this place and my perception, not his power or presence."

Blessing #3: If there was a friendly pilgrim nearby, perhaps they might travel together and offer each other fellowship and security.

And blessing #4: those wicked thoughts introduced through this valley had not been his own at all; he could see that now. In fact, those voices, which had invaded his heart and mind, were familiar to Christian. He'd heard them before—in his dreams, in the City of Destruction. They were repugnant to him then, as they were now, and he would rebuke them if they spoke again.

Christian rose and returned to the path. He had taken only a dozen or so steps when the sun burst forth from above the valley head. Lovely, purifying light! Christian cried out, "He turns the shadow of death into the morning. Jehovah is his name!"

The smoke behind him and the dark cloud of confusion above thinned away, burnt off by the light of the rising sun. Then Christian looked back—not out of a desire to return, but just to see by the light of day what hazards he had gone through. And when he saw the ditch and the quag and how narrow the path had been, he was amazed that he had made it through. He also saw the goblins, satyrs, and dragons of the pit, but now all far off, not daring to come out into the light. Christian thought of the words of Job: *He uncovers deep things out of darkness, and brings out to light the Shadow of Death.*

As he looked back at the dangers he'd faced, the new light made them not only conspicuous to him, but absurd. Christian returned All-Prayer to his back and again drew his sword, hacking here and there at vines, ropes, and tripwires spanning the path. It became immediately clear to him that, while the first part of the Valley had been dangerous, this final ascent was even more so, filled as it was with snares and traps, deadfalls, pitfalls, and nets. Had he tried to pass through here in the dark, he was sure he would not have made it—even if he had a thousand souls.

The thanks and praise overflowed from his heart. Even just knowing that it was now morning was a great relief to Christian. And then an even greater cause for praise: he saw another man up ahead, scaling the last and steepest steps out of the valley.

"Ho! Wait!" Christian called out, sheathing his sword and beginning to run. "Wait for me, friend!" He'd taken only a few steps when his foot broke through a thin, brush-covered lattice and his body dropped into an open pit. His right hand snagged a thick vine and he found himself dangling over a grid of spikes, glistening with poison, ten feet beneath him.

"Help!" he called out. "Help me! Please!" His hand, still stiff from the wound he'd received the day before, began to cramp and the vine itself began to slip. Christian looked down into the pit and knew that if he fell, he would die, although certainly not quickly.

"Does anyone hear me? Lord, send your angels or your mortal servants! Or . . . anyone!" He felt his right hand letting go and the vine slipping through it, then a sudden rough grip around his wrist and he was lifted, slowly and painfully, out of the pit.

"That's some heavy armor," his rescuer said, plopping

down next to him. "And some rather well-made armor. Where on earth did you procu—wait . . . *Christian?* Is that you?"

"Faithful? It is you! I caught you!" They both rose to their feet and embraced.

"You caught me?" Faithful laughed. "I've been trying to catch up to you since I set out from Destruction. Oh, man! I passed you back—didn't I?— at the . . . Oh, we have much to talk about!"

"Indeed we do. I can't wait to hear *everything* about your journey so far!"

"Let's walk and talk," Faithful replied and the two of them came up from the second valley in far higher spirits than they had entered with.

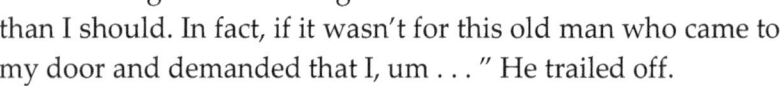

"So tell me," Christian said, "how long did you stay in Destruction after I set out?"

"As long I could. Longer than I should. In fact, if it wasn't for this old man who came to my door and demanded that I, um . . . " He trailed off.

Christian followed his gaze and saw that the ground was littered with bones, ashes, and mangled bodies.

"The giants," he said. "Those fleeing men warned me that we would find these things beyond the valley—evidence of two giants living in a cave nearby. And look—there!" He pointed to the open maw of a massive cavern a hundred feet back from the path. "Those men were right about the creatures in the valley. And it seems they were right about these giants—Pontiff and Pagan, they called them."

"I don't think we need to worry," Faithful said, giving his companion's arm a brief tug and then continuing pulling him along through the midst of the bones. "I've heard of these giants. Pagan is said to have died a long time ago. And, while some recent sightings have been reported here and there, it's always far from his former home. And as for this one . . . "

They passed by the entrance of the cave and saw a fat, droopy-eyed giant sitting just inside, his stubby fingers covered in rings and jewels. "Well, from what I've heard, due to his age and the many shrewd brushes of his younger days, he is now so crazy and stiff in his joints that he can do little more than sit there in the mouth of the cave, biting his nails and grinning at pilgrims as they go by."

"What is he mumbling?" Christian asked.

"Oh, I don't know. Ignore him."

Pontiff looked up at the pilgrims, pulling on his lip and saying, "You will never mend till more of you are burned."

The pilgrims said nothing until they had cleared the bones and debris and made some further progress, shoulder to shoulder on the Narrow Way.

Christian broke the silence. "So, you were saying someone showed up at your door and prompted you to set out?"

"Oh. Right . . . You know, it's a long and strange story."

"Well, it's a long and strange road."

The Taking of Linger-After-Lust

That first stretch of the Narrow Road—just on the fair side of the Wicket Gate—is an odd place. There, every pilgrim is filled with joy at having entered in, most brim with exhilaration at having narrowly escaped some desperate attack by Beelzebub (from his fortress not far away), and all are unsure what they might find on the as-yet-unfamiliar Pilgrim Road Proper, laid out before them. For this reason, the stretch of road between the gate and the Place of Deliverance is most dangerous, and should be crossed over most quickly, save for the Interpreter's House, where the old mystic (though he looks quite frail) has been known to defend his guests from horrible satanic attacks—and has sent even Apollyon himself fleeing back to his own dominion, lion's tail between his legs.

But even after losing one's burden at the cross, the danger endures for a time. Those newly relieved and newly clothed in the garments of their Master still often make easy marks for the agents of the Enemy.

Case in point: Linger-After-Lust had finally come to the gate after dawdling near it for more than a fortnight. He had camped off the Way, on the left-hand side (nearest the Broad Gate and Beelzebub's garrison), where he had spent a good deal of time hobnobbing with the people on that side. This, any seasoned pilgrim will tell you, is particularly inadvisable, and when Linger-After-Lust (or just "Linger," as he was known to his friends) finally determined to knock on the Wicket Gate, he was taken aback by the questions the gatekeeper posed.

"Who are you? Where do you come from? And what would you have?"

These he answered in the straightforward way: "They call me Linger, I come from the town of Fleshly Provision, and I would enter this gate in order to enter the Good King's service, to avoid the coming judgment, and to inherit a dwelling place in the Celestial City."

But then, Goodwill asked another question (for it was at his discretion what he should ask each traveler): "Why have I seen you milling about by the gate for weeks now, consorting with those who serve Beelzebub?"

"Is there some rule against this?" the pilgrim asked, with a touch of indignation. "Wasn't it the Celestial Prince himself who commanded us to be sure and count the cost and who modeled for us a habit of mixing with those who would walk the Broad Road, even if this prompts the outwardly religious to look down upon them and judge them?"

"And this is truly what you were doing?" Goodwill asked. He was quite certain all this was a cover for a heart that was not fully sold on holy pilgrimage, but he did not press the issue, since pilgrims themselves might not be aware of their every secret motive. And if this man would come in now, put his hand to the plow, and not look back, it would not be right to shut the door on him, especially given the burden on his back—meager as it was.

"Just one more question," Goodwill said. "How did you fare against the enemy's final attempt to drag you away or kill you before you reached this gate?"

The pilgrim shrugged. "I was not the victim of any such attack."

"I wonder why that is . . . "

"Perhaps I outsmarted the enemy by becoming a bit of a

fixture on the border of his own lands before I came here, so that he didn't realize I was bent on pilgrimage until it was too late."

Goodwill opened the gate to this man, but offered a stern warning as he entered: "I have admitted men like you before, and a better part of them have fallen away or turned back before they ever were relieved of their burdens. Be sober and alert."

"You need not worry about me," said Linger. "I know how to deal with their kind."

But all his boasting notwithstanding, this man took nearly three weeks to cover the ground between the gate and the cross. No sooner had he begun to walk the Narrow Path than he discovered thick vines spilling over the wall on the left-hand side and some very sweet fruit on them, and so he walked along the wall, not on the Narrow Way itself, thinking the only thing that really mattered was whether he made progress in the right direction. He traveled slowly, of course, as the ground here was neither paved nor well-trodden . . . but he had never been one to hurry, and considered it a virtue that he ambled along and took full advantage of this tasty fruit.

Of course, he saw many pilgrims walk right past him at a much quicker pace, both Christian and Faithful among them, but he just laughed to himself at these frantic, fanatical souls who did not know how to enjoy life.

As evening approached, that first day, Linger-After-Lust heard laughter and chatter from just the other side of the wall. The voices of young women. Now, you should know that Linger had been known as a bit of a ladies' man back home in Fleshly Provision (and he knew, deep-down, that was the reason for his continually gravitating toward the Broad Gate before finally entering in here), and this whole day, he had seen only a few dozen women walking the Narrow Way—and they were all quite dour and grave looking, dressed plain and modestly, carrying heavy, filthy burdens upon their backs.

And so, using the sturdy vines growing over the wall as a

ladder, Linger climbed up, high enough as to make him a bit nervous, and looked over the wall. There he saw a gathering of beautiful women, adorned with gold, their hair braided and faces painted. There Linger-After-Lust lingered for a long time, watching them, wishing he was on the other side, where he could make their acquaintance, make them laugh at his own wit, and find some excuse to here and there brush against them, and perhaps more.

Thus, Linger's progress was slowed all the more, stretching out the hour's walk to the Interpreter's House over many days. His practice was to sleep late, then travel a dozen steps or so before peering over the wall, yearning for whatever he saw: young men drinking to excess, men and women cavorting, or people doing absolutely nothing, lying idle and lifting their heads only to laugh at some coarse joke offered up by one of their fellows.

When a week had passed, Linger awoke one day feeling particularly enlivened to make some real progress along the Way, and he traveled at a good clip—still up against the wall separating the King's land from Beelzebub's, until he thought he saw the Interpreter's house up ahead, on the right. But then he stopped to rest and, out of habit, climbed back up on the vines and found himself looking down at a place where women went to bathe—out in the open, as shame was a rare commodity on the other side of the wall.

And so he camped in that spot for many days. Each morning, he would rise and break his fast with some of the fruit plucked from the vines on the wall, intent on finally going the last few paces of his journey to the house ahead and the Deliverance beyond. But first, just one last peek over the wall. And then, as day turned to night, he would settle into what had become a very comfortable bed of moss and vines, and tell himself that tomorrow was the day when he would leave this place behind, return to the center of the path, and walk the strait and narrow, only to repeat this process yet again the next day.

It was three weeks to the day after he'd passed through the gate, as he was standing on the vines and calling down to a damsel on the other side of the wall, when he felt a hand grip him around the ankle and yank him roughly back. He lost his footing, fell hard against the wall, became momentarily tangled up in the vines, and finally landed on his side, where the soft ground he'd prepared undoubtedly saved him from a broken bone or two. He noticed as he rolled onto his back that his burden had shrunk to the point of being almost unnoticeable.

A flash of rage was replaced by confusion, then shame, as he looked up to see Goodwill standing above him, his face stern.

"I'm not supposed to leave the gate," he said.

"Well then, why have you?"

"Because I have seen you tarrying here, just as you tarried on the other side of the gate, only longer yet and with no evidence of a pilgrim's heart."

Linger-After-Lust rose to his feet, standing nine inches taller than the gatekeeper, but nowhere near as stout. "Why don't you just mind the gate, hmm?" he said. "Mind your own business."

"This is my business," Goodwill said. "And if you will not go without delay to the door of the Interpreter's House, I will drag you back to the Wicket Gate, and put you out by force."

Linger glanced back at the vines on the wall, for the first time seeing how withered and sick they looked and how the fruit drooped down heavy like a blister ready to pop, and he felt a sense of guilt overtake him.

He nodded. "I am sorry for lingering here. It is my nature, but that is exactly what I need to be cured of. And I am grateful to you for pulling me down from that wall. Before long, I doubtless would have fallen, probably to the other side."

Goodwill grabbed him by the shoulders and spun him around to face toward the east. "I think you'd better go right now," he said, whacking a hand against his burden, which had returned now to its former girth.

"I am gone," he said. "God bless you, Goodwill. I will not forget this."

Linger ran the last fifty yards and just about tore the knocker off the door of the Interpreter's house. There he was admitted and shown quite a few wonders, which touched him deeply.

There was a man in an iron cage, the sight of whom stuck terror into his heart. There was a bird eating a centipede, and many others. Finally, he was taken to a great dining hall, where a man who was dying of thirst continually ate salty foods and licked a block of pure salt, looking to slake his thirst. This, the Interpreter told him, was the state of any man trying to find satisfaction in the passions of the flesh. Linger wept and thanked his host profusely for the lesson.

He dawdled not between that house and the place of Deliverance, where he was relieved of his burden and his tattered rags, washed and clothed in the garments of the King, and given a new name: Godly Affections. As he descended that holy hill, he was filled with hope and life and a great desire to make progress each and every day.

But then he came upon a place where the wall to his left was again visible, and there it was so short that he could see an orchard on the other side, and even some branches of those trees hanging over into this land. He felt the pull of the old self inside of him, to go that way and taste that fruit. But as he took his third or fourth step off the path, he heard a man shout, "Ow! What is this? I'm trying to sleep here!"

Looking down, he saw three men and a woman, all curled up cozily on the ground, their legs shackled.

"Sleeping?" the pilgrim asked. "Why? It's not even noon."

The others stirred and regarded him with no little annoyance. "Why do you care?" one of them asked.

"Oh, be nice," the young woman said. "My name is Dull. I've just made the acquaintance of these fellows a short time ago, and haven't quite been able to tame their manners."

One of them laughed and swatted at her playfully. "I apologize," he said. "My name is Simple. These are Sloth and Presumption. And you know Dull. What is your name?"

"Linger-After-Lust," he said, without thinking.

"Well, Mr. Linger," Simple said with a mighty yawn, "you ask why we're sleeping. I might ask why you're not. It is a beautiful day—sunny but with a cool breeze—a day made for relaxing and enjoying."

"I'm not sleeping," the pilgrim replied, "because I am on pilgrimage to the Celestial City. I've already turned aside more than once, and I've determined not to do it again."

This brought a laugh from all four of them lying on the ground. "I used to say the same thing," said Sloth, "until I realized that the Lord of that city is a hard taskmaster, the sort of man I have no interest in serving. And then I spoke with these two men, who enlightened me as to the state of your so-called 'good land,' which is not half as good as you think it will be. And, of course, both the road and the city itself are full of meddlesome, troublesome busybodies."

"I suppose he'll fit right in," Dull said with a laugh.

"I highly doubt all of that. Have you not heard of the bread of God and the comforts he provides for his children, and the righteous travel and labor of pilgrims on this road?"

"Husks," said Sloth.

"Mere fancies."

"Things to no purpose."

"Lie down for just a while and see if you don't change your tune," Presumption said.

And so, Linger-After-Lust first sat for a while and talked with these idle fools, and then leaned against a tree trunk, and finally lay down alongside them. As he drifted off to sleep, he was thinking that he'd be sure to get up before dark and continue along the road. But maybe, first, he'd have another look over the wall.

The Crown Incorruptible

aithful and Christian practically talked themselves hoarse over the course of several hours, catching each other up on their progress so far. As they walked, the landscape had grown all the bleaker, until they were surrounded by what could only be described as wilderness on all sides. They barely noticed, though, as they joyfully recounted their experiences on the Pilgrim Road, discovering that they had never been far from one another, even though they hadn't known it.

"Did you ever see Pliable again after I set out?" Christian asked. "I assume he made it back home?"

"Yes, he did. That's how I knew about some of your earlier adventures—how you fell into the Slough of Despond (which I avoided, since I was warned by him ahead of time). But if that little man expected to be celebrated for turning back, he had another thing coming. Everyone in the city mocked and derided him. His former friends broke contracts with him. I fear he's now ruined, or worse."

"I don't understand. Why should our townspeople be so set against him? They despise the Way and he forsook the Way. Sounds like a match made in—well, *Hell*, I guess."

"I don't know, but the day before I left, a mob had gathered against him, saying, 'Hang him! He's a turncoat! He was not true to his profession.'

"Perhaps God stirred up their sinful hearts to make a proverb of him for others who might be tempted to forsake the Way."

"Did you ever talk to him?" Christian asked.

"I saw him once in the street, and called out to him, but he leered away on the other side, as one ashamed of what he had done."

Christian shook his head. "A sad tale. I truly had high hopes for that man. But it sounds as though he will perish in the overthrow of that city. It's like King Solomon wrote, *as a dog returns to its vomit and the washed sow to her wallowing, so a fool returns to his folly*. I suppose the opposite is true as well: you avoided my own failure altogether, having heard the tale of the Slough. Did you see the steps passing through?"

"I did. And I'm thankful for them, and for the signs warning me ahead of time. It sounds like it was a real trial of faith."

"Oh, yes. That slough was among the worst moments of my pilgrimage so far—right there at the outset, too—perhaps only surpassed by the most recent trials: my battle with Apollyon and the horrors of the valley we've just left. How did you fare against those?"

"Apollyon I did not meet. Although, in the Valley of Humiliation I was hounded by two lying spirits who wished to turn my heart to wax and thus turn it back from the Holy City. But after that, I had sunny skies all the way through that valley and the next one."

"Huh. That sounds rather . . . is there a word that means 'pleasant for you, but ultimately unfair?'" He laughed.

"Yes, well, don't get me wrong; I have certainly faced troubles of my own—namely three that continue to vex my spirit."

"Tell me of them," Christian said.

"First, that same man who drove me out of my house chased me up Hill Difficulty and beat me nearly to death! I begged him for mercy, and he told me he did not know *how* to show mercy. I fear he would have killed me had I not been . . . are you all right, Christian?"

"You need not tell me this story, for I was there. I hid among the trees while the lawgiver thrashed you—although I did not recognize you for your wounds. Oh, forgive me, Faithful. Had I stopped to offer my aid, we might have be been together from that moment on."

Faithful grinned. "I was given aid by another."

"I know. I saw him too."

They walked in reverent silence for a while, before Christian asked, "What were the other two trials?"

"There was a woman. Wanton. She tried to seduce me to leave the Way and follow her home."

"I think I saw that woman along the road—before the Wicket Gate. I made sure to avoid her, having read in my book just that morning how even a few words from her lying mouth cast the Patriarch Joseph down into the darkness of Pharaoh's dungeon for years."

"I wish I'd been as wise as you. I offered to walk with her for a time. You cannot imagine what an enticing, flattering tongue she had. She promised me all manner of content."

"Oh, she promised you the content of a good conscience?" Christian joked.

"You know what I mean. All carnal and fleshly contentment. She knew my past. She knew my besetting sins. She was . . . *very* convincing."

"Thank God you escaped her. She's brought down many strong men."

Faithful's voice dropped to a whisper. "That's just it. I don't know that I did wholly escape her."

"Did you give in to her enticements?"

"No, not to defile myself. I quoted a proverb at her, and she railed on me and I ran right to the gate."

"See? You did make good your escape. What was the third test?"

Faithful's face went pale. "Well, it wasn't another woman. It was an *old man*: Adam the First. He offered me so many convincing promises, and I truly considered taking his offer. But by God's grace it burned hot in my mind that he intended to sell me as a slave. I told him to be gone and he reviled me, and promised to send such-and-such friends of his after me,to make the Way bitter to my soul . . . Empty talk, you know. But then, as I  turned to leave him, I felt him take hold of my flesh and give me such a deadly jerk back that I thought he had pulled part of me after himself. I cried out, 'Oh, wretched man!' Then I threatened to kill him and made a lot of bluster about it, but even as I ascended the hill, that part of me which he pulled back—I continued to feel it, still turned back, oriented toward *his* house and *his* daughters and *his* empty promises of wages and happiness and an earthly inheritance."

"Do you feel it still?"

"I think I do. Especially when I'm under the—"

"Hello, gentlemen!" A man came walking briskly up beside them, greeting them bombastically. He was tall, his clothes and hair immaculately kept and his very long beard well-groomed and oiled.

"Good day to you," Faithful said.

"My name is Talkative," the man said. "I am on my way to the heavenly country."

"As are we. I'm Faithful and this is Christian."

"Please to make both of your acquaintance. Or . . . acquaintances? Acquaintances. Anyway, if we are headed to the same place, would you be averse to some company along the way?"

"I don't know," Christian said. "The two of us have just been reunited and have been catching up on our respective journeys so far, and—"

"Come now, Christian," Faithful said, "these aren't dark secrets we're sharing. Rather, we've been relating how our King has kept us safe through every trial. We'd love to hear from you as well, if you're up to it."

Talkative rubbed his hands together. "You're singing my tune, Faithful. I've always said, 'To talk of things that are good is the greatest good.' Agreed?"

Christian squinted in thought. "I'm not sure that's—"

"And I am very glad to talk of such things—with you or with any other. I've been disappointed and rather troubled at how many pilgrims along this way waste their time, when they could be deep in good conversation."

"That is a thing to be lamented," Faithful said. "After all, I can think of no better use of the mouths God gave us than to speak of holy things."

"I like you," Talkative pronounced. "I like how you speak with conviction. And I would agree that there are so many good things to talk about that it boggles the mind when people waste the opportunity. There's the history or mystery of things. Or miracles, signs, and wonders. Or doctrine and the particulars of Scripture."

"Yes," Christian said, "but not just to talk of them, right? Our aim should be that we are profited by our conversation."

"Yes, of course, of course. Talking of these things is most profitable. That's what I said. It helps us see the benefit of things above and the vanity of things below. To speak of the insufficiency of our own works, the necessity of the new birth, and the imputation of Christ's righteousness. This is how people learn to repent and believe, to pray and suffer and all the rest."

"I agree wholeheartedly," Faithful said. "For lack of instruction, many ignorantly remain in the works of the law, which cannot save them."

"Right? I believe we are kindred spirits, sir."

"Hold on a minute," Christian said. "This heavenly knowledge is the gift of God. Therefore, it is not obtained by mere talk or even by great human effort."

"I know this indeed. Salvation is 100% grace and 0% works; I could give you a hundred Scriptures to prove it."

"No need," Faithful said, "we are of the same mind on this."

"I should probably apologize," Talkative said. "My zeal gets the best of me sometimes when I get to talking. I can talk on almost anything: things heavenly or things earthly; things moral or things evangelical; things sacred or things profane; things past or things to come; things foreign or things at home; things essential or things more circumstantial—provided that all be done to our profit, as good Christian has said."

Faithful laughed. "You're an odd fellow, Talkative, but I'm glad for your company."

"I'm not sure your, uh, *friend* feels the same way." He gestured at Christian who was now trailing behind by a dozen steps or so, hugging the outside of the path.

"Hm. Let me have a word with him," Faithful said, falling back to walk alongside his friend. "Christian, I'm sorry if I should not have invited him to join us. I just figured, the fewer the better fare, but the more the merrier."

"Do you truly not know this man?" Christian asked, quietly, falling back yet further in his steps. "He's from our hometown."

"Now that you mention it, I do believe I sold his father a set of horseshoes. Oh, what was his name?"

"Say-Well. Of Prating Row, father of Talkative, who is well-known to be a sorry fellow, his fine tongue notwithstanding."

"Seem alright to me."

"That's just it. He is better abroad, but the nearer he is to home, the uglier he gets—not unlike certain painters whose pictures are best viewed at a distance."

Faithful laughed. "Very well put."

"I wish I were joking. I'm hesitant to say too much, for fear of falling into gossip, but be warned about this man. As he talks now with you, he will also talk on the ale-bench. And the more drink he has in his crown, the more words he has in his mouth. Sometimes foul words, sometimes religious. And yet, fill his mouth as it may, religion has no place in his heart or house or life. You will find no prayer in his home, nor any sign of repentance. Bear this proverb in mind: *they say, and do not*. This man is a saint abroad and a devil at home, as they say."

"That seems a bit harsh. You are sure of all this?"

"Do you know one Wanderlust?"

"Yes, we've met here and there."

"Well, that man has travelled to the distant East many times and done business with many shrewd and cunning street merchants, and he told me he'd rather deal with ten of them than with Talkative. From a pilgrim's point of view, this man—by his righteous talk and empty life—has caused many to stumble and fall and, unless God prevents it, will be the ruin of many more."

Faithful scowled. "Now you *are* getting into gossip. I tell you what: let us test this man's doctrine and see for ourselves if it truly be heresy—or just hearsay."

"I suppose you're right. You lead the way, Faithful."

The two of them picked up their pace and rejoined Talkative. "Sorry about that," Faithful said. "We'd be happy to walk with you for a time."

"Finally. I thought we should have had a great deal of talk by now."

"Then let us waste no more time. The topic will be this: how does the saving grace of God manifest itself in the human heart?"

Talkative grinned. "I see we will be talking about the power of things! I like it! Now, then. There are several answers to your question. First, the grace of God causes a *great outcry against sin!*"

"Well put," Faithful replied, throwing a triumphant grin at Christian.

"Why thank you. Secondly, it gives rise to great knowledge of Gospel mysteries. And third, it does—"

"Hold on just a minute there."

The three of them wheeled to see a familiar man coming up from behind them.

"Evangelist!" Christian rushed in to hug him, but bounced off Faithful, who beat him to the embrace.

"Is this a greeting or an attack?" Evangelist laughed.

"I apologize," Faithful said. "It's just . . . it's good to see you. And look who I found along the way!" He grabbed Christian by the scruff of the neck and gave him a shake.

"*Owww.*"

Evangelist looked happily from one man to the other, and then to Talkative, who stood beyond them, tapping his foot and looking dubious.

"Talkative," Evangelist said, nodding. "Good to see you."

"Yes, yes, hurray, you're here. But we were just in the middle of a most productive conversation before you interrupted and—"

"I heard; you were discussing the evidence of God's saving grace. I would love to join the discussion, if I might."

Talkative turned his back and resumed walking up the road, saying "I do not enjoy talking with you, sir."

The others followed him and Evangelist said, "Fair enough. But I'd like to put in my tuppence, just the same, if I might; perhaps it will benefit these other pilgrims."

"I doubt it, but—"

"Talkative, I believe you said that the first sign of God's saving grace in the heart is that it stirs up a great outcry against sin. Do you two gentlemen agree?"

Faithful nodded. "Sound doctrine indeed."

"I'm not so sure," Evangelist said. I think you should rather say that God's saving grace inclines the soul to *abhor* its sin."

"Oh, here we go again with the semantics." Talkative looked at Faithful and rolled his eyes. "This man would split a hair and then split it again. What difference is there between crying out against sin and abhorring it?"

"A world of difference."

"Well, this I've got to hear," Talkative mumbled.

"A man might cry out against sin by principle alone. But he cannot abhor it except by a God-given hatred in his heart, which accompanies a God-given love for his Creator. I've heard many cry out against a sin in the pulpit, and then make nice with that selfsame sin throughout the week. Or think about Potiphar's wife, who cried out with great indignation as if she were very holy, but would have most willingly defiled herself with Joseph. Or consider this: I once saw a mother whose child nearly ran into the river scold her so sharply you might think she despised the little girl. But then she began to cry and held her close and kissed her again and again. She cried out against the child, but did not abhor her."

"You are nitpicking again, I think."

"I'm not trying to. At any rate, back to you. What did you say was the second evidence of God's saving grace?"

Talkative sighed heavily. "Never mind."

"I believe he said, 'Great knowledge of Gospel mysteries,'" Christian supplied.

Talkative shook his head. "I suppose you have some issue with that as well."

"I was thinking it should have been first," Faithful said.

Christian shook his head. "First or last, it's also off-base. For great knowledge might be obtained in the mysteries of God without any work of grace in the soul. Knowledge itself does not make anyone a child of God; in fact, alone, it tends only to puff up."

"I agree," said Evangelist. "Christ did not tell his disciples, 'Now that you know these things, blessed are you just for knowing them.' Or, 'Blessed are you if you go on talking about them.' Rather, it was 'Blessed are you if you do them.' I suggest there are two types of knowledge: that which rests on mere speculation and that which is rooted in the grace of faith and love, which conforms the heart to the will of God. The former will satisfy those who wish to sit and chat in rooms for hours, but it rings hollow to the true pilgrim."

Talkative scoffed. "None of this is for edification. You are just laying traps with your words—just as the Pharisees and Sadducees did for our Lord."

"I assure you, that is not my intention. You were about to share a third evidence of God's saving work when I came upon you. Would you share it now?"

"I see that we will not agree, so . . . no."

"Do you mind if I share one?"

Talkative shrugged. "Use your liberty."

"The work of grace in the soul bears witness both within, to the one being saved, and without, to those looking on. To the one who would be saved, it convicts him of sin (especially the sin of unbelief, for which he is sure to be damned if left to himself). This then gives birth to sorrow and shame for his sin and defilement. Then Christ comes into view and all that he offers, and the sinner is granted faith and begins to hunger and thirst after his Savior. And the stronger his faith, the more joy and peace he has and the more love of holiness and desire to serve Christ in this world. A new heart brings forth new affections within.

"From without, others bear witness to this work of grace by hearing his confession of faith and by observing his life—a life of holiness. He will put sin to death in his own heart and root it out of his house and promote holy living and thinking among his family—not by talk alone, like a hypocrite, but by true submission to the power of the Word." He looked at Talkative and said, "Have you experienced all of this? Does your life bear witness to your speech, or is your religion all in your tongue?"

Talkative grappled for words and then settled on, "I beg your pardon, sir, but I cannot seem to recall appointing *you* as my catechizer. I would also love to know who appointed you to be my judge that you would ask me such questions and talk to me this way."

"I ask you these questions, Talkative, because everyone knows that you are a man whose religion lies in talk only, and that your life makes a liar of your profession. That is why, when Mr. Great-Heart offered to see you safely to the city, you sent him away after only an hour, because he asked you hard questions and would not accept your easy answers. He learned the truth of what many have said: that you are a stain among Christians, that some have already stumbled at your wicked ways, and that more are in danger of being destroyed by them. And I will not see you draw either of these men into your empty form of religion, which is just as at home drunk on the ale-bench or slandering and swearing in the midst of vain company as it is in the pew on the Lord's Day."

"Well . . . since you are so ready to rashly judge me, I must assume that you are a peevish and melancholy man, and not fit for conversation with the likes of me. And so . . . *adieu.*" He began to walk comically fast, disappearing into the distance.

"That was a bit rough, no?" Faithful said.

"Not a bit, for a little leaven will leaven the whole loaf. And Talkative's brand of leaven spreads particularly fast and wide. As the Apostle James has written, faith without works is dead, even as the body without the soul is but a dead carcass. For he tells us that the soul of religion—pure religion—is the practical part: visiting the fatherless and widows in their affliction, and keeping oneself unpolluted by the world."

"He did remind me a bit of the serpent in the Garden," Christian said, "so ready to talk and equivocate, but with no real interest in obedience. After all, hearing and saying alone do not a true pilgrim make. To hear is to sow the seed. But how does one know if the seed has been sown successfully? Not by talking of it, but by observing actual fruit. The Scriptures compare the end of the world with a harvest, and those who harvest regard nothing but fruit."

"Yes, I suppose you're right," Faithful said. "On the last day, a naked profession will be useless. And the Apostle Paul declared that all the great talkers of his day amounted to a sounding brass or clanging cymbals. I do wonder if we might have persuaded him of all this, though."

Evangelist shook his head sadly. "I have spent many, many hours trying to do just that. I will go on praying that the seeds sown will one day germinate, take root, and bear fruit. For now, though, we have dealt plainly with him, and so we are clear of his blood should he perish. And now we can speak of things that are truly profitable, for words are far more valuable when they are tied to life and experience. Speaking of which—Christian, are you still writing those hymns, like the one you showed me near Morality?"

Faithful punched playfully at his old friend's shoulder. "Hymns? Really?"

"I mean, I don't know if they're hymns or poems or—"

"It makes sense," Faithful said, "This man has always been a writer. Ink-stained hands since we were lads." Turning back to Christian, he demanded, "Well, let's hear one."

"Oh, I don't know."

"We won't stop pestering you until you relent."

"*I* won't pester you," Evangelist promised.

"I will. Let's hear it. Let's hear it. Let's hear it. Let's hear it."

"Do you think we could catch up to Talkative?" Christian laughed. "I suddenly miss the sound of his voice."

"I mean, if you're *afraid* to share your hymns . . . "

"Oh, fine! I'll recite one. I composed this in the depths of the Valley of the Shadow of Death, which—*for some of us*—was quite an ordeal:

> *O world of wonders, I can say no less*
> *That I should be upheld through deep distress*
> *What I have met with here, O blessed be*
> *His mighty hand which hath delivered me*
> *From dangers, devils, hell, and sin,*
> *A veil of darkness hems me in*
> *A world of snares and pits and nets,*
> *Of goblins, satyrs, dragons, threats*
> *That might have tripped and cast me down.*
> *But since I live, let Jesus wear the crown.*

Faithful swallowed hard. "That is good, Christian. *Since I live, let Jesus wear the crown.* Pretty good. What do you think, 'Vange?"

"I think . . . I am glad for your experience—not that you have met with trials, but that you have been victors. It does me so much good to see you both together, and so far along this road, and to hear you sing the praises of our King. I am reminded of the words of Jesus in John's Gospel: that the one who sows and those who reap shall rejoice together. And, brothers, you will reap if you do not faint. The crown is before you—an incorruptible crown. Run, that you may obtain it."

Evangelist came to a stop and looked first Christian, then Faithful, in the eye. "But hear me," he said, "You are not yet out of the gunshot of the devil. In your struggle against sin, you have yet to resist unto bloodshed. Let the kingdom be always before you, and believe steadfastly concerning the things that are invisible. Let nothing that is on this side of the other world get within you. And, above all, look well to your own hearts and the lusts within, for they are deceitful above all things, and desperately wicked. Set your faces like a flint; you have all power in heaven and earth on your side."

Faithful's face went grim. "Why are you speaking like this now? What's— what's coming up on this road?"

Evangelist placed a hand on each man's shoulder. "My sons, you know the Word of God: that through many tribulations you will enter into the kingdom of heaven, and that in every city, bonds and afflictions await you. And so you cannot expect to go long on your pilgrimage without them—in one form or another. I'm sure you can see that you're almost out of the wilderness. You will soon come to a town that will beset you on all sides. And there, it is very likely that one or both of you will seal his testimony with blood. Be faithful unto death, and the King will give you a Crown of Life."

"Can we not just go around this city?" Christian asked.

"Stay on the Narrow Way. If one of you does die there, although your death will be unnatural, and your pain perhaps great, you will be the envy of the other—not only because you will arrive at the Celestial City soonest, but because you will escape many miseries that the other will meet with on the rest of his journey. But when you come to that place, quit yourselves like men, and commit the keeping of your souls to your faithful Creator."

"You're not coming with us?" Faithful asked.

"No, I'm not. I passed through that town three weeks ago and was expelled—violently, for the third time. I have no fear of that place. But tomorrow I am needed in Carnal Policy. Souls hang in the balance. Godspeed, my friends. I will see you again, in the City of our King, if not before."

They embraced again and parted ways, both Christian and Faithful noticing that their previous speed and enthusiasm as they walked and talked had evaporated, replaced by a slow and dragging pace. As evening approached, they came out of the wilderness and saw a town in the distance before them. Within a few minutes, they passed a sign along the road, which read "Vanity: 1 Mile." Beneath it was tacked a placard, which boasted "Fair open 365 days a year!"

Faithful took a deep breath and said, "Tell me again, Christian—how did that hymn go? Since I live . . . "

"Let Jesus wear the crown."

They were entering a clearing, which led up to the gates of the city when they came upon a man playing an annoying, trilling song on a penny whistle. He was a silly person in a silly hat, which came to a point straight above his head, and yet he had something of a sad countenance about him. When he heard the pilgrims approaching, he stopped playing, looked up at them, and burst out laughing.

"Are you quite alright sir?" Christian asked.

"Oh my goodness! Look at the two of you! Are you lost?"

"On the contrary, we are pilgrims on the Narrow Way. And the Narrow Way passes through this town, which I surmise is called Vanity?"

"Oh, you *surmise?*" He laughed again. "Have you never heard of our town? Have you never heard of Vanity Fair? Why, this place is famous!"

"We are not from nearby," Faithful said. "We were both born in the City of Destruction."

"You look like you've never been to a fair in your life!"

"There was a fair in our city every year," Faithful said, "which lasted several weeks. I'm ashamed to say I spent more time there at the end, when pleasure had replaced commerce."

"Oh, several weeks you say! Am I supposed to be impressed? Our fair never ends! And this is no newly-erected business or temporary gathering. It is a thing of ancient standing—thousands of years old! Ever growing! The great founders of the fair—Beelzebub, Apollyon, and Legion (with some other companions)—decided to establish a continual festival in this city for the very reason that pilgrims must pass through it."

"What is for sale there, sir?" Christian asked.

"Call me Inanity."

"Okay. What is for sale there . . . Inanity?"

"Oh, anything you might want! Lands, honors, titles, kingdoms, lusts, pleasures and delights of all sorts—including, but not limited to: harlots, wives, husbands, children, slaves, lives, blood, bodies, souls, silver, gold, pearls, precious stones, and the like. But don't think it's chaotic like so many other fairs. It is vast, yes, but there are rows and streets under very proper names, where these wares and those services can be found. And also by country: there is a British Row, a French Row, an Italian Row, a Spanish Row, a German Row, where all sorts of vanities from that land can be purchased. I've lately been bingeing my way through all the merchandise of Rome, which many consider to be the best and most celebrated items here. It's not exactly my cup of tea, but it's certainly a wonderful way to pass the hours. And of course the taverns of bottomless drinks to take the edge off, amidst clouds of fragrant, mind-binding smoke form the North. Truly, a lovely way to wile away the days."

"You said hours."

"What?"

"A moment ago, you said 'a wonderful way to pass the hours.' Now you speak of wiling away whole days."

Inanity folded his arms. "And what makes up days if not hours? Let's not be difficult, gentlemen."

"Well," Faithful said, "I suppose we will see for ourselves."

"I wouldn't go in dressed like that," Inanity warned with a dark giggle.

"Why not?"

"Those embroidered coats. And those foreign marks on your heads . . . " His face darkened so much and so quickly that it seemed to dull the sunlight in the clearing. "They've *done things* to people wearing such garments here. Terrible, unspeakable things." He suddenly brightened. "But there are ways around it. I suggest you remove those coats and fashion them into some sort of turban to cover your foreheads and perhaps affect some sort of exotic accent. Make a curiosity of yourselves and you might slip through unmolested."

"We will do no such thing," Christian said. "Goodbye, sir—or, Inanity."

The man waved them off and went back to playing his whistle.

Christian and Faithful approached the gate of the city and entered beneath a massive arch, bearing the name "Vanity Fair" in bright, colorful letters. Beneath it, in smaller print, were the words "Eat, Drink, and Be Meaningless, Meaningless."

"Oh, very clever," Faithful mumbled.

No sooner had they entered the city than they found themselves in the midst of the fair itself. After such a long time spent either in solitude or encountering only a handful of people here or there, the sight of the crowd was overwhelming, not to mention the sounds and smells.

From what must have been the center of the fair, a towering maypole rose up well into the sky, colorful ribbons and streamers wrapped around its top and staked to the ground all a great distance away, creating the illusion of a huge open-air tent. The sounds of multiple songs, wafting in from different directions, competed for their attention.

As they walked deeper into its midst, they saw jesters and jugglers, conjurers, wild beasts chained up, dwarves, giants, and rope-dancers. Women and men alike rushed about in the most immodest clothing, openly displaying their lusts.

"If I had to sum all of this up in one word," Faithful barked down Christian's ear, "*diversions.*"

"I agree," Christian answered. "Diversion from the state of man's heart and the ultimate, eternal destiny of the sinner."

Just then, they passed a toppled booth, upon which one man was beating another, shouting, "You cheat! You thief! Give me my money back! That was rigged and you know it!"

They learned quickly to watch their step, as the muddy ground was full of ruts and potholes, vomit and excrement. They also realized that Inanity had been telling the truth about their dress; despite the wide variety of clothing and costumes present, the two pilgrims stood out and drew curious and hostile gazes wherever they went.

"Hey, you! You in the armor!" The pilgrims looked down to see a young boy holding a bundle of fresh-cut flowers. "Buy a flower?" he asked, pushing his bottom lip out, pathetically. "*Pleaaase?*"

Christian smiled and reached for his moneybag, tied up beneath his breastplate. "I don't have much, but I'll happily buy one flower if it will be a help to you."

The moment his purse came into view, the boy snatched it and made to run into the crowd, but Faithful grabbed him by the collar and lifted him up off the ground.

"Easy there, lad," he said. "Let's have that back."

The fairgoers in their immediate vicinity were now watching intently and whispering to each other as the boy tossed the purse contemptuously back to Christian, who withdrew three coppers, handed them to the boy—still twisting and kicking, a foot off the ground—and took a flower in return.

"You remind me of my youngest son," Christian said. "And I hope you will listen where he has ignored me. The Best of Books tells us that no thieves, nor greedy, nor drunkards, nor revilers, nor swindlers will inherit the kingdom of God." The ground tremored a bit beneath their feet and Faithful dropped the boy, who stared up at Christian, eyes wide, frozen with the look of a deer about to bolt. "But please, listen, young man: our Prince died to pay for our sins. And yours. Put your faith in him and you will be saved."

The ground shook again, violently enough to overturn tables, spill drinks, and topple merchandise. Then it ceased.

The boy ran off and an eerie sense of calm and quiet descended—like the stillness before a storm. The pilgrims looked around to find every eye in the fair locked on them—looks of malice and murder.

Faithful put a firm hand on Christian's shoulder and said, "Since we live, let Jesus wear the crown."

"Indeed. And if we die—all the more."

Vanity Fair

The Prince of Princes continued along the Narrow Way.

His step had been lighter coming up from the river, just off the path a few miles back. There, his kinsmen had plunged him beneath the waters, and all present had heard the voice of the Father above: a heavenly coronation, perfectly fit to this earthly mission.

But as the Spirit compelled him now more forcefully along the road, he felt a growing weight within. He knew what lay ahead: the town of Vanity, with its lusty fair and all its wickedness, distractions, amusements, and enticements. The Prince had no use for such things. And yet, he had to enter in. After all, he had come to rescue not only the hapless victims of this place, but its vilest offenders, if they would have him. And, of course, there was no way back to his own country without passing through Vanity Fair—not without going out of the world itself. This was the very reason its founders had chosen the site.

The Prince prayed as he walked. He recited Scriptures to himself and sang psalms, hymns, and spiritual songs. Presently, he saw the city gate drawing near. And there, waiting for him, were the founders of the fair: Legion, Apollyon, and the great Beelzebub himself, all of them grinning and panting for his arrival. And yet, as the Lord drew near and Beelzebub spread his monstrous wings in welcome, his two companions

shrunk back and hid behind them, their smug confidence waning at the slow approach of infinite power in the form of this
humble man.

"This is quite a welcoming party," the Prince said.

Beelzebub chortled. "Nothing but the best for you, good
Prince. The best of common food troughs for your cradle. The
best of dung-smeared pasture-men for your royal court. The
very best of filthy, backwater blights for your hometown . . .

But now, it's time you had some luxuries actually fit for a king, if you would but take them. In fact, I intend to personally walk you through the midst of our great fair and see that you have every comfort and dainty you could possibly desire."

"Lead the way if you like. But I will buy nothing."

"This road you've been walking passes through nothing but wilderness, for some time. You must be hungry. Thirsty."

"I have food you know nothing about."

"And *we* have food you've only dreamt of. Dates. Fine meats. Exotic nuts. We have delights of all sorts in this place. And worry not about the cost. There are great bargains to be had here. Prices so low you'd be mad to pass them up."

"Are you going to stand here and talk all day? Or will we actually enter the fair at some point?"

Beelzebub smiled and refolded his wings behind him, revealing his two companions, who shrank back all the more. The Dark Prince then stepped aside and motioned for the Heavenly Pilgrim to pass through the gate and under a massive arbor, draped with fragrant flowers and dripping with honey.

When he was no longer in sight, the prince of demons drew his sword and pointed it at Apollyon. "Did you just *soil yourself?*"

"I'm sorry, my lord. I—I've never—"

"Be gone!" He struck Apollyon across the face with the flat of his blade, and the beast turned and scampered into the woods.

Turning his attention to Legion, Beelzebub said, "And you—I have an assignment for you. There is a lost and desperate man near the graveyard of the Gadarenes. Do you know the place?"

"Yes. A haunt for unclean beasts and unclean spirits alike, for many years."

"Make haste, then, and do what you do best. I will deal with this gentle Jesus, meek and mild." Legion saluted his master and departed in an explosion of flapping wings.

As Beelzebub passed beneath the arch, into the city and its raucous fair, the flowers began to wilt and shed their pedals. He spotted the Prince of Princes and moved quickly through fairgoers and revelers, shoving and knocking them from his path until he was walking alongside him.

"I see you're drawn to the finer things—as a prince should be! Look here: such an endless expanse of cakes and casks. Choose one. Any of them. All of them. Let your flesh be your guide."

The Prince barely glanced at the lavish food and drink as he walked by. "Man does not live by bread alone," he said, "but by every word from the mouth of God."

"What is it you want then, hmm? What secret desires dwell within? Not women, no. And not men. Not slaves or fleets. You're a man of honor. *Yessss.* This way, then, your *highness*. We have honors aplenty."

Beelzebub beckoned with his long, thin fingers and led the Good Prince to the maypole at the center of the fair, around which a large wooden platform had been erected.

"We will make you the Lord of the Fair. A fitting title, no?" He gestured at a laurel crown on a finely crafted table, next to a beautiful wooden box. "These will be yours. Put this crown upon your head and everyone in the city will bow as you walk by." Running his hand along the polished rosewood, he added, "This beautiful case contains ease and opulence and the praise of men. You need only promise to stay here with us and you may have all these things at no cost."

The Prince looked Beelzebub in his dark, sunken eyes and said, "There is always a cost. You would do well to count the cost before you put the Lord your God to the test."

"How noble," Beelzebub murmured. "But you are right; it was a test." He began to lead the Lord down another row. "And you passed, of course. One little fair—one little town—is nothing. You deserve much more."

They came to a colossal ornate tent, over which a hundred

different flags and standards whipped in the growing wind. Beelzebub drew back the flap from the entrance and motioned for the Prince to enter the tabernacle. The interior smelled of exotic spices. In the low light, he saw dozens of tables covered in glinting crowns and scepters.

"These can all be yours," Beelzebub said. "Every nation, all the kingdoms of the earth. The price is obscenely low. Simply take a knee and kiss my ring, and I will hand you these." He stretched out his left hand, in which was clenched a fat ring of golden keys.

The Lord's eyes flicked down to the keys and the ring for just a moment before he answered, "It is written: you shall love the Lord your God and worship him only." He stepped closer and added, "And when the time comes, I will simply *take* those keys. I will not buy them. And on that day, you will be the one to kneel." He ducked back out of the tent, into the oppressive afternoon sun. Beelzebub followed him out, flustered and blustering.

"Come back here, you filthy, homeless wretch! I'm not done with you!"

The Prince of Princes came to a stop, alongside a long, low wooden cage containing several gaunt children.

"Like what you see?" The vendor leaned in, raising an eyebrow. "Running a special today. Buy one, get *uh*—" He met the Prince's gaze and fell silent, then fell back a step, shaking his head stiffly.

The Prince ripped the door of the cage open. "Come, little ones. You're free." The children hesitated a moment, then spilled out and fled along the Narrow Way, which went out from the city just a stone's throw away. Several nearby merchants began to object.

"What do you think you're doing?"

"We're running a business here!"

A holy fire burned in the Lord's eyes. He grabbed the nearest table and threw it on its side as if it weighed nothing, spilling documents and golden amulets. Then he overturned another. And another.

The traders and traffickers made to intervene, but all stopped short and thought better of it, first backing away, then turning tail to run from the melee.

Within a few moments, the Prince was alone amidst piles of money and merchandise—save for one man who cowered behind his booth, his shaking hands held up before his face as if to ward off an attack.

"Matthew," the Prince said.

The man lowered his hands tentatively. "Do I . . . know you, sir?"

"Not yet. But you will. And, more importantly, I know you. Come, follow me."

The young man came out from behind the booth, eyes wet, and asked, "Where are we going?"

"Look to the East, Matthew," the Prince said. "Do you see the shining light?"

Faithful felt a hand grabbing at his sleeve, pulling him toward a collection of occult books, trinkets, and talismans. "Look, sir. Whatever ails you, we've got a solution here, don't we?"

The pilgrim wrenched his arm free, not looking back.

"Let's step lively," he said. "It would be foolish to stay here any longer than absolutely necessary."

"Agreed," Christian said.

"Hey! You!" A fairgoer jeered from behind them. "Where'd you get that coat? You're a bold one to wear that here!"

Others who crossed their path mocked and laughed. Some spat on them. All the while, vendors flattered and fawned: "Oooh, we've got visitors from a far-off land. You must be wealthy to afford such raiment. Have a look here. Bring some vanities home to your little ones."

Despite their best intentions to get out quickly, the deeper into the fair they went, the thicker the traffic and the slower their pace. This left them captive to the pitches of every huckster along the way. There came a point at which Christian was so overwhelmed that he put his fingers in his ears to avoid the temptation. "Lord, turn my eyes away from beholding vanity!" he shouted.

Again, the cacophony of the fair went silent, and every eye fixed on the pilgrims.

"If you want none of our wares," a vendor spat, "then why are you here?"

"We are simply passing through," Faithful said. "That is all. Our trade and traffic is in heaven." The ground beneath them quaked once again and a display case full of lustful paintings toppled over. The crowd began to shout and harass the pilgrims.

"So-ho! Christian! Faithful!" came a voice from a grand pavilion one row over. They looked up to see Talkative, at the head of a long table, holding court over a dozen men and women, slumped against their drinks. Talkative raised his  tankard and said, "Making friends in your signature way, I see!" He then laughed derisively and turned his attention back to his new companions.

Faithful grabbed Christian by the arm and made to force his way through the crowd, but a battle-scarred mountain of a man stood blocking their way.

"You don't just *pass through* Vanity Fair," he growled. "This is a place of commerce. What would you men buy?"

"We buy the Truth," Faithful said, standing his ground. Another tremor overturned several tables and Faithful tried to grab the distraction and slip past the man, but people were now pressing in on every side.

"You're not going anywhere," the big man said, pointing to a coat of arms affixed to his garment. "You may think this is a lawless place, but it's not. Come with me." He placed his hand on his sword and gestured with his chin toward a stone building in the distance.

"Shall we fight him?" Christian whispered, looking down at his own sword. He was perplexed at his lack of courage. As impressive as this man was, he was half Apollyon's size and no more than flesh and blood.

"No," Faithful answered. "This crowd would tear us to shreds. Besides, Evangelist did not tell us to defend ourselves here, but rather to be willing to suffer and even die for our faith. We will not return evil for evil." He then said to the guard, "Lead the way, sir."

The crowd parted, allowing them to enter the building, which was divided between a long, dank cell of iron bars on one side, and a rather well-appointed guardhouse on the other. Several men wearing the same badge as their fellow sat around a fine table, playing cards over a pot piled high with gold and silver.

With no regard for the game and no apology, the pilgrims' escort swiped everything from the table in one motion and ordered them to sit.

"Hey! I was about to win a fortune!" one of the men complained. Then, turning his anger from his hulking superior to the two oddly dressed men, he smashed a fist into Faithful's side, and, when he had doubled over, knocked the pilgrim's head against the table. He then barked orders for cards and coin alike to be relocated to a nearby drinking tent and, within a few moments, the group had gone.

The hulking guard who had arrested them sat across from the pilgrims, the chair complaining under his weight and said, "Alright—who sent you?"

"Sir?"

"You have created chaos in our fair. And, while we do enjoy some chaos in the form of strategic indulgent release, we will not tolerate the sort of bedlam that interferes with commerce. You two men are either mad or you came here as saboteurs with a design to undermine and spoil our fair and our fair city. So I ask again: who sent you?"

"We are pilgrims, sir," Christian said. "And while you do not like the answer, we wish only to pass through your town on our way to the Celestial City."

"Give me your bags," the guard demanded. "And you—I'll take that sword."

Christian glanced at Faithful, who nodded subtly, and the two of them handed over their belongings.

"Stand up and put your hands out," the man ordered. A moment later, he was affixing a set of irons to Faithful's wrists. He then shoved him roughly into the cell.

Christian, eyes closed in prayer, felt his own wrists secured and then a tug on his helmet. Then another, harder yet.

"Take it off," the guard growled.

"I can't."

Another jerk at the helmet brought a flare of pain, as if the guard would pull the pilgrim's head clean off.

"Huh. Won't do you any good anyway—not at the end of a noose." The guard laughed and shoved him in with Faithful.

"I'll be back in a little while," he said, locking the cell door and exiting the building.

"What will they do to us?" Christian asked.

"I do not know."

"Maybe we should have bought something. Something harmless. Some tea or truffles."

Faithful regarded his friend. "Christian, what fellowship has light with darkness?"

They sat in silence for ten or fifteen minutes, until the guard came back in, leading a train of angry men.

"Alright, my little provocateurs," he said, "these men all have valid grievances against you. I myself am a witness to that. But to make everything nice and official, let's get something on record." He gestured to a wormy little man who sat at the nearby table, opened a writing case, and prepared his pen.

One by one, the merchants and rabble of the fair cataloged the damages they'd sustained as a result of the pilgrim's presence, while the clerk wrote it all down. When they'd all said their piece, the guard turned to the pilgrims and asked, "Do you deny these charges?"

Christian stood. "This is a farce," he said. "By their own admission, any losses incurred by these fellows were the result of theft by opportunistic fairgoers or else no real loss at all—just simple offense at our presence in their midst, for which I do not apologize and, frankly, do not believe we can be held responsible."

"You're wrong there," the guard said. "We have laws against defaming the fair or giving rise to any sense of shame by your word or conduct. In fact, these are among the only laws of our city. And you have undoubtedly broken them. For that, you will be punished."

He then unlocked the cell and dragged Faithful and Christian out into the midst of the fair, where a mob was waiting. There, starting with the men who had lodged complaints, each one of them smeared the pilgrims with muck and filth, called out insults and blasphemies, and otherwise made sport of them, pelting them with rocks and rotten produce, knocking them to the ground again and again, only to command them to rise and endure more.

This went on for the space of an hour, the pilgrims enduring it all with a quiet dignity, until a few people in the crowd began to object.

"That's enough," one of them called out.

"You've made your point," said another. "If these men have broken a law, let's try them properly!"

A few shouts of agreement arose from here and there.

"Show of hands," the chief guard bellowed. "Who thinks these men have endured enough abuse?" A dozen hands went up. "I believe we've identified their confederates," he declared, and ordered those sympathetic souls to be placed in the stocks for two days' time. "As for these men," he said, "if it's a trial you want, that can be arranged. For now, to the dungeon!"

A cheer came up from the main part of the crowd, and with great fanfare, Christian and Faithful were paraded along a circuitous path, up and down every row, until they arrived at the heart of the fairground, where an elaborate columned courthouse awaited them.

The pilgrims were practically carried through the front doors and then led down a flight of stone steps and along a dark and musty hall, past several rusty metal doors on either side.

"Your room, sirs," the guard said, mockingly, then ordered, "You—open it."

A familiar man slid a key into the lock, and with a deep, ominous creak the door swung open.

"I tried to warn you," Inanity said under his breath. "Why didn't you listen to me?"

"We knew the cost," Faithful replied, trying to look him in the eyes, but Inanity only studied the dirty floor.

"In!" the guard ordered, fairly tossing the men into the stark chamber.

"We'll come for you when we come for you. For now, enjoy your stay here at Vanity Fair."

The door slammed shut.

Christian examined their accommodations, such as they were. Only a sliver of daylight spilled in, through a narrow, barred window up near the low ceiling. There was no furniture of any kind—only a bucket next to the door.

Faithful sat against the wall and patted the floor next to him. "What a blessing," he said.

"I'm sorry—a *blessing*? Are you joking?"

"By no means! They could have put us in separate cells. But here we are together! Now we can encourage each other, pray together for wisdom and endurance, praise our Lord together!"

Christian sat next to him. "Encourage each other, you say? Alright. You go first, I guess"

It was several hours later, while the two were deep in prayer, when a slat at the base of the door slid open and two bowls full of some sort of slop were pushed into the room.

"Thank you," Faithful called out.

"You're, um . . . yes," came a voice from out in the hall.

"Inanity? Is that you?" The man's face appeared in the opening for a moment, upside down, and the pointy hat fell off his head. "It's me," he said. "You should eat up. You'll need your strength." Then the slat slid closed.

The pilgrims gave thanks and began to sup. Thankfully the light was failing now, and they could not see what they were consuming, for Christian was quite sure he'd have been unable to choke it down otherwise. When they'd finished their meal, they spoke about Evangelist's words and prayed all the more for courage, strength, and perseverance.

At about midnight, they began to sing songs of praise to the King of the Heavenly Land.

> *A hymn of glory let us sing,*
> *New songs throughout the world shall ring;*
> *Alleluia, alleluia.*
> *Christ, by a road before untrod,*
> *Ascendeth to the throne of God,*
> *Alleluia, alleluia.*
> *Alleluia, alleluia. Alleluia!*

Faithful laughed. "I can't carry a tune to save my life. You sing. I'll listen."

"No," Christian said. "You sing too. I insist."

> *To whom the angels, drawing nigh,*
> *"Why stand and gaze upon the sky?"*
> *Alleluia, alleluia.*
> *"This is the Savior," thus they say,*
> *"This is His noble triumph day."*
> *Alleluia, alleluia.*
> *Alleluia, alleluia, alleluia.*

The floor beneath them began to shake and a soft, warm light filled the room.

"Keep singing," Faithful said.

Again shall ye behold him so
As ye today have seen him go,
Alleluia, alleluia.
In glorious pomp ascending high,
Up to the portals of the sky.
Alleluia, alle—

The door of the cell swung open and two armed men charged in, wordlessly pulled Faithful to his feet, and shoved him out into the hall, slamming and locking the door.

A moment later, Christian was all alone in the still darkness. He lay there on the cold ground until he drifted off into a restless sleep.

The morning came with the sounds of revelry wafting in amidst birdsong and dappled sunlight, but Christian felt no sense of renewed mercies. He neither prayed nor sang—only sat there, dejected, until the slat opened again, and another bowl of slop appeared.

"I need the bucket," came Inanity's voice.

Christian pushed the waste pail through the opening, thinking that there was little difference between what it contained and the breakfast he was about to endure.

"Hey," Inanity whispered, "your friend is safe. Just across the hall."

"Is that supposed to comfort me?"

"He thought you'd want to know."

"Go away, you silly halfwit," Christian spat. The slat remained open for a moment, then an empty bucket bounced back into the cell and the little door closed.

Christian forced himself to give thanks, although he felt no appreciation and was only able to choke down about half the bowl's contents. He thought of the lavish feast he'd enjoyed by the roaring fire in the Palace Beautiful and wished he had stayed there.

For three days, this continued. Twice a day, the slat would open and Inanity would empty Christian's bucket and provide him more of that gruel to eat. Inanity said nothing else to him until the morning of the third day, when he reached his hand in through the opening and offered half a loaf of bread. "It's from my own house," he said.

Christian thanked him and wolfed it down, but still felt no real gratitude—to Inanity or to the King of Heaven. He was now caught in a cycle of bitterness and regret, wondering what Mr. Legality was eating this morning or whether Mr. Worldly Wiseman had ever had to suffer like this. He thought of Simple, Sloth, and Presumption lying under the warm sun. How unfair that this was his reward. Loneliness gripped him and Christian began to wonder aloud what had been the point of being briefly reunited with Faithful, only to be torn away from him again after such a short time. It seemed a cruel cosmic joke.

The nights were the worst. Christian longed for company, only to feel an evil presence with him in the cell. He heard whispers—taunts, temptations, more of those dark and blasphemous thoughts he'd heard deep in his being in the Valley of the Shadow of Death, only he lacked the strength or will to rebuke them. When he slept, he had horrifying nightmares. Apollyon's glistening fangs, the chalk-white goblins from the mouth of hell.

Then, on the fourth morning, the door swung open and the familiar voice of the chief guard ordered him to come out into the hall. There, he saw Faithful, his countenance no darker than it had been the night they'd dragged him away. Beside him stood Inanity, his eyes downcast.

The guard grinned at Christian. "It's time for your trial."

- Mr. & Mrs. Timorous, at Home -

Mercy shifted the earthenware dish of baked apples onto her hip and knocked gently on the front door of the small house. A moment later, it opened just a few inches and a man peered out. He studied her warily for half a minute before craning his neck to peer around her diminutive form, as though there may be untold dangers lurking there.

"Hello, Mr. Timorous," Mercy said, pleasantly. "It's me; just me. I've brought dessert like we discussed." She stood there, awkwardly, while the man hung in the doorway, seemingly undecided as to how he should proceed.

"Is . . . Mrs. Timorous home?" she finally asked.

"*Thweetie!*" he called back into an unseen room, "*Merthy'th* here!"

"Well, invite her in, you silly goose," came the barked response.

The man frowned at the young woman for a moment and then opened the door wide and gestured for her to enter.

"Welcome. *Pleathe* come in."

Mercy entered the familiar house and placed her dish on the table. "How are you today, Mr. Timorous?" she asked.

He narrowed his eyes. "Why do you *athk*?"

"No reason, just . . . making conversation. I assume you are coming with us this evening? Normally, with a widow, just we women would bring some food, of course, but since it was *Mrs.* Endearing who died, we thought it would be improper for us to—"

Mrs. Timorous blustered into the room, apron covered in flour and meat drippings, wielding a large wooden spoon. She gave Mercy a brief kiss and chided her husband for his lack of manners.

"It looks like you've been cooking up a storm," Mercy said. "Shall we go?"

Mrs. Timorous met her husband's gaze for a moment and said, "Oh, I'm not sure. You know how we hate to travel at night."

"At night? Why, it can't be later than four o' clock."

"Ah, but Mr. Endearing will invite us in and he'll talk with us at length. And I never know what to say in those situations. By the time we leave, the sun will have set and we'll have to return under cover of darkness. Who knows what scoundrels might be lurking in the shadows."

"But Mrs. Timorous," Mercy said, "we volunteered to bring some food and some cheer to that poor man today." She gestured at her dish, growing cold on the table. "I made my best dessert and you've certainly been working hard in the kitchen; I can see that. What a shame it would be if we failed to deliver it. Come now. I promise, there's nothing to fear."

"You can't promise that."

"No, but *you* promised this wouldn't happen again. Didn't you?"

Mrs. Timorous rapped the spoon against the table. "Oh, it's so very easy for you, isn't it?" she spat. "You spend your days roaming and playing with those children and gabbing and gossiping with their mother, carefree as can be. Meanwhile, we are reminded of the dangers that lurk in every corner each time my poor husband opens his mouth!"

"Okay. Mrs. Timorous, I know you don't like Christiana or her husband, but—"

"Do not speak of that man in my house!"

"I'm sorry, it's just that I—"

"It's all her fault!"

"How is it his—?"

"Oh, I've long suspected she drove that man out on his so-called *pilgrimage.* Poor Mr. Timorous was simply looking out for him. And if that foolish man had just listened, all would be well. But *noooo,* he had to be a hero and push ahead. And do you know what happened to my dear Timorous?"

"Yes, he was burned—"

"He was burned through the tongue with a hot iron!"

"And not *jutht* me," Mr. Timorous said. "My dear friend *Mithtrutht ath* well!"

Mrs. Timorous rubbed his back tenderly. "The King's men built a stage specifically to make an example of these good citizens. And now look; you've upset him. We certainly can't go out now."

Mercy sighed. "I'm sorry for what you endured. Truly, I am. But you can't really think such a thing might happen here in our town."

"*It'th thertainly pothible!*"

"Well . . ." Mercy's voice cracked.

"I'm *thorry, ith thomething humorouth? Amuthing? Thith ith theriouth!*"

"I know. I'm—I'm sorry." Mercy glanced again at her dessert and said, "Perhaps we could bring the food tomorrow morning, in the daylight."

"Dear, you know we don't travel during the busy part of the day. Not since I was nearly trampled by a carriage six months ago. People are so preoccupied with their own business, they don't even see you! Why don't we just stay in? It just so happens that I have enough dinner for all three of us. And we could eat your lovely dessert."

"Mrs. Timorous, it does not 'just so happen.' You have extra food because you made some for that mourning widower. I'd bring it myself, but that would be inappropriate. How about noon-time, tomorrow?"

"Pish-posh! Tomorrow, Mr. and Mrs. Light-Mind will be bringing food to the widower," Mrs. Timorous said. "We don't want to overwhelm him. Besides, he'd probably rather be alone, don't you think? Let's stay in tonight. We'll have dinner and play cards together. Sounds cozy, doesn't it?" She opened the lid of Mercy's dish and fanned it, letting the aroma fill the room.

"I suppose I could make another meal tomorrow," Mercy mused, "and bring it to Mr. Endearing, if the children were with me."

Mr. Timorous's face lit up. "*Doeth* that mean you'll *thtay?*"

Mercy looked out the window and then back to the table, where she noticed three place settings already waiting. "Yes, I'll stay."

"*Thplendid,*" Mr. Timorous said.

Faithful

Mr. Great-Heart approached the tavern quietly, head-down, his sword obscured by the wing of his cape. He felt no tingling nerves nor rush of excitement; this was not a dangerous assignment—not for Great-Heart. And it would be brief, which was becoming something of a pattern, of late.

Three months had now passed since Great-Heart had finished his last long-term appointment, escorting an old man—one who had only passed through the Wicket Gate in his later years—all the way to the Celestial City. The journey had been an honor and a great benefit to both of them, but had also taken a toll on Great-Heart, who had seen many close brushes with destruction along the way.

Since then, he'd found himself sent on short excursions, here and there, executing these one-off jobs between longer periods of mandated rest—which he knew he needed, and yet struggled to fully embrace. A month at the Palace Beautiful, singing and reading, smoking pipe with Watchful and swapping old stories with Steadfast, seemed at first like heaven-on-earth . . . but within a week, he grew antsy and began to pray for an early end to his repose—a prayer which had been answered with orders to come here.

The door creaked loudly as he entered the small, ramshackle tavern and the few patrons—all of them inebriated—looked up at him for just a moment, before turning back to their drinks. He spotted his man immediately, sitting on the ale bench, flanked on either side by dark figures in heavy cloaks.

"Mr. Generosity, is that you?" Great-Heart called out with a smile. The man turned and squinted at him.

"Do I *kno'ye*?" he slurred.

"It's your friend, Great-Heart!"

"Oh, yeah *isss* Great-Heart," the man repeated, teetering on the bench. "It's Great-Heart. *D'know'im.*"

"And who are these two fellows?" Great-Heart asked, whacking the dark figures on their backs.

"These are, *uhhhh* . . . I don't 'member. They're just always, ya know . . . with me."

"Are they now? You know, we've missed you on the Narrow Way. Missed your kindness and joy. Your service to your fellow pilgrims. What on earth are you doing here in the County of Idleness on Sloth?"

"Oh, just . . . " He laughed. ". . . drinking, mostly."

"How about you come back with me instead?" He snapped at the innkeeper and said, "Do you have any coffee for my friend here? Oh, hey! Mr. Generosity! Don't fall over." He hefted the man back up onto the bench. "Come on, now; we can head right back to where you left off the Pilgrim Road."

The two dark figures stood in unison and turned to face Mr. Great-Heart. Their skin was a pale gray, their pupilless eyes hung heavy, sagging like a dead man's, and their hands were obscenely long and gnarled.

"He is ours," one of them said.

"*Yessss*," the other hissed. "He *sssssstays.*"

Great-Heart took a step back and carefully pushed a table aside, opening some space on the floor. "Alright," he said, "we can dance if you like. But before we do, tell me your names."

The two just glared at him.

"Names!"

"Intemperance," said one of them, floating up over the bench and lighting on the floor before it.

"I am Compulsion," said the other, coming down beside his companion. "And when I have had my way with you, this place will be your prison as well."

"I guess we'll find out." He reached beneath his cape and pulled the shield from his back, securing the straps tightly to his forearm. "I'm going to be forthright with you; I've felt a little restless lately. And, as a result, I might make this last a little longer than it needs to."

With that, he spun and slammed the shield into Compulsion's face, throwing the creature back against the bar, where it crumpled to the ground.

Intemperance lurched forward, clumsily, hideous hands outstretched. Great-Heart stepped into him and brought the edge of his shield straight up with all his might, connecting with the creature's knobby chin and snapping its head back.

Great-Heart looked from one inert enemy to the other and said, "Come, now. That can't be all the fight you've got."

Both ghouls came rushing up at him in a blur of darkness, but Great-Heart's sword was out, cutting them down before they could reach him. They staggered back, mouths hanging wide, revealing several rows of sharp, rotting teeth. Mr. Great-Heart stepped forward and buried his sword, first in Compulsion's chest and then Intemperance's.

"Hey, innkeep!" he called. "I don't smell that coffee. Am I talking to the floorboards here or what?"

"Oh! *Yuh-yes sir.*"

"I'd also like a heaping bowl of whatever that man is eating. It smells . . . good enough. And one for my friend too."

Mr. Great-Heart sat on the bench with his charge for nearly three hours, until the man had sobered up. He then left payment and a generous tip for the innkeeper, saying, "I'd apologize for the mess, but you're the wicked fool who profited off the work of these vile creatures. Now you can deal with them."

As he ushered Mr. Generosity out the door, he asked, "Do you know the way back to the Pilgrim Road?"

"Yes, I do. Sadly, it's a trip I've made a few times." He looked Mr. Great-Heart in the eye and said, "Thank you for putting those things to death and dragging me out of that awful place."

"I'm sorry to tell you, but those two are not dead. Hard as it is to believe, even I cannot kill them outright. Nor can you. In fact, you'll meet with them again and again on your journey. And each time, it will be a fight for your life. Only when you reach the Celestial Gate will they finally be executed at the command of our King."

Generosity nodded. "Understood. I don't suppose you're going to see me back to the Narrow Way?"

"I'm afraid not. I'd love to, but I don't write the orders; I just obey them. Christ be with you, Generosity, and Godspeed."

The two men grasped hands and Generosity headed off into the woods, back toward the Narrow Way.

No sooner had he disappeared from sight, than a horse and rider came thundering up the road from the south, wearing the colors of a royal messenger.

"Mr. Great-Heart, I presume."

"None other."

"This is for you." He extended a document, sealed with the King's crest. Great-Heart broke the seal and read the orders. A smile broke out on his face. "Oh, I've heard of this gentleman. Been wanting to meet him." He looked up at the messenger and asked, "Just out of the city? No further?"

"No further."

"Alright, then." He re-rolled the document, gave it back to the rider and said, "I am on my way."

As Christian and Faithful came up from the dungeon, it seemed as though the entire city was packed into the courthouse, waiting to mock and jeer at the prisoners. Some pelted them again with clods of dirt, to which the guards turned a blind eye.

Entering the courtroom proper, they saw the jury fenced off to the side, their faces grim. Of the twelve men, four had been among their most prominent abusers on the day they first entered the town. Three of them wore clown makeup and two of them frilly collars, as though they'd been pulled mid-performance from their work in the fair and herded directly into the jury box.

"Sit here," the pilgrims were commanded as their shackles were removed.

No sooner had they obeyed, than a herald announced, "All rise while the honorable Lord Hate-Good takes the bench!"

The judge was short with dead, sleepy eyes and a small pickedevant beard. "Sit," he bellowed. "Now, Mr. Accuser, rehearse for me the charges against these men, that we might get these proceedings over with as quickly as possible."

The prosecutor stood and said, "Your honor, these men have been enemies to, and disturbers of, the trade and amusements of this place. They have made commotions and divisions in the town, and have even won a party to their own most dangerous opinions, in contempt of the law of our prince and founder. The gallery behind me is filled with witnesses ready to attest to this, should these men deny the charges."

Lord Hate-Good looked down his nose at the pilgrims and asked, "Well? Do you deny them?"

Faithful stood and answered, "Your honor, if I have set myself against anyone or anything, it was only against that which itself opposes him who is higher than the highest."

"Speak plainly!" the judge barked.

"I have only been faithful to my God. As for the 'disturbance,' I make none, being myself a man of peace, as is my companion. The so-called 'party' that was won over to us is no

more than a few good men among you who took umbrage with their baser neighbors and their cruelty. If anything, we're guilty of helping them turn from the worse to the better. And for that I say: you're welcome. And, as to this prince you speak of, am I correct in understanding him to be none other than Beelzebub, the enemy of my Lord?"

"You are correct, sir."

"Well, then . . . I defy him and all his angels and I say to hell with them and the sooner the better!" The crowd began to shout and froth anew.

"Order," Lord Hate-Good shouted. "I will have order in these proceedings!" When the crowd had settled down once again, the judge addressed Christian. "Do you share this man's views?"

"I do," Christian said, without standing.

Lord Hate-Good sucked his teeth for a moment. "Given these offensive and damning statements, I wonder if there is even a need for witnesses in this case. But I suppose we must keep up the sense of propriety here. I will allow two or three witnesses. Whom will you call?"

"First, I call Envy," Mr. Accuser said.

"Come up," the judge droned.

When he'd taken his seat, the prosecutor asked, "Do you know the prisoner at the bar?"

"I have known this man for a long time," Envy said, "and will attest upon my oath before this honorable bench that he is a—"

"Hold! Give him his oath," the judge ordered.

"Right. Do you swear upon the name or our lord and prince Beelzebub that you will give reliable testimony concerning these things?"

"I do."

The judge waved his hand. "Proceed."

Envy leaned back in the witness chair. "My Lord, this man, notwithstanding his plausible name, is one of the vilest men in our country; he regards neither prince nor people, law nor custom, but always does whatever he can to infect others with his own disloyal notions, which he calls 'principles of faith and holiness.' And in particular, I heard him once say that his Christianity and the customs of our town of Vanity were diametrically opposite, and could not be reconciled.

"In thus speaking, he condemns all our laudable acts and traditions, our beliefs and customs, and, therefore, he condemns all of us, doesn't he?"

"I see," said Lord Hate-Good. "Is there anything else?"

"I could go on, but I don't want to be tedious to the court. Unless you have further questions?"

"Stand by, Mr. Envy," the judge said. "Mr. Accuser, call your next witness."

"I call Superstition to come forward."

When they had sworn him in, the prosecutor pointed at Faithful and asked, "Do you know this man?"

Superstition apprised the pilgrim as if he were a sick horse not worth the trouble of treating. "My Lord, I have no great acquaintance with him, nor do I desire to. However, I do know that he is a very pestilent fellow! While briefly interacting with him the other day, I heard him say that our religion was naught and that, by following it, no man could please God.

"As we all know, Vanity is a place of love and acceptance and tolerance. But according to this man, our churches with their bright and welcoming flags are *worthless* and do nothing whatever for those who worship there! I jest not! I heard him say that those who fill her pews stand yet condemned in their sins and finally shall be damned!"

"No further questions," Mr. Accuser said.

"You may step down," the judge told him. "Oh, and I believe I see my good friend Flatterer there, waiting to take the stand. Come up, sir, if you will."

Flatterer took the stand, was placed under oath, and said, "My Lord, let me first begin by saying that you are doing a fantastic job so far at providing a fair and equitable trial for these men, even though we all know what sort of men they are."

"Thank you. Yes, thank you. Now, what is your testimony regarding this fellow?"

"Your honor, good men of the jury, and all of you kind and wonderful people of Vanity gathered here today . . . First, let me thank you for taking time away from our splendid fair to deal with this matter. You are all patriots. Now, as to this man. I have known him for a long time, and have heard him speak things that should never be uttered.

"He has railed on our noble prince Beelzebub, and spoken with contempt of his noble friends, whom we all hold in high honor: Lord Old Man, Lord Carnal Delight, Lord Luxurious, my old Lord Lechery, Sir Having-Greed, and others of our nobility. And in addition, he said that if all men were of his mind, these lords would be considered nobles no more! And be assured, this is no temporary frenzy distemper upon an other-wise good man. These last few days, I've spent time with another visitor to our town—one Talkative—who is well acquainted with this man and assures me that this is the pris-oner's normal way of speaking. I'm sure Talkative would gladly take the witness stand as well, although I'm not sure we'd ever get him to conclude his testimony."

Some mild laughter followed and Lord Hate-Good said, "I think I have heard enough. You are dismissed, sir." The judge then turned his attention to Faithful and said, "You, sir, stand accused of being a traitor, a heretic, and a fugitive. Have you heard these words of testimony against you?"

"I have," Faithful said. "May I speak a few words in my own defense?"

"Sir, you deserve to be slain at the earliest convenience of this court, but so that no one can accuse us of not being fair and gentle, let us hear whatever vile justifications you might make for your crimes."

"I will be brief," Faithful said. "In answer to Mr. Envy's accusations, I did identify certain laws and customs of your people that stand opposed to the Word of God. If I was wrong, convince me of my error and I will recant.

"As to Mr. Superstition's charges against me, all I said to him was that true worship of God requires a divine faith, and that requires a divine revelation of God's will and a submission to it on our part. Therefore, a human faith based on the shifting sands of culture and fancy can never profit a man, eternally speaking.

"And finally, Mr. Flatterer, the notorious pickthank. He has spoken truly, I suppose, although I would question his choice of terms, that I did 'rail' and the like. I did say that the prince of this town, with all the rabble of his attendants, (including all those he named) were fit for hell. Because they *are*. And so, the Lord have mercy on me, for I can see that you will not."

Lord Hate-Good laughed. "I see that we have four witnesses against the accused today, the last being the accused himself! Gentlemen of the jury, you have heard what these worthy gentlemen of our town have witnessed against this man—a man who came to our peaceful fair to create uproar and unrest. You have heard that he denies none of these charges. His fate is now in your hands.

"Before we hear the verdict, though, let me remind you all of our ancient laws. There was indeed an act ratified in the days of Pharaoh the Great, servant of our prince, that, lest those of a contrary religion should multiply and grow too strong for him, their males should be thrown into the river. There was also an act declared in the days of Nebuchadnezzar the Great, another of our prince's servants, that whoever would not fall down and worship his golden image, should be thrown into a fiery furnace. Further, a similar act was made in the days of Darius, that whoever would call on any god but him, should be cast into the lions' den. Now, the substance of these laws is directly applicable to this rebel here, in thought, word, and deed. Held up to this standard, this man is intolerable to our good city."

Glaring down at Faithful, the judge said, "Sir, you may be accustomed to court proceedings in which the jury goes off in secret to reach a verdict. Not so in this place. Here, each man will announce his views publicly, so that a record exists of what he has said—a record which may later be used against him should he stand trial for similar crimes. And so—" he turned to the jury, "when the clerk calls your name, please assess your verdict."

"Mr. Blindman."

"Guilty."

"Mr. No-Good."

"Guilty as sin, your honor."

"Let's keep the commentary to a minimum, gentlemen," the judge said, biting down a smile.

"Mr. Malice."

"Guilty."

"Mr. Love-Lust."

"Guilty."

"Mr. Live-Loose."

"Guilty."

"Mr. Impetuous."

"Guilty."

"Mr. High-Mind."

"Guilty."

"Mr. Enmity."

"Guilty."

"Mr. Liar."

"Guilty."

" Mr. Cruelty."

"Guilty."

 "Mr. Dark-Heart."

"Guilty, your honor."

"Mr. Implacable."

"It's unanimous. I find him guilty as well."

Lord Hate-Good squeezed out a self-satisfied smile and announced, "The prisoner stands convicted. It is the opinion of this court that hanging would be too good a death for the prisoner. You, sir, are a vile heretic and truly insufferable. It is the ruling of this court that we will adjourn these proceedings for today in order to carry out the sentence of death, according to the procedures laid out in the Handbook of Legion. We will reconvene another day to try his compatriot." He stood and summarily disappeared into his chambers.

Several guards came up and laid hands on Faithful.

"Say goodbye to your friend," one of them taunted.

Christian began to weep. "Faithful. No."

"Be comforted," he said.

"Yeah," one of the guards sneered, "You'll be joining him soon!"

"And don't worry; we'll let you watch!"

Faithful wrenched free from the grip of the guards and embraced Christian, whispering into his ear, "They can do nothing to me now, Christian. Don't lose faith. Don't lose heart. I will see you again in the Celestial City." The two men were violently separated with more blows than were needed and the entire circus of the trial moved out into the midst of the fair.

There, the throngs from the courthouse and the waiting crowd outside began to beat Faithful with a sense of pure delight. They laughed and mocked as they punched, kicked, and slapped him. Some pricked him with their swords or lanced his flesh with knife-blades.

Christian tried to turn away, but the ruthless guards all around him forced him to watch, taunting and laughing all the while. Faithful endured all with a courage and strength that could only have come from God himself.

When they grew bored of beating him, they began to hurl stones in his direction, but not with the intention of killing him immediately. Rather, they threw them just hard enough to prolong his suffering. Each time he was knocked down, Faithful stood again.

"Lord, do not hold this sin against them!" he shouted.

Again the ground began to shake beneath their feet and the crowd drew back a bit, spooked. At Mr. Cruelty's suggestion, a gag was tightly wrapped over Faithful's mouth, many times over to keep him from speaking any more of his hateful words.

Then Faithful's coat was pulled from his back and tossed aside. Leading him to a large wooden pole, they bent him over, tied his hands to it and scourged his back until it was little more than ribbons of bloody flesh. They then straightened him up, pressed his back to the pole, and tied him to it with thick ropes, his raw back screaming against the rough, splintered wood. Children began to pile logs at his feet.

Christian sobbed uncontrollably at the sight of all this, oblivious to the jeering of all those around him. He silently prayed, "God if you are good at all, do something to save my friend. *Do something!*" We looked to the west, hoping to see a vast army ride up, Steadfast at its head. But no one came. He looked eastward, thinking the heavenly host might overtake them now, rescue Faithful, and bring the vengeance of God upon all these godless people.

Someone tossed a glowing firebrand at Faithful's feet and the wood began to burn. Faithful twisted in pain as his clothes were scorched and began to smolder. His flesh was singed and the gag fell away from his mouth. Looking up into heaven, he cried out, "Lord Jesus, receive my spirit!" Then his eyes fell to somewhere behind Christian, and he said, "Oh. Oh, that's beautiful."

Christian turned and saw a chariot behind the multitude, its wheels made of churning orange flame and a horse of fire standing ready to ride, its mane burning blue. Ready at the reins was one of the Shining Ones, standing a head taller than anyone in the crowd. No one else seemed to take notice of this, but Christian saw his friend Faithful, now serene and wearing a white linen robe, take the hand of the Shining One and step up onto the chariot, which carried him off in a grand blaze of glory until he was out of sight.

Christian fell to the ground, weeping before his friend's charred, smoldered corpse. He refused to get up, even when the guards kicked and threatened him. Finally, they lifted him up and carried him back to his cell in the dungeon, where they dumped him unceremoniously on the hard floor and locked him in, his wrists still unchained.

The pilgrim lay there, motionless, for hours.

Dinner time came and went, but Inanity did not deliver a meal. Which was fine. Christian was sure he could not eat tonight anyway—certainly not the swill they served here. His tears were renewed at the thought that such slop had been Faithful's last meal and he wondered how long it would be before they came back to try, condemn, and execute him. If only they had just killed him alongside his friend.

Christian wanted to pray. He knew that Faithful, had their roles been reversed, would be praying. But he felt hopeless. And so he confessed his hopelessness to the Lord. Then he began to confess other things: how he'd been tempted to compromise in the streets of Vanity, how he had truly wanted the vainglory offered there, in a way that Faithful clearly had not.

Then the prayers began to flow in earnest. He asked for comfort in his afflictions and that he would be a worthy witness to his Lord when the time came. From there, words of praise began to pour out from his heart. He sang Psalms. He sang the hymns he had written. Then he wrote another verse, for his departed friend.

> Faithful one, you followed true,
> Despite faithless fiends, who vied for you
> Forever may your name survive
> For, though you die, you're yet alive!
> Those who keep the faith through fire
> Are flames eternal, which never expire

Christian sat up, feeling a sense of enduring peace descend upon him. It was about midnight, he guessed, and he thought about the last peaceful moments he'd had with Faithful, joyfully singing hymns together in this very cell.

"Let Jesus wear the crown," he whispered.

Suddenly the room shook—an earthquake beyond any they'd experienced since their arrival. The walls shuddered for a full minute and, when they stopped, the door of his cell creaked open.

Standing tentatively, Christian tiptoed to the doorway and looked out. The hall was empty and mostly dark, the only light coming from a single candle, on its side, rolling toward him along the floor. Christian stepped out of the cell and moved as quickly and quietly as he could to the stone staircase, then up into the courthouse.

Peering out through the windows, he saw the nightlife of Vanity Fair cautiously resuming after the violent earthquake. Men righted booths and food stands. Some were putting out fires. Women ran laughing through the chaos, chased by boisterous young men. Christian slipped out the door and darted along the side of the courthouse, keeping to the shadows.

He waited there, by the rear of the building until a roving band of merrymakers had passed, swallowed up into the debauchery of the fair proper. Then Christian ran for it, having to brave the open for a moment until he was safe behind a large drinking tent. Just the other side of the canvas, he could hear all manner of wickedness transpiring. Repulsed, he moved along the rear of the tent and tried to get his bearings.

Just then, two men staggered around the corner of the tent, swilling from large jugs. Christian froze and stared at them.

"Look at this guy!" one of the men announced, gleefully. "You headed out to battle? What's with the whole suit of armor? He's like a little tin soldier!"

"Wait, I know this fellow!" his companion shouted. Christian stepped back, into the shadows. "He was at the trial today. Remember? The defendant!"

"We killed that fellow, though. I think we killed him."

"No, the other one. The one we didn't kill!" He glared at Christian. "What are you doin' out here? Where do you think you're goin'?"

Christian smiled sheepishly for a moment, then turned and sprinted as hard as he could toward the darkness at the edge of the fair.

The two men gave chase, one of them shouting, "Hey! Guard! Over here! Escaped prisoner!"

Christian could feel them at his back, neither gaining on him nor losing ground, but he knew he could not keep up this pace much longer. Ahead, he saw a stand of dense trees, stretched across with dozens of hammocks, most of them seemingly unoccupied. A long banner hung twenty feet off the ground, identifying the place as "The Grotto of Love," although the word "Love" had been crossed out and "Lust" written above it.

The pilgrim poured the last of his reserves on the fire and charged all the faster into the midst of the trees. He ducked under an empty hammock, crunched through a few yards of brush, and then crawled beneath another hammock, this one containing at least two writhing bodies.

"Lord, take me from this wicked place!" he prayed.

Christian could hear his pursuers entering the grove behind him and, in a bit of panic, he dove into an empty hammock and went limp, trying to remain completely motionless. Through the canvas, he could hear the three men checking searching methodically for him, peering into hammocks without apology, drawing ever closer to the pilgrim's position.

Then Christian found himself summarily dumped to the ground and looking up at the same guard who had arrested and beaten him four days earlier. The city's vulgar coat of arms prominently pinned upon his tunic, shimmered in the moonlight.

"We meet again," the guard said with a grin, letting loose with a savage kick against Christian's side. The two other men came up, flanking him, grinning even wider, like a pack of dogs at an injured hare.

"You know what our law says about fugitives?" one of them asked. "It says we can have fun with 'em before we bring 'em back!"

"Gentlemen," came a voice from behind Christian. "This

man is under my protection. I'll ask you to step back now."

"Yeah? And who are you?" the guard demanded.

Christian scrambled out from between these men as they faced off—three against one.

"They call me Great-Heart and I've been tasked with bringing this pilgrim safely away from this depraved town." The man was tall and broad shouldered and looked to Christian like he could have been Faithful's older brother. "I'll give you this one chance to walk away," he said, tossing the cape back over his left shoulder to reveal an ornate sword at his side.

The three brigands glanced at each other, snickered, and rushed the intruder. Great-Heart ducked one blow, absorbed another, and then delivered two in swift succession to the guard's nose, audibly crunching through the cartilage. One of the other men rushed in, intent on tackling Great-Heart to the ground, but only found himself flying through the air and colliding with a tree, right where his neck met the base of his skull. He rolled to his hands and knees, attempted to stand, then staggered and fell again to the ground.

The last man leapt at Great-Heart from behind, a jagged rock in his hand; Christian shook himself from his stupor and rushed the man, colliding hard with him and knocking him off course. Great-Heart turned just in time to drag the attacker to the ground and keep him there with a well-placed blow. The big guard was rising now, shaking his head violently, hand moving toward his sword. But Great-Heart was faster, drawing his own blade and holding it a few inches shy of the guard's throat.

"Uh-uh-*uhhhh*," Great-Heart sang. "Let's see those hands. Put them up high. Now, wiggle your fingers. Come now, you can wiggle them better than that. With feeling! Very good." Great-Heart sheathed his sword and punched the guard again in his broken nose, before reaching over the man and pulling his tunic down over his head. With a twist of his hip, he tossed the man right out of his cloak and into a hammock.

"Behind you!" Christian called out.

Great-Heart stepped aside and watched his rock-wielding attacker run headlong into the same hammock containing the guard, the two becoming entangled. He then cinched it shut like a canvas cocoon and ordered, "Christian, quickly—there's a coil of rope hanging from my belt. Wrap it around these gentlemen a few times." The guards were struggling and kicking now, while Great-Heart fought to keep his grip. "A little tighter maybe. Even tighter yet."

"You just keep a length of rope on you?"

"In my line of work, it comes in handy more than you'd think. Maybe a couple more loops, but leave some for me. There you go. Do you know any good knots?"

"I can manage," Christian said, tying it off several times over.

Mr. Great-Heart drew his sword once again and ordered the dazed man on the ground to turn onto his belly, hands behind his back. He then hog-tied him with the same length of rope and, finally, tied the end of it to a nearby tree.

"That should occupy them for a while," he said. Glancing around in the moonlight, it seemed to dawn on him that no one else in the grove had even bothered to investigate the violence that had just transpired. The sounds of snoring and fornication continued, unabated.

"Ugh. This wicked town. Come, Christian. Let's get you out of here." He grabbed up the guard's tunic from the ground and wrapped it around himself. "I'll just be borrowing your cloak for a moment," he threw over his shoulder.

As they emerged from the stand of trees, Great-Heart whispered, "Act like you're my prisoner."

They travelled a few hundred yards before a guard shouted, "You there! Where are you going with that one?"

"There was an escape attempt," Great-Heart answered. "So I'm relocating him. Is that a problem?"

The guard waved him on. And they approached the place where the Narrow Way left the town of Vanity, on the side nearest the Celestial City.

"I can accompany you no further," Mr. Great-Heart said. "I will watch over you to ensure you get safely out of this town. Beyond that, if you move carefully and keep low, you should be fine by morning. But keep moving. No sleep, Christian. Not tonight."

"How do you know my name, sir?"

"I was tasked by our King with seeing you safely away."

"But . . . why didn't you come earlier? If you had, there would be not one, but two pilgrims headed back on the Narrow Way."

Mr. Great-Heart put a hand on Christian's shoulder and met his eye with all sympathy. "I'm sorry. I don't write the orders. I just obey them. And if I'd been here yesterday, a man named Generosity would be dead on the ale bench by now."

Christian nodded and wrapped his arms around Great-Heart, who stiffened a moment, a bit uncomfortable with the embrace, before giving Christian's back two friendly pats.

The pilgrim took two steps toward the edge of Vanity, then hesitated. "Will they come after me?"

"I doubt it very much. By the time anyone discovers your absence, you will have quite the head start."

"There's one man who's sure to find me gone first thing in the morning. I can only assume he will raise the alarm."

"Then we shall pray to the One who overrules all things, having the power of this city's rage in his own hand, that he will allow the blood of Faithful to have quenched their blood-lust, even as it is already sowing seeds of faith among many wicked men. But now, you really do need to go. Christ be with you, Christian. And Godspeed. We will meet again, along the road or in the City."

Christian took off like a shot and, before he knew it, Vanity Fair was well at his back. Still, he felt his heart pounding against his ribs for more than a mile. The thought of Mr. Great-Heart covering his exit brought him comfort. But how long would that man stay there? For all Christian knew, the three men they'd bested and restrained had already freed themselves and were even now gathering a vengeful mob to track and overtake him—to drag him back and put him to death.

Christian tried to walk briskly without making noise, certain that he could feel someone behind him, gaining on him.

"No," he thought. "I'm imagining it. I've got a window of safety." But then he heard the snap of a twig no more than ten feet behind.

He spun and gazed into the darkness.

"Mr. Great-Heart? Is that you?" he called out. No answer. Then he saw the silhouette of a man, standing in the middle of the path. "Who are you?" Christian demanded, inching closer to him.

The man said nothing.

Christian took three more steps and felt his heart sink. He recognized the man's face. It was Inanity. Only, he was not wearing his pointy hat or his usual filthy garments.

No, he was wearing . . .

"How dare you?" Christian said, drawing yet closer. Rage began coursing through his veins.

"I'm sorry?" Inanity said.

"You took his coat? Like some kind of trophy? Some—curiosity? Is that funny to you?" He took another step, vengeance building in his heart. "I should not be surprised, I suppose. If the Romans gambled for the cloak of Jesus, it only makes sense that a man like you would—" Then Christian saw the sword in his pursuer's hand and wheezed a defeated laugh. "Oh, I see. You're here to bring me back."

The man looked down at the sheathed weapon in his hands, confused. Then he held it out to its owner. Only then did Christian notice the mark on this man's forehead.

"My name is no longer Inanity," he said. "You can call me Hopeful. And I am here to join you."

Hopeful

To Faithful, the music was transcendent, beautiful. True, it was just two regular men—one of them half-tone deaf—singing in the echoey confines of a prison cell, but from time to time Faithful felt as though he was granted the ears of the angels, to hear the praise of men and women and children as it came forth from their hearts.

> *In glorious pomp ascending high,*
> *Up to the portals of the sky.*
> *Alleluia, allelu—*

The heavy metal door swung open and two armed men strode in. One of them pointed at Faithful and the other grabbed him around the neck and dragged him out into the hall, shutting and locking the door behind them.

Faithful felt himself slammed hard against the stone wall. He snickered. "Was our singing really that bad?"

The taller of the two guards buried a fist in his stomach, sending him down to the floor.

"Get up," he barked. "You two can await trial separately. That way you don't have the chance to get your story straight."

They shoved him into a cell across the hall. He landed in a heap just as the lock turned. Looking around in the faintiest of moonlight—creeping in through a vent above—Faithful saw that this cell was a good deal smaller than the last, which he supposed was no hardship, as he was alone in here.

Or was he?

Scrambling to his feet, he struggled to survey the darker corners of the little rock-hewn room. There. In the deepest shadows, beneath an uneven wall, someone was sitting, legs drawn up beneath him.

No, beneath *her*.

I've been waiting for you, Faithful, said Wanton.

Inanity had four meals to deliver this morning, which was just one shy of his record for a single day. In fact, there were only eight cells down here and to Inanity's knowledge there had never been a time when all eight were occupied. While a certain type of order was very much prized in Vanity Fair, there were not many offenses that would actually land someone in the dungeon.

He carefully set the tray containing the four bowls on the ground, in the midst of the cells, and carefully lifted one of them, to make his first delivery. This would be the tricky one. Mr. Carnal Fury was known to lie in wait by the little opening in the door and try to reach out and grab Inanity while he delivered his meals. For this reason, he used a four-foot-long pole to open the slat and used the same pole to slide the bowl full of food in.

He opened it without incident, and saw that the empty bowl from the night before was near enough to withdraw using the pole, which was unusual, and therefore seemed a bit like a trap. He gripped the pole tightly, ready to fight for it if need be.

"One of these days . . . I'll kill you," the prisoner gritted from within the cell.

"Of course you will. But today, I need your bucket. And if you knock it over this time, you'll have to do without for a week. That's no fun."

The bucket—precisely the same size as the opening—came skidding out into the hall. Inanity emptied its contents into a barrel, singing a rude little song he'd learned as a boy, and returned it to the prisoner, shutting the slat with the pole and thanking his lucky stars he still had all his fingers.

Next, he visited the door of Mr. Judgmental, who cooperated as always, albeit while condemning every aspect of Inanity's person, from his appearance to his character to his inefficient method of emptying waste buckets.

Then he came to the new prisoners, whom he'd met outside the city gate the day before. Surely, these would not attack him—physically or verbally—and yet, Inanity was dreading these interactions most.

He opened the access port of the first cell and slid the steaming bowl in.

"Thank you," the gentleman said.

"You're welcome. I need your bucket."

"It's empty."

"Alright then. Have a nice— or, I guess . . . goodbye."

"Inanity?"

He hovered there, hand on the slat. "Yes?"

"Could you do me a favor?"

"No, I'm afraid I'm not allowed to—"

"Could you just tell my friend that I'm okay? Tell him Faithful's okay? That's all."

"Sure. I will."

"Thank you. And Inanity?"

"Hm?"

"You have a good day too. I'll be praying for you."

Inanity laughed, bombastically. "Oh, ha ha! I like that! Your humor is as twisted as mine, pilgrim!" He closed the port and made his way over to Christian, murmuring, "He'll pray for me. Priceless." All at once, he stopped laughing and stood there, looking down at the bowl of mush in his hand. "Thank you," he said.

That night as he brought the prisoners their evening meal, Inanity lingered at Faithful's door, the slat still open.

"What is it?" called a sympathetic voice from within.

"Well, your friend called me a 'silly halfwit' this morning."

Faithful chuckled. "Surely other prisoners have called you worse."

"Yes. Of course. But for some reason, I did not expect it from him."

"He didn't mean it. He's upset, frightened, and perhaps feeling a bit abandoned. Were I still a betting man, I'd put a few coppers down on him apologizing soon."

"Well, we'll see. Can I ask you something, Faithful?"

"Please do."

"What is it that you're so cheerful to be imprisoned for? To possibly die for? I just don't get it."

"It intrigues you, doesn't it? It even troubles you."

"No, not so much intrigues me. I find it amusing."

"Interesting word choice," Faithful said. "A-musing. 'A,' meaning *not*, and 'muse,' meaning *to think*. This whole town and its fair are set up as continual *a*-musements. They keep you from musing about things that matter. About what's worth living for, worth dying for. What's the meaning of our brief lives? If every moment is spent in amusement and fleshly gratification, you can avoid these questions. For a time."

"I have to go feed your friend."

Faithful laughed. "Well, I'm not going anywhere, if you'd like to continue our talk when you're done."

Inanity left Faithful's food port open as he tended to Christian—something he'd never done before—and then sat down next to it, his back against the solid cell door. He imagined Faithful leaning against the same spot, on the other side.

"My whole life," he said, "I've chased after the delights that are seen and sold at our fair. But I will not lie; I've always hoped there was something more to live for."

"I can relate," said Faithful. "And your hope would best find its resting place in the Celestial City, if you would move along from this place and its amusements. I'm guessing that, deep down, you already know this: not only are all these vanities useless—unable to ultimately satisfy you—but they will, in the end, drown you in perdition and destruction.

"I was once just like you, Inanity. Just like you. I delighted in reveling, drinking to excess, swearing, lying, rioting, fornicating, Sabbath-breaking, and all manner of uncleanness. All the things that scratch the itch of the flesh for the moment, even while they erode the soul."

"You are correct," Inanity said. "I do know the truth of what you say. These things which make up my life and make feel 'alive . . ' the end of them is death."

"That is the hard truth," Faithful agreed. "And for the sake of these very things, the wrath of God is coming upon the children of disobedience."

"Oh, but what's the point of this?" Inanity said. "At least I'm not locked in a cell! You have your religion and you'll die for it, but I have my freedom. And I'll go on living in it as long as I can. That's all anyone can really hope for, I suppose."

"Inanity, please consider that—"

"Enjoy your night, Faithful. I'm sure you'll have a great time here in the dungeon. I, on the other hand, have a date with a lady! I wouldn't call her 'beautiful,' per se, but she endures me, and we have a good enough time. We'll be stuffing ourselves at the tavern and taking in a raucous show at the Vanity Playhouse. But hey—I'm sure whatever you have planned will be just as fun. Ta-ta!"

When the slat closed again, Faithful lay back on the cold, hard rock and looked up into the darkness.

Are you ready to talk to me now? The voice of Wanton.

"I told you to leave me."

But you're all alone.

"Exactly. Leave me *alone*. I'd prefer solitude to your company."

He covered his ears, but remembered that he'd tried this the night before, when Wanton had hounded him so much he'd barely slept a wink. The voice, it turned out, was coming from without and within at the same time.

Just talk to me. Let me help you escape this filthy place, even if it's just for a little while. He felt her hand brush gently along his arm. He shimmied a few more feet away from her.

Wanton sat up, the moonlight glistening off her shiny hair and soft bare shoulders.

Did I do something wrong?

"I'm going to get some sleep."

I can help with that.

"How about a compromise? Do you do those?"

Of course, darling. I love compromise.

"You let me sleep, and we'll talk in the morning, okay?"

You've got a deal. She snuggled up to his side.

"No. You go away. Let me sleep in solitude. *That's* the compromise."

She sat up again, piled her hair atop her head and, through a pouty expression, said, *Fine. Be that way.*

Faithful slept well that night. He dreamt of the Celestial City and the wonders he would encounter there. When he awakened, the narrow strip of broken sunlight coming in through the small vent above was projected directly onto his eyes. Faithful rubbed them and stood, waiting for the floating shapes to dissipate.

When his vision came back into focus, he was pleasantly surprised to find himself alone. Then Wanton spoke, from behind him.

You're up. She reached around him and ran her fingers over his chest.

"I said we'd *talk* in the morning. But hey—if you're not willing to listen . . . "

I'm a great listener. You can tell me anything. Your deepest, darkest secrets.

"You stay there." He walked across the cell, leaned against the opposite wall, and regarded her for a moment. "Okay. This is what I wanted to tell you. When I was out in the midst of Vanity Fair, it was like being thrown suddenly back into my life in the City of Destruction. My old life. The place was thick with wicked men and the sort of women my father used to warn me about. He called them 'loose lasses,' which is not very kind, I suppose. But here's the point: in the midst of Vanity Fair, I had a completely new perspective. You see, after I met you by the gate, I prayed that the King would grant me the eyes of Jesus, that I would see people as *he* sees them. And out there, in the fair, I saw those women not as conquests to be had or as sinners to judge or even as temptations to be defeated. I saw them as broken, precious women, made in the image of God, and loved by him. Broken and fallen, as all of us are before we come to the Place of Deliverance. Precious, precious souls."

Wanton yawned. *Is there a point to this?*

"Indeed there is. For when I look at you, Wanton, I see none of that—only your true form. You are a reflection of my own shameful lusts, memories of my wicked past. You are the world and the flesh projected like a lantern onto the form of the enemy. Darkness masquerading as some dim, mottled light."

Wanton shook her head and began to pace around the room, quicker and quicker.

"I am disgusted by you, Wanton, because you represent all that remains in me of the old self. Wicked appetites yet to be destroyed." As she paced, Wanton began to change in appearance. Her soft, smooth shoulders fell and took on a knobby, reptilian appearance. "You are the very provision for the flesh that I have vowed to avoid." The creature's hair became stringy and sparse and its ears grew until they hung like dead fish.

"You are that sin nature, which I am bound to put to death."

Wanton was stalking frantically around the room now, a small impish creature, stooping low and emitting a rutting guttural grunt with every step. Faithful reached out his hand and caught the creature by its neck.

"And I will put an end to you," he said. He then stuffed Wanton into the waste bucket, which did not even come up to Faithful's knees. And yet, with a dozen savage stomps, he managed to crush the creature all the way down into the vessel. Just then, the slat came up and Faithful slid the bucket out into the hall.

"Good morning, Inanity," he said, cheerily.

"And to you."

"You don't sound very happy today. I take it your night was not all you'd hoped?"

Faithful's breakfast appeared, through the opening, along with a spoon.

"I'm not supposed to give you that," Inanity said. "Could be sharpened into a weapon. Please don't make me regret it."

"I won't. And I greatly appreciate it. Thank you, my friend. Now, do you want to tell me why you're so down this morning?"

"I suppose it's your fault."

"*My* fault? How?"

"Well, last night, when you said—"

"Hold on a minute," Faithful said. "I'd like to eat while we chat. I believe any distraction from this food is a good thing. No offense. Heavenly Father, thank you for this nourishment you have provided and for this kind man who has served it. And even for this spoon, a reminder that your mercies are new every morning. Through Christ my Lord and only Savior, Amen." He began to eat. "Mmm . . . It's a little better today," he said. "Did you add salt?"

"No."

"Huh. Well, then. Tell me how your bad mood is my doing?"

"You must know. You spoke last night of the emptiness of my life—something which has vexed me off and on for years. I spent the whole evening thinking of how much I love those things you call sin, how impossible it would be to part with these old companions, and how miserable I always am during seasons of conviction when they come.

"I mean, when you called the distractions and pleasures of the fair empty, I could relate. But at least that misery remains under the surface. The thoughts *you* prompted brought it up into the open. Last night was a series of troublesome and heart-affrighting hours, which I could scarcely bear."

"Well, clearly you've learned to banish these thoughts in the past. Why do you suppose they keep coming back?"

Inanity sighed. "So many things might trigger one these spells. Meeting a good man in the streets, hearing someone read the Scriptures, having a headache, learning that a neighbor has fallen ill, hearing the bell toll for a dead man (which, of course, makes me consider my own inevitable death), and especially thinking of that one fearful fact, which is indeed planted in all of us from birth: that when I die, I must quickly come to judgment."

"You must have found some mechanism of easing your conscience in the past," Faithful said, "albeit temporarily."

"No, not I. My first thoughts during hours of conviction of sin have always been to bury myself in that selfsame sin until I've completely forgotten any sense of guilt or shame. That worked for a while, but eventually . . . any thought of returning to my sin would only double my torment. And so I determined –again and again—to mend my ways so that I would not be damned."

"I see. And how did that go?"

"Well, I did flee from my sin at times. And even from sinful company, hard as that is in this place. And it might surprise you that I even gave myself to religious duties; praying, reading, weeping for sin, speaking the truth to my neighbors, and many other good deeds of various kinds."

"And did that cure what ailed you?"

"Again, for a time. But only for a time. Soon my troubles would come tumbling upon me again, burying my attempts at self-reformation. Have you never experienced this?"

"Oh, for certain I have. And it's a good thing, too. The Law is a teacher, Inanity, not a savior, and if you try to give him that role, he will assail you endlessly and mercilessly. Trust me; I know. But make him your teacher and he will show you that all your righteousness is filthy rags, that doing all the good works in the world will never save you or even profit you, and, in fact, all your self-made religion amounts only to a pile of manure in the sight of God. This is true for all of us. We can make the pile bigger, but we can't make it into anything else."

"Very encouraging," Inanity laughed.

"It is, though. Not for the flesh. But confidence in the flesh is for fools! Think of it this way: say you run a hundred pounds into the shopkeeper's debt. And then you begin paying for everything as you buy it . . . your old debt still stands uncrossed in that man's books. He could sue you for that sum and cast you into prison, unless the debt is paid."

"But if all my prayers and weeping and good deeds can't do away with that debt, how can—"

"Oy! You there!" came a thick voice from down the hall. "We don't pay you to sit and chat with the prisoners! Get on with it!"

"Yes, sir," Inanity called out. "Sorry!" He lowered his voice and said, "I'll need to be quick serving dinner tonight; I have to mop the floors upstairs. But we can talk again in the morning. Good night, Faithful."

Faithful peered out through the port in the door while Inanity stood and said, "It's been nice chatting with you, sir."

"You too," Inanity said, groaning as he straightened.

"Did you hurt your back?"

"No, I think it's just the extra prisoners. Stooping down so much to deal with bowls and buckets and the like. I just feel kind of . . . stooped over."

Faithful spent the balance of the morning reading from the Holy Book (which, in God's providence, he'd been able to spirit in, within the sleeve of his jacket) and spent the afternoon praying for wisdom and for the right words to say to Inanity when he returned. Even a few brief words exchanged during a hurried interaction might plant some good seeds.

As the time for the evening meal approached, Faithful sat cross-legged, facing the metal slat, waiting for it to rise. When it did, he was taken aback.

Another familiar voice greeted him, and this one brought a lightning bolt of alarm up his spine.

"Hello, young man. Remember me?"

"I do."

"Adam the First. I offered you a job once and—"

"I said I remember you. What do you want?"

"I want to bury the hatchet. We've had our differences, yes, but I'm content to let bygones be just that."

Faithful leaned down and peered through the opening to see the old man's wild eyes and crooked grin. "As you can see," he said, "I'm rather indisposed at the moment. Go bother someone else."

"But that's just it—just what I'm offering you. I have the key to this door. See?" He flashed a large metallic object. "And I can open it for you and help you make good your escape."

"You senile old fool. You already admitted to me that, if I went with you, you'd sell me as a slave."

"So what if I would? That would be better than dying here, no? Besides, we both know you'd be able to escape from me. Look at you: young and strong. I am old and weak. I'll help you escape and then you can get away from me whenever you want!"

Faithful thought for a moment and then came to a decision. "We have an accord," he said, and reached his hand through the port in the door.

"Good to hear," the Old Man said, and gripped the proffered hand firmly.

Faithful squeezed harder. He felt bones crunch and heard Adam the First cry out in pain, but he squeezed harder still, and wrapped his other hand around the old man's bony wrist. Then he braced his feet against the door, one on either side of the small opening, and began to pull the Old Man through. Narrow as his shoulders were, they were twice the width of that little square opening. Still, Faithful was intent on pulling this enemy in, tearing him apart.

"I told you what I'd do if we met again," Faithful shouted, feeling something give on the other side of the door. "Did you think it an idle threat?"

He dug deep, pulled with his arms and pushed with his legs, with all his might, feeling the tearing and popping he'd been waiting for. With one final pull, Faithful found himself sliding back along the floor of the cell, empty-handed. Adam the First had disappeared in a puff of sulfurous yellow smoke.

Faithful looked up again. The slat was closed. He smiled and thanked his God for this victory, knowing that he would never again have to contend with that old enemy.

The following morning, Inanity brought another gift with Faithful's breakfast: a loaf of fresh-baked bread.

"Oh, thank you," Faithful said. "You have no idea what a gift this is. You are a good friend to me, Inanity. But could I trouble you to give this half to my brother, Christian?" He broke the bread and extended half of it out through the opening.

"I'll do it," Inanity said. "For you."

"Thank you very much. Your kindness is a truly a bright light in this dark and dismal place. Now, what were we talking about yesterday, when we were so rudely interrupted?" Looking out into the hall, he saw that Inanity's burden had grown immensely and was now larger and more cumbersome than his own had ever been.

"You were saying that all human religion and reformation can do nothing to cancel the debt of our sin. Remember? Owing the shop-keep a hundred pounds and all that."

"Oh, that's right! Now that I think of it, I could have gone even further with that analogy. Because you have to admit that, even in your most serious seasons of cleaning up your act and living a good life, you certainly continued to sin. Meaning you were yet piling up *more* debt! I've been there, my friend. And I can attest that during my most successful day of self-reformation, I committed enough sins to send me to hell forever, even if my former life had been faultless."

"So it's hopeless then?"

"Hopeless? Inanity, I have a hard time imagining you *hopeless*. But where do we find hope? That's the question. The only possible way is to obtain the righteousness of another—one who never sinned."

Inanity balked. "That is . . . that is not the turn I thought this discussion would take. Is this some sort of dark magic?"

"Of course not! And if you've thought about these things, you know it's the only possible way to clear your debt, to sanctify your present, to secure your future."

"But . . . where can I find such a man? And would I not be sinning all the more to deprive him of his own well-earned righteousness?"

"Oh, that's the beautiful part, Inanity. Not only does he *want* to bestow it upon you, he has in his person enough righteousness to save every last man and woman who ever lived or ever will live, without becoming even the slightest bit less righteous himself."

"*Who?*"

"Jesus the Christ. The Prince of the Heavenly Land. He is the one who dwells at the right hand of the Most High. And by trusting in what he has done in the days of his flesh, when he suffered for us and hung on the tree, you can be justified by him."

"But how can one man's righteousness count as another man's before a just God?"

"The Lord Jesus *is* Almighty God and he did what he did and died as he died not for himself, but for you and me, so that by his sacrifice our sins would be imputed to him and his righteousness (and, with it, his worthiness) imputed to us."

"This is truly fascinating," Inanity said. "But I cannot believe that such a God would save me. I know my own heart too well. And my own past, and—"

"Please believe me, Inanity, when I tell you that I was twice the sinner you are in my day. Yet I received him. And he received me. He paid my hundred pounds, covered all my present and future debts, and gave me untold endless storehouses of treasure beyond. Go to him and see."

Inanity sniffed. "I couldn't presume to—"

"It's not presumption! You are invited to come! Here, this—*this* is your invitation." Faithful extended the small book out into the hall and felt Inanity accept it.

"Suppose I do go to him? What do I do? What do I say?"

"Approach him on your knees, with all your heart and soul. Ask the Father to reveal the Lord Jesus to you."

"Suppose he responds with wrath."

"He will not. You will find him upon a mercy-seat, where he sits all the year long, to give pardon and forgiveness to all who come. Say to him: 'God, be merciful to me, a sinner, and cause me to know Jesus Christ and to believe in him, for I see that, without him, I will be utterly cast away.' Tell him, 'Lord, I have heard that you are a merciful God and have ordained that your Son be the Savior of the whole world, and that you are willing even to bestow him upon such a poor sinner as I—for I am indeed a sinner. Lord, magnify your grace in saving my soul. Through your son, Jesus Christ. Amen.' Tell him that, and see what he does."

"I— I will try it," Inanity said.

Faithful did not sleep that night. Instead, he prayed. For Inanity. For Christian. For his own courage in the face of the final trials that were undoubtedly fast approaching. And yet, despite having no sleep, when the sunlight appeared in his room and the sound of distant birds danced in, he felt well-rested.

Inanity came to the door much earlier than usual, and seemed more dejected than Faithful had ever seen him. He was bent so low that he could peer through the meal-port without stooping any further.

"Did you do as I told you?" Faithful asked.

"Yes. Over and over, and over again."

"And did the Father reveal the Son to you?"

"He did not."

"No? But here you are, talking to me again, telling me how you did not leave off praying—but rather went to him again and again? Why?"

"Because I believe that what you told me yesterday is true—that without the righteousness of this Christ, all the world cannot save me. So I pleaded. And as I pleaded with your King, I thought to myself, 'If I leave off, I die. And I am unwilling to die anywhere but at the throne of grace.' And then I found this in the book you gave me—" he flipped to a marked page. "'For still the vision awaits its appointed time; it hastens to the end—it will not lie. If it seems slow, wait for it; it will surely come; it will not delay.'"

"And so you will continue to beseech him."

"If it takes a thousand years, as long as I am still—"

"Open the door, Inanity!" came a gruff voice from out in the hall. "It's time to rid our city of these intolerant fanatics!"

Inanity watched the trial from the balcony of the courthouse. He was tied up in knots, anticipating the moment when the judge would call for any witnesses to speak on behalf of the accused. When that happened, he knew he would have to respond. He also knew what this would mean for him; he'd seen the abuses heaped upon the men and women who'd dared to speak up for the pilgrims outside the guard house. Still, he was willing to endure that for Faithful.

But the call for sympathetic witnesses never came.

Before Inanity knew what was happening, the crowd had dragged good Faithful out into the fairgrounds and was beating him mercilessly.

Helpless, Inanity could only look on, his heart breaking, thinking that if Faithful only looked his way, he would no longer find it hard to imagine this light-hearted man utterly hopeless.

Someone pulled the embroidered jacket from the pilgrim and tossed it aside, disdainfully, as if it might infect him with the odious convictions of its owner. The mantle landed at Inanity's feet. Already bent down by the weight on his back, he picked it up and held it close to his chest.

Faithful was enduring the flogging with a stoutheartedness Inanity had only read about in poems and epics. The blows came one on top of another and the blood flowed freely. Still, Faithful did not cry out. Inanity, however, could take no more and withdrew, back to his secret spot—a wooded area where he often went to be alone and play his whistle during breaks from work.

Gripping the coat, he fell to his knees and cried out in his spirit, "Father, I come to you again. Show me the Son! Give me what Faithful has, even if it means giving me a death like his! Just . . . show me Jesus."

And then it happened.

He did not see the Lord with his bodily eyes, but with the eyes of faith, of understanding. The eyes of his soul.

He saw Jesus looking down from heaven upon him, saying, *Believe on me and you will be saved.*

"I will believe, Lord," he answered. "But I am a great, a very great sinner."

The Lord responded, *My grace is sufficient for you.*

"But Lord, what is 'believing?' What do you require?"

Hear these words and understand: he that comes to me will never hunger and he that believes on me shall never thirst.

Inanity stood. "I do see. I see that believing in you and coming to you are the very same thing. That my heart and my affections running after your salvation is indeed me believing on you. But, Lord, I still struggle to believe that you will accept such a great sinner as I am."

He that comes to me, I will in no way cast out. I went into the world to save sinners, even the chief of sinners. I died for your sins and rose for your justification. I came to love you, to wash away your iniquity by my own blood.

"Yes. I see it now," Inanity said, tears streaming down his face. "Satisfaction for my transgressions can only be found in your blood. I see it so clearly. Righteousness can be found in no one else."

Inanity realized that the tears he'd grown so accustomed to shedding when he thought of spiritual things were now tears of joy, not of sorrow or hopelessness.

Then he became aware of a rushing sound behind him and the heat of a great fire. Turning, he saw a fiery horse and chariot, being driven by a great Shining One. And at his side, Faithful, smiling and extending his hand to Inanity. "Come," he said.

"Am I going with you to the Celestial City? Already?"

"Not just yet," the Shining One said. "We'll be making a special stop for you."

As he stepped up onto the chariot, Inanity held the embroidered coat out to Faithful and said, "I kept this safe for you."

"Keep it," Faithful said with a wink. "Oh, and you'll probably want to hang on." With a woosh, they took off at a frightful pace. Inanity saw cities and forests and rivers fly by, and then it all became a blur as they travelled he-knew-not-where with supernatural speed. Just as quickly, they came to a stop.

Faithful embraced his friend for the first and last time, and said, "I will see you again. In the Celestial City. For now, what you seek is at the top of this hill. You know what you will find; go there straight-away. Godspeed."

Inanity stepped off the chariot and when he turned to wave goodbye, it was already gone. A road stretched out before him, walled in on both sides.

"Well, onward and upward," he said, and began to move quickly up the incline. The growing weight on his back had become excruciating over the past few hours, but Inanity put the pain out of mind and pushed ahead, step by step along the road as it grew both steeper and narrower.

Within an hour, he reached a leveling, where the road curved, bringing him to the mouth of a rock-hewn tomb. He leaned in, hoping to see the risen Lord here, but instead he heard the words of the book in his head:

> *He is not here. He is risen!*
> *Go . . . on the mount you will meet him.*

Running now, he resumed his climb up toward the summit of the hill, where he could now see a large wooden cross. Suddenly, he stopped his ascent. Something was different. He stood straight and felt his spine decompress. The crushing weight was gone!

Again he ran until he reached the cross and fell down at its foot, praising the Lord who died there for him. He kissed the cross again and again as the tears flowed.

"Peace be with you." He wheeled to see three Shining Ones approaching. One of them he recognized.

"Back so soon?" he said with a smile.

"Your friend is safe in the Celestial City, happier than he

has ever been on this earth. But we are here now to attend to you." He raised a hand and said, "You are a new creation. No longer will you be known by your fleshly name. Instead, you will be called Hopeful."

"Hopeful," he repeated.

"And know, Hopeful—truly *know*—that all your sins are forgiven."

Another Shining One came forth and pulled the cap from his head. He then undressed him of the filth-stained work clothes he wore and dressed him in clean, new garments. Then, taking the embroidered coat from Hopeful's hand, he helped him put it on.

"It fits perfectly," the pilgrim marveled.

The third approached him and placed a mark on his forehead and a scroll in his hand with a seal upon it. "Keep this close to you at all times," he instructed. "Look upon it for comfort as you travel and present it at the Celestial Gate."

Hopeful stayed at that place for hours, praising God for his goodness and mercy and power and holiness. It was nearly midnight when it sunk in that he had no idea where exactly he was or how to get back home, much less in the dark. But he'd left his duties undone. Men were going hungry because of him.

"I suppose I should just continue along the Narrow Way," he said to himself, and began to descend the hill. Within ten minutes, he recognized the terrain. It was the lazy descent into Vanity Fair, on the north end of town. He could have traversed it blindfolded.

As the lamps and fires and the glow of tents came into view below, it occurred to Hopeful all at once what his next move must be. That man Christian was almost certainly back in his cell, destined to die just as Faithful had.

Hopeful could not let that happen.

He circled around to the courthouse, dark and empty, and, using his key, slipped in the front door. By feel and memory, he made his way to the storeroom beside the judge's chambers and let himself in. A few fireworks exploded outside and, by their light, Hopeful saw what he was looking for: Christian's sword. He grabbed it and turned to leave.

"Who goes there?" a man growled. "Show yourself!" He held a lamp out over his head, spilling light onto a hate-filled face.

Hopeful sighed. Of all the guards, this was the last man he wanted to deal with. He took a dep breath and came out into the light.

"You?" the man said. "You're a little late with the evening meal, aren't ya? You should have heard Carnal Fury going on and on about it. You'd think he— Wait . . . what are you wearing? Is that the coat we pulled off the prisoner today?"

Hopeful swallowed hard. "Yes, it is."

The guard stared at him for a long moment, then burst out in howling laughter. "Oh, that is good! I needed that tonight. I can always count on you to make me laugh. Oh, Inanity . . . "

"That's not my name anymore," he said. "And I do not wear this garment as a joke. I have been bought by the blood of the Lord Jesus and I belong to him."

The courthouse shook violently, throwing Hopeful to the ground and sending the guard lurching forward, off-balance, tripping over Hopeful and sprawling into the storeroom. The earth still rumbling, Hopeful pulled himself awkwardly to his feet, slammed the storeroom door, and locked it, leaving his key in the door.

A massive statue of Lord Self-Love, the first man to serve as judge in Vanity, came crashing down. Hopeful leapt out of the way just in time, and the statue slammed against the storeroom door. An aftershock arose and subsided. Hopeful heard shouts from behind the door, along with the rattling of keys, but it would have taken ten men to dislodge that statue.

"Sorry," Hopeful called out. "Truly, I am. I'm sure someone

will help you out in the morning. Sleep well." Hopeful rushed down the back steps to the dungeon, only to find the door to Christian's cell standing wide open and the room empty.

A rescue now unnecessary, Hopeful's plans evolved.

"He can't have gotten far," he thought as he rushed up the stairs and out into the night. He stood on the courtroom steps and gazed out into Vanity Fair, his eyes peeled for his fellow pilgrim.

- Letters from the Road -

Christiana returned from the market to find yet another letter snugged between door and frame, tied with a blue ribbon. This particular shade of pale blue was her favorite color, something which Christian had used to undiminishing returns during their courtship, as each note of love, each sonnet and song he wrote for her, was carefully tied with just this color of ribbon — possibly from the very same spool as the piece she now untied. Before opening the folded page, however, she unloaded the produce she'd just bought onto the board in her kitchen, and washed each piece. She'd been prepared to go and fill the basin with clean water, but that had already been done.

This was not the first time that a kind and helpful act had seemed to mysteriously carry itself out lately. Broken items were mended, dishes washed, firewood chopped and stacked. Christiana had first assumed this was the doing of her eldest, Matthew, who was very keen to take on adult roles of late, but he had denied it.

Then the letters began to arrive and she had put the two together. While he was on a journey of his own — on his own — Christian yet provided for them in every way, and far more attentively than he had before he'd left. It was an intriguing mystery to Christiana and, if she was honest with herself, it had begun to break down the barriers she'd erected between herself and the idea of pilgrimage.

When she had finished preparing the produce (and had

mentally rehearsed the ingredients needed for tonight's dinner, confirming they were all in place), she retired to the parlor, where she sat and opened the letter.

My Dearest Christiana,

Greetings, from the Pilgrim Road.

All is well at present. Although I have recently faced great trials, my King has seen me through, and my new companion, Hopeful, has been a great comfort.

Still, I miss you greatly. You are on my mind every day. Every hour. In fact, it would not be much of an exaggeration to say that there is never a time when you are not in my thoughts—if not always in the center of them, you are never far off. I thank God every day for you and for our lovely boys, who are growing into good and reliable men.

My one prayer, though, for all of you, is that you would join me on the Narrow Road. I would love to share this journey with you. In fact, I want nothing more than to see you making progress, as I am, along the Narrow Way. Indeed, I myself would stay behind in Destruction and perish in the flames if it meant you and our boys travelling the road to the Celestial City.

Please consider this an invitation to walk beside me once again. We've been through a lot during our lives together, but this last journey would be more meaningful and more rewarding than all that came before it. Grace and peace to you.

All my love,
Christian

She set the letter on a low table and dabbed her eyes with a handkerchief, reminding herself to hide the letter away before the children could see it. This simple page would join a dozen others in a keepsake box beside her bed, and the small piece of ribbon she would tie into her hair with all the others—a way of keeping her husband close without raising difficult questions from her neighbors.

With each new letter, Christiana felt herself drawn that much more to this "Wicket Gate" her husband spoke of so fondly. And yet, even as she felt the mysterious pull of that place and the promises Christian had conveyed, there was

something holding her back—like a chain, which could not be broken even if the pull she now felt were increased a hundredfold.

Tears began to flow more freely—an odd intermingling of gratitude, longing, and frustration. The sound of her sons, James and Samuel, laughing as they ran past the house, snatched her back from the sorrow she felt. She dried her eyes and walled off the pain.

Looking down at the letter, she could see it now as the very culprit of her tears. She marched into the bedroom and stuffed the page into the box, which she lightly kicked, sending it skidding deeper beneath the bed.

Glancing up, she caught her reflection in their looking glass. She looked tired and spent, and she reminded herself that this was Christian's fault. He had left her in this impossible position. The pool of tenderness which had been forming in her bosom hardened. "No," she thought, "I did not marry a pilgrim and I never agreed to leave behind everything I've ever known or loved, to follow him on a fool's errand."

She caught her own eye in the glass and felt as though she looked away first, heading off to the kitchen to get an early start on dinner—something to occupy her thoughts.

As she walked, she was oblivious to the two ill-favored ones flanking her, moving deftly with her, petting her head, hardening her heart, whispering poison into her soul.

Lucre

Demas stood at the craggy apex of Hill Lucre with the posture and poise of a gentleman. He wore a wire collar with lace trim atop slashed doublet and sleeves. Despite the heat, he did not fan himself nor make any other such fuss—only stood tall beneath the wide brim of his hat, which he had pinned up on the right side, rather than the left, so as to provide some protection from the sun, hovering in that quadrant of the sky. This was his only gaffe, in fashion or bearing, and Demas was quite sure no one would take any notice of it.

The gorge of the enormous mine to his back, he gazed out intently upon the Narrow Road and felt a surge of excitement—like the crackling of gunpowder up his spine—as two young pilgrims came into view around the bend, engrossed in conversation with one another. He guessed them to be husband and wife, which pleased him all the more.

As they drew nearer, the two of them seemed to notice the silhouette of the gentleman in the wide-brimmed hat at the same time, peering curiously and pointing up toward him.

"Ho! Turn aside!" Demas called.

"For what?" the man called back. "Are you hurt, sir? Are you stuck up there?"

"Not at all! I am in good health, good spirits, and much wealth. And I am as free as any free man can be!" He raised his arms above his head and drew in a deep breath. "Come up here and I will show you something wondrous, which will leave you both in the very same state as I!"

"It's a bit of a climb," the woman said, "and we are tired. What will we see?"

"A vast silver mine," Demas answered, "and a few people digging in it for treasure, to great effect. Believe me, dear woman, for very little work you and your husband may find yourselves quite rich when you resume the road!"

He could half-hear them conferring below—not taking in every word, but getting the broad strokes: that these travelers were overdue for a rest at any rate, and that both were content to add some profit to their respite. They came up the steep rocky ascent with no little difficulty and came to stand precariously beside Demas, who turned and gestured broadly at the mine with a grand flourish as if he were, in that moment, bringing it into existence.

The two pilgrims gaped at the deep, sunken pit, which gaped back all the more. Drifts and shafts could be seen here and there, blocked off by single ropes stretched across. Apart from that, all was still.

"Has much silver been found?" the man asked. "It looks abandoned."

"Oh, a veritable treasure. Even today, much has been recovered. You can see piles of the stuff gathered against the nearest wall here, just below our feet. See for yourself, but be careful."

The two travelers glanced at each other, their eyes dancing with the promise of easy wealth, then leaned precariously over the edge, eyes searching.

"I don't see anything," the man said. He shuffled a bit closer to the ledge. "Wait—maybe . . . "

"Oh, it's down there," Demas said.

Suddenly, the man flailed, flapping his arms frantically like a bird, dangling out over the deadly expanse for a panicked, breathless moment, before recovering his balance and taking a long step back from the edge.

"That was a close one," he wheezed, wiping his brow.

"Ahhh, but you saw, did you not? The gleaming silver?"

"No, I saw nothing that shimmers. I'll take your word for it, though."

Demas frowned. "I see. Perhaps you're a bit too timid for this work. That's fine. Easy as it is, it's not for everyone. And, of course, the Celestial City awaits! Tell me, would you two like some tea before you head off on your way? My name is Demas, by the way, and I am a fellow pilgrim, at your service."

"Pleased to meet you. I'm Mr. Go-Along, and this is my wife, Cupidity." Turning to her, the man said, "And now, my little cupid, perhaps we should scale back down and have a proper, um . . . Oh dear, please don't stand so close to the edge."

"I can see it," she said. "I see the silver."

"Please, dear. Come back just a—"

A shriek and the sound of sliding rock, and she was gone.

"*Noooo!*" Go-Along shouted, reaching out after her. He flailed once again, arms grasping at nothing, his balance shifting out toward the chasm. Demas grabbed the back of his coat and held him firmly, stretched out over the pit, gazing down at the mountain of corpses below.

An involuntary wave of relief washed visibly over the man, swallowed immediately by renewed shock and sorrow. "Oh, my little cupid," he sobbed. "What did you do?"

"My heart breaks for you," Demas said. "In fact, I wouldn't be able to live with myself if I didn't reunite you two."

He released his hold on the coat and watched Mr. Go-Along fall to his death. Demas looked down at his latest victims and issued a dark, self-satisfied chuckle before turning his gaze back out toward the road, waiting patiently for more pilgrims to happen by.

As Great-Heart had instructed, Christian and Hopeful walked through the night, speaking all the while in thin whispers. As they travelled, Hopeful related the events which had led him up to the place of Deliverance—Faithful being so kind and patient, so forgiving yet unyielding, that Hopeful had been able to simply follow him, a step at a time, up to the cross of Christ, as it were.

As they spoke of Faithful, both men broke down more than once. They were overwhelmed with sorrow at each thought or mention of their departed friend. Knowing that the brave pilgrim was even now safe and happy in the Celestial City, while they yet made their way down this dark and dangerous road, enemies at their back and tribulation ahead of them, was some comfort to their souls—but not enough to quell their tears.

Ashamed at the memory of his own ill treatment of the dungeon-servant-turned-servant-of-the-Great-King, and convicted by the tales of Faithful's kindness, Christian halted his steps, gripped his new friend by the shoulders (tightly enough to raise an alarm in the man's eyes), and pleaded, "Oh Hopeful, please forgive me. I should have been doing exactly as my companion was—filling your ears with the Good News of our King and showing gratitude for every meal and every service you provided. My words and my actions, to say nothing of my heart, were not worthy of the One I serve. The One *we* serve."

"There is nothing to forgive," Hopeful said with a smile. "And don't sell yourself short; my journey to that holy hill began on the day you two entered our town, as I watched you and Faithful both endure abuse with such courage and grace as I had never seen before. The both of you sowed seeds. Faithful watered them. And God caused them to burst forth from the soil. I am grateful to all of you. And I trust that you will help in pruning and watering all the more, so that God might bear great fruit through my life!"

They resumed walking as the sun now broke forth above the horizon, beginning in earnest a new day for these blessed pilgrims.

"And it wasn't just me, you know," Hopeful said.

"Pardon?"

"It wasn't just me who watched in awe as you and our brother bore witness with unmatched confidence, willing even to face death for your King if need be. These past few days, there has been increasing talk among fairgoers about this King and his country and the Narrow Way. We may have left that place only two, but there will be many more people of Vanity who will take their time and follow after us."

"I pray you are right," Christian said. "I can think of no better tribute to Faithful's witness than for his blood to bring forth a harvest of souls."

They stopped briefly for breakfast—some cold meat and cheeses and dried fruit, which Hopeful had brought with him—and then resumed their progress, now swapping tales of their youth and the towns of their origin. Before long, they came to a surprising conclusion: while the average citizen of Vanity or Destruction would laugh at the idea that these two towns had more than the most superficial things in common, from a pilgrim's perspective they were practically the same place. Each was set firmly, in its own way, on keeping its population from moving on along the Narrow Road. They were prisons without bars or guards, but prisons all the same.

It was mid-morning when they came upon two well-dressed men making their way up the path at a leisurely pace.

"Hello," Hopeful called, cheerfully. "How are you gentlemen this fine day?"

"Quite well," the two said in unison, then looked at each other and burst out laughing.

"I assume," said Hopeful, "that, like us, you two men are on pilgrimage to the Celestial City?"

"We are indeed," said the taller of the two. Both wore expensive wigs and boots, crafted more to impress society types than for comfort in travel. "We have come from the town of Fair Speech," the tall one said. The other man busied himself counting coins, one at a time, and replacing them in his purse.

"Fair Speech?" Christian repeated. "Does anything good live there?"

"Touché. But remember, that's just what they said of our Lord, is it not? That nothing good can come from his hometown. Careful with such generalities."

"I was thinking of the proverb found in Scripture," Christian answered. "'Believe not the man of Fair Speech, for there are seven abominations in his heart.'"

The man with the coins chuckled. "Only seven?"

"What's your name?" Christian asked.

"Well, at present, I am a stranger to you. But if we're going the same way, perhaps we could get to know each other along this road."

"That suits us," said Hopeful. "I've actually heard some good things about your town, sir. They say it's a very wealthy place."

"So it is. I do all right myself, and I have many rich friends and kinfolk there." He nudged his fellow and said, "including this gentleman, Mr. Money-Love."

His companion sneered and grumbled, "Curse you, By-Ends, I've lost count now and must start over." He fished the coins from his purse.

"Who are some of these relations of yours, if you don't mind my asking?" Christian said. "Perhaps I've heard of them if they're as prominent as you say."

"Almost the whole town is related to me in some way. Let's see, there's my Lord Turn-About, Lord Time-Server, Lord Fair Speech, from whose ancestors the town first took its name. Not to mention Rev. Two-Tongues, the parson of the Pleasant Chapel, our local church. He's my uncle. A well-respected man."

"Sounds like you come from very good stock," Hopeful said.

"Yes and no," the man replied. "I have become a gentleman of some quality, yes, but my great grandfather spent his life looking one way and rowing another."

"He was a waterman?" Hopeful said.

"Indeed. And I got most of my estate by the same occupation."

"Nothing wrong with that," Christian said. "Are you married?"

"Yes indeed. And my wife is a very virtuous woman, and the daughter of a virtuous woman—one Lady Feigning. Perhaps you've heard of her. I very much 'married up,' as the say. My wife is the apex of breeding, and yet she can consort with prince and peasant alike."

"And you serve the King who rules these lands and sets his throne in the Celestial City?" The words came out more like a challenge than Christian had intended.

"Well, yes. In our way. Our religion does differ from those of the stricter sort in a couple of small points."

"Such as?"

"First, we never strive against wind and tide. That is the core of our creed. *Never strive against wind or tide*—has a certain ring to it, doesn't it? Secondly, our zeal grows in relation to the approval of men. I know it sounds odd to just come out and say it, but in Fair Speech, we believe in simply putting it out there: we are most devoted and fervent in our faith when the sun shines upon it. Most men live this way; we simply own it. When the multitudes applaud Religion himself—when he goes out in his silver slippers—then we proudly walk in his train."

Mr. Money-Love, seemingly satisfied with his sum, returned the purse to his belt and said, "By-Ends, I wonder that he we haven't yet caught up to the others. Might we have passed them?"

"By-Ends?" Christian interjected. "You're Mr. By-Ends of

Fair Speech? I believe I've heard of you."

The man rolled his eyes. "That's not my real name. Rather, it is a silly nickname given to me by some who cannot abide me—" he shot a look of reproof at Money-Love—"and I, being kind-hearted and patient, must content to bear it, as a reproach. Just as other good men before me have borne similar names."

"Your friends gave you this name, you say?" Christian asked.

"Yes, and I catch your meaning. I suppose I should think of it as just some good-natured ribbing."

"Actually, I was thinking, who knows a man better than his friends? And I was wondering if you'd ever considered why those who know you best might have named you after selfish motives? Has your behavior invited such a name?"

Mr. By-Ends scoffed heavily, overselling it. "Never! No, not ever! If anything, I've simply been lucky—lucky enough to always jump in with the present way of things, and, therefore, to make the most profitable move in a given moment. Quite by chance, I've found my fortune swelling of late and, well, I choose to see it as a blessing, rather than focus on the jealousy of my so-called friends." With a crooked smile and a wink, he added in a stage whisper, "Especially those who spend their time counting and re-counting the same thirty coins."

Hopeful frowned. "It seems to me that your nickname may suit you more than you think."

Mr. By-Ends chuckled. "Well, I can't help how it seems to *you*. But I am still willing to go along with you until we find the rest of our party." He shielded his eyes against the sun and peered off into the distance. "They went ahead to see if there was some finer food to be had along this stretch . . . "

"You may certainly walk with us if you like," Christian said, "but you will have to go against wind and tide to do it, which of course goes against your creed. And you must own Religion when he is in rags or bound in irons, as well as when he wears silver slippers. And you must not abandon him when the crowd leaves off applauding, and instead mocks and reviles him."

By-Ends belched out a haughty, superior laugh and said, "Oh, I *must*? Do not presume to impose your views on me, sir. Who are you to lord it over my faith? Leave me to my liberty and let us simply walk together."

Christian came to a sudden stop and grabbed Hopeful by the elbow, pulling him back as well. "Not another step unless you agree to my conditions. We have no fellowship with the sort of fair-weather faith that you propound."

"Well then," said By-Ends, "we will part ways, for I am unwilling to desert my old principles, which are as harmless as they are profitable." He turned to his companion and said, "Double-time, Money-Love. Let us catch up to our countrymen and have some civilized company."

The two men hurried on, growing stiff and tired, for they were unused to exerting themselves. But within the space of an hour, they came upon Mr. Save-All and Mr. Hold-the-World, both of whom greeted them triumphantly, waving fresh-baked bread and a few small wedges of parmesan. "Gentlemen!" Save-All announced, "the hunt was a success!"

Mr. By-Ends accepted some bread and cheese, and began to nibble them as they continued on.

"Well, look at this fellow," Save-All said. "We locate the finest food this road has ever seen and he looks like we've force-fed him sour grapes! What's got you down, By-Ends?"

"Well, it's just—may I ask you gentlemen something?" They all grunted their ascent. "How long have we known each other?"

"Since boyhood, boy-o," Mr. Hold-the-World answered. "Schoolmates at the great Lovegain Academy in Coveting County. Under that dreadful Master Gripeman. I can still sing the school song if you like!"

"Spare us," said By-Ends.

"I wouldn't call Gripeman dreadful," Mr. Money-Love put in. "He did teach us the Art of Getting in all its forms: either by violence, deception, flattering, lying, or even using the guise of piety. It was a comprehensive education, no doubt."

"Agreed," said By-Ends, "I would drink to the health of Mr. Gripeman any day. I believe he taught us well enough that any one of us could open such a school if we so desired."

"Yes, yes," said Save-All. "But why all this nostalgia? Are you homesick already, By-Ends?"

"No, it's these gentlemen we encountered along the way. Far countrymen. They were so rigid and so in love with their own notions, and clearly thought so little of the opinions of others, that even an exceedingly godly man, if he does not jump with them on all things, finds himself thrust quite out of their company."

"He means himself," Money-Love said.

"And you as well."

Money-Love shrugged. "Honestly, I was hoping for an out. They seemed a bit dour and overly serious for my tastes."

"I've read about such men," said Save-All. "Excessively religious and overly rigid, condemning all but themselves. Sadly, they are all too common on this road. I'd rather hoped we were past that, as a civilized people. But they remain still. I assume these men had you feeling like your religion was worth less than theirs. If not worthless altogether."

"They tried at least."

"Tell me," said Save-All, "where exactly did their religion differ from ours?"

By-Ends thought for a moment. "From what I gathered, they see it as the duty of all pilgrims to rush ahead through any weather in a headstrong manner, rather than waiting for wind and tide. For, of course we never strive against wind or tide."

All the men clucked in agreement.

"But these two insist on hazarding all for God and Gospel, while level-headed gentlemen like us take every advantage to secure life and estate, even while holding religion in high esteem. But what troubled me most is the way they would hold fast to their beliefs, though everyone be against them, without a thought to the times or even to their own safety!"

"Not to mention," said Mr. Money-Love, "that they are for religion in rags and contempt! They said as much!" He laughed grandiloquently.

"So these men are fools," said Mr. Hold-the-World. "They have the liberty to keep what they hold, but are stupid enough to lose it! We, on the other hand, are wise as serpents . . . just as the Good Book says. We are clever enough to make hay while the sun shines, just as the Good Book says. And for my part, I'll take my religion with the security of God's blessings; after all, he has seen fit to give us the good things of this life," he hoisted what remained of his cheese wedge, "so he must want us to go on enjoying them for his sake!"

Mr. Save-All nodded vigorously. "Right you are. And this is the natural way of things. Have you noticed how the bee lies dormant in the winter and only stirs when she can have profit and pleasure . . . "

"As the Good Book says!" Hold-the-World interjected.

"I'm not sure these are all from the Good Book. But, all the same, God has given us this great example in nature, as well as the examples of Abraham and Solomon, who grew rich through religion. And, yes, Mr. Hold-the-World, those men *are* from the Good Book. As is Job, who calls it good for men to store up gold as dust. Do you suppose the two pilgrims behind us have ever even read about these holy men?"

By-Ends shook his head, sadly. "I wish I'd thought of half of this when I was speaking to them. It irks me no end that we have both Scripture and Reason on our side, and yet these men still thought to critique our religion, simply for being tolerant of the times and for valuing liberty and safety."

"I'll tell you what I would ask those two narrow-minded dogmatists if they were here," Mr. Save-All said. "I'd say this: suppose a man (be he a tradesman or a minister of religion or whatever the case—it doesn't matter)—suppose he learns about a possible advantage to his situation, which he might lay hold of, but only by appearing to be quite zealous in certain points of religion—points in which he had never really meddled before. May he not use these means to attain this end and still be an honest man?"

"Oooh, is that a trap?" By-Ends asked.

"Trap or not," Mr. Money-Love said, "the answer is obvious. Let's suppose the man *is* a minister. And suppose he is a worthy man, but has only a very small parish and has his eye on a much larger church with far greater honors and a plumper purse to boot. And suppose that, by being more studious, preaching more frequently and fervently, and perhaps altering some of his own principles, he can attain this goal. I say he can *and should* do so. And here are my reasons:

"First, his desire is lawful. This cannot be contradicted, since the opportunity was set before him by God's own providence. His conscience is therefore clear concerning his new appointment. Secondly, if his desire to climb the lattice makes him more studious, more zealous in his preaching, and all the rest, it therefore makes him a better man. This must be in keeping with the mind of God, who desires all of us to become better men."

"Hear! Hear!" they all agreed.

"'But,' some might say, 'is it not a sin to abandon one's principles for gain?' On the contrary, was it not the Great Prince of the Heavenly Land who told us to deny ourselves? Is that not what such a minister would be doing? And what can go wrong with adopting a sweet and winning demeanor? I would argue that all this makes him more, not less, fit for his ordained position."

"Oh, you are on a streak, my friend!" said By-Ends. "Now do the tradesman!"

Money-Love thought for just a moment and said, "Suppose this tradesman is just barely scraping by. And he determines that, by becoming quite religious, he might mend his market and gain far better customers in his shop. This could, in turn, lead to a rich wife and a life of relative ease. I find no problems whatsoever in such a course of action. And I'll tell you why."

He rolled up his sleeves while the others shouted, "Tell us!"

"First off, to become religious is a virtue. It does not matter *why* he becomes virtuous; the end is the same! Secondly, it is not unlawful to gain more customers or to marry a rich wife. And thirdly, it's all good! Here's what I mean by that: he gains what is good by means that are good, by becoming good himself! What is not good in this equation? A good wife, good customers, good profits, all by becoming religious, which is itself good! Can anyone object to all this goodness and still consider himself good? I think not."

The men of Fair Speech clapped Money-Love on the back and praised his intellect and rhetoric. Then By-Ends folded his arms and glowered. "Where was all that verbal dexterity when we were walking alongside those men?"

Money-Love shrugged. "I didn't know you felt so strongly about them."

Save-All nudged Mr. By-Ends and whispered. "But look!

Coming up behind us now—is this not them? Let's have a return match and show these men that the religion of Fair Speech is not to be slandered."

"Ho there!" Mr. Hold-the-World called back toward the two pilgrims. "May we walk and talk with you?"

As they approached, Christian's eyes passed from Money-Love to By-Ends to the two newcomers. "Talk about what?" he asked, walking past them.

The men of Fair Speech picked up the pace and drew up alongside. "I am Mr. Hold-the-World and this is Mr. Save-All. And I believe you've met our two friends."

"We have," Christian said. "But we found that, while we may be in the same place at the same time, we are not truly walking the same road. So we decided to part ways."

"So they said. And that is what I would like to understand. Could I pose to you a question, which we were just now discussing as we walked along the path? I think your answer could be eye-opening for all of us."

"Let's hear it," Christian said.

Hold-the-World took a deep breath and carefully crafted the question. "Suppose a minister or a tradesman learns about a possible promotion to a higher station, which he might achieve by appearing to be far more zealous in certain areas of religion, which he had up to that point neglected. May he use these means to attain this end and still be an honest and upright man?" He raised his eyebrows and grinned at the pilgrims.

Christian glanced at Hopeful and rolled his eyes. "That's it? Even a babe in religion could answer ten thousand such questions."

"I would hear your answer to just this one," Hold-the-World said.

"If you will hear it, then listen carefully. In his earthly ministry, the Lord Jesus rebuked the crowds who followed him for loaves and fish. Is it not far viler to make of him and of true religion a Trojan Horse to acquire and enjoy the things of this world? It is the height of wickedness. Only heathens, hypocrites, wizards, and devils would dare deny it."

"I think you've tipped your hand and given me the trick," said Hold-the-World. "To try and refute me by saying that only rogues and devils and such share my opinion—without giving specifics—is as good as admitting defeat!"

"Oh, you'd like specifics! Alright, let's begin with a specific heathen. Are you familiar with Shechem, who wanted to gain the daughters and cattle of Jacob and so offered to adopt the mark of Israel's covenant? I'm sure you remember the story from the writings of Moses; it did not go well for him or for his subjects."

By-Ends half-raised his hand. "I don't know that I've read the passage in question."

"Well," Christian said, "After taking Jacob's daughter by force, the wicked Prince Shechem tried to erase his crimes by proposing marriage to her, even offering to circumcise himself and to command all of his men to do the same, in order to appease her brothers. The sons of Jacob accepted this offer. Then, on the third day, when they were all at their sorest—" Every man grimaced and took a few smaller steps—"on that day, all of Jacob's sons rushed into the city and killed every last man to avenge the honor of their sister. This is the fruit of the heathen who would try to use true religion for gain." He furrowed his brow in thought as he walked. "Let's see . . . what was next? Heathens . . . "

"Hypocrites," Hopeful supplied. "And I can fill that one in. The hypocritical Pharisees were also of the same sort of religion. They postured with long prayers and showy piety, but with the goal of devouring widow's houses to their own gain. And this brought all the greater damnation from God. Our Lord Jesus himself declared seven woes against them for such things."

"Absolutely," Christian said. "Then there are the devils. Of course, Judas himself was filled with the devil. He followed Jesus so he could hold the money bag and skim for himself what he would. But ultimately, he was lost forever, the son of perdition. But at least he gained those thirty cursed pieces of silver." He glanced at Money-Love.

"But you said wizards," Save-All said. "Surely you misspoke."

"Not a bit. Simon the Wizard was of the same religion, which you celebrate in Fair Speech. The physician Luke recounts this sorcerer's tale in his chronicles of the Holy Apostles. This man tried to buy the gifts of the Holy Ghost, as if the third person of the Blessed Trinity might turn him a profit like a trained monkey in the street. But Peter, the Rock, rebuked him, saying, 'May your money perish with you!'

"And know this: any man who will take up religion for the world will throw it away just as quickly, for the world. That is what Judas did. He followed the Lord for gain and he sold his Master for the same. And so, for anyone to answer your question in the affirmative is heathenish, hypocritical, superstitious, and devilish. And his reward will be according to his works."

The four men of Fair Speech stared at Christian, slack-jawed, none offering a response. After an awkward moment, he wished them good day and he and Hopeful continued on their way, By-Ends and company falling back a hundred yards or so.

Christian turned to Hopeful and said, "If these so-called pilgrims cannot stand before the sentence of men, what will they do with the sentence of God? And if they fall silent when dealing with vessels of clay like you and me, what will they do when rebuked by the flames of devouring fire?" He fell silent himself for a moment and studied the ground in thought.

Hopeful put a hand on his shoulder. "Are you alright, Christian?"

"I . . . I am just missing Faithful. He would have shown us perhaps a better way—a kinder way—to engage these fellows and bring the truth to bear. In the end, it does break my heart that they are so lost, even while they believe themselves bound for the Celestial City."

"I fear that whole town is lost, right down to the parson of their local church," said Hopeful. "In Vanity, everyone spoke highly of the town of Fair Speech. It was considered sophisticated and quite clever how they would wear the outward trappings of religion when it suited them, while each man was secretly a rioter and a rake. In fact, on their city's banner is written their true motto: 'Do what thou wilt.' That is the sum of their law. Beneath the veneer of their devotion is much drinking, wenching, and banqueting. This is celebrated in Vanity Fair, but cannot be championed by a true pilgrim, on the Way."

"'Do what thou wilt?' Really?" Christian's head hung low. "That is written on the flags of Beelzebub's kingdom."

"Aye. And it flies over the chapel in Fair Speech, right next to the steeple."

Just then, they rounded a bend and saw a high, jutting hill ahead of them and a man standing at its peak, waving for them to come up.

"Ho! Turn aside!" he shouted.

"To what end?" asked Hopeful.

"I will show you something amazing!"

Christian frowned. "What is so amazing that we would

want to turn out of the Way to see it?"

"Why, it's a silver mine, and a few people digging in it for treasure, with great results. If you will but come up here, with very little effort you men can become very wealthy."

"I've never seen a silver mine," Hopeful said. "Let's go have a look!"

"That would be unwise, my friend. I have heard of this place. Many have been slain here. Others have been broken and maimed so that, to their dying day, they could never be their own men again. The treasure of which he speaks is a snare to those who seek it, holding them back from their pilgrimage."

"What are you fellows talking about down there?" called the gentlemen. "Deciding how you'll spend your fortune?"

"Is that place not dangerous?" Hopeful asked.

"Only to careless folks. Come up and see for yourself!"

Christian strode up to the foot of the rocky hill and said, "Demas, you are an enemy of the Lord of this road and of all who walk along it. You have already been condemned for turning aside, and now you want nothing but to turn others to the same condemnation!"

"You have me wrong, friend," the man said, doffing his hat and giving a little half-bow. "I am of your fraternity. If you will only join me for a moment, you will see how wrong you are."

"Did I call you by the right name?" Christian demanded.

"Yes, my name is Demas; and I am a son of Abraham!"

"I know just who you are. Judas was your father and Gehazi your great-grandfather. You follow in their steps with your devilish prank, but we true pilgrims know that your father was hanged for a traitor, and by the very lips of our Lord he would have been better off had he never been born. And now, we continue on our way to meet that great Lord in the City where his throne is established. Good day, sir."

As they departed, they heard Demas shouting again, "Ho there! Turn aside, good gentlemen!"

Looking back, they saw the four travelers from Fair Speech coming around the bend, calling back up to Demas, "Turn aside for what, good sir?"

"Oh, this is not good," Hopeful muttered.

"I will show you something to dazzle the senses!"

"Gentlemen," Christian shouted, "I beg of you: do not listen to him! He wants only to turn you aside from the Narrow Way, to your our own very great destruction!"

"O pish posh," said Mr. Hold-the-World. "We've had quite enough of you two killjoys. On your way!"

Hopeful cupped his hands to his mouth and cried, "Believe us, he will promise you riches, but take your very lives!"

By-Ends dismissed this with a wave of his hand and began climbing Hill Lucre. The others followed.

Hopeful and Christian tried several more times to call them back, but within a few minutes, they'd climbed out of sight and the two pilgrims resumed the road ahead of them.

Hopeful asked, "Do you think they fell into the pit?"

"I have no idea. It's likely, I suppose. Or perhaps they will go down into the mine to dig and be smothered by the toxic fumes, which fill the place. Or perhaps they will see the mine for what it is and come back down of their own accord."

They traveled on without much conversation for two hours. They had just determined to find a shady spot for a mid-afternoon meal, when they came upon what appeared at first to be a strange monument: the likeness of a woman, reaching out, her mouth slack and her empty eyes pained.

"This is . . . rather macabre," Christian said.

"What is it made of?" Hopeful wondered. "Quartz?"

"I don't think so," Christian said. He rubbed his finger along the woman's palm and held it to his lips. "It's salt." Looking up into the hollow cavities of the woman's eyes, he felt a sense of dread welling up within him. In that moment, he felt certain that she was reaching out to him for help, only he had arrived many years too late.

"There's something written over here," Hopeful said, from behind the monument. "I can't read it, though. *Memores estote . . .* "

Christian broke himself away from the woman's gaze and read the brass plate affixed to a small stone pillar. "' . . . *uxoris Loth.*' It means, 'Remember Lot's wife.'"

"This can't truly be her, can it?"

"I believe it is." Christian now saw that she was not reaching out for deliverance, but reaching back toward the City of Destruction, longing for what was behind her, rather than the salvation that lay ahead. "This is quite timely," he said. "Her covetous heart drew her back while she fled to safety and now she has become a spectacle for all who pass by. Just as we would have been had we gone over the edge of Hill Lucre."

"Christian, I am so sorry that I wanted to go and have a look. By all rights, I should be just as this woman before us. I cannot see the difference between her sin and mine." He rubbed his temples. "Actually, I can. She only glanced back. I had a desire to climb up and take in the whole view. I am ashamed that such a thought ever entered my heart."

"Every pilgrim's heart entertains such thoughts, Hopeful. Do not despair. Instead, let's take notice of what we see here, for surely the King of this country has placed her here for a reason. This woman escaped one judgment—destruction in Sodom—yet she was destroyed by another."

"Yes," Hopeful agreed. "May she be both caution and example for us—that we should shun sin, lest such a judgment overtake us as well. And I see something else: her eyes and her hands are pointed backward, toward the cities destined for destruction no doubt, but more immediately toward the silver mine that lay just down beyond that Valley. I see the top of Hill Lucre. Which means that Demas and everyone who stands at its peak cannot help but see this woman standing here as a terrible warning against turning aside—or even looking back!"

"It confounds the mind," Christian said. "But desperate people do foolish and desperate things. Like the man who picks pockets in the presence of the judge or snatches purses beneath the gallows. Consider that the land of Sodom was second only to Eden in its lushness and natural beauty, and yet their lives were filled with every wickedness and abomination before the Lord. This kindled his jealousy all the more so that their plague was as hot as the fire of heaven could make it."

Hopeful fell to his knees and said, "Thank you Lord for your mercy that neither Christian nor I were made such an example. Especially me, a pilgrim so recently mired in sin and filth. We thank you and fear you and pray that we always remember Lot's wife!"

"Amen," Christian said.

They continued on their way, not willing to share a meal at the foot of this eerie monument or in the shadow of Hill Lucre. And soon they found the Narrow Way following along a pleasant river.

They passed a young woman, fishing on the bank of the river, a shield upon her back and a sword at her hip.

"Pardon me, miss," Hopeful said. "Do you know the name of this river?"

She looked up with a smile and said, "It has more than one name. The great king David called it The River of God. But John the Apostle referred to it as the River of the Water of Life. In either case, its water is cold and crisp and satisfies the thirsty who drink of it, enlivening their weary spirits. Enjoy it as you make progress along the way.

"And don't miss the green trees growing on its banks. They produce nine kinds of fruit, all of which are sweet to the mouths of pilgrims and agreeable to their stomachs. And even the leaves are edible, and protect against many of the diseases that tend to afflict travelers."

"You know an awful lot about this place," Hopeful observed. She flashed another smile and turned back to her fishing.

"Thank you," Christian said.

"Christ be with you both," the young woman answered.

The road followed the river around a lazy bend and soon the pilgrims found themselves in the midst of a sprawling meadow, carpeted with lilies, spreading out as far as they could see on either side of the river.

Here they sat down and ate their dinner, followed by a piece of fruit from the green trees and long pulls of sweet, cold water, which quenched their thirst like nothing ever had. Then they lay down, knowing they were safe here.

When they awoke, they gathered more fruit from the trees with which to break fast and drank more of the water from the river. Then they lay down again and rested in the meadow. This they did for three days and nights.

Then, on the fourth day, strengthened and rested, they determined to depart, for they were not yet at their journey's end.

Doubting Castle

T he holdings of the Giant Despair were vast.

A royal charter had been granted by Beelzebub himself, many, many years ago, and no one under that prince's rule dared encroach upon the giant's property, although his land was wide open on three of four sides. No walls or fences indicated its edge. No posts or signs warned of the certain tragic fate that awaited all trespassers. Still, there was no question where the public land ended and Doubting Estate began.

The trees were thinner here—not dead, but devoid of lushness and color. The earth was packed hard and covered, not with grass, but with some invasive creeping vine that tripped and snared the feet of travelers. The air too was thinner and entirely devoid of birds, save for crows, which cawed loudly day and night. Most of all, though, a traveler could sense that he'd stumbled into the dark domain of Doubting Estate by the pervasive sense of hopelessness, which grew ever stronger the closer one came to the center of the sinister giant's plot and his home, Doubting Castle.

This morning, Despair had just finished his rounds, scouring his lands for intruders—a daily habit of his. Ironically, this was the only pursuit that offered him anything akin to hope these days. The giant loved discovering foolish wayfarers who'd stumbled unawares over his borders. He loved falling

upon them with a speed that belied his massive frame and snatching them up by the scruff of the neck while they kicked and fought to no avail. He loved tossing them into the cage beneath his dungeon, locking the door with a clang, and syphoning away his captives' joy. Then their hope. Then their very will to live.

But today had been fruitless in that regard. In fact, it had been nearly two months since his last catch, and a sense of urgency was weighing on the giant's mind. He walked a bit faster and passed the stag's carcass from one hand to the other, gripping it by the eight points of one broad antler. It was a fine animal and could easily feed two giants this evening. But it would only feed one. This beast would never do. Not for The Giantess Apprehension.

Despair glanced down at the animal's vacant eyes and shared a brief moment of mutual dread. Something had to happen soon or there'd be no living with her. Perhaps tomorrow, the giant would venture out beyond his own lands, try to snatch a pilgrim or two from the King's Road and drag them over the wall.

No. That would never do. The sun shone more often in that land, which invariably brought on one of the giant's fits, leaving him more than vulnerable . . . which could be deadly beyond the wall, where Sir Great-Grace, Mr. Great-Heart, and Lady Daring were known to frequent that stretch of the Narrow Road, where it ran along the meadow near the stile at Indolent Pass. At his best and on his own land, the Giant Despair feared facing such foes. With the advantage theirs, it would mean certain death, he had no doubt.

As he approached Doubting Castle, he looked up into the gray sky, toward the crooked tower of Beelzebub in the distance, and steeled his nerves for the coming confrontation. Upon entering the castle's great hall, he tore the stag open and, with a knife from his belt, cut away a good deal of meat. He then roasted the flesh over the fire before adding it to the pot of bubbling stew, which had been cooking for nearly a week, continually refreshed with new ingredients. To that end, he added some more carrots, garlic, and a gallon of bullion-infused beer. He sat by the iron pot while it cooked and the sun went down, until the dancing fire was the only source of light. He then filled a large clay bowl with the savory dish.

Snatching a torch from the wall and igniting it in the fire, he mounted a broad twisting staircase to the chamber at the very top of the castle's keep. He wrapped his bloated knuckles gingerly against the heavy wood door and called out, "I've brought dinner. May I come in?"

A long, drawn groan from beyond the door was the only response and Despair took it as an invitation, entering the dark room. It was cold up here, as the giantess liked it. And sparsely furnished. Along the outer wall sat a long, deep straw-filled mattress, piled with so many blankets that Despair had to let his eyes adjust before he could see the rise and fall of Apprehension's breath beneath them.

Some years earlier, Despair had purchased the giantess a fine canopied bed with a white poplar headboard, which he had presented to her at the feast of the New Year. But true to form, she had grown suspicious of him and his intentions and, ultimately, of the bed itself, which she broke into pieces and pushed out the narrow windows of the tower, sending it plummeting down to the earth below.

Holding the bowl up to where he guessed her nose must be, he troubled the bowl of stew, hoping the aroma would awaken her appetite. Or at least awaken her. She did not stir.

"I brought you food," he said, his façade of gentleness threatening to crack. "Rise. Eat."

Slowly, the blankets fell away and a long, hollow face came into view in the torchlight—two sunken eyes framed by gaunt cheeks.

"What is it?" she asked.

"Meat. You'll like it. Try some."

The Giantess pushed her nose into the bowl and sniffed. Then recoiled. "I do not want venison."

"I know, but . . . "

"I want *men*. Women. Pilgrims wandered in off the road, drained of hope like a stag bled dry."

"And I'll provide it. In the meantime you have to eat something," Despair said, "to hold you over until another pilgrim presents himself."

She pulled the blankets back over her head. From beneath them, her muffled words were loud and clear to the Giant Despair.

"Go and find me a pilgrim. Or find me dead from your lack of provision."

For days, life had been like a dream for Christian and Hopeful. The road continued to follow the winding river with its cool, crisp water. The fruit and leaves of the life-giving trees were always near at hand. But then, as they knew it eventually must, the two diverged, the Narrow Way going one way, and the river another. Unwilling to go out of the way, they each took one last long pull of that heavenly water and filled their packs with the fruit before leaving these blessed resources behind.

Immediately, the ground became rough and rocky, and the pilgrims' began to feel the sort of weariness they hadn't felt in many days. Their feet became raw and blistered. And not only their soles, but their very souls were affected, and they soon grew impatient because of the Way.

They traveled for a full day and suffered a cold and restless night of tossing and turning along the side of the road, where they found the fruitless, leafless trees yet too green to provide a fire.

Christian and Hopeful awoke to find the sky gray and the air cold. They returned thanks before eating some of their gathered fruit—which was far less appealing when not freshly picked—and began to discuss the day ahead.

"It smells like rain," Hopeful observed.

"Yes, it will certainly rain today," Christian agreed. "I can feel it in my knee."

Hopeful laughed and poked at his friend. "You are so old."

Christian just nodded. "Older every day. And closer to the City each day. Today is no exception."

Hopeful pushed his toe at the uneven ground beneath them. "But if it rains and these ruts fill with water, that would be . . . I wonder if we should perhaps wait it out. No? Just wait and see?"

Christian stood and stretched. "Hopeful, who was it who told you pilgrimage was a fair-weather pursuit? It wasn't Faithful. And certainly not me. Was it perhaps Mr. By-Ends?" He winked at his fellow-pilgrim, who chuckled sheepishly and followed him back onto the way, their faces set to the Shining Light, beaming dimly through the haze.

But as they went, the sky grew darker and the road became rougher. And by noon they were both wishing for a better road. And that is when the Narrow Way passed within twenty feet of the stone wall to their left. And just at the point where the two almost met, they saw a well-worn path from road to wall, and a set of wooden stairs up over it.

"Look at that," Christian said. "I wonder why the King would place a stile over the wall here."

"How do you know it was the King who placed it?"

"Well, if nothing else, he failed to tear it down. And that's something. I'm going to have look."

He carefully ascended the steep wooden steps and gazed out over the wall.

"What do you see?" Hopeful asked.

"It's a beautiful meadow! There's a sign here identifying it: Bypass Meadow. I'll tell you, the ground looks soft and even, and there's a clear path beaten down, starting just the other side of the stile, where many pilgrims must have gone before us."

"But you're always saying that we should never leave the Way."

"That's just it," Christian mused. "I don't believe we would have to. The path itself follows along the wall, just opposite the pilgrim road. We'd be on much softer ground and give our feet a much-deserved rest, while remaining within a stone's throw of the Narrow Way!"

Hopeful opened his mouth to speak, then looked back and seemed to think better of it. "Where you lead, I will follow," he said, and followed Christian over the stile and down into Bypass Meadow.

"You were certainly right about one thing," Hopeful said, stepping out onto the soft ground. "This is far easier on my feet. What a relief."

"And look," said Christian, "as far as the eye can see, this path remains only a small distance from the wall. I suppose that's why they call it Bypass Meadow. Here pilgrims can skip the difficult terrain without losing their way. Why endure what we need not endure? Wisdom is still a virtue, is it not?"

They walked this trail for hours. As they went, the path veered, slowly and steadily, away from the wall until it was barely visible in the distance. Then the sky grew darker with clouds and the air began to thin.

"I have an ill feeling about this place," Hopeful said. "I can scarcely make out the wall in this failing light. We are on unfamiliar ground and, for all we know, this path will take us straight back to the City of Destruction or some other—"

"Look!" Christian pointed at a man walking the trail ahead of them, in the same direction. "Ho, sir!" he called out.

The young man looked back at the approaching pilgrims, smiled, and beckoned them, but he did not slow his gait. Christian and Hopeful increased their own pace until they overtook him. They then clasped hands by way of greeting, still walking briskly all the while.

"What perfect timing to encounter another pilgrim just now. We were starting to have doubts. I am Christian and this is Hopeful and we are on our way to the Celestial Gate."

"Pleased to meet you," the man said. "I am Vain Confidence and I too am headed to the that gate and to the holy city that lies beyond it."

Christian turned to his companion and said, "See? I told you this path would not take us off course. Have a little faith in me."

They walked alongside Vain Confidence for a time, but he was not much for conversation, speaking only of himself and his exemplary progress and his unmatched speed, until said speed pulled him away from Christian and Hopeful and he disappeared into the gathering darkness.

"I can't keep up with him," Christian said, his breath short.

"Nor can I. And I can't see . . . anything. Only ten yards or so ahead of us." He looked around with growing concern. "And, while I'm sure the sun has not yet set, I cannot find it for the clouds."

Christian motioned impatiently. "Well, we're doing ourselves no favors standing still. To carry on, we need only see the very next step, and I can see the next dozen. Let's go!"

A shriek pierced the darkness up ahead, and Christian took off running in the direction of the sound, drawing his sword as he charged down the well-trodden path.

Suddenly, the ground was gone from beneath his feet and he felt himself falling into a deep, dark void. Then, just as suddenly, he was jerked violently back. Christian landed hard atop Hopeful, then rolled onto the earth and lay there for a moment, willing his heart to stop pounding. He sat up and gazed at the massive pit into which he had very nearly fallen.

"Hopeful, you . . . you . . . " He crawled up to the edge and peered down into the never-ending darkness.

"Are you alright, Christian?" Hopeful asked, drawing up next to him.

"I am. Thanks to you. But tell me: can you see the bottom of this pit? I fear our man Vain Confidence may have fallen in."

"I see nothing," Hopeful said. "But listen." They could hear the faintest of groaning and shallow, broken breathing from down below.

Christian sheathed his sword. "We have to pull him out. Oh, I wish I'd heeded Mr. Great-Heart's advice. A coil of rope would be most useful right now."

A crack of thunder and the sky lit up for a moment, searing the gruesome image of Vain Confidence, his body twisted obscenely at the bottom of the pit, into both of their minds. A moment later, the floodgates opened above.

"I don't think rope would do us any good," Hopeful said. "Even if that man is somehow still alive—which I can scarcely imagine after such a fall—he is gravely injured. And with this rain, the bottom of that pit will fill with water in a short time, drowning him."

They sat in the downpour for a few minutes, listening to the rumbling thunder.

"Christian, where are we?" Hopeful asked.

Christian said nothing.

"We should have stayed on the Narrow Way," Hopeful

muttered. "I knew this was foolishness."

"Then why didn't you say something?"

"I did. I offered a . . . gentle caution if you'll recall. I would have spoken more plainly, but you are older than I, and more experienced on this road, as you continually remind me."

"I'm sorry, brother. You have saved my life, though I have greatly wronged you. My pride and my aversion to suffering have brought us out of the Way and into grave danger. I beg you, forgive me. It was not out of evil intent."

Hopeful smiled. "I forgive you. And I believe God will work even this for our good." Another flash of lightning and the smile died on his lips.

"What's wrong?" Christian asked.

"Did you see the size of that pit? The depth? What manner of man or engine could possibly dig something so enormous?"

Christian stood and took several steps back from the deadly chasm. "Only a giant," he said.

"Aye. We are on dangerous ground, Christian."

"All right, let's keep our heads here. Up ahead, there may be pitfalls and mantraps aplenty, but the road behind us is safe; we've seen it. We can backtrack and—"

Hopeful shook his head. "Not in this downpour. Look." He gestured at the ground beneath them, a muddy mess of battered grass and gushing channels, further obscured by the sheets of rain and the dark.

"Okay." Christian nodded. "New plan. The wall is that way. It must be. So we travel in that direction—slow and careful—until we hit the wall. Then we follow it back to the stile and over to safety."

"Agreed," Hopeful said. "I'll go first."

"No, please. This is all my fault to begin with. Let me go before you so that any tripwires or deadfalls out there will claim my life, not yours."

"Christian, no. Your mind is troubled and I fear you might lead us astray yet again. This time, you follow me."

Christian nodded his ascent.

"And don't despair, my friend. Remember the words of the prophet: *Let your heart be toward the highway, even the way you once went: turn there again.*"

Christian looked down at his shoes, soaked through and bogged down in the mud. "One thing's for sure: it is easier going out of the way when we are in, than going in when we are out. Let's get moving while we still can."

They travelled with all care, but the terrain tended downward and the waters rose up and it crossed Christian's mind more than once that they both might be drowned before they ever saw the Narrow Way again. Still, they pressed on—persistently—choosing every step with care. By the time they reached the high stone wall, night had truly fallen, and the darkness had thickened all around them.

"I can't go on," Hopeful said, resting his hands on his knees. The water was nearly up to their waists now and it was clear to both men that a second leg of this journey was out of the question tonight.

"Nor I," Christian said. "So what are we waiting for? Give me a boost."

Hopeful cradled his friend's foot and lifted him up along the wall, high as he could, but the slick stone offered no traction and Christian slid right back down, falling once again in the muck. As he stood, dripping wet, he began to shiver.

"I'll try again," he said. "Just a minute. Let me catch my breath."

"You'll catch your death," Hopeful amended. "This is no good. We can't get back tonight. We need to find somewhere dry to ride out this storm." Looking up to the heavens with hands held high, Hopeful cried out, "Oh Lord, deliver us! Point us to the way of life!"

Just then, a crooked bolt of lightning connected with the top of a nearby hill, filling the air with a heavy chemical odor.

"There!" Hopeful said. "High ground. We'll find no standing water there. I'll fashion a shelter—a lean-to of some kind. Some measure of protection from the elements. It's our best chance."

Abandoning caution, he fairly dragged Christian the two hundred yards to the top of the hill, where—in another flash of lightning—they saw a modest stone building, still and dark inside.

Hopeful tried the door, expecting it to be locked. It swung open. The first thing that hit him was the smell of clean straw, followed immediately by a most welcome warmth. Hopeful shut the door and felt around in the darkness until he discovered the heap of dry straw, where he helped Christian lie down. And, after another moment of searching, he found several incredibly large saddle blankets. He spread three of them over his companion and, lying down next to him, wrapped himself in the fourth.

And there, despite the pounding rain and crashing thunder, the two of them immediately fell asleep.

The sound of a heavy door creaking open snatched Hopeful from his dreams. He opened his eyes only to be blinded by the dull gray daylight shining into their shelter around the massive silhouette of a giant—a nightmarish image coming more into focus with every passing second. Hopeful remained perfectly still, trying to melt down into the pile of straw beneath him. As his eyes warmed to the light, he sensed Christian beside him, shrinking back beneath the blankets. Neither of them so much as breathed.

The giant entered the building and only then did Hopeful notice just how high the roof was. The doorway must have been ten feet tall, and still the giant had to duck his head on the way in. Yet holding his breath, Hopeful squeezed his eyes shut, realizing how infantile an impulse it was to try and disappear in his own darkness.

"I see you both," came a grim and surly voice. "Awake, arise, and face your fate."

Christian leapt up from beneath the blankets and put a hand on his sword.

The giant smirked. "What? Would you kill me here, on my own land? Within my own walls? What sort of miscreants are you?"

"We are not miscreants, sir. We are pilgrims bound for the Celestial City. And if we are trespassing, we apologize. There was a great storm and we got turned around. We very nearly died before we found your storehouse here."

"Ye still might."

Hopeful stood at Christian's side, craning his neck up to meet the giant's malicious glare.

He could sense that he and Christian were thinking the same thing: if they would have any prayer of defeating this monster, it would have to be in here. The walls were tall but narrow, and the space was tight. Plenty of room for the pilgrims to maneuver, but the giant would find himself bumping, crashing, and tripping in the confined space. Hopeful glanced at his brother pilgrim.

"Well?" the giant demanded. "If you are honorable pilgrims, as you say, you will want to face the consequences of your crimes with honor, no? You have trampled in my grounds, made your bed on my land, and now you must go with me."

He stepped back out into the dreary morning and beckoned them.

"What should we do?" Hopeful asked. "We can't outrun him. And I don't like our chances in battle."

"Nor do I," Christian said. "And he's right that we did trespass. If there's any justice here our punishment should be light. After all, we meant no harm."

"Come out now," the giant growled, "or I'll bring the roof down on your heads."

"Before we do," Christian called, "tell us your name."

"I am Despair, Beelzebub's champion and rightful owner of Doubting Estate, where you now transgress."

The two pilgrims came out, shoulder-to-shoulder through the massive doorway.

"I'm not gonna take your blade," Despair said, "but if you draw it on me, I'll force-feed it to you. We clear?"

Christian nodded. "Where— where are you taking us, sir?"

"Look yonder," he said, pointing to a crooked bulwark rising up above the horizon in the distance. "That's Doubting Castle. And that's where you meet your fate."

The two pilgrims trudged along, the giant on their heels. He continually jabbed at them, cajoling them to move faster, but the closer they got to the castle, the slower they walked. A sense of despondency weighed on them so heavily that both checked to see if their burdens had reappeared.

By the time they entered the great hall of Doubting Castle, they were resigned to their fate, and any sense of fight had left them.

A fire roared on the hearth, and a large iron pot bubbled with some savory smelling food.

"Are you hungry?" he asked.

"Very much so," said Christian.

"So is the giantess," Despair said, grabbing up the pilgrim's by their necks and carrying them down a dank stairway to a stinking dungeon, where he stuffed the two of them in a large iron cage suspended from the ceiling. Slamming and locking the cage door, he looked at them with wild eyes and added, "so be quick about it!"

A moment later, he was gone.

The cage would have been too small for one man, let alone two. There was no room to stretch out, no room to stand up. Even sitting meant hunching over and within an hour both men were aching and beginning to feel the frenzy of confinement setting in.

"How long do you suppose he'll keep us here?" Hopeful asked.

"How should I know? A week? A day? I don't think I could survive even that."

Hopeful sneered. "What was it you promised before we came over the wall? Much softer ground without ever leaving the Narrow Way? How well that worked out!"

Christian kicked at the bars. "The only thing soft here is you. Not used to being on this side of the cell door are you? I've been a prisoner, Inanity. I know what it's like. And I have no intention of staying here."

"Alright, alright. Let's stop sniping at each other and form a plan. The giant has got to come back—if only to feed us at some point. And when he does, you draw your sword, and we will both attack him."

"Do you have a weapon?"

Hopeful jerked and twisted until he could access his bag. "Not exactly a weapon, but dangerous enough." He pulled out a paring knife in a leather wrap. "He went through my bag; I'm surprised he left it. And you, your sword. It will prove a fatal mistake."

Christian chuckled darkly at the tiny blade in Hopeful's hand. "Did you see that...*creature?* What are you going to do with that thing—pick his teeth?"

"Then lend me your javelin—All-Prayer, is it?"

Christian reached up to his back and pulled at the weapon, but he couldn't draw it in the confines of the cage. Likewise, his sword would slide only six inches or so in its sheath before striking the bars.

"We need to get out first," said Christian. "Then we fight. I with my sword, and you with the spear."

Despair knocked lightly on the giantess's door. When she did not answer, he entered, walking softly—for a giant.

"I have news," he blurted, loudly.

"Unless your news is that you've snatched me a pilgrim, be gone."

"I am still here."

She sat up, wincing in pain. Despair looked down at her,

not quite managing to hide his alarm at her appearance. Her once ample arms hung down in waves of dappled skin. Her cheekbones seemed to be pushing out against her face in an attempt to free themselves from it. She was truly disgusting to him, and yet the giant could not help but swell with pride as he asked her, "What shall I do to prepare them for you, my love?"

Her face twisted into a vicious grin like a carved pumpkin from the pagan North, left to dry in the sun. "Let them suffer through the night, and in the morning . . . *beat them*. Beat them without mercy."

Promise

The Castle of Prince Beelzebub was just off Broadway, not far from the Wide Gate. From its turrets, his sentinels could see for miles in every direction, on both sides of the wall. In the heart of the fortress, the prince himself passed the days in all manner of self-gratification and indulgence, seated on his high throne while an endless train of meat, various dainties, and every form of forbidden fruit was set before him.

In the evenings, and sometimes at noonday, he would stalk about his domain, marking victims for his agents to target, and sometimes falling upon them himself. This was not work for the dark prince; rather, it was the culmination of the day's leisure.

From time to time, though, duty called, usually in the form of a scout or messenger relaying something of note. Reports, updates, strategy, decisions—these things were necessary evils, although they were among the least enjoyable of all evils as far as Beelzebub was concerned.

Such was the case this morning. Two impish messengers padded into his courtroom, folding the stretched hide of their wings up behind them and bowing low before their prince, who wiped the blood and juice from his chin and gestured curtly for the two to stand and report.

"What is it?" he demanded.

The gaunter of the two stepped forward. "My prince, we are here to report that two pilgrims have wandered into Doubting Estate, where they were captured by the Giant Despair, and are now locked in his dungeon."

Beelzebub sat silently for a beat. "There had better be more to it than that. As it stands, you may as well interrupt my breakfast to tell me that water yet flows downhill. This giant you speak of captures careless pilgrims. He leeches them of all hope and comfort. He feeds them to his revolting wife. This is the natural way of things. What in this report justifies my suffering you . . . *fringe* sullying my halls with your presence this morning?"

The other messenger stepped up next to his companion. "Sir, we recognized one of these men, and we were certain you would want to know of his status." He opened his mouth as if to add something else, but then swallowed it back down in fear.

Beelzebub leaned back in his throne and studied the messengers until a look of recognition spilled across his face. "You two," he said. "You brought me word some time ago that my champion had been bested in the Valley, did you not?"

He turned his head to glare at the creature Apollyon, whose massive body was stretched taught against the rock wall of the chamber, a chain pulling him down by the ankles and another stretching him up by the wrists.

"We did," the messenger said, bowing. "And yes, this man Christian, who defeated Apollyon, is the same pilgrim who finds himself now starving in the giant's dungeon."

"Well," Beelzebub sneered, "it seems that the simple brute has accomplished what my cunning captain could not."

"My Lord," Apollyon called out, gritting in pain.

"Did I ask you to speak?"

"Forgive me, my Lord. But perhaps I could vindicate myself by return—"

"*Forgive* you? When have you ever known me to *forgive*? You will suffer there, a spectacle of humiliation for all to see, until I determine that you've paid for your crimes." He turned his attention back to the messengers. "Who is this other pilgrim?"

"No one of consequence, my prince. A low-level servant escaped from Vanity Fair."

"Oh. *Yessss*. I had forgotten that this Christian was in our grasp once before, locked securely behind iron bars, yet somehow slipped through our fingers." He stroked his beard in thought.

"Let me fly to our outpost near Doubting Castle," Apollyon cried. "I will keep watch and assure that—"

Beelzebub gestured to a slave, who cranked the wheel half a turn, stretching the dragon's body all the further and bringing a cry of pain from deep within him.

"The Giant Despair is not a tool of precision," the prince mused. "He is not clever. He is a . . . cleaver. A mallet. And yet, he rarely loses a pilgrim once they've fallen into his grasp." To the messengers, he said, "Return to that outpost and keep watch. Report back any developments. Let us see what these pilgrims are made of." He laughed hoarsely and added, "as I'm sure the giant himself will do, quite literally, while he picks the meat from their bones."

The next morning, the pilgrims awakened again to the sound of a door creaking open. The cage door.

Christian's spirit leapt into action, but his body was stiff and weary from the night spent crammed and cramped in the cage. He found himself plucked out and thrown easily over the giant's right shoulder. A moment later, he saw Hopeful dangling over the other and they were taken up the stairs like two small children carried off by a scolding parent.

Despair brought them out of the castle and a few dozen paces further out under the canopy of clouds, before dumping them to the ground in a rocky place.

He then picked up a grievous crab-tree cudgel and grinned at them.

"So it's to be combat," Christian said, rising and pulling his sword. Only it stuck once again after only a few inches of draw. He jerked on it over and again while the giant laughed.

"Can't pull that thing here, can ya? It's a common problem."

Christian then turned to All-Prayer, lashed to his back. It too was locked fast in its place, and he was unable draw his weapon in the face of the Giant Despair, who rushed in on the pilgrims and began to beat them viciously. He struck them both with all his might, again and again. Christian cried out—in pain, yes, but also in frustration that the giant's strength (and his skill in delivering these blows) seemed to render his armor useless. The two pilgrims were equally battered and broken over the course of nearly an hour.

More than once, Christian thought he could endure not one more strike of that terrible club, only to feel it again and again. When the giant had beaten them nearly to death, he grabbed them each by an ankle and dragged them back down the steps into the dungeon. He then stuffed them into the iron cage and locked the door. Christian almost laughed at the memory of his own grousing and complaining the night before. How uncomfortable the cage had felt when he was whole and unbeaten. The pain was magnified now, perhaps tenfold.

Despair's ugly face and stinking breath hovered just outside the bars. "This is life for you two," he said. "From now on, this will be all you know. This cage and my club. I think you know what to do."

"What are you saying?" Christian asked.

"End yourselves," the giant spat. "You have the means. And mark my words: you will surely do it eventually. Why endure what you need not endure?" He laughed as he climbed the steps out of the dungeon, repeating the words, "Why endure what you need not endure?"

Christian began to weep—quietly at first, but before long it came in heavy, doleful wails.

"Stop that," Hopeful said. "Please. I'm sure it's music to our captor's ears. If you must cry out, cry out to our Lord!"

Christian dried his tears and slumped back against the iron bars. "If only I'd listened to you," he said. "If only we'd stayed on the Narrow Way. Our feet would hurt, but . . . " A hollow, cackling laugh filled the dungeon. "Our feet would hurt!" He winced in pain and fell silent, waiting for Hopeful to speak words of encouragement. But he never did.

That whole day, they only exchanged a few short lamentations, and wondered aloud if the giant ever intended to feed them or give them water to drink. As evening approached, they fell into a weak, fitful sleep.

Despair returned to Apprehension's chamber again that night and reported what he had done.

She sat up on her bed—a good sign in the giant's mind—sipping mulled wine from a goblet, and twisted her wax-like features up in thought. "Will they follow your instructions?" she asked. "I will only accept them if they perish for lack of hope."

"I know not. They are broken and teetering on the edge for sure. But I can see the light of the enemy King still shining in them. I stripped their provisions from them and have given them nothing to eat or drink . . . and yet they seem to have food of some other source."

"Give them another day to accept their fate," the giantess said. "If they do not break, show them the bones. That will do them in."

The Giant Despair awoke early the next morning and prepared some porridge and pork, which he brought down into the dungeon with him, waving the platter about, to spread the pleasing aroma through the room. The two prisoners awakened and looked longingly—pitifully—at the breakfast.

"Well, would you like some?" Despair asked.

Both of them began blubbering, *yes sir, yes please,* . One of them reached his bloodied arms out through the bars, filthy fingers reaching.

Despair laughed and tossed the food to the floor. "You can

watch the rats eat it. But you two will never have another morsel of food in your miserable lives. Your tongues will never be wetted again. They will swell in your mouths and fill your throats." He watched the lion's share of what little hope they'd retained drain away.

"Why not just end your suffering now? Hmm? You've got a blade in there. Make a clean end; keep some dignity."

The pilgrim wearing the armor grabbed the bars of the cage and pulled himself up to meet his captor's gaze. Despite his hunger and many wounds, he managed to look the giant in the eye and say, "You may have us in chains now, but you are destined to be destroyed. Greater is he that is in us than all the villains in the world. Why don't you just save yourself some trouble and let us go?"

Despair felt a surge of rage filling up his massive frame.

"You want me to let you go?" He patted at the sides of his belt. "Oh, I don't seem to have my key. How about this instead?" The giant gripped the cage by both sides and squeezed with all his considerable might. The metal bars complained and then began to bend, pushing the two prisoners closer and closer together. "I'll crush your bones!" he shouted. "I'll make a—" A shaft of sunlight shown down the staircase and caught him square in the eyes. The giant stumbled back, reeling.

The sun's unencumbered rays were so rare in this land, much less down here in his dungeon that Despair was thrown for a moment as to what was happening.

Then he felt the dreadful effects.

The giantess called them his "sun spells"—fits, prompted by the brightest light of day, during which he lost the use of his hands. Despair looked down at the useless things, hanging by his sides, and let out a cry of rage and madness as he rushed out of the dungeon and up the steps.

"Perhaps he's right," Christian said when the giant had left.

"About what?"

"That we ought to put an end to ourselves. I can draw my sword just enough to use the blade against myself. You could do the same. Or better yet, your paring knife! Hand it over."

Hopeful just stared at him in shock.

"Oh, what hope have we down here?" Christian bellowed.

"No one knows where we are. No one is coming to save us!"

Hopeful balked. "The Great King knows we are here. The King who sent Mr. Great-Heart to save you from the Fair and sent Help to pull you from the slough."

"Yes, while we were on *his* land," Christian said. "While we were in the light. Now we languish here in darkness, beyond the wall, beneath the earth! Perhaps he cannot see us here." He sighed. "God help me, in my heart, I feel that he cannot. And if he can, he must have chosen to hand us over to this giant—a rather disproportionate punishment for us simply wanting a short break for our feet. Perhaps we've been wrong all along and this King doesn't love us. At the moment, it seems to me that he hates us."

"How can you say that, Christian? Even here, there are little mercies—undeserved mercies!"

"Mercies? You mean no food? No water? Constant beatings and the like? I don't know how much more 'mercy' I can take."

"You know that's not what I mean. I mean, for one, that in attempting to crush this cage our captor has elongated it just enough for us to both stretch out."

Christian looked at his companion, basking in the beam of sunlight, legs fully extended, and realized that he himself was still curled up, stiff and cramped. He stretched out, feeling his spine and knees crack—painful at first, but then a great relief.

"A miniscule mercy, if that," Christian spat. "More like a happy accident. And, by the way, the only happiness we're likely to know. The life that we now live is miserable. For my part, I confess that I am torn between continuing in this state and dying by my own hand. My soul would choose the grave over the dungeon, I think. My friend, shall we really be ruled by this giant?"

Hopeful reached over and squeezed his brother's shoulder. "If you do this wicked thing, only then will you truly be ruled by the giant, for that's what he has commanded you to do. You are right that our present condition is dreadful, and death would be far more welcome to me than to abide here forever. But we are not our own masters, Christian. We were bought with a price.

"And the Lord of the country to which we are going has commanded us, 'Thou shalt not murder.' And if that applies to slaying another, how much more does it forbid us slaying ourselves? Remember: to kill another man is only to murder his body. But to kill oneself is to kill body and soul at once. For when you speak of 'ease in the grave,' you have forgotten that hell awaits all murderers. Dare we tempt God in this way?"

"Then we are stuck in every sense," Christian said. "We cannot live. We cannot even die. And I am back to questioning the love of this King."

"Christian, remember that others have been taken in by this giant before us and yet have escaped. Perhaps God, who made all that is—seen and unseen—will cause the Giant Despair to die. Or he may take us out again to taunt or beat us and forget to lock the cage. You saw him just now; he is mad for sure. Or maybe he'll have another of those fits we just saw—at just the right moment—and give us an opening. I am resolved in this: if even the slightest opportunity to escape should open up to us, I will quit myself like a man, and strike with all my might or flee with all swiftness. Until then, brother, let us be patient and endure for a while."

"All right, Hopeful. I will endure with you a little while longer. But I am afraid that I will soon be so weak from lack of food or water that, even if the giant should turn us loose, still I would die before I reached the Narrow Way. I may even now be too weak to even climb out of the cage."

"Then let us pray for patience and strength," said Hopeful.

"You pray. I cannot."

"But you and Faithful sang songs of praise in the dungeon at Vanity. I heard you."

Christian turned his back to Hopeful. "That was a different place and a different situation. This castle—this dungeon—is devoid of all hope. Besides, in Vanity we had you bringing us gruel twice a day. Hey, I don't suppose you have any of that stuff on you now? I'd give all I own for a spoonful."

The two of them laughed. And Hopeful prayed over his friend. Then he sang songs of praise into the evening, all the while hoping that Christian would join him. But he did not.

The giant returned to the dungeon late that night and flew into a rage when he saw them yet alive—although they were barely alive, able to do little more than breathe and moan.

When he opened the cage and dragged them out, Christian again reached for his sword, but was unable to pull it from its scabbard. The giant knocked him to the ground and commanded him to stand again. He then prodded and shoved them both down a dark and musty passage, deeper into the dungeon. He held a burning torch in his hand, and he waved and poked it at them if they moved too slowly. Finally, they entered into a round room with a domed ceiling.

"Look here," Despair said, holding the torch out over the center of the floor. The pilgrims gaped in terror at what they saw: a huge mound of bones, human remains, piled high like gold in a dragon's lair.

"These were pilgrims like you," the Giant said. "They trespassed on my grounds, as you have. I kept them in that cage until I'd dripped them dry of any hope. Or faith. Or devotion. And then, when I saw fit, I tore them to pieces. And sometime soon, I will do the same to you. Agony beyond your worst nightmares awaits you. Unless you should, uh, shuffle off of your own accord."

He then knocked both of them to the hard ground with savage blows and ordered them to stand and return to their cage. He tripped and struck them the whole way, then punished them for falling or dragging their feet. By the time they reached the cage, both men crawled back in willingly, if only to make this abuse stop.

"Think on it," the Giant said, locking the cage. He left them, this time also locking the barred door of the dungeon itself. "You've nowhere to go but deeper into hell," he called back, from the darkness of the staircase.

"Surely you can see now that he's right," Christian croaked.

"Oh no," Hopeful said. "Do you mean to tell me, Christian, that he struck you so hard on the head that you've lost your memory?"

"What?"

"Do you not remember how valiant were before coming to this place? Apollyon could not crush you. The whole wicked town of Vanity could not break your spirit. Even the Valley of the Shadow of Death you survived. You have faced hardships, terrors, and amazements and now you are nothing but fears?

"Look at *me*, Christian. Well, it's too dark, but think of me. Picture me in your mind. I am far weaker in stature than you, far newer to the pilgrim's life, and I know a fraction of what you do about the Celestial Land and its Great King. I too have been beaten and starved and left in the dark. But I am not ready to give in.

"We might face death, yes, but such was the case in Vanity Fair, and you did not faint or falter. You and Faithful stood tall, fearing neither cage nor chain nor the burning stake. Let us honor Faithful's memory and glorify our King by bearing up with patience as well as we can."

Christian grunted his ascent. "Oh, all right. I'll do it." He chuckled darkly. "I don't expect to survive long anyway. How many days have we been without food and drink?"

Hopeful thought. "Three days, I believe. Which would make it late Saturday night. Or early Sunday morning; I know not which. Huh. The Sabbath. Let us get some sleep, Christian, and praise our King properly in the light of morning."

"I don't think I will, Hopeful. There's something I've never told you: when I had not yet come to the Place of Deliverance, I went into the home of a man called The Interpreter. An odd fellow, but wise. He showed me many wonders, one of them being a man stuck forever in an iron cage. A man past all hope, for whom even repentance was unattainable. This cage we are in looks very much like that cage. And I feel very much like that man."

"Christian, listen to me: you are not that man. You are bought with the blood of Jesus Christ. You say, 'I am a great sinner.' And Christ says, 'I will in no wise cast you out.' 'But I am a pitiful, backsliding sinner,' says you.' And Christ says, 'I will in no wise cast you out.' 'But I have no good thing to bring with me,' says you. And Christ—Great and Merciful—says, 'I will in no wise cast you out!'"

"Yes," Christian said. "You're right. *I* may be wallowing in doubt and despair, but *he* will not cast me out. He will never leave us or forsake us. Let us rest, Hopeful, and see what comes in the morning."

They both dozed a bit and, when they awakened to the feeble gray light snaking its way down into the dungeon, Hopeful seemed a bit off. Almost as if he were drunk. He snickered and pointed deliriously at Christian.

"What?" Christian demanded.

"I see the key," Hopeful slurred. "We can leave. There's the key. We can leave."

"Are you alright?" Christian looked down at his breast-plate. Indeed, there was a key there, or the image of a key. An inlay of a key. Or . . . could it be?

He remembered the words Charity had spoken in the armory of the Palace Beautiful: *This is the breastplate of righteousness. It will guard your heart and give you courage in facing the Enemy. But look here. This is Promise. It will help you never to forget the promises of God, and may indeed save your life one day.*

"What a fool am I!" Christian exclaimed.

"Huh?"

"What a stiff-necked, thick-headed—! I thought of Promise as a symbol, merely something decorative to adorn my outer garments and rest upon my heart—something for the world to see. It never occurred to me for a moment that it might actually have the power to set me free. And so, I chose to lie here in this stinking dungeon, when at any time I could have walked at liberty."

Christian dug his fingers into the breastplate and began to pry at the silver key. It took some time and effort, but it started to move. And as it did, he felt not only the metal separating from the molded leather of the breastplate, but the Key of Promise itself coming forth from inside his heart. It hurt horribly for a moment, but the pain was followed by a surge of hope, as the key came free.

Crawling over his companion, Christian reached through the bars and inserted the key into the padlock. It turned easily, and the lock fell away. With great difficulty, the men climbed out of the cage and dropped to the hard ground below, grunting in pain.

As quietly as they could, they approached the locked cell door at the entrance of the dungeon and, once again, the key turned easily, and the bolt gave back. Shushing each other incessantly, even while they leaned upon one another, they ascended the stairs and were met with yet another door, this one leading to the castle yard.

"Are you with me, Hopeful?" Christian whispered.

"To the end," Hopeful said. "To the City."

Breathing a prayer, Christian fit his key into the lock of the huge iron door and tried to turn it. No movement. The key wouldn't budge. He tried again to no avail.

"Hurry," Hopeful said. "I believe it is nearly morning and the giant seems to rise early."

"Then help me," Christian said. Hopeful placed his hands upon Christian's and the two turned with all their might. The grinding of the lock as it turned was like music to their ears.

The deafening creak of the door as it opened—not so much.

"We've got to run now," Christian said. "That must have awakened him."

The sound of the giant's thundering steps down the winding stairs confirmed their fears. The two pilgrims pushed themselves out into the yard, feeling sluggish and stiff. They were a few rods away when Despair came charging out into the yard, closing in on them, his mouth frothing.

He was gaining steadily, but still Christian thought they stood a decent chance. They'd seen how the giant was easily winded when he'd marched them here and there over the past few days. If only they could put some distance—

Hopeful cried out in pain as a vine snagged his foot and dragged him to the ground. Christian had no choice. He came to a stop, pushed Promise back into his heart, and spun to face the giant, drawing his sword. It came forth smoothly.

"Face me if you will, you wicked son of Anak" he cried out, "but it will be your death. The Lord will deliver you into my hand, and I will leave your flesh for the birds of the air and wild beasts of the earth. I bested Apollyon and I will vanquish you."

Despair drew back for a moment. Then, looking down at Hopeful, he smiled and snatched up the fallen pilgrim.

"Drop your sword," the giant barked, "or I'll pop him like a tick!"

"Don't do it!" Hopeful shouted, then cried out in pain as the giant's hands twisted him.

Christian froze, paralyzed by indecision.

"Don't underestimate me, pilgrim," the Giant growled. "You don't know who I am."

"If God is for me," Hopeful grinded through his teeth, "then whom should I fear? We know exactly who you are. Look me in the eye, if you dare, and tell me you don't fear our King."

Despair ceased crushing his victim for a moment and pulled the little pilgrim up to meet his gaze. He was like a rag doll in the giant's massive hands. "I don't fear your—*Arrghhh!*" Just then, the sun came out from behind a cloud and the giant's grip loosened. He then dropped Hopeful to the ground, convulsed, and cried out in rage and agony.

Christian saw the handle of Hopeful's paring knife protruding from the giant's bulbous right eye. Blood streaked down his face. Desperately, Despair grasped at the weapon, but his hands had lost all strength and he only managed to fall to his knees, shouting in pain.

Hopeful caught Christian's eye and nodded. "You know what to do."

"Yes I do," said Christian. "What David did to the Philistine, what I promised I'd do to you, Despair. I will have your head." He was approaching the giant, sword held high, when a horrific shriek echoed down from the window of the castle's tower. A long, hollow face appeared—a giant's face. She was even bigger than Despair himself.

"What have you done?" she shouted. "I'll kill you! I'll kill you!" Her face disappeared from the window. Despair was running away now, staggering back toward Doubting Castle, his hands hanging limp at his sides. Hopeful tugged on Christian's arm.

"There's another giant," he said. "At least one more. We need to go."

"Right."

The two of them ran with a speed that defied their aching bodies and empty bellies. In the bright light of day, they could see the path tamped down by so many erring pilgrims before them, and they followed it back to the stile, amazed at how close it truly was.

Weakness and weariness catching up to them, they climbed with great pains up the stairs on the one side of the wall, and descended the other side with unspeakable relief.

"Back where we started," Christian laughed.

"And wiser for it. Not to mention praising God all the more for his mercies."

"The sooner we leave this place behind, the better," Christian said. "But perhaps we should take some time to destroy this stile, to keep other pilgrims from adding their bones to the pile in Doubting Dungeon."

Hopeful agreed, but as they inspected it and assessed their own weak condition, they determined that the thing was too well-built to demolish it today.

"At least let us place a notice here," said Hopeful.

"That's a good idea," Christian said. It took some time, but they fashioned a sign and carved on it the words "Over this stile is the way to Doubting Castle, which is kept by Giant Despair, who despises the King of the Celestial Country, and seeks to destroy his holy pilgrims. Be ye warned."

They were in the process of affixing the sign across the steps when the same young woman they'd seen fishing along the River of God came walking briskly up the path, a hand on her sword.

"I know you two," she said. "But my, if you don't look like you've aged ten years since I last saw you. What was that—a week ago?" She read their sign and nodded in understanding. "I see. Oh, sorry—introductions: I am called Lady Daring and I was sent to look after two pilgrims who had wandered into Bypass Meadow four days ago. I don't suppose that would be you two?" She smiled warmly.

"It was indeed," said Christian. "And I think that explains the extra decade you see hanging upon us. We last met you in the midst of that cool, crisp water and the fruit and leaves of those mysterious trees. I did feel young there."

The lady produced a skin and held it out to them. "I brought some of that water with me if you'd like a drink. Somehow it remains just as cold in the vessel as it was running through the river."

The two pilgrims took turns drawing deeply from the life-giving water. When they apologized for how much they'd taken, Lady Daring laughed and told them the skin was theirs, and all the water it held. She then produced two of the fruits from along the River and handed one to each of them.

"Nothing has ever tasted this good," Hopeful said, juice dripping down his face.

"I take it you've learned something valuable here" she said.

Christian nodded. "Yes, my view on shortcuts has rather changed."

"That is good to hear." Then, looking from Christian to Hopeful, she said, "Christ be with you as you go. And for your sakes ,and the glory of his holy name, stay on the Narrow Way." She waved and continued on, toward the Shining Light in the far distance, which was once again visible to them, on this side of the wall.

The two pilgrims resumed their work, reinforcing the sign.

"Yeah, she's pretty," Christian said.

"What do you mean?"

"I mean, she left five minutes ago and you're still grinning. It's . . . off-putting."

"I'm just glad to be out of that dungeon is all."

"Sure, buddy."

They finished their work and resumed the Narrow Way, munching on wild raspberries growing along the path as they went. They'd travelled only a half an hour or so when they crested a hill and saw the beauty of the Delectable Mountains spread out before them in all their majesty.

"I just remembered," said Christian. "It's the Sabbath."

"Yes, it is. And I can think of no more fitting a place to worship our King than here, overlooking his magnificent handiwork."

And so the two men sat down to read from the Holy Book, to sing the praises of their King, and to thank him for his unspeakable faithfulness, whether in this lovely place, overlooking a breathtaking vista, or in the darkness of the Dungeon Despair.

- Turn-Away, of the Town Apostasy -

Turn-Away met the lady Good Soil near the Place of Deliverance, on the side nearest the Celestial City. He saw her walking with a lightness that belied her age, eyes fixed on the shining light in the distance, her gray hair bouncing with every step, and came up alongside her, offering to accompany her.

He had heard the tales, he said, of thieves and brigands attacking lone travelers, even along this road, and if he was quite honest, having lost his mother at a young age, he loved the idea of a spiritual mother to help guide and encourage him along the Way.

They walked together for many miles, stopping occasionally for Good Soil to rest, and relating to each other the details of their journeys so far, particularly what had transpired since passing through the Wicket Gate. At Good Soil's gentle prodding, Turn-Away recounted the tales of many mighty deeds he had done in the Lord's name, some of which sounded to her like miracles.

"I assume you received your name for the way you've turned away from your sins," Good Soil, said, as they settled down to a simple lunch, "but I think I'll call you by a nickname: Rapid Growth. I cannot believe how much you've grown in such a little time. The stories you tell! And, I almost hesitate to say this out of fear of flattery, but I believe I've seen you grow in your faith even since we've been travelling together."

Turn-Away blushed a bit, actually turning away. "That's kind of you to say, but I don't know about that nickname. It doesn't exactly roll off the tongue."

"Oh, I think it will stick," Good Soil said, with a laugh.

When they'd finished eating, they resumed the road and their conversation shifted to how they might be of service to others, even as they made progress toward the city.

"I think we just need to keep our eyes open for people who might—" Good Soil came to a stop.

"Are you alright?"

She pointed off the path a bit, and there they were met with the oddest sight: five people sleeping in the grass, their ankles shackled.

"Should we awaken them?" Good Soil asked.

"Certainly, if only to satisfy my curiosity about this. You there! Wake up! It's the middle of the day; why are you sleeping?"

One by one, they lifted their heads to squint at the two pilgrims, confused and annoyed.

"What do you want?" the man nearest them asked.

"Why are you sleeping?" Turn-Away repeated. "And why are your legs bound?"

"Oh, again with these same irksome questions. Leave us alone, pilgrims. Be gone!"

"I think I can break your chains for you," Turn-Away offered, picking up a particularly sharp rock and holding it out.

"Why don't you just mind your own business?" another of them said. "And do it, like, over there—way, way far away . . ."

"You there," said Good Soil, pointing at the man furthest from them. He had been resting his head on the belly of a woman, her garment pulled up indecently around her thighs. "You don't belong. What's your name?"

"I'm Dull," the woman answered. "Why?"

"No, I'm talking to you, sir. You in the pilgrim's coat. What is your name?"

"Linger. Uh, Linger-After-Lust."

"Really?"

The man sat up with some difficulty and rubbed the sleep from his eyes. "Wait, no," he said, his face twisting in thought. "No, that's not my name anymore." He looked back down at the woman, who beckoned him to return to his slumber. Instead, he rose to his feet, unsteadily, trying to find his legs like a newborn calf. The two pilgrims rushed to his side and held him up as he took a few tentative steps.

"My name is Godly Affections," the man said. "And you're right, ma'am; I don't belong here."

"Well, let's get you on your way," Turn-Away said.

"Oh, leave him *beeee*," one of the slumbering fools droned. "He's one of us."

"No, I'm not," Godly Affections said. "I forgot who I was for a long time. But thank God for these pilgrims, who cared enough to call me back to the road." He looked up to see a family of five running eastward, and buried his face in his hands. "Oh, it's right there!" he cried. "It's been fifteen feet away this whole time!"

Good Soil pulled his hands down and gazed into his bloodshot eyes, saying, "You've wasted some time, yes, but let's not waste a moment more." Bending down, she held the chain connecting his legs taut against a boulder. With three well-aimed strikes, Turn-Away broke it apart, and the three pilgrims began shuffling up the Narrow Way, Godly Affections in the middle, his withered legs barely holding his weight, dragging the two halves of the broken chain behind him.

As they walked, he recounted how he'd been charmed by the sounds and sights from beyond the wall and how his progress had slowed to almost nothing, until he abandoned it all together.

He wept as he spoke, confessing his sin and asking the King to forgive him.

"Godly Affections, look," Turn-Away said.

"What?"

"You're walking all on your own. And your legs . . . "

He looked down to see that, not only had his atrophied muscles returned to their former strength, but the shackles and the chains had vanished.

"Praise the Lord!" he shouted, running ahead and leaping for joy, before doubling back. "What a gift!" He jumped and spun a few more times before falling in step with his new companions. "And now," he said, "I must again confess that I have been singularly focused on myself the entire time we've been walking together. I haven't even asked your names."

"No worries. I am Good Soil and this is Turn-Away, although I call him Rapid Growth."

"'Rapid Growth?'" He laughed. "That's not very catchy."

"Maybe not, but you should hear his stories. And I'm sure you will. But when we came upon you and your companions back there, we'd been discussing the future, not the past— namely, how we might be of service to our fellow travelers along the Way."

"Well, you've already made all the difference for one back-slidden pilgrim," Godly Affections said. "I say we just keep doing what you've been doing. We've got Good Soil, we've got Rapid Growth; sounds like a recipe for bearing fruit!"

"And Godly Affections!" Turn-away said. "Don't sell yourself short. Although I think we should shorten the name. If anyone here needs a nickname, it's the man with the five-syllable name."

"Hm, seems like a job for me," Good Soil said. "How about 'Feksh?' No, that's terrible. Maybe 'Shawn?'"

Turn-Away laughed. "As in 'Godly *Affeck . . . shawn . . . s*?"

"Eh," she shrugged.

"I fear this may not be your gift, dear lady," Turn-Away

laughed. "How about just 'Godly?'"

"'Godly' it is," Good Soil said.

They walked together for the remainder of the day, singing hymns as they went, reciting passages from the Holy Book, and speculating about the incomparable glory of the Celestial City. As the sun began to set behind them, Turn-Away said, "We should think about a place to lay our heads and, if possible, to get a bite to eat. I don't suppose you have any food with you, sir?"

"No," Godly said, "I'm afraid I was eating the fruit spilling over the wall. And oh, how I would love a real, hearty meal to satisfy my hunger."

"We are also out of food," Turn-Away said. "What little we had, we ate for lunch."

Good Soil halted her steps and pulled her companions back by their elbows. "Do you smell that?"

"I certainly do," Turn-Away said, drool pooling in his lower lip. "It smells amazing! I believe it's coming from down here." He pointed at a footpath diverging from the Narrow Way and winding off to the left.

"Be careful," Godly warned. "I am probably hungrier than the two of you combined, but I know first hand the dangers of leaving the Narrow Way. It's nothing to be trifled with."

"No one's suggesting we actually leave the Way. This is an exit, a little place of rest, probably put there by the King himself. I suggest we follow this path for a little while, and see what we encounter. If any one of us wants to turn back, we'll *all* turn back. Sound good?"

"I trust you," Good Soil said.

"I guess I'm game," Godly said. "But let's keep our heads up and our wits about us. The night is coming fast."

They followed the trail around two bends in the space of two furlongs, after which it straightened out. There, a sign announced, APOSTASY: 3 MILES.

"Apostasy," Godly read. "I'm done. Let's head back."

"No, look!" Turn-Away pointed to a simple building, bearing the words: THE HIGHER STANDARD: FOOD & DRINK. "That is the source of that heavenly smell," he said. "We've come this far; I suggest we go in."

"Are you mad?" Good Soil said. "We may find ourselves in the very seat of scoffers!"

"What have we been talking about half the day?" Turn-Away said. "Wanting more opportunities to proclaim the word, to reach out to the lost. Isn't that our whole mission as we walk the Narrow Way? I'm not suggesting we move in. It's a meal in a public house, situated more or less along the Pilgrim Road."

"I guess I can't argue with that," Godly said. "What do you think?" he asked Good Soil.

"I suppose I'll trust our leader here. Let's have some dinner and bless some souls. Possibly win some souls."

They entered the windowless building to find the light low—mostly supplied by the roaring fire in the hearth—and the room all-but-filled with a single large table. At the far end, seven men were huddled together, drinks in hand, embroiled in lively conversation.

They took no notice of the three pilgrims as they sat and ordered roast chicken and corn pone. But when the food arrived and the pilgrims paused to return thanks, the room went suddenly silent. Upon saying "Amen," the pilgrims found themselves the objects of scornful looks.

"I suppose you three blew in here from yonder religious road?" said a man with a scraggly beard and fur-collared coat. "We are pilgrims, if that's what you mean," Turn-Away answered.

"And, like other pilgrims, are the three of you dead-set on converting others to your way of thinking?" The man absentmindedly spun a coin on the table as he spoke.

"It's not convincing others to think like us that makes a difference," Good Soil said. "It's proclaiming the Good News and trusting the Spirit of God to draw sinners to the cross."

"I see. Then I suppose you would not be interested in hearing my objections to the pilgrim creed. I wouldn't want to upset your quaint little applecart."

"On the contrary," Godly said, "a pilgrim is always ready to give an answer for the hope that lies within."

"And," Turn-Away added, "to destroy arguments and every lofty opinion lifted up against the knowledge of God."

The bearded man flattened the coin against the table with palm of his hand and said, "But what if each of us had an objection. Would you hear them all? All seven? Or would you be too busy 'destroying our opinions?'"

"We would hear them," Godly said, "if you would hear us as well. Go ahead; speak your mind."

A portly man sitting half in the dark at the corner of the table said, "I will speak first. I believe your 'faith' to be based in fear. You motivate the masses through oracles of doom, dangling your own journey as the only possible escape. But, if your teachings are true, why would you need to resort to such cheap tricks?" The man tipped back in his chair. "You may not believe it, but I once walked that very road and believed that doing so made me bold and courageous. It was only after I left the Narrow Way for good that I could see the truth: leaving was the truly *bold* move. I no longer walk in fear of some vengeful 'king,' who comes under the banner of love, only to crush me for my failings. I am freed from such fear."

"So, you are sure there will be no reckoning for your sins?" Good Soil asked. "Truly?"

"I believe you people overstate the consequences of so-called 'sin.' In fact, much of the happiness in my life today is the direct result of what you would call 'sin.' Pilgrims often speak of faith and fear as though they are opposites, but I submit to you that they are only such in the sense that two sides of the same coin are opposite each other."

"But consider this," Godly began to say, but Turn-Away motioned for him to keep silent.

"Let us hear all seven before we respond," he said. "We may find them to be redundant, or perhaps we can answer more than one objection at once." Godly nodded his ascent, and Turn-Away gestured for the next man in line to speak.

"I have only a question for you," the man said. A simple, two-word question: *Why hell?* Why would a supposedly kind and loving God even conceive of such a thing—to send even some of his kindest and most loving creatures into eternal punishment? Yes, you'll say, 'He is loving, but he is also holy and just.' But how can a just king create me as I am, with lust or pride or jealousy in my heart, and then punish me for living these things out? It's such nonsense. I would expect small children to embrace such notions, but not grown men and an old woman."

"Okay, I'm not *old* —"

Turn-Away patted the woman's hand and gestured to a young, clean-cut man. "Have you something to say?"

"My objection," the man practically shouted, "is that the entire enterprise of pilgrimage is built on a foolish and anti-intellectual foundation! Why, to even entertain the idea of 'miracles' flies in the face of two and a half centuries' worth of scientific revival! Just throw all that knowledge right out the window! No rational person believes a man can walk on water, or ascend into the sky, or be swallowed by a whale and live! And certainly no one can return to life once he's died!" He inspected the three pilgrims for a moment, before pointing at Turn-Away and saying, "You especially surprise me, sir. These others perhaps do not know any better. But you strike me as someone with the potential to be sophisticated. An intellectual."

"That sounds awfully elitist," Godly said.

"You are the elitists!" a bald and wizened man declared, pointing his stubby finger at the three of them. "Of all the religions of all the people in all the world, for all of history . . . only *your way* is right? Such arrogance!"

Good Soil shifted in her seat, clearly wanting to give a response, but instead, she swallowed it down and asked, "Is that
all, sir?"

The little man laughed. "Yes, that's *all*—just that your narrow view of the universe is laughable and naïve; nothing
more!" He threw up his hands.

"And let us not forget the hypocrites," a finely dressed man
said, leaning dramatically into the light of a burning candle. "I
have spent a little time on that road of yours, and I have noticed
that many a scoundrel walks it. Many who prefer cruelty to
love, who hold to greed and slander and gossip and even
worse. There are some on that road who would claim to be the
very light of the world, while obscuring their own wickedness,
and that of their friends and fellows in the shadows. If that road
of yours is travelled by such wicked people, why should anyone want to walk it?"

"I raise an even more foundational question," the next man
said, swilling his drink around in its tankard. "Why would
anyone want to walk that road when they are made to *submit*?
To give up their autonomy, even their identity? Are you a
sheep? A follower? Or a leader? It seems clear to me that this
religion of yours preys upon the simple minded and weak-
willed, in order to benefit the few."

Godly's eyes drifted down the row of barflies. "By my
count, we've one more grievance yet to hear," he said. "But I'm
not sure who—"

"It is I," said the man with the scraggly beard, now flipping
the coin deftly between his knuckles. "And for last I have saved
the most obvious flaw. You claim that your King is all-powerful, all-knowing, and all-loving. And yet there is still suffering
in this world. Unspeakable, nonsensical suffering, beyond what
any man could catalog. This does not require a philosopher's
mind or great learning; it was clear to me when I was but ten
years old. My mother fell ill and I prayed for her, that your King
would heal her, but he did not. She died."

"I know how that feels," Turn-Away said. "My mother died when I was young. It never truly leaves you, does it?"

"Did you not pray for her?"

"Well, it was an accident, not an illness."

"An accident beyond your King's ability to prevent?"

"No, but—"

"You mother—was she a pilgrim, like you?"

"No, she did not walk that road. But she was a good woman. A kind and wonderful woman. I miss her greatly."

"A good woman, you say? Not good enough for your king! By your doctrine, he has tossed her aside into burning brimstone, simply because she did not walk his Narrow Way, in his particular narrow way! Perhaps she followed her own heart, her own path; could he not love her and reward her for that?"

Godly Affections planted his hands on the table and half-stood. "How can you speak this way? The King of Princes died for us—suffered and died for our filth and sins and rebellion, so that we could have a way of deliverance: one way to escape eternal death and have eternal life! And instead of praising him with all your being, you complain that he should have died a dozen other deaths so that you could have some choice in how you are saved?"

"That's not what he's saying and I think you know it," Turn-Away snapped. Then he recomposed himself and said, "I understand this man's frustration and I think we have all shared it. Why must the Narrow Way be so . . . narrow? We all keep these doubts hidden deep in our hearts, but they must come forth at some point. The question must be answered: who is this King to use us as playthings in his game of cosmic chess?"

"Turn-Away," Good Soil said, "what are you doing . . . over there?"

He looked down and saw that he was now sitting on the opposite side of the table, in the midst of the Seven.

Across from him, the two pilgrims gaped at how quickly

this reversal had taken place. "Turn-Away, do not rush into anything," Godly said. "To doubt is not sin, but your doubts are not your friends either. As the poet said, our doubts are traitors. And how do we treat traitors? Give them a fair trial, yes, but then put it to death!"

But the Seven were now plying Turn-Away with strong drink and whispering dissension in his ears.

Good Soil reached for his hand, but the table was too big. "Turn-Away, think of the Place of Deliverance. Think of the new name you received."

"Yes," Godly said, "and think of the empty sepulcher and the hill where your burden was taken from you. Think of the cross we saw there. In fact, as I think back to it now, I saw the Prince himself dying there, suffering for my sins. Did you see it?"

"Listen to how their memories shift to ward off reason and doubt," one of the men said, again filling Turn-Away's cup.

"You were there, Turn-Away," Godly said. "Think back!"

TURN-AWAY WILL NOT LISTEN TO EVANGELIST.

He shook his head, slowly. "No. No, I wasn't. My name has always been Turn-Away. And I met up with the Pilgrim Road east of the hill, taking an old path directly from my hometown. There was a man there—one *Evangelist*—who laid hands on me and tried to guide me to a gate some miles back, but I was unwilling to start at the beginning. I've always been a quick study, after all."

He locked eyes with Good Soil. "And then I met you, good woman, and you spoke so transcendentally of that holy hill—

the transport of the place and the freedom you received, that I just went along with it."

"But your coat," Godly began to say, but in this light, they could see that it was a counterfeit. And the sweat trickling down his brow was cutting through the mark on his forehead. "Oh, Turn-Away, I know what it's like to be tempted by our old sin, our old selves, and—"

"Don't bother. There's nothing you can say that I don't already know. If anyone ever really knew this King, I did. I prophesied powerfully in his name and did many great wonders for his glory. And yet, I feel nothing but relief to quit that Narrow Way. Leave me now. I will never walk that road again."

"We can still go back," Good Soil said. "Come with us; we'll accompany you back to the Wicket Gate."

But the Seven had closed in around Turn-Away so that they could no longer see him.

"Where was his hometown?" Godly asked.

"He never said," Good Soil answered. "But I think I know. The Town Apostasy. He comes from that place and now he will go back willingly."

"You should forget you ever knew this Turn-Away," said the bearded man. "He was never yours to begin with. And he never belonged to your king."

"He's right," said Good Soil.

"But were we wrong to come in here?" asked Godly. "Was Turn-Away misleading us when he said he that our mission along the road is to reason with the lost and to point them to the Gate and the Place of Deliverance?"

"No, he was right. And we will encounter many more on the road, some of whom may say the very same things we've heard here tonight—only earnestly, and seeking truth, not by way of dragging a pilgrim into the pit of hell. These Seven are not men seeking God. They are dogs and swine, and our Lord has forbidden us giving holy things to them, lest they trample them under foot, turn, and tear us to pieces. We should go."

"Or maybe we'll keep you here with us!" the leader of the Seven said, leaping upon the table and scrambling over it impossibly fast on hands and knees. But as he wrapped his hand around Good Soil's wrist, it sizzled and burned, and he let out a hoarse shriek. By reflex, she pushed him away. The simple blow sent him sailing across the room, where he slammed into the wall and crumpled to the ground.

The two pilgrims stood and made their way out into the night, looking back sadly for their friend, but not seeing him.

When they'd gone, the Seven dispersed, returning to their seats. They kept filling Turn-Away's cup with strong drink and his ears with the seeds of unbelief—as well as the dung to fertilize them—well into the night.

"I'm so glad I found you guys," Turn-Away slurred, looking around at his tablemates. "Whoa. I think I may have had too much. You're . . . you're changing." And they were. Their faces were transforming—some into canine form, brows pulled low, the sharp gaze of a predator. The others took on the visage of wild boars.

Turn-Away looked down into his cup and chuckled. "Dogs and swine. *Ha!* That's too much."

"Don't worry," the leader said, his tusks emerging from the bedraggled beard. "You're just over-warm from the fire. Let's take this off." He helped Turn-Away remove the coat, which he tossed into the flames. He then withdrew a brand, the end glowing red.

All at once, Turn-Away's drinking companions converged on him, savagely pinning him to the table, pulling his shirt up to expose his bare back.

"Since the mark has melted from your head," the bearded swine said, "Let's give you something more permanent."

A Glass, Darkly

Christian awoke the next morning to find the lingering stiffness from the giant's cage all but gone. He stood tall and stretched, filling his lungs with the crisp morning air. A few feet away, Hopeful was yet sleeping by the glowing embers of their fire, hugging his thin blanket in a way that reminded Christian of his young son Joseph.

"I'll let him sleep," Christian thought. "He needs it." While their time in the dungeon had been more of a test for Christian in the moment, Hopeful seemed more shaken by the battle with the giant. Christian thought back to his own first grave encounter—his combat with Apollyon—and was thankful that Hopeful had not had to face his test alone.

Hiking up a few dozen steps from their campsite, Christian stood at the overlook of the Delectable Mountains and drank in the majesty of the sight once again. They'd spent hours in worship, facing out toward this majestic view, but the beauty struck him anew this morning, cloaked in mist, both powerful and serene. What he wouldn't give now for a cup of Steadfast's thick, aromatic coffee to sip while he watched the sunrise here.

That was out of the question, of course, but a tasty breakfast enjoyed here at the overlook might be just as good. Christian thought back to the wood strawberries growing along the path no more than three miles back, upon which they'd snacked while travelling the previous morning. If gathered in large enough quantity, these might be the base of an enjoyable meal to start this new day.

Christian crept back into camp, quietly strapped on his sword, and began retracing his steps from the previous day. As he listened to the birds and the swish of the leaves in the morning breeze, they sounded to him like the voice of the Great King, declaring his love and protection over pilgrims.

He'd been walking only about fifteen minutes when he noticed a peculiar rock formation, just where a little well-trodden path came snaking in from the north—and a sudden sense of alarm gripped the pilgrim. He reached for his sword, but the sound of a dagger being drawn behind him and the prick of its point against his spine, just above the stiff fabric of his embroidered coat, froze him in his tracks.

"Well done, bandit," Christian said. "I didn't even hear you approach."

"I'm as quick as I am stealthy, so don't even think of pulling that sword," the thief said, pushing the tip of his blade into the pilgrim's neck just enough to coax out a drop of blood, which Christian felt trickle down and pool against his collar.

"I've already admitted, you got the drop on me."

"And we've got you outnumbered too," said a thick-necked brawler of a man appearing from behind a bush, alongside another—as willowy as his companion was stout. The burly man wielded a club, which he swished back and forth menacingly as he approached. The other held only a cloth bag. He too advanced, although his sunken eyes projected fear and he seemed to somehow shrink back more with every forward step.

"Let me guess," Christian said, pointing at the men in turn. "Deep-Doubt and Faint-Heart." The two stopped in their tracks. "And I presume that's Guilt skulking behind me like a coward."

Faint-Heart took a staggering step back, glancing uneasily

at his club-wielding brother, who also seemed thrown, uncertainty diluting his former swagger.

Christian smirked. "Oh, it frightens you that I know your names? I know more than that! I have heard tales of this place—Dead Man's Lane—of the ruthlessness of you three brothers. And your cowardice." He squeezed the hilt of his sword. "Perhaps you should run along. As it is, you've ventured up to the King's Highway. This is not a safe place for you, as you must know."

"We will be gone just as soon as you hand over your valuables," Deep Doubt snarled.

"Yes," Guilt said, behind him, "give us your treasure . . . "

Christian scoffed at this. "I have on my person—and *in* my person—greater treasure than you three hooligans could ever imagine. But because of your carnal, wicked bent, you would not recognize its value if it bashed you *in the nose!*"

In one fluid motion, Christian pulled his sword, spun, and knocked the dagger from the robber's hand. Before he could lay a blow upon him, though, Deep Doubt came charging up behind him and ran face-first into a blow from the pilgrim's elbow. He grunted, choking on his own blood and teetering like a tree about to fall.

Faint-Heart lunged as well, tentatively, and Christian simply rolled to the ground and watched him collide with Deep Doubt, both of them bouncing away like billiard balls. As he came back to his feet, Christian used his momentum to slam the cross-guard of his sword into Guilt's nose, propelling him to the earth as well.

While the three brothers collected themselves, Christian removed the shield from his back and buckled it down to his arm. "Naturally, I meant to do that last bit earlier, right after I said the thing about my treasure bashing you in the— Oh, never mind. Have you common thieves had enough?"

The three had regrouped now and rushed the pilgrim again—this time as one. Christian ran to meet them, slamming his shield into Guilt's chin and dodging a blow from Deep Doubt's club. Pivoting on his heel, he rushed Faint-Heart, wrapping his left arm around the man's concave chest and lifting him off his feet. Three steps later, he slammed the villain into the wide trunk of a tree. Immediately, the pilgrim turned and swung his sword, deflecting a blow from Deep Doubt's club and then blasting him to the ground with a savage stomping kick.

"You three presumptuous fools have not caught this pilgrim asleep or wandering the woods unarmed. Take a moment to count the cost and cut your losses. Or face death at my blade."

The three of them rose again, slower this time. They silently conferred, seemingly considering this out. Then Deep Doubt scooped up a heavy rock and heaved it at the pilgrim, catching him in the helmet, just above his eyes. Christian reeled, and that's when Faint-Heart rushed in from the side, tackling him around the legs, and bringing him down.

Christian tried to stand, but a boot to the head spun his helmet, covering his eyes. Another kick to his side put him flat on his back. Then he felt hands yanking up on his breastplate and more hands reaching in beneath it, searching for his pockets. Then five cold fingers directly upon his heart, and a gripping fear—far colder than ice—filled his chest. Out of the corner of one eye, he could see Deep Doubt's massive legs planted beside him. For a moment, Christian was inclined to just play possum and let them take what they would and leave him be.

Then he remembered the frantic day he'd spent without his scroll, and the fear melted away. Reaching out to where his sword had fallen, he grasped the hilt and swung it up toward the burly man's calf, intending to hamstring him, but the blade came up harder yet and severed Deep Doubt's leg below the knee.

Rolling to his feet, Christian righted his helmet and, with a wide swing of his shield, dealt a crushing blow to Guilt's cheek-bone, connecting so hard that the bandit's head and feet switched places for a moment, before gravity jerked him ruthlessly back to the earth with a crunch. Deep-Doubt was cursing and grunting as he tied off his left thigh.

Only Faint-Heart stood among his brothers now, a stiletto blade clenched in his thin, veiny fist. He trembled, staring at Christian like a hart before the hunter. Christian looked from the thief's thin blade to his own blood-streaked sword.

"Mine's bigger," he said. "And I have won the day. Go back over the wall to your damned land. And lug this *trash* with you."

Faint Heart dropped the weapon and began to draw in a deep breath. Christian strode quickly to him and pushed the edge of his blade against his enemy's sunken cheek. "I see you preparing to call for your master. But how will you do so without your tongue?"

Faint-Heart shook his head, stiffly, and set about helping Deep Doubt to his remaining foot. Guilt rose on his own, but staggered in a crooked line as the three strongarm thieves slowly made their way back toward Beelzebub's land.

When they'd gone, Christian fell to his knees and thanked the King for his love and protection.

When Christian returned to the campsite, Hopeful took one look at him and dropped the firewood in his arms, asking, "What on earth happened to you?"

Christian smiled wryly and said, "I went to get us some berries." He sat heavily on a log and warmed his hands.

"Well . . . where are they?"

Christian looked down at his empty hands and laughed. "I guess the task was too much for me. But it looks like you've got some breakfast on the fire." He pointed at the small pot hanging from a trivet, boiling.

"Cow parsley and wild onions," Hopeful said. "It's no feast, but we'd have given anything for such a meal a day ago."

"Right you are, brother. And I thank you for preparing this meal—and our King for causing it to grow."

They ate slowly, savoring what little nutrition there was to be gleaned, and both men were still hungry when the pot was empty—a hollow ache, yet unsated, from their days in the Dungeon Despair. Still, after dousing the fire and packing up their few belongings, they set off toward the Delectable Mountains with a spring in their step.

They walked quietly for some time, drinking in the beauty of the mountains ahead. Then Hopeful broke the silence. "So, are you going to tell me what really happened this morning or leave me to imagine it?"

Christian considered this for a moment. "If you must know, let me begin by telling you a story."

"I'd rather hear one of your songs than one of your stories."

"I haven't had time to write this one yet. But this is a tale that was told me by a great Teacher in the study of the Palace Beautiful. It's about a pilgrim named Little-Faith, of the town Sincere. A good man, but not so stout-hearted. The thing was this: one night, Little-Faith bedded down, all alone, right where a winding road comes in from Broadway Gate to merge onto the Narrow Way, on the left hand side. This road is called Dead Man's Lane, both because of a rock formation there, which looks like a skull and crossbones, and because of the many murders that have been committed at that place."

"A rocky skull? Did this Little-Faith not see such a glaring omen?" Hopeful asked.

"No. Just as you and I did not notice when we passed it yesterday. Only this morning, as I walked back toward the City of Destruction, was it clear to me. But, back to Little-Faith. While he slept, poor Little-Faith was set upon by three sturdy rogues: Faint-Heart, Deep Doubt, and Guilt. These three brothers threatened poor Little-Faith, beat him, and made off with one of his purses, containing most of his spending money."

"What of his scroll?" Hopeful asked.

"His scroll they did not see," Christian said. "Nor his second purse, which contained his jewels—although this was by no cunning of his own. Rather, by God's good providence, the pilgrim had landed upon these things when he fell and, thinking they might have heard one Mr. Great-Grace coming their way, the thieves fled back to their lair beyond the wall."

"He must have been thankful for that mercy."

"You'd think so," said Christian, "for in addition to his scroll and his jewels, he had a little odd money left as well. But he was not wise about how he spent it, and before long Little-Faith was reduced to begging until his journey's end."

"Still, though," Hopeful said, "it must have been a continual comfort to him that they missed his jewels and his certificate."

"Aye, it might have been, had he used them as he should. But because of his great dismay at losing his purse, he hid them away and practically forgot about them. And the few times he sought their comfort, they only reminded him of his loss, and these bitter thoughts would swallow up all."

Hopeful shook his head. "Poor heart. That's a lot of grief to bear."

"For certain, as it would be to any of us, had we been robbed and wounded in such a frightful place, in the dead of night. It's a wonder he did not die with grief, and for the rest of the way, he issued nothing but doleful and bitter complaints, telling any-one he encountered all about his troubles, and only about his troubles, often showing his scars and recounting his wounds."

"Yet he was not reduced to selling some of his jewels?"

"Selling his jewels?" Christian gaped for a moment before grabbing Hopeful's head and pulling it near to examine his scalp.

"What are you doing?" Hopeful complained, pulling away.

"I was just looking to see if some of your shell was still on your head!" he laughed. "For what could he pawn his jewels? Or to whom could he sell them? For if he did, he would have been turned away at the Celestial Gate—which is worse than the villainy of ten thousand thieves."

"Why so contrary, brother? I seem to remember that Esau sold his birthright for a bowl of red stew. And that birthright was his greatest jewel. If he could do it, why couldn't Little-Faith?"

"You are right about Esau, and many others besides, who have excluded themselves from the heavenly inheritance. But there is a world of difference between these two men. Esau's belly was his god; not so with Little-Faith. Esau was dragged about by his carnal desires for a savory dish (whether of the stew variety or the Hittite woman variety) and he saw no fur-ther than the satisfying of those lusts; not so with our pilgrim. Little-Faith feared he would die at the hands of those three brig-ands, but Esau declared himself at the point of death, simply because he was hungry after a strenuous hunt, posing the foolish question, 'What good will this birthright do me in the grave?'

"You did not hear the good story, but you should have known the difference between these men, in this: it was Little-Faith's lot to have but a little faith, and yet that little faith kept him from trading his birthright and led him to prize his jewels even if he did not sufficiently use them. On the other hand, I defy you to show me in the Scriptures where Esau had any faith at all. If he did, he would not have sold his soul. Those whose minds are set upon their lusts will have them, whatever the cost. Little-Faith, on the other hand, could never have made such a foolish trade. Will a man give a penny to fill his belly with hay? I think not. And that is your mistake."

Hopeful studied one foot and the other, as he walked. "I acknowledge it; still your severe rebuke . . . almost makes me angry."

"Severe? Why, I only compared you to some of the *brisker* sort of birds who will run to and fro in untrodden paths with the shell upon their heads. But get over that and consider the real topic of discussion, and all will be well between us."

Hopeful scowled. "I still think I'm right. If these three fellows were not, at their core, a company of cowards, why would they turn-tail and run at the noise of someone coming up the road? It seems to me that Little-Faith ought to have strengthened his heart, plucked up his courage, and put up a fight."

Christian thought for a moment and said, "You are correct that there is cowardice at the heart of these thieves. But in the time of trial, it is hard to see. And Little-Faith himself had no great heart to speak of. You asked where I was this morning; I was fighting these three brothers myself. And if it had been you whom these cunning outlaws had surrounded so suddenly, I believe you would have a different perspective.

"When our enemies are out of sight, it's easy enough to boast about our own courage and prowess. But see them closing in on you, and you may have second thoughts. Something you should know about these rogues, Guilt, Faint-Heart, and Deep Doubt: they choose their victims at will and keep most of their spoil, but they are employed by another—the king of the bottomless pit, who has been known to come to their aid if they call for him. When I was engaged as this Little-Faith was, I found it a terrible thing. I determined, as a Christian, to resist. But they proved themselves worthy adversaries and I knew that they might call for their master at any moment. Even outfitted as I am with this holy armor, I nearly despaired of hope. No man can tell you what he will do in combat until he has tasted the battle himself."

"But you said they ran away when they thought this Mr. Great-Grace was in the Way."

"True. They have often fled—both they and their master—when Great-Grace appears, for he is our King's champion. But there is a great contrast to be seen between Great-Grace and Little-Faith. Or between Great-Grace and you or me. All of a king's subjects are not his champions, Hopeful. Eleazar mowed down the Philistines until his sword froze in his hand. Do you suppose a little child could have done the same thing? And yet, Jesus called a little child up to sit on his knee as an example of the type of faith we must have. Some are strong, some are weak; some have great faith, some have little. This Little-Faith was one of the weak, and therefore he went to the wall."

"I wish it *had* been Great-Grace they stumbled upon that day," Hopeful said.

"If it had been, he might have had his hands full. Though Great-Grace is mighty and skilled with his weapons, these three—Deep-Doubt, Faint-Heart, and Guilt—can get *within* a man and bring him down, and then he might find himself at their mercy, of which they have none.

"The Teacher also told me quite a few tales of Great-Grace. To look at his face is to see the many scars of battle. And scars are proof that a man has been opened, and bled. Great-Grace will confess that he once even despaired of life when he faced these foes. And it was these same foes who made King David groan and mourn and roar! And Mighty Peter, the prince of the apostles, though he would draw his sword and stare down the mob, was laid low by a servant girl when these three enemies had their way with him."

"But that's just it," Hopeful said. "Had Peter known them for who they were, he—"

"You're not listening, Hopeful! If their master is about, he will come to their aid. Let footmen like us never desire to meet with such enemies or boast that we would have done better when we hear that others have met their match. And above all, let us never be tickled with thoughts of our own strength and courage; that was Peter's downfall, and David's, and it will be ours as well if we follow in their footsteps."

"How then should we respond?" Hopeful asked. "And how can we prepare ourselves when we hear of such violent crimes committed on the King's Highway?"

"Two things become a pilgrim in such cases," Christian said. "First, we must be sure to take a shield with us. If we lack that, our enemies fear us not at all. Remember, the apostle tells us 'Above all, take up the shield of faith.' And secondly, we should travel in a convoy."

"There are only two of us," Hopeful observed. "I'd hardly call that a convoy."

"You are right that we would do better to find a band of pilgrims with whom we might travel more securely. But I mean that we should ask the King himself to go with us. When David was in the Valley of the Shadow of Death, the thought of our God going with him caused him to rejoice. And don't forget the great Moses, who would rather die where he stood than take one step without his God.

"My brother, if He will go along with us—and He will!— we need not be afraid of ten thousand enemy soldiers. But without him, even the greatest warriors fall. Yes, I have faced down Apollyon—and others as well—and I remain, by God's grace, alive. But I cannot boast of my heroism. And I pray that I should meet with no more such adversaries, though I fear that we are still not beyond all danger."

They walked again in silence until late afternoon, when they arrived at the Delectable Mountains. As they climbed, they passed through gardens and orchards, vineyards and fountains, from which they drank, finding the water to be as cold and refreshing as that from the River of Life.

"Christian," Hopeful said, "I still feel the grime and hopelessness of the giant's dungeon clinging to my outer person. Do you think it would be proper for us to bathe here in this fountain?"

"I was just thinking the same thing," Christian said, stripping off his armor and kicking off his boots. "These mountains belong to the King of this land and I am sure we will be safe to take a moment to let down our guard and be cleansed of any dust or grit from Beelzebub's land."

When they'd finished washing, they dried in the sun, got dressed, and once again followed the Way up the mountain. As they passed through still more vineyards, they ate the heavenly fruit and found it to be delicious and satisfying.

Before they knew it, they had reached the highest ridge, along which they saw nothing but lush green grass and many sheep happily grazing.

From here, they could see the other mountaintops as well, equally fertile. Where one might expect to find snowcaps, there was only vegetation.

As they walked along the ridge, they came upon three shepherds standing by the roadside. Taking hold of the opportunity to rest (as well as to learn something of this place), they approached these men and, leaning upon their staffs, asked them, "Sirs, whose sheep are these?"

The youngest of the shepherds—who still looked to be older than Christian and Hopeful put together—answered, "These are Emmanuel's sheep and this is Emmanuel's land. They are here because they know his voice when he calls to them, and they know he will lead them into green pastures and beside still waters, and will protect them from wolves, even with his very life. And we, his under-shepherds, are called to emulate him."

"Is this the way to the Celestial City?" Hopeful asked.

"Yes, you are just in the Way."

"How much further?" Christian asked.

The oldest of the shepherds, his eyes as white as his beard, said, "Too far for any but those who shall arrive there."

"I . . . see. Is the way dangerous?"

The old shepherd said, "It is safe for those for whom it is safe; but transgressors shall fall therein."

Hopeful caught Christian's eye for a moment and half-shrugged. He then asked, "Is there any relief here for tired pilgrims?"

"Of course," said the other shepherd. His robe was as brightly colored as Joseph's, and his skin as dark as the bark of an oak tree. "The Lord of these mountains has charged us to always entertain strangers." He spread out his hands and said, "The good of this place is before you, and your perseverance will be rewarded. For few who begin to walk this holy road ever show their face on these mountains."

"What are your names, if I might ask?"

"I am Knowledge," said the man in the colorful robe. "This is Sober, and the patriarch of our order is called Experience."

Just then, a youth came running up, laughing, a shepherd's

staff in his hand and a playful lamb on his tail.

"And this," the old man Experience said, "is Sincere." He reached out both his hands to the pilgrims and they each took one. These shepherds then brought the pilgrims into a wide tent, where they fed them fresh bread, cheese, and pastries.

"And now," said Knowledge, "I invite you to stay a while and be acquainted with us. It is nearly dark now, and this is a safe and comforting place to sleep, here among Experience's many cushions." He laughed.

With only a brief look between them, both pilgrims agreed to stay till the morning.

They sat up well into the night, as each of the four shepherds came, in turn, to converse with them, between shifts of keeping watch and their own sleep. Finally, Christian and Hopeful retired to the corner of the tent, where there was indeed an enormous collection of cushions and pillows. After praying together and bidding each other good-night, the two pilgrims drifted off into the deepest sleep they'd known in weeks.

They awakened the next morning to the smell of strong coffee, which Knowledge offered to them mixed with fresh sheep's milk. The taste was heavenly to both the pilgrims and filled them with the energy to set out once more.

"Would you mind if we walked with you for a time?" Knowledge asked.

"We would love it," Hopeful answered.

Leaving Sincere to tend the flocks, the other three Shepherds accompanied the pilgrims along the mountaintop road. As they walked, Christian and Hopeful were nearly overwhelmed by the beauty on every side. When they'd gone perhaps half a mile, Knowledge stopped in his tracks, looked at his fellow shepherds, and asked, "Well? Shall we show these pilgrims some wonders?"

The other two agreed, as did Christian and Hopeful, and a short time later, they found themselves following these three mysterious men up a hill called Error. As they reached the top, the pilgrims drew back, seeing how incredibly high and steep it was.

"Yes, be careful," said Sober, "but look down to the bottom, and tell me what you see."

Hopeful reached over and grabbed his brother's sleeve, peering carefully over the edge. "I see several men," he said. "Or they were once men. Now they are but bones, decaying clothing, and precious metals. Clearly they fell from this peak and were dashed to pieces."

"What is the meaning of this?" Christian asked, unable to tear his eyes from the terrible sight.

"Have you heard of those who hearkened to the teaching of Hymenaeus and Philetus regarding the resurrection of the dead?"

They answered, "Yes."

"These are the shattered people you see below," Knowledge explained. "They remain unburied to this day as an example to others who would come near the brink of this hill. Remember always what you have seen here."

"I will never forget," Christian said.

"Nor I," said Hopeful.

"Good. Now follow me; there are more wonders to show you."

As they descended, Christian said to Knowledge, "You remind me, sir, of the Interpreter whose house I visited between the Wicket Gate and the Place of Deliverance."

Knowledge smiled. "Ah, you speak of my brother, who once lived with us in these mountains, until he was called to minister near the head of the road, rather than to those approaching its end." When they reached the bottom of the hill, they began to ascend an even higher peak, the name of this one being Caution.

When they'd climbed about halfway to the top, Sober pointed out toward a distant graveyard, and told the pilgrims to look.

Christian shielded his eyes against the sun and squinted. "I see some movement among the tombs," he said, "but I cannot tell who it is or what they are doing."

"Here." Knowledge held a spyglass out to them.

Christian received the instrument and inspected it. "I've never used one of these before. How is it done?"

"I have," Hopeful said, snatching it up to his eye and carefully adjusting the focus. "I see men walking among the tombs alright, but they continually stumble and fall."

He handed it to Christian, who, mimicking his fellow-pilgrim, looked through the smaller lens and said, "They seem to be trying to get out from among the graves, but they cannot. Are they blind?"

"They are," said Experience. "Tell me, did you notice, some miles back, a stile that went over the wall on the left-hand side, just off the way?"

"We . . . did, yes," Christian said.

"From that place, a path leads directly to Doubting Castle, which is kept by the Giant Despair. And these men—" he pointed out toward the tombs, "who came once on pilgrimage, as you do now, thought the Narrow Way too rough, and went over that stile, into Bypass Meadow. And there they were taken by the giant and cast into Doubting Dungeon. And when that wicked monster grew tired of them, he put out their eyes and cast them among the tombs, where they wander to this day. For it is written, *Those who wander out of the way of understanding shall remain in the congregation of the dead*."

Christian and Hopeful dried their tears and said nothing to the shepherds about their own experience with the giant.

As they descended the hill a different way, Sober brought them to a door in the mountain itself. "Open it," he said, "and look inside."

Christian did as the shepherd instructed and found that it was dark and smoky within. A deep rumbling noise, like a great fire, the scent of brimstone, and the cries of tormented souls came up from the depths.

"What is this place?" Hopeful asked.

"It is a byway to hell," Knowledge said, "for hypocrites—namely, those who sell their birthrate as Esau, or their Master, as Judas."

"And," said Experience, "for those who blaspheme the Gospel with Alexander, or conspire with Sapphira."

Hopeful stared into the terrifying void. "And yet, each of these walked this road as a pilgrim."

"Yes, and for a very long way, some of them even farther than these mountains before they were miserably cast out."

Hopeful looked at his fellow pilgrim with bloodshot eyes and said, "You are right indeed, Christian. I should not have presumed how I would fare in Little-Faith's shoes, nor should I long for glory in battle against the enemies pressing in, for stronger men than I have fallen, and nearer the end than I am now."

"It is a difficult lesson," Christian agreed. "I too am still learning it. And you have learned it without falling yourself! I admire you for that. And . . . sorry I said the thing about the shell upon you head. It wasn't even that funny."

Hopeful laughed. "I think I've removed the last of it today." He looked up at the sun, climbing in the sky, and said, "If we are leaving this place today, we should do it soon."

"Aye," said Christian. "We've imposed on these good men long enough."

The shepherds accompanied them back up to the Narrow Way and walked with them to the end of the mountain ridge, where they found young Sincere watching the flocks.

"Before you leave these mountains," Sober said, "there is one more thing you must see." He pointed into the distance. "From this vantage, the gates of the Celestial City are visible."

The two pilgrims squinted toward the shining light, which was now far closer and much larger to their eyes than it had been before.

"Perhaps this will help," Sober said, offering them a small pane of amber-tinted glass in an ornate gold frame. Looking through it, the overwhelming light of the place was dimmed just enough that Christian could make out a pair of tall towers, which he assumed flanked the entrance. The gate itself, though, was too distant to truly see. He handed the device to Hopeful who, after peering through it for a moment, asked, "Sir, may I borrow your spyglass again?"

"Of course," Knowledge said, handing it over.

Hopeful instructed his companion to hold the tinted glass up before him and, lining up the spyglass behind it, he suddenly gasped.

"Did you see the gate?" Christian asked.

"I think I did! But I confess I am so rattled by what we saw behind that door that my hands are shaking, and I saw it for only a brief moment. Here, you try."

They switched places and Christian adjusted the focus until

he too gasped and jerked the instrument down from his eye.

"I saw something like a gate," he said. "And I saw some of the glory of that place. I cannot wait to reach it." He looked up at Hopeful. "We have to go." Handing the spyglass back to the shepherd, he made to head out.

"Yes, this is where we must part ways," Knowledge said. "But we do not leave you empty handed." Reaching beneath his colorful robe, he withdrew a rolled document, which he handed to Christian. "A map," he said, "of the remainder of the Way. Remember the door in the mountain, and see that you are not yourselves led astray so close to the end."

"Some food for your Journey," Experience said, handing them a sack full of bread. "And with it, I offer this word of warning . . . " He place a hand on each of the pilgrim's heads and solemnly uttered the words, "beware the Flatterer."

"As one who is watchful and vigilant," Sober said, "I implore you both not to sleep upon the Enchanted Ground. The importance of this cannot be overstated."

"Understood," Hopeful said. Then, looking down at the framed glass in his hands, he laughed and held it out to Sincere. "I nearly walked off with your mystical tool."

"You can keep it," the young man said, with a hearty smile. "And Godspeed to you."

There was once again silence between Hopeful and Christian as they descended the mountains—but this silence was borne, not of conflict, but of awe.

Both men would have been content to simply meditate on what they'd just seen for the rest of the day, but a little below these mountains, they happened upon a very brisk lad coming up to the Narrow Way from a crooked little lane on the left.

"Hello, young man," Christian said. "Where are you coming from on this lovely day?"

The young man beamed and answered, "Sir, I was born in the country of Conceit, which lies at my back. That's where I'm comin' from, and the Celestial City is where I'm going."

"But how do you plan to enter at the gate?"

"You know," he shrugged, "as other good people do."

Hopeful shot Christian a look and asked the young man, "Do you have anything to show at the gate, that it should be opened to you?"

"Well, I know my Lord's will. I've lived a good life so far. I pay every man what I owe him, I pray and fast. I tithe and give alms. And, of course, I've left my own country behind for the one to which I'm headed. I should think that will do the trick."

"But you did not come in at the Wicket Gate," Christian said. "Rather, via some crooked lane. Young man, I fear that, whatever you may think of yourself, when the Reckoning Day shall come, you will be found a thief and a robber, and barred from entering the City."

The young man narrowed his eyes. "What's your name?"

"I am Christian, and this is my friend and brother, Hopeful. And you?"

"They call me Ignorance. And save the jokes and barbs; I've heard them all. It's just a name. And you may think that you know me by it, but you don't. In fact, you don't know me at all. So, as utter strangers to me, be content to follow the religion of your country, and I will follow the religion of mine.

"And since you seem to come from a land that is even more distant from the Holy City than I do, I find it utterly laughable that you would attempt to school me on it. How could you even know the way to this distant place, let alone exactly who will gain entry, and how? Can you not be content to simply walk this pleasant lane and make pleasant, polite conversation?" Before Christian could answer, the man fell back a few paces to distance himself from the pilgrims, muttering all the while.

In a low voice, Hopeful said, "This man is wise in his own conceit, but ignorant of the things of God. There is more hope for a fool than for him. Shall we continue to walk and talk with him or pull ahead and leave him to think on what we've already said?"

"I say we leave the seed of truth planted and see if God might cause it to grow into understanding."

"Agreed," Hopeful said. We can speak with him again tomorrow."

So they went on, and Ignorance followed. The two of them stopped for an early evening meal from the food the Shepherds had given them. They determined to offer some to Ignorance, should he join them, but he yet trailed at a distance.

After dinner, they resumed the Way, and soon found themselves at a fork in the road.

Christian looked down at his feet, right where the road split. "Well, this is new."

"I assume," said Hopeful, "that we should take the road to the right, as the other would bring us closer to Beelzebub's land."

"Ah, but the true Way has several times brought us close to the wall between the two realms."

"True," Hopeful conceded. "Perhaps we should just try one and see what it looks like. If it seems to be the wrong way, we can turn back."

"And if it proves deadly?"

Just then, they were overtaken by a tall, thin man in a long, sparkling coat, which reflected the light of the sun behind them, practically blinding them with it. The man followed the road to the left about twenty feet, before turning back and calling, "If you two be pilgrims, you would do best to follow me."

Straining to make out the man's features against the glaring

light, Christian said to Hopeful, "Well, I suppose that's our answer. Let us follow this Shining One."

"You have chosen wisely," the man said, "and such wisdom will be rewarded richly."

But as they followed him along the path, it turned by degrees until the Celestial City was at their back and the setting sun before them, further blinding them.

"Christian," Hopeful whispered, "I think we made a mistake in following this man. We are headed the wrong way."

"I agree," he said, and called out, "Sir! Why are we headed back toward the land of Destruction?"

The man stopped and whirled toward them, hurling a large net, which hit the two pilgrims with such force as to knock them to the ground. They began to thrash about, trying to free themselves, but only getting more and more hopelessly entangled.

The man approached them, laughing as he shrugged off the sparkling garment. Without it, the pilgrims could see him clearly: a fearful creature indeed. His coarse hide clung tightly to his bones and sinews, especially upon his ghoulishly elongated limbs. Long, silky hair cascaded down his shoulders, framing a hideous face: yellow eyes and wicked fangs and, between them—where his nose should be—only a puckered cavity of tarrish flesh.

Working quickly, the monster pulled the net taught and tied it with a long, black rope, which he then tossed up over a tree limb, some twenty feet in the air. With great pains, he then began to raise the confined pilgrims up off the ground. When they were only a few feet shy of the pivot, he tied the rope to another nearby tree trunk.

He then searched through his discarded garment and came out with a small pyrotechnic flare, which he embedded in the ground with a thin rod. He then produced a flint, with which he lit the touch paper, and quickly backed away as the rocket shot up into the sky and exploded into a massive red starburst.

The creature sat down on the earth, his back to them, and

looked out toward the wall dividing the land, just visible in the distance. "My Lord Apollyon is on his way," he said, without looking back at the pilgrims. "You've cost him much suffering and he is eager to see you again."

In the distance, Christian saw a plume of black smoke, growing closer by the minute.

- Back to Hell -

The Pilgrim Contrite passed beneath the arch at the entrance of Vanity Fair and found his senses immediately assaulted by the goings-on. Rows and rows of crass commerce as far as the eye could see, amidst fighting, drinking, and cavorting. Contrite put his head down and pushed forward, intent on passing through this place as quickly as possible.

Within ten steps, he bumped into a burly fairgoer, who shoved him, hard, sending him tripping to the muddy ground. All around, people pointed and laughed at his predicament. The pilgrim was so stunned at this turn of events that he lay there on the ground for a full minute, before finding himself lifted to his feet by a portly man in a long, hooded robe.

"Are you alright?" the man asked.

"Yes. And thank you for your concern. It seems to be in short supply here."

"It is indeed, although the citizens of this place will tell you that empathy and concern are among their chief products. Perhaps I can help you navigate the fair today," the man said. "It seems as though you could use it. My name is Compromise."

"Contrite," the pilgrim said, gripping the man's hand. "And I am thankful for your help."

"Contrite and Compromise," the man sang, leading the newcomer toward the north end of the fair. "It has a nice ring to it."

"Sir, why are we going this way? I really just want to pass

through this town and continue on toward the Shining Light. The quicker the better, in my book."

"Trust me, pilgrim," the man said. "This may not be the most direct route through, but it is the wisest and safest."

As they walked, it became clear to the pilgrim that he was the object of much ridicule, among those buying and selling alike. They pointed at his embroidered coat, laughing, scoffing, even threatening him.

"Why is it," Contrite asked, "that my clothing is met with nothing but derision and yet your odd garment seems to pass unnoticed? Are you some sort of wizard or mystic?"

Compromise laughed. "No, no. Nothing so interesting as that. It's just that I've been here in the fair so long that everyone's used to me. Stay close and no one will dare harass you. Ah, yes! Here we are!"

They had reached the entrance to an enormous tent, the flap of which Compromise pulled back, gesturing for the pilgrim to enter. Contrite peered in, and took a staggering step back at the sight of the shameless wickedness on full display within.

"No," he said. "I will not go in there."

The hooded man grabbed Contrite around the wrist, hard enough to stop the blood. "I know your reservations, pilgrim, but trust me," he said. "It's for the best. You'll be out of here before you know it, and on your way to your City." He pulled unyieldingly, slowly drawing Contrite in, the pilgrim's feet sliding through the muck.

"No!" Contrite cried. "Release me!" A wave of laughter and mockery—from within the tent, as well as those around it—was the only response.

Then a man came charging up from behind the tent flap and struck Compromise with a savage blow, blasting him down into the mud. The man placed himself between Contrite and Compromise. He wore boots up to his knees, a pack on his back, and a hat with a brim so wide it drooped a bit on the sides.

"Have a care, good pilgrim," the man said, pointing at the prone figure before them. "This is no fellow sojourner. This is one of Beelzebub's agents. Look at what he conceals beneath his robe."

Contrite saw that the man's legs—or rather the creature's legs—were furry and behooved like those of a goat. Compromise cursed his attacker and made to rise, but the man in the wide hat stepped quickly to him, pulling the hood roughly from the creature's head and revealing two curling horns. Then, pulling a dagger from a sheath on his belt, he yanked back on one of the horns and pushed the blade up to Compromise's exposed throat.

"Now, will you make yourself scarce or shall I make you extinct?"

Compromise swallowed hard and said, "I yield. Let me be."

The man sheathed the dagger, grabbed Contrite by the arm, and began walking him quickly back toward the maypole at the center of the fair.

"I shouldn't have done that," he said, looking furtively around. "That man has many friends in the fair, and he has eyes everywhere. In fact, this whole town belongs to Beelzebub, who is effectively its god. We should make good our escape as quickly as possible."

They weaved their way deftly through the crowds and were seemingly on their way out of the cursed place when they came upon a frothing mob that filled the lane and blocked their path.

"Oh, what now?" Contrite's new companion muttered. The two of them pushed their way into the crowd until they saw the subjects of the unrest: two men, one of them in armor and both of them smeared in filth, being mocked and reviled, pelted with rocks and rotten fruit, and beaten, while a massive guard kept watch, smirking all the while.

"We have to stop this," Contrite said. "These men are pilgrims, as we are." Looking to his left, he saw a man in cassock and gown and said to him, "Are you not a minister, sir? Put a stop to this!" The man just raised his hands and backed away, his face pale.

"That's enough!" someone called from deeper in the crowd.

"Yeah, you've made your point," another cried out. "If these men have broken a law, let's try them properly!"

Contrite opened his mouth to add his own objection, but felt his new companion squeeze his arm. "Let's see how this plays out," he whispered. "A grievance has been lodged; there's no use in you bearing the consequences, without furthering the cause of these poor men."

"Show of hands," the guard bellowed. "Who thinks these men have endured enough abuse?"

Contrite made to raise his hand, but his guide held it down. "It's a trap," he whispered. "Just wait."

This advice was seemingly confirmed when the guard ordered everyone with a raised hand to be gathered up and placed in the stocks. He then commanded the crowd to disperse and dragged the two pilgrims away.

As they set their faces toward the Shining Light and the outer limits of the fair, Contrite said, "I feel eyes on us."

"As do I." Hand on his dagger, the man glanced about. "The last thing we need is to be snatched up at the border or followed into open country. Let us remove all suspicion by purchasing something innocuous."

He led Contrite up to a vender's booth, covered in woodcuts, which he perused briefly before purchasing two of them. He held both out to Contrite and invited him to choose. One print depicted a rather silly-looking goat in a pen and the other, a man lying pleasantly beneath a tree. Contrite took the latter, rolled it up, and placed it in his satchel.

"Now you'll have a token of your time in Vanity Fair," said the other man, folding his own print and sliding it beneath the strap of his pack. "It will serve as a reminder of how our Great King saw us through." They resumed their travel, and within a quarter hour, they had left the fair behind.

"I have a proposition for you," the man said. "I have business further down this road a stretch. Perhaps we could travel together for a time."

"That would be most welcome. My name is Contrite. And you are…?"

"Mr. Toehold."

"That is certainly an unusual name. I assume there's a story there?"

"Ah, yes. My mother—a very pious woman—named me in the biblical fashion, if you can believe it. She gave birth to twins: myself and my brother—fraternal, not identical. We were born much like Jacob and his twin brother Esau, him grabbing at my foot as we emerged. Of course, with the patriarch and his brother, it was the heel and with us it was my toe. And so she called me Toehold, rather than Heel-Grabber."

Contrite laughed. "I suppose you find yourself telling that story quite frequently."

"Indeed, I do."

"Can I ask you something, Toehold—what is on your back? Surely you haven't made it this far without losing your burden."

"Of course not. These are supplies for the journey. I prefer to sleep in as much comfort as possible, even while traveling. I carry with me a good-sized tent (big enough to protect us both from the elements), some cooking supplies, and other things needed along the way. Although I must admit I do grow rather weary of carrying it." He flashed a grin at Contrite and said, "I have a second proposition: if you relieve me of my load for the next couple of days, and pitch the tent for us, I will do all the cooking. And believe me when I tell you that I am quite skilled at preparing a good meal. Is that agreeable?"

"I can hardly say no after you saved me from that monster back there. But all debts aside, it does sound like a fair arrangement." They paused on the Narrow Way to transfer the pack onto Contrite's shoulders.

As they resumed, Mr. Toehold said, "Now I have a question for you; why you were alone back there?"

Contrite nodded sadly. "I had been travelling with a small band of pilgrims, but, some weeks ago, they stopped to rest, and I continued on. When I realized my mistake, I retraced my steps, but never could find them again. How about you, Mr. Toehold? Why are you alone?"

"I was on pilgrimage with my brother."

"Your twin brother?"

Toehold smiled. "Yes, although I'm the handsome one. Some time ago, he decided to go a—a different way." Grief stole over his face.

"I'm so sorry to hear it."

"Ah, thank you, my friend. And I do have hope that I will see him again. Perhaps even soon."

As they walked, both men recounted their experiences along the way, their trials and triumphs alike. The conversation was good, and it was a comfort to Contrite that he was no longer walking alone. And yet, the weight of the pack on his back continually called to mind the weight of his former burden in a way he could not quite understand, and he suggested before the sun had even begun to set that they stop and make camp for the day.

Per their agreement, Contrite set about pitching the tent, after which he gathered some wood for the fire and stones to contain it. Then Toehold, his oddly named new companion, made good on his promise, preparing a delicious, exotic-tasting stew, which he proudly presented to his fellow traveler.

Looking down at the contents of the bowl, Contrite chuckled. "Red stew—another reminder of your biblical counterpart, who sold his birthright for a bowl of the same." He had another spoonful and added, "There's a taste here I can't quite identify . . . some spice from foreign lands?"

"That would be the secret ingredient. The legacy of my dear brother, if you will. It's his recipe."

As the sun was setting, they made their beds—Contrite's in the tent and Toehold's next to the pleasant fire. "I'm a very light sleeper," he explained. "The least snap of a twig rouses me to full diligence. Unless you would rather establish a watch schedule, I suggest I spend the night out here and you in the tent, and we both get a full night's sleep."

"That works out well, I suppose, as I am an incredibly deep sleeper. But let me know if you do want me to take a watch. I'd be happy to." And with that he crawled into the tent and fell asleep, exhausted from a day of trouble and travel.

When he awoke, Contrite's arms and legs felt tingly, and his eyesight was a bit blurred. He exited the tent and stood, hoping it might help to get the blood flowing, but no sooner was he upright than he found himself doubling over, feeling as though he might vomit.

"Toehold," he called, "I fear I may have eaten something turned or toxic yesterday."

The man rushed to his side and helped him sit. "That's odd. I feel fine. What did you have for breakfast?"

"The only thing I ate the whole day was your stew."

"Well, that can't be it. I ate the same thing. Perhaps you encountered some unlawful spice or narcotic in the fair. Or it could be that the vile beast Compromise dosed you with something dark and mind-altering; he's been known to do that. I'm sure it will pass with time. Can you stand, do you think?"

"Yes, just . . . give me a moment."

"Alright, but when you can, let's get moving. It will do you good to breathe the fresh country air. I'll even carry the pack for you."

Their progress was slow that day, further encumbered by the terrain growing stark and rough underfoot. By early afternoon, Contrite could go no further and all-but-collapsed onto a bed of moss, imploring of Toehold, "Can we please just camp here tonight? I'm sure I'll feel better in the morning when this has left my system."

Toehold regarded him with concern and said, "Yes, of course. You rest; I'll pitch the tent."

Contrite faded in and out of consciousness for a while until the sound of the mallet striking the tent pegs snatched him from his fever dreams. The dull sound came again and again, continuing for several minutes, each blow feeling as though it would split his skull open.

Finally, he rolled to his knees and crawled over to where Toehold was still on the second of four pegs. He kept hitting them at a glancing angle. Any progress he made in driving the stake in with one blow was knocked loose with the very next swing of the mallet.

"Here," Contrite said, taking the tool in his sweaty hands. "I'll—I'll do it. See, you've got to hit the head of the stake head-on and swing like you're trying to crush the thing. Like this." It took him only a few minutes to finish staking the tent, but he was completely depleted when it was done. He again curled up in the moss and faded from consciousness.

The sky was orange when Toehold shook him awake and offered him more of the red stew. "I'm sorry," he said. "This is all I have. I hope you're not tired of it."

"Not at all," Contrite managed to say, but he had a hard time muscling it down, as the taste of the mystery spice was now even more overpowering than it had been the night before. He fell asleep beside the fire and woke up beneath the stars, a blanket having been placed over him. He looked all around and could not find Toehold anywhere. The man's bedroll was there, just across the fire from him, and his boots as well, but the man himself was nowhere to be seen.

"Perhaps he's gone into the woods to relieve himself," he thought. Then realized that no man goes off into the forest, in the dark, barefoot.

"Mr. Toehold?" he called out into the night. "Are you there?" His head pounded in response to his own voice.

"Yes, I'm here," came the reply, from out in the darkness. "All is well; I'll be back in a moment. Go back to sleep!"

Contrite closed his eyes and drifted off.

When he awakened, it was morning and he felt even sorer and more disconnected from his extremities. His neck was stiff, his body sluggish. He was unable to help pack up camp and, in order for the two men to make any progress, Toehold had to both carry the pack and allow Contrite to lean against him for balance and support as they traveled.

They stopped several times throughout the day, and made camp even earlier than the night before. Contrite apologized profusely, but Toehold would have none of it.

"How about I don't pitch the tent tonight?" he said. "I know how the sound of the mallet hurt your head last time. Let's both sleep by the warmth of the fire again. It will do you some good."

Contrite thanked him, slumping onto his blanket. He dozed off and on through the early evening and awakened to the now-familiar smell of the red stew. With great difficulty, Contrite sat up and accepted the bowl, the smell of the stuff turning his stomach.

Toehold noticed this reaction and said, "You know, I'm growing tired of this dish myself. I think we need a change tomorrow. I suggest we take the day off from travel. You're not feeling up to it; today's progress is proof of that."

"I do apologize," Contrite said, "But you're right. I am so slow and so stiff and dizzy that I would only hold you back."

"Then let's remain here for a day. You can rest and recover, and I'll set some snares to trap some hares. How does that sound for dinner tomorrow?"

"Sounds good," Contrite nodded. He looked down at the stew in his bowl and knew he could not eat it. But not wanting to hurt his friend's feelings, he pointed off into the darkness and said, "What is that?!"

Toehold craned his neck. "What? Where?"

Contrite sloshed the pungent stuff off into the brush, realizing as he did it that its smell might attract a predator during the night. "I could swear I saw something. A bear or a lion—a beast of some kind."

"I'll have a look." Toehold drew his dagger and disappeared into the darkness. Contrite clambered over to where the stew was seeping into the ground and turned the earth over with his spoon, frantically trying to bury it.

He heard his companion returning and crawled back to his bed.

"I saw nothing," Toehold said, shrugging.

"It may have been my fever I suppose. Sorry; I don't know what's come over me." Contrite mimed eating a few bites before setting the bowl down by the fire.

"Get some sleep, my friend," Toehold said. Then, as he had the night before, he pulled the floppy brim of his hat down over his eyes and almost immediately began to snore.

Contrite also drifted off, and again he awakened in the dead of night, the glow of coals and the nearly full moon the only sources of light. He could feel some vitality returning to his mind and body.

He sat up and noticed immediately that Mr. Toehold was gone once again. Only his boots remained, sitting next to his pillow.

Hunched and hurried, Contrite made his way over to his companion's bed, head still pounding. He felt a shock of fear and horror as he looked down into the tall boots. They were lined with silk, tapering gradually down, almost to a point. Contrite thought of the cloven hooves of the creature Compromise.

Then he heard a rustling from out in the darkness, and the sound of whispered conversation. Stepping as lightly as he could, Contrite made his way to the edge of the woods and peered down into a shallow ravine, where he saw the silhouette of his travelling companion. It was too dark for him to see the man's feet and his broad hat obscured the view of whoever he was conversing with.

Contrite could not make out their words, but he could sense from the tone that they were nearing the end of their conversation. The pilgrim slunk back to his bed and feigned sleep, just as Toehold came creeping back into camp and crawled into his own bed, again pulling the hat down over his eyes.

Contrite did not think he would fall asleep that night, but the next thing he knew, the sun was beating down on him, closer to the top of the sky than it was to the eastern horizon. Toehold was gone again, having left a note that he was off setting traps to catch their dinner.

Grasping the opportunity, Contrite opened the man's pack and rifled through it. At first, he found nothing of note—just supplies for the road—but then, in a hidden compartment, two pages, folded over each other.

The first was the woodcut from Vanity Fair—the image of a goat, now looking evil and foreboding. The other was a schedule of sorts.

> *Day one—A pinch*
> *Day two—A level teaspoon*
> *Day three—A rounded teaspoon*
> *Day four—One gill*
> *Day five—The remainder*

He slid the pages back into the compartment. Then, remembering his own woodcut, he pulled it from his satchel. A sense of dread rose up in his entrails. The picture of the man resting beneath the tree was now of a dead man, his head a yawning skull, a crow perched atop it. "No," he thought. "I will not die a victim of this creature's cunning."

Toehold returned an hour later to find his companion in bed, breathing raggedly, wide eyes jerking from one invisible horror to another. He smiled and set about preparing two rabbits on the fire. The smell of the meat brought an audible growl from

Contrite's stomach, and he feigned waking just as the dish was ready. Having not eaten in two days, even the thick red coating could not dissuade the pilgrim from having some of the meat.

Doing his best to continue the charade of ever-increasing illness, Contrite pulled away the rabbit's skin and cut a portion from the center of the animal, with shaking hands. But even the deepest meat was saturated with the earthy spice, and he spit it surreptitiously into his hand.

"I don't ... feel well," Contrite said, and collapsed back onto his bed. Toehold seemed hardly able to mask his happiness at this turn, eating his own dinner down to the bones and cleaning up the dishes with a barely-contained sense of glee.

As night fell, he approached Contrite with a thick cup of hot liquid. "It's a medicinal tea," he said, "to grant you healing sleep."

Contrite took one sip and recoiled at the familiar taste of the red spice. He made a show of fighting against the heaviness of his eyelids for a few seconds before letting the cup slip from his hand, its contents spilling into the earth.

Toehold laughed, darkly. Through interlaced eyelashes, the pilgrim watched him remove his boots, set them side by side next to his pillow, and begin to dance, both in and around the fire.

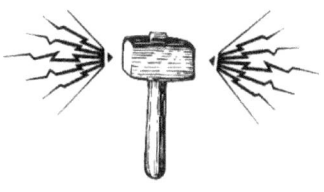

Compromise walked upon his cloven hooves, his heavy robe dragging leaves and needles along behind him. He came to a stop and drew back his hood, revealing his horns. This was the meeting place, as it had been the night before. The darkness all around did nothing to quash his exuberant spirit. According to the last update, they were on the very precipice of taking yet another pilgrim.

He smiled at the sight of the floppy-brimmed hat coming down into the ravine, in the moonlight. But the smile quickly faded. Something was off. As the man drew closer, he also drew his dagger. He then removed his hat, which he threw aside.

"Were you perhaps expecting someone else?" the pilgrim Contrite asked. "No horns upon my head, nor hooves upon my feet." He kept the dagger pointed directly at the heart of Compromise.

"So this is what you do," Contrite spat. "Two sides of the same coin. If you cannot drag a pilgrim into that den of iniquity, your brother will get a toehold and inch him along to the same effect."

Compromise grinned. "You are far from the first," he said. "Nor will you be the last."

"I wouldn't count on that," Contrite said. "I found your secret ingredient in the toe of your brother's boot. Or what would be the toe if he had any for you to grab—a whole bundle of that wicked red spice."

Compromise shrugged. "So, you found it. What of it? You're still in the dark, in the wilderness, outnumbered two to one. No one will hear your screams."

"Two to one? Are you sure?"

Compromise felt his innards pull taut. "What—what does that mean?" he asked.

The pilgrim sneered. "What do you think it means?"

Compromise drew back, pulled a pouch of corrosive powder from the folds of his robe, and ejected it into the pilgrim's face, sending him spinning and coughing. He then knocked him to the ground and rushed up the slope to the campsite. There he saw his brother lying unnaturally upon his back in the dancing orange light of the fire, furry legs akimbo, his vacant eyes staring up into the sky.

He cried out in despair. Drawing closer, he saw Toehold's mouth gaping wide and the encrusted red powder caked upon his cheeks. "Oh, my brother. *Noooo!*"

The light and heat of the fire were suddenly blocked by the pilgrim's presence behind him. "How much did you give him?" Compromise sobbed.

"All of it," he said, his voice hard and unyielding. "No more half-measures. No more glancing blows."

Compromise looked back to see the pilgrim holding the mallet high above his head.

"And now, loathsome creature Compromise," the Pilgrim Contrite said, *"back to hell with you."*

The mallet came down with a brutal, sickening crunch, and Compromise was no more.

Discourse & Discipline

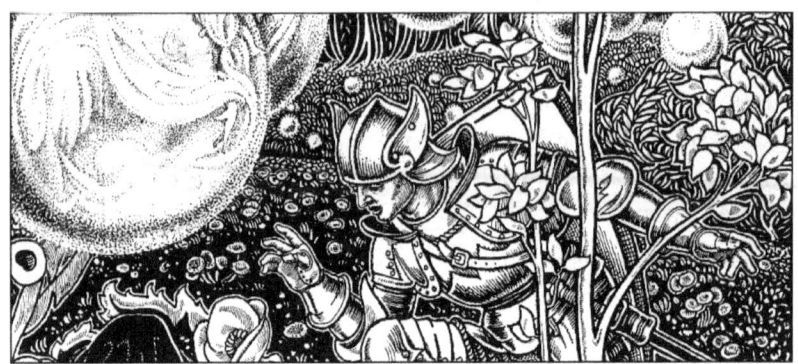

Christian and Hopeful had been hanging in the net for nearly two hours when the last purple light of day gave way to true darkness. They'd said nothing to each other up to this point, afraid that any commiserating would anger the wicked creature sitting a short distance off, guarding his prey and waiting for the Destroyer to arrive. From the moment he'd turned his back, he'd said nothing more, but it was easy to imagine him bringing swift and vicious reprisal upon the prone pilgrims should they try to plot an escape.

The gaunt, wicked creature was still there—Christian was certain—but for some reason the darkness emboldened him to twist uncomfortably against the pull of his own weight, until his mouth was as close to Hopeful's ear as he could manage, and whisper, "How far off do you think he was when last we saw that telltale smoke?"

"I don't know," Hopeful responded, louder than Christian would have liked. "We are on high ground, and suspended higher yet, above it. He might have been thirty miles. Or maybe it was ten. I've never been good at estimating distance. My question is: if this is Apollyon, why hasn't he simply flown up here? He can fly, no?"

"I have seen him fly, yes, but I believe he can only sustain it in short bursts."

"Like a peacock," Hopeful said. He squelched a laugh and then gave in to a wave of giddy giggling.

"*Shh!* Why are you laughing?" Christian demanded. "When I was free to fight him with all my strength, I barely defeated the beast that comes our way now. What will become of us when he finds his prey neatly wrapped in a net like a bunch of apples at the market?"

"You're right," Hopeful said. "But if I don't laugh, I'll wail. And if it's not funny, it's at least absurd how we left the Delectable Mountains as if in a race to see who could be the bigger fool—and more quickly than the other."

"I don't know if I'd go that far . . . "

"No? We were given a map of the road, which we did not consult, opting instead to follow the first shiny thing to happen by—never thinking it might be a distraction to keep us from seeing the monster beneath. We were given a solemn warning: *Beware the Flatterer.* This we also ignored."

"You think this creature is the Flatterer?"

"Of course! He came along in our moment of indecision— as if we merited our own heavenly escort, as if we needn't be bothered seeking wisdom or having a look at the map we'd just received, or opening the Scriptures to read those heavenly words, *The man who flatters his neighbor spreads a net for his feet.* And here we are, in a net. He praised our great wisdom and promised we would be rewarded richly for it. What is all that but vanity and flattery?" He sighed. "I confess, I thought the Flatterer would be more obvious." Hopeful was silent for a moment, then added, "There was a man in my hometown by that name. I've known him my whole life. He's a lot more transparent than this Flatterer."

"I remember him," Christian said. "I believe he was the last to testify against Faithful and me. And you're right; a child would see through that sycophant."

"Yes, and still there were some who loved to receive his empty praise, Lord Hate-Good among them. But this Flatterer, who sits beneath us to deliver us into the enemy's hands, is far cleverer."

"This we should have expected," Christian said. "The Apostle Paul tells us that Beelzebub often masquerades as an angel of light and his servants as messengers of light. And King David, in one of his holy songs, wrote, *Concerning the works of men, by the word of your lips I have kept me from the paths of the Destroyer.* By neglecting the Word of his lips, we are not only in the Destroyer's path—we are now his destination."

"We have faced hardships on this Pilgrim Road before," Hopeful said, "both by our own foolish disobedience and by God's unsearchable providence. We have cried out to him in both cases and have every time been delivered. Let us stop chastising ourselves and instead confess our sins, humble ourselves, and pray that our God will come and save us from this beast. If we are to be chastised, let him do it when he has delivered us."

The two of them prayed well into the night. And then, having cast their cares upon their Lord, they fell into a deep sleep.

It was in the first predawn light that Christian awoke to find Hopeful's foot, which had somehow come out of its shoe during the night, pushed against his face. He wretched and shoved it away, only to find the net pulling it right back in.

"Hopeful," he whispered, "what happened to your shoe?"

It seemed Hopeful was already awake. "My shoe? Really? I hear heavy footfalls approaching us, and the guard beneath us rises to his feet . . . but you're worried about my *shoe*."

"Take heart," Christian said, trying to project a sense of spiritual leadership. "The sun is rising, I think. And every morning, our Lord's mercy are—"

But as they looked, it was not the sun that they saw coming

up from the East, nor was it their dark enemy, Apollyon. Rather, a Shining One came rushing up the hill, his very countenance bursting with light. In his massive fist, he held a glowing whip.

The Flatterer drew back, his long, clawed fingers tensed, preparing for battle. But when the Shining One reared back and cracked his whip, the shockwave knocked the Flatterer to the ground, even as it sent the two pilgrims spinning and swinging in the net. The Flatterer scrambled to his feet and immediately found the whip snapped taut around his neck. He shrieked in pain and fought in vain as the Shining One drew him unyieldingly closer. When he was within arm's reach, the heavenly warrior jerked back on the whip, sending the Flatter spinning twice-round and falling in a heap.

"Rise. Now," the Shining One commanded. "If you flee, I will spare you."

The creature stood on shaky legs and began to stumble and trip his way into the distance.

As he regathered the whip, the Shining One looked appraisingly up at the pilgrims in the net, as if they were a string of sausages in a butcher shop. "Who are you and where are you going?" he demanded.

"Sir, we are humble pilgrims," Christian said, "and we were headed to the Celestial City when we were deceived, and followed that Flatterer, who took us off the true Way, bound us, and suspended us here."

"Could you not see that the Flatterer was a false apostle, presenting himself as an angel of light?"

"We see it now," Hopeful croaked, "quite clearly."

"Would you have me let you out?" the Shining One asked.

"Please, sir," they both pleaded.

The Shining One let the whip out again and with two wide swings, cracked it, first against Hopeful and then against Christian. The moment it touched them, they felt as though a bolt of lightning had struck them from the sky. Though neither was grounded, the jolt seemed to be anchored in the heavens, not the earth. They cried out in pain and fear. The third crack of the whip rent the net and the two men fell out, landing hard in a tangle of arms and legs. A moment later, Hopeful's shoe landed in his lap.

They scrambled to their knees and held their hands up in defense before the Shining One, although they knew this would do nothing to protect them from another crack of the whip.

"Fear not," the Shining One said, "and remember the words of your King: *Those whom I love, I rebuke and discipline. So be earnest and repent.*" He coiled the whip and hung it on his belt. "This instrument leaves no scars, no stripes. For your sins were paid for on the back of your Savior. By his wounds you have been healed. His discipline now is only to help you grow and learn. And you pilgrims are in grave need of such remedial lessons. In an exceedingly short time, you forgot the map you had in your possession. You forgot the warning you received. And you forgot the most basic principle of pilgrimage: anyone who would lead you away from the City is not sent of the King."

"Yes, we understand," Christian said. "And thank you."

"Now," the Shining One said, "I will stay here and deal with the enemy Apollyon when he arrives. You two, go back to where you left the path, and resume the Narrow Way. And this time, be careful to heed all the wisdom of the shepherds."

The pilgrims needed no further prompting and ran without rest until they were back at the fork in the road. Doubled over there, to catch their breath, they observed two things: first, they could both now see, with absolute clarity, that it was no fork at all. What had seemed before to be the right-hand branch was clearly just the continuation of the Narrow Road, albeit with a slight curve to the right. The left prong of the fork was actually a diverging path, not only leaving the Pilgrim Road at a significant angle, but wider and covered in sandy soil, in stark contrast to the thick clay of the Narrow Road at this point.

The second thing they saw was that Ignorance was just now ambling toward them in the distance, closing the space between them.

"He must have called it an early night," Hopeful said.

Christian laughed. "And walked quite slowly today." He chuckled as he watched the loner behind them drawing closer. Then his face fell.

"What is it?" Hopeful asked.

"Here we stand laughing at that young man's lack of progress. And yet, had he followed with us, he would have spent the night fearing for his life in a devil's net, tasted the heavenly lash this morning, and been no better off at this point than he is now."

"That is true, brother," Hopeful said. "May this whole unfortunate episode humble us, if nothing else."

Resuming the Narrow Way, the two pilgrims walked quickly, trying to make up for lost time, and due to the rigor of their toil, they said nothing to each other for several hours.

Then Christian pointed up ahead and said, "Do you see a man coming this way?"

"I see him," Hopeful said. "Another lone traveler coming softly, his back toward Zion. Let's be wise and watchful, Christian. He may be a Flatterer as well."

They stood and watched the man approach until he came to a stop a few feet shy of them and, with a mocking smile, said, "Hello, gentlemen. How are you this fine day?"

"We are well enough," Christian answered, guardedly. "And you?"

"Even better," the man answered. "Do you mind if I ask where you are headed?"

"To the Celestial City," Hopeful said.

At this the man doubled over in laughter.

"What is the meaning of this?" Christian demanded, but the man was unable to answer, waving them off through tears as he continued to laugh and convulse.

The two pilgrims were about to leave the man to his hysterics when he wiped his face on his sleeve and said, "I'm so sorry. That was rude of me. My name is Atheist. And you?"

"I am Christian and this is Hopeful. And I ask again: what is the meaning of your laughter?"

"No offense, but I laugh at what ignorant people you are." He held up his hands. "Forgive me again. I don't mean to come across as I do. It's just that I cannot understand how anyone would take on such a tedious journey when you are likely to have nothing but blisters for your pains."

"Are you suggesting we won't be received there?"

Atheist laughed again. "Received *where*? There is no such place as this 'Celestial City' in all the world!"

"But there is in the world to come," Hopeful said.

"Look, I don't mean to laugh *at* you men," Atheist said. "In fact, I heard the same sort of thing in the country where I grew up, and I spent nearly twenty years seeking this so-called 'City.' And yet, I saw no more of it during that time than I did on the very first day."

"Be that as it may," Christian said, "we both have heard, and now believe, that the City is real, and have kept our eyes fixed upon it for the space of our entire journey thus far."

Atheist did a full turn, looking up and all around him. "Well, where is it? I see it not!"

The pilgrims gazed off to the east, but at this point in the road, a craggy peak and some thick trees stood between them and the shining light. "It is obscured from this place," Christian said. "But from the top of the Delectable Mountains we saw the very gates of the City, as clear as day."

"Oh, as clear as day? Tell me, was there anything carved on them? Any inscription?" Atheist smiled sympathetically at their silence. "Don't get me wrong, had I not believed as you now believe while I was in my native land, I would never have come this far to seek it!"

"You confuse me, Atheist," Hopeful said. "A moment ago, you were baffled that anyone would undertake such a 'tedious journey,' as you put it. Now you're a very veteran of the road."

"Touché," Atheist said. "I suppose I need only think back to my own former ignorance and gullibility to understand your motivations."

"But why do you assume that you are correct?" Christian asked, "when you are no older than me and, as far as we can tell, no wiser than either of us?"

"I will answer that question with one of my one. Tell me this: from which direction did I just come?"

"From the east," Christian said.

"Which means that I went farther than you in my seeking, and still found nothing. If there were something out there, I would certainly know about it. And, honestly, I wish there had been! It's a nice idea, although naïve, and I truly did cast aside everything I had to come seeking it. And now I head back home to seek solace in those very things I tossed away to chase such fairy dreams." He looked earnestly from one pilgrim to the other. "Gentlemen, waste no more time on this nonsense. For my sake, and for your own." And with that he tipped his hat and continued back toward the land of Destruction.

"Hold on a minute," Christian said to Hopeful, as they watched Atheist approach Ignorance, who was resting on a felled tree, drinking from a water skin. "I want to make sure this man does not beguile that poor nave back there." But Atheist simply offered a friendly greeting to the young man and continued on his way.

"Good," Christian said. "I fear he would have won over poor Ignorance."

"Yes. I confess he was a little convincing," Hopeful said. "When he pointed out that he had been further along the road than we are, I admit I began to wonder if he was telling the truth about The Celestial City."

"He may have taken more steps on this road and perhaps spent more days walking it, but by his own admission he got no nearer the city than he was the day he set out. His description of pilgrimage was on the mark—if only for him. For twenty years, he put one foot in front of the other and received only blisters for his reward. His words lose their punch when considered more closely."

Hopeful agreed, and began walking again. "Yes, this man was quick to offer his own experience as iron-clad proof, but quicker still to dismiss ours out-of-hand. And yet, if he truly walked this road for decades and never saw the light of the City ahead, he must be the most unobservant man to ever take up pilgrimage—or the most disingenuous. Meanwhile, we both saw the gates of the City, albeit through a glass darkly and with shaking hands."

"What's more, are we not to walk by faith? This is the very heart of pilgrimage, and clearly it is something that has evaded Mr. Atheist. And it now occurs to me that he is misnamed. For 'atheist' means 'no God,' and yet this man is blinded by the God of this world and serves him with singlemindedness. He may not realize that he serves him, he may not think that he serves him—but that just makes him Beelzebub's ideal servant."

Hopeful looked behind them and saw that Ignorance was once again on the move. "That youngster is still lurking at a distance."

"Yes, he surely does not desire our company."

"I'm not so sure," Hopeful said. "He could have easily overtaken the two us as we spoke with Atheist, and yet he sat and waited until we began to move again. Perhaps we should speak with him some more."

Christian agreed and called back to Ignorance, "Join us, young man! Why do you loiter behind?"

Ignorance shrugged broadly as he approached them and said, "I prefer to walk alone, rather than with company. Unless it is the best sort of company, of course."

Christian winked at Hopeful and said, "Would you consider walking alongside us for a while anyway, and redeeming the time with some conversation?"

"What sort of conversation?"

"Tell us, how is it between God and your soul?"

"It is well. At least, I hope so. I am full of positive thoughts that enter my mind and comfort me as I walk."

"Such as . . . ?"

"Such as thoughts of God and of heaven. I can't imagine I'd be comforted by such if it were not well between the Lord and me."

"Hmm," Christian said, his brow furrowed.

"If you've something to say," Ignorance spat, "then say it. I may be young, but I can bear up under your scrutiny."

"I was just remembering that even the devils think of these things—of God and of heaven."

"Ah, yes," said Ignorance, "but unlike them, I have a desire for these things."

"The Best of Books tells us, *the soul of the sluggard desires, and gets nothing.*"

Ignorance rolled his eyes. "You're not hearing me. I not only think of these things and want them, but I am no sluggard; I have left everything behind for them!"

"Have you, though?" Christian asked. "To leave all is a very hard thing—harder than many think. Tell me, how do you know that you've truly left all for God and heaven?"

"Why, my heart tells me so."

"But does not the Word of God tell us that the man who trusts in his own heart is a fool?"

"That is spoken of an evil heart, sir. Mine is a good one."

"How do you know?" Hopeful asked. "If the heart of man is deceitful above all else, and desperately wicked, as the Scriptures say, it seems likely that an evil heart could convince a man it was good."

Ignorance sighed. "Again, I say: because it comforts me with hopes of heaven. I feel we are going around in circles."

"But how do you know it's not a false comfort, meant to deceive you? Isn't that just what a deceitful heart would offer?"

"That is a good a question," Ignorance said, "and I have a good answer. You see, my heart and my life agree. Therefore, my hope is well-grounded."

"Who told you that your heart and your life agree?"

"Why, my heart tells me so!"

"I think you are correct; we *are* going around in circles," Hopeful said. "Your heart tells you that it is good and not deceitful, and that your life bears witness to that. But if your heart is lying, how would you know? Can't you see that, unless the Word of God bears witness in the matter, all other testimony is worthless?"

"You men are overcomplicating everything," Ignorance said. "And, since you brought it up, *this*—" he gestured between them—"this right here is why other travelers have not sought out your company. It is common sense that a good heart has good thoughts. And it is plain as the nose on your face that a good life is lived according to God's commandments."

"I agree entirely," Christian said. "But it's one thing to assume you have all this and another to truly have them."

"Let me question you now and see how you like it," Ignorance said. "You tell me—since you are so very wise—what would you consider good thoughts and a good life, lived according to God's commandments?"

"That's a big question," Christian said. "There are so many different kinds of good thoughts: about ourselves, about our King, and many other things. What specifically are you—"

"Start with good thoughts about ourselves."

"Well, any good thought about ourselves must agree with the Word of God and, therefore, it must pass the same judgment upon us that the Word passes, which is to say that, of ourselves, there is none righteous—no not one. There is no one who does good or seeks God, and every inclination of the heart of man is only wicked, all the time, even from youth."

Ignorance shook his head. "I will never believe that my heart is as bad as all that."

Christian shrugged. "In that case you have never had one good thought about yourself in your whole life. And if your thoughts are not good, it only stands to reason that neither are your actions. For the Word of God says that man's ways are crooked and perverse, and that by nature we turn our backs on the good and seek only self-satisfaction, self-promotion, and self-glorification, all of which are the grossest forms of idolatry. It may seem backwards to the carnal mind, but these are the foundation of every good thought about self, because they are in keeping with God's Word."

"Just say what you mean," Ignorance demanded.

"What else have I been doing? The Word of God tells us that man's ways are wicked, crooked, and perverse—not good. And what's more, in our natural state, we don't even know it. In his great sermon inaugurating his Kingdom, our Great King of Princes opened with these words: *Blessed are the poor in spirit.* That is where we must begin. We are by nature proud and haughty in spirit, and convinced of our own goodness, but this is self-deception, and it stands as an impassable brick wall between us and our God. Only when our thoughts and judgment agree with the thoughts and judgment of God can the wall come tumbling down, as it did by his mighty Word in Jericho."

"You have not convinced me," Ignorance said. "But I am now morbidly curious; what would you call 'good thoughts' about God?"

"Again, they are thoughts that agree with His Word, particularly what it says about his character, his perfections—his power and holiness and all the rest."

"Call the town crier!" Ignorance shouted. "I believe that, even by your narrow definition, I do have right thoughts about God. I recognize that he is all-powerful, all-knowing, *et cetera.* And it pleases me to think about these things."

"But right thoughts about God would necessarily lead to good thoughts about yourself. For a God who knows all knows every secret inclination of our hearts and, in fact, knows us better than we know ourselves. He can see the depth of our sinfulness—even sins of which we are unaware or only partially aware. And recognizing that all this is a good thing and can propel us further down this road of sanctification . . . *that* is a good thought about God and about self, and in it we see that God is so holy that all our own righteousness stinks in his nostrils."

Ignorance rolled his eyes. "Christian, you act as though you're teaching me some deep, unknown mystery of the faith. But I already know—and have known for some time—that I must believe in Christ for justification and cannot approach God on my best performance. That is elementary!"

"Huh," Christian said. "Then understand my confusion when your earlier answers made it clear that you do not see your need for Christ. And yet you say you must believe in him for justification? You don't seem to grasp original sin, nor the heaps of sin that we have all built upon that rotten foundation. Your heart is *good*, you say, and you will enter the City as other 'good men' do, by the good life you have lived. How do you reconcile that with a need for justification by faith in Christ?"

"I believe well enough for all that. Let us move on to—"

"No, hold on . . . *what* do you believe well enough?"

"That Christ died for sinners and that I will be justified before God and delivered from the curse through his gracious acceptance of my obedience to his laws. Worry not about me; I see my need for Christ to make my good deeds and religious duties acceptable to his Father, by virtue of his merits."

Hopeful grimaced. "*That* is your confession?"

"It is, and I stand by it. And will not be able to upturn it, although I see you will try. My confession is firm, like a table with four stable legs."

"Rather, it is four-times faulty and bound to collapse beneath any weight at all," Christian said.

"What do you mean, 'four-times faulty?'"

"Let us examine these four legs holding up your faith, shall we? First of all, yours is a fantastical faith—very creative indeed, but nowhere found in the Scriptures. Creative, in that you speak of justification, using the same language as the Holy Book, but you speak of something else entirely. Secondly, it is a false faith, in that it removes justification from Christ's own personal righteousness and applies it to your own. Thirdly, it is a misplaced faith, for such a thing makes Christ the justifier of actions, not of people. And fourthly, it is a deceitful faith, which will leave you under God's wrath on the Day of Judgment!

"True faith makes us horribly aware of our own sin and our lost condition, and sends us flying to the cross, where we find refuge in Christ's perfect righteousness. And true justification does not make our own feeble (and often sinful) efforts at obedience acceptable before God. Rather, it declares *us* righteous and acceptable before God, *despite* our best attempts at keeping the law. Our own lives are not *shined up* by Christ's blood, until they look good enough to the Father. Rather, our sins and rebellion—including our most righteous deeds, which are but filthy rags in his sight—are laid on Christ's shoulders as he dies, and his own righteousness is placed upon us in exchange. Can you not see the difference between this beautiful, mysterious truth and what you confess?"

Ignorance chuckled. "I don't believe you've thought this through. If a person is justified by Christ, completely apart from his own conduct . . . well, that would unleash everyone who calls himself a Christian to follow his own lusts and live as the heathen do. By your doctrine, it would make no difference how we live, would it?"

"You are aptly named, my friend," Christian said. "Your very answer proves what I've been saying. You are ignorant of what true justification is, and just as ignorant of its true effects, which are that it wins over the heart to Christ, so that we love his name and his Word and his ways and his people. We hate those things we used to love in the flesh, and love what we used to despise."

"Ask him if he ever had Christ revealed to him from Heaven," Hopeful said.

"Ask me what?" Ignorance laughed. "Oh, I see. You buy into revelations and the like! It's all coming together! Your fanatical yammering has been the fruit of disturbed brains!"

Hopeful frowned. "Young man, Christ is so hidden in God from our natural comprehension that no one can know him as Savior unless God the Father reveals Him."

"That is your faith, not mine. And I'll have you know, mine is as good as yours, although it involves fewer whimsical fancies!"

"Be careful, Ignorance," Christian said, gravely. "You should not speak of these things so lightly. Pray to God that you will be awakened and see your own wretchedness and fly to the Lord Jesus, who is God himself, for his righteousness, so that you might be delivered from condemnation!"

"Oh, I can't keep up with you. Your pace is as frantic as your doctrine. Besides, I am growing rather sleepy—undoubtedly a side effect of your dizzying interrogation. I think a short rest would do me well. Farewell, you two." He then slowed to a very crawl.

Christian and Hopeful carried on apace, and Ignorance trailed behind once again. Before long, though, their own pace slowed as well and they found that both their eyelids and their limbs were growing quite heavy.

The road before them appeared to be a dark and foreboding lane and, from behind them, a hideous noise—scurrying feet, snarling, snorting, and wailing—was suddenly closing in. Looking back, Hopeful saw a group of demonic creatures, packed tightly together drawing ever-closer, and it was all he could do to throw himself out of the way and pull Christian down beside him.

Lying there in the tall grass, they watched as seven devils—some of them with canine features and some of them resembling swine—passed them by, shoving and prodding a shirtless man along the road, his face downcast and his hands tied at the wrist.

"There's something written on that man's back," Christian said, "some words burned into it."

Hopeful stood and squinted in the low light. "I can't make it out." He took a step after them and said, "I have to know." Against Christian's objections, he quietly ran alongside the unholy band for the space of thirty steps. He then returned to find Christian strapping on his shield for battle, although he was pale and visibly shaken, in addition to the lethargy they both felt.

"Well?" Christian said. "What did it say? Should we intervene?"

"I don't think we should," Hopeful answered. "The man was bound with seven strong cords, and on his back, it read 'Damnable Apostate,' as though seared in with a brand. He is lost now in the darkness, but I saw them drag him up a crooked path that doubled back and began to ascend. I can only assume this is some back way to the door we saw in the side of that mountain, to reach it without encountering the Shepherds. I wonder who he was."

Christian returned his shield to his back and said, "I got a look as he passed us, and I thought he might have been a certain Turn-Away from the town Apostasy, a man with whom I had several dealings in my own hometown. But he hung his head like a thief caught in the act, and I couldn't say for sure."

"Was that man a pilgrim?"

"No. At least not when I left the City of Destruction. But good Faithful told me that many followed me out in the days and weeks after I departed. I would be quite saddened to learn that Turnaway was one of these, but then made up his mind to turn back to his own cursed hometown."

"The shepherds did say that many would be turned off the Way into that fearful door—some who had come not so far as the Delectable Mountains, and some who had passed well beyond them."

"Yes," Christian agreed. "And yet, it is no less horrifying a sight for having been warned to expect it. I suppose we should make some more progress, although I am quite exhausted."

"So am I," said Hopeful. "Perhaps we should have a short rest. It's as if the air here is making me drowsy."

Christian looked all about him, feeling an odd lag between seeing his surroundings and comprehending them. "Something is amiss for sure," he said. "Look at this." He stooped down and pointed to a black weed growing along the road. It reminded him of the terrifying tree in the Valley of the Shadow of Doubt.

"What about it?" Hopeful asked.

"Just wait. . . " A moment later, a drop of water came up from a puddle beneath the weed and gathered itself at the tip of a long, serrated leaf, where it then pooled back along its veins. Behind it, tall, fan-shaped mushrooms seemed to be blooming and then shrinking back into nothing before growing up a distance away, repeating the process continually so that they seemed to be surrounding the pilgrims.

"Is this some dark magic?" Hopeful asked, rubbing his eyes. He sat back in thought for a moment. and then turned onto his hip, half-lying on the ground.

"Get up," Christian barked. "Do not slumber!"

"Just a few minutes of rest," Hopeful mumbled. "Then I'll feel restored for the journey."

Christian grabbed his friend and bodily hauled him to his feet. "'Beware the Enchanted Ground!' That's what the shepherd said. Shall we ignore yet another warning from these sages? How can we be aware if we are asleep?"

"You are right, brother," Hopeful said, shaking his head roughly. "If we lie down here, we may never wake up. Let us not sleep, as do others, but let us watch and be sober. Thank God you were here to remind me of the shepherd's words."

"Two are better than one," Christian recited. "And if not for you, Hopeful, I would have met my death more than once along this Pilgrim Road. Let's pass over this enchanted place as quickly as we can."

"What about Ignorance? We can't just leave him here to whatever gruesome fate awaits him. He's probably already asleep."

"Ignorance!" Christian called back. "Do you hear me?"

"Yes, I do" came a sing-song response from out in the odd purple light. "And I still don't wish to walk with you."

"Dear God, keep that young man from falling asleep on this ground," Hopeful prayed, "and give us another chance to direct him back to the Wicket Gate. Oh, and keep us awake and alert in this mystical place."

"Amen," said Christian, and the two pilgrims set out once again over the Enchanted Ground.

Enchantment

Hopeful was dragging.

Each step seemed to cost him half of what little energy he had left and, as such, he suspected he would find himself depleted before achieving a dozen more.

He suspected that Christian was just as exhausted, but was putting on a strong face for his friend, injecting each step with a spring he neither believed, nor successfully executed. Still, his friend's commitment to bringing them both over and out of this land—and his confidence that it could be done—was truly a boon to Hopeful.

"Let us occupy our minds somehow," Christian said. "Keep ourselves alert and awake."

Hopeful laughed. "Good idea. Perhaps you could write a hymn about this place. I'd love to watch the master at work."

"I'm hardly a master," Christian demurred. "And I have a better idea: why don't you try writing one?"

Hopeful considered this. "I've never penned a song before. But I've always been somewhat musically inclined. I used to play the whistle, you know."

Christian chuckled. "Yes, I . . . heard. Maybe we could just start with the words to the hymn."

Hopeful mimed pulling a knife from his side and held the

invisible weapon out to Christian. "Does this belong to you, sir?" he laughed.

"I didn't mean to insult you! I just—"

Hopeful waved his hand and laughed again. "Worry not, Christian. After all, it's not your fault you don't appreciate fine music. Lyrics it is."

Their steps grew quicker and lighter as they spent the next twenty minutes piecing together a short stanza, Christian offering his two pence here and there, but mostly letting his companion author the piece.

"I think we've got a worthy verse," Hopeful announced after nearly half an hour.

> *When saints do sleepy grow, let them come hither,*
> *And hear how these two pilgrims talk together;*
> *Yea, let them learn of them in any wise,*
> *Thus to keep open their drowsy, slumb'ring eyes.*
> *Saints' fellowship, if it be managed well,*
> *Keeps them awake, and that in spite of hell.*

"So what do you think?" he asked.

"It's a start. We can tighten it up a bit; the meter is off. But we've certainly got time."

"Nope, too late," Hopeful countered. "I'm already composing the whistle solo in my head."

Christian laughed at this and said, "I find that this sort of creative work quickens the mind for a time, but soon begins to deplete my mental resources. Perhaps we should set our hymn aside for a bit and return to some profitable conversation."

"If you'd prefer. What shall we talk about?"

"I have yet to hear the details of your conversion. I know the broad strokes, of course, but despite being just a few yards away, I was utterly unaware of the miracle taking place right across the hall."

"That I will always discuss," Hopeful said. "Of course, you are already somewhat aware of the wicked and licentious life I led in Vanity Fair, but as I told Faithful, there were many times, even before your arrival, when I experienced a deep sorrow and a sense of clarity at the hopeless and empty life I was leading. This was likely the first preparatory workings of the Holy Spirit on my heart, and these caused me to squeeze my eyes shut against the light, if you will. For, as the evangelist tells us, men prefer darkness."

"That is a fascinating thing to recall, is it not? I remember a similar season in my own former life, dwelling in Destruction. Enlightened as we now are, it is hard to fathom we responded with such revulsion to the initial working of the Spirit and stirring of our souls."

"It is a more recent thing for me," Hopeful said, "and I do recall quite well what went through my mind. I was ignorant, of course, that this building sense of spiritual panic was the work of God. No one had ever told me that this is how God begins the process of awakening a sinner—not even Mr. Liberty, the pastor of our parish. There was a disconnect because sin still felt very sweet to my flesh, even as my soul suffered as a result of it. I desired the end of the suffering, but not the departure of the sin itself. These old companions of mine were truly precious to me. And as soon as the terrifying time of conviction was over, I walled it off in my heart with all the others and never brought any of them to mind again."

"That too sounds familiar," Christian said. "And if you're anything like me, you were sometimes rid of this deep disquiet for a time."

"Indeed. But despite my best efforts, it would come to the fore again and again, and I would find myself each time worse off than I had been before."

"Yes," Christian agreed, "like birth pains, waves of conviction seem to come amidst times of relative peace and relief. And as with birth pains, they come with increasing severity, leading up to the birth—or rebirth in the case of the convert."

"And yet," said Hopeful, "during those times of ease between those seasons of spiritual suffering, although my mind was turned against my sin, a single thought could drag me back down into it. And that would be a double torment to me."

"And so you would redouble your efforts at reformation," Christian said.

"Yes, for I saw that I was on the road to damnation, for certain. And for a while, I would feel utterly free, until at last it came crushing back down upon the neck of all my self-improvements. This was my exact condition when I first met you and Faithful. And he told me that unless I could obtain the righteousness of a man that never had sinned, neither my own righteousness, nor all the righteousness of the world, could save me."

"And when the Father finally revealed the Son to you, did you find your spirit set free from this cycle of suffering?"

"Absolutely. It made me see that all the world is in a state of condemnation, It made me see that God the Father, while perfectly just, can justly justify the sinner who comes naked, filthy, and broken to the foot of the cross. It further made me greatly ashamed of the vileness of my former life and confounded me with a sense of my own ignorance. Suddenly, I wanted nothing but to live a holy life, that I might honor the one who saved me! In that moment, I knew that, had I a thousand gallons of blood in my body, I would spill it all for the sake of the Lord Jesus."

They walked in grateful, contemplative silence for a little while, before Christian held his hand up and said, "Hold, brother. Do you hear that?"

"I hear nothing."

"Exactly. This whole time, the sound of Ignorance's shuffling steps has echoed up from behind us, but I hear it no more."

The two pilgrims locked eyes for a moment and then, without a word, turned back, retracing their steps and calling out for the young man.

They found him nearly a hundred paces back, curled up on

the roadside, snoring and drooling.

"Well, his head may be propped on a rock," Hopeful said, "but this is not the sleep of Jacob, with ladders coming down from heaven."

"No it is not," Christian said, sitting the man up. "This is a place where ladders come up out of hell to drag poor pilgrims down." He shook Ignorance roughly at the shoulders until his eyelids fluttered.

"Oh. What do you want?" he complained.

"Get up, Ignorance," Christian commanded. "This is not a safe place to sleep."

"Go away," the young man said, his head lolling back, mouth hanging open.

Hopeful grabbed him by the collar and dragged him to his feet. As he stood, they heard the distinct sound of jingling chains, although they saw no shackles on the man's ankles.

"Stand and walk!" Hopeful shouted. "We will not leave you be until you are on your feet once again, and walking with us along the Narrow Way."

Ignorance pushed the pilgrims away and smoothed his garment. "I am now refreshed," he said, "and that is why I will continue on my journey. Not because you two busybodies insist that I do."

"That suits us just fine," Christian said.

"And I continue on *alone*."

Christian turned to his companion and said, "It seems the thanks we get for saving this man's life is to be sent away, posthaste."

Ignorance somehow yawned and scoffed at the same time. "Waking a man from a nap and saving his life or two very different things. Do you two have to be so dramatic about everything? Go on. I'll follow presently."

"How about you go ahead of us?" Hopeful asked. "That way you can walk alone, and we can have peace of mind that you haven't fallen asleep again."

Ignorance laughed. "I see your plan. You think you'll catch up to me and draw me back into conversation. But you underestimate Ignorance to your own peril. You will only ever see my backside again until we've reached the city. First me, and then you. Enjoy the view! And with these words, I bid you farewell: your shirt has come unbuttoned there."

Christian looked down and refastened the errant button.

"There," Ignorance said, "now I've saved your life too." Then he spun on his heels and marched off, eastward, at a good clip.

"I fear it will go ill for him in the end," Christian said.

"I agree. And there are many in his condition—not only in Conceit, but in Vanity Fair as well."

"And in Destruction," said Christian, "and all along the Way. As the Book says, *He has blinded their eyes, lest they should see.* But tell me, what do you think of such people? Do they ever have times of conviction as you had in Vanity? Do they ever fear that they are in a dangerous position?"

Hopeful gave a deep shrug and said, "You tell me. You are the elder brother."

"I think they might. Although, in their ignorance, I doubt they recognize such convictions as being for their good. Rather, a fearful feeling descends upon them, and they immediately try to stifle it—not only by gratifying the flesh, but by flattering themselves and their own hearts as Ignorance has done whenever we bring up the topic."

"You've hit on something there," Hopeful said. "For, while the pilgrim is called to be strong and courageous, fear is often vital in sending sinners out on the good road."

"The right kind of fear, yes. The Word itself says, *The fear of the Lord is the beginning of wisdom.*"

"What do you mean by 'the right kind of fear?'"

Christian thought for a moment. "I think right fear is marked by three things: it begins with a conviction of sin, it drives the soul to hold fast to Christ for salvation, and it results in a growing reverence for our Great King. Even as we near the city, such holy fear keeps us from turning to the right or to the left, lest we dishonor him in the sight of his servants—or even his enemies. I fear that Ignorance and his ilk may have some form of conviction, but not the kind that brings them to that place of holy fear."

"Yes, I have seen this many times," Hopeful said, "the stifling of conviction, before real godly fear can take hold. There is self-delusion in this. A man convinces himself that these fears are from the devil, not of God. 'After all,' he thinks, 'why would a good God wish to frighten me?' And so he resists with all his might, convinced that he is undertaking the good fight. After all, if faith and fear are opposites (and in the right context, I suppose they sometimes are), then any fear must be a great danger to his faith, such as it is. This is what he tells himself, and this sort of foolish oversimplification has helped many an ignorant man justify the hardening of his heart against the work of the Spirit."

Christian nodded. "I believe you have struck the nail on its head, Hopeful. And, of course, there is the fact that godly fear, which accompanies conviction, threatens to bring down the house of cards that is their pitiful self-holiness. By carnal instinct, then, they resist with all their might."

"How much farther?" Hopeful suddenly asked.

Christian laughed. "You remind me of my boys on a long journey. Is our conversation that tedious to you?"

"No. But if I knew how much longer, I would be less tempted to rest. Besides, we have a map, and we've already been rebuked once for failing to use it."

"Fair play," Christian said, pulling out the document and unrolling it. They stood in the middle of the path and alternated between squinting at the map and gazing off into the distance.

Finally, Hopeful pointed at a tall, rocky spire off the Way, on their left. "That must be Castle Rock. And if that's the case, we are only about two miles from the end of this Enchanted Ground."

Christian looked to the top of the rocky structure and mused, "I have half a mind to climb that thing to see if the City Gates are visible from there too, but I don't know if—"

"I'm willing," Hopeful said. "Let's go!"

"It's awfully high . . . "

"You wait here. I'll be right back."

He dashed off toward the rock formation, leaving a cloud of dust behind. The thought of ascending to such heights—or even watching his friend do so—turned Christian's stomach and tilted his senses, compounding the sleepiness of the place. He turned his back to Castle Rock and time seemed to crash to a halt, even as his mind came rushing back to full vigilance.

Hovering there before him was his enemy Apollyon, a wicked sneer on his frightful face.

Without a moment's hesitation, Christian pulled his sword, rushed forward, and made to sever the monster's legs. Apollyon's form disappeared in a wisp of black smoke, and the pilgrim's blade passed through unimpeded, just as the apparition

reappeared to his left, circling Christian and laughing uproariously.

"Let me fear only you," Christian prayed as he fastened his
shield down to his forearm. He felt the Spirit burning within
him, a source of strength and courage.

"I know you fear me," Apollyon spat. "Why deny it?"

Christian forced a smile. "You know, I heard you were punished by your master, when I opened you up and sent you fleeing from the valley some time ago. Nothing like a little insult
for your injury, am I right?" Apollyon's wicked grin faltered for
a moment and Christian pressed in. "You wonder how I know
this," he said. "Your Flatterer. He's awfully loquacious.
Apollyon, I have no reason to be wary of you, but you have
learned the hard way to fear my sword. I assume that is why
you're afraid to face me hand-to-hand again, instead hanging
here as a vaporous specter."

Christian felt a pang of conviction, and knew he was in danger of boasting against his enemies—the very thing he had
warned Hopeful against. He prayed for humility as Apollyon
continued to circle him, growing larger with each pass. "And
then, of course, I'm curious: how did it go when you arrived at
the site of that shredded net and faced the Shining One? If I was
able to defeat you once, surely that great warrior could best you
every day of the year."

Apollyon came to a stop and his yellow eyes glowed bright.
"I smelled your trap from miles away, and further followed the
scent of your sloth and fear to this place, where I chose my am-
bush and have been waiting for you. And be assured, if I appear
to be an apparition, that is in you, not in me. You are quite ill-
equipped to deal with the air in this place, pilgrim. Why don't
you just close your eyes and—" Suddenly, the demon's own
eyes flew wide, glowing with alarm and fixed upon something—or someone—behind Christian.

"The Shining One," Christian thought. "He's tracked this
filthy monster down and has come to finish the job."

Apollyon turned and disappeared into the wind—tendrils of black smoke. Christian faced again toward Castle Rock, preparing to kneel before the great heavenly warrior. But instead, he saw Hopeful, breathing heavy, cheeks red, his hair goofy and wind-blown.

"We were right about the distance, I think," he said. "I'd say another two miles or so."

Christian gaped at his friend. Had Apollyon just fled at the sight of Hopeful? Or was it a coincidence?

"Are you all right, Christian? You look like you've seen a phantom!"

Christian shook his head and said, "I'm fine. I was just listening to your assessment and remembering when you said the black smoke was either ten miles away or thirty."

Hopeful laughed. "Sure, I'm not great with distance. But the map clinches it. And I wish you had come with me. The climb has left me drained indeed, but the sight of the shining glory beyond this land has stoked the flame of my zeal all the more. Let us press on toward the goal."

As they resumed the Way, Hopeful said, "I'm quite relived, and a bit surprised, that we haven't come across Ignorance catching another nap. Perhaps we misjudged him."

"I hope so," Christian said. "But I think it may be spite propelling him forward, more than longing for the heart of the King." He fell silent for a moment before abruptly asking, "Tell me, Hopeful, did you always live in the town of Vanity?"

"Born and raised."

"Did you know a man from around your parts, named Temporary? He was known quite a few years back as an up-and-comer in the world of religion. Came from a town with a pretentious name, which I can't recall."

"Pseudogratsia!" Hopeful exclaimed. "Yes, I know him. That town is just a mile or so off from Honesty, which put him only three miles from my boyhood home."

"You knew of him or you knew him?" Christian asked.

"Perhaps somewhere in the middle. I was a lad when he briefly became the talk of the town. As I recall, he lived next door to a man named Turnback."

"In his early days, yes," Christian affirmed. "He even dwelt under the same roof with him. I bring up this man Temporary because he doesn't seem to have fit into either category that we've been discussing: neither a pilgrim who overcomes to the end, nor an ignorant soul who stifles all conviction and never catches sight of his sins. Rather, this man seems to have had a true awakening to the gravity of his transgressions, and their wages to boot."

"I must agree," Hopeful said. "My house was not far from his, as I mentioned, and he often came to see my late father, weeping and wailing, so that you could hear him coming a long way off. I pitied him greatly then. And now, as I think back to his deep sorrow, and the pious reputation that he built up afterwards, it seems as though he must have been to the Place of Deliverance."

"If only," Christian said. "Not all who cry, *Lord, Lord* will enter into the kingdom of heaven, but he who does the will of the Father. Temporary did once tell me that his mind was made up to go on pilgrimage. He spent a great deal of time stockpiling supplies for the journey, and was nearly finished when he became acquainted with a man named Save-Self. After that, the idea of pilgrimage faded from his thoughts, and he used what food he'd gathered to throw a party for that man and his friends."

Hopeful shook his head. "So sad. I wonder what could possibly prompt someone, after feeling the sorrow for sin and tasting the excitement of pilgrimage, to suddenly backslide like that."

"I have thought a lot about this," Christian said, "and have come to the conclusion that it happens in three steps. First of all, though their consciences are awakened, their minds remain unchanged. As a result, when the power of guilt has waned, their motivation to be religious goes with it, and they naturally return to their own way, just as a dog returns to its vomit without thinking about whether that vomit is truly a good meal or why it was expelled from his body to begin with. He simply wolfs it down because that is a dog's nature.

"While we have observed that fear often works to our good in bringing us to repentance, if fear of hellfire alone motivates us, rather than a fire for serving heaven, it will always be temporary, for such fear fades with time, leaving the man worse off than he was before.

"The next step, I believe, also has to do with fear—this time, the fear of men, which according to King Solomon, is a great snare. As the terrors of hell ebb away over time, the world stands by to tell them that it's all nonsense, and urge them to be wise (or, at least, worldly-wise), not risking all they have in this world to obtain they-know-not-what."

"That was surely prevalent in my hometown," Hopeful said. "There was a worldly shame attached to religion there. People tended to be proud and haughty, while religion—and especially pilgrimage—was seen as low and contemptable. Now tell me, how do you describe the third and final step?"

"At this point, what little guilt or fear remains in their hearts becomes odious to them. It may have initially pushed them toward the cross, but upon further reflection, that awakening was only a brief stirring in the midst of a deep slumber. Once again asleep to the wrath of God and the reality of hell, they set about hardening their hearts, once and for all, and all the more."

"It makes me think of a felon," said Hopeful, "quaking before the judge. He seems to be repenting as heartily as any man might, but only the fear of the gallows is on display. He has had no change of heart, or mind, or will. Should the judge give him his liberty, he will be a thief and a rogue still."

"That's a good analogy," Christian said. "So what do you think of my three steps? Is that how a man like Temporary, who has all the outward signs of repentance, might fall?"

"I have no quarrel with what you've said, but it seems rather vague. Let me tell you what I've seen in specific cases, even before my own conversion. After a short time, someone who seems a pilgrim (perhaps a new convert or perhaps a veteran of the Way) begins by letting his thoughts drift away from the remembrance of God, from death, from the judgment to come. And to that end, he begins letting slide his private duties, such as prayer, curbing his lusts, repenting of sin, and keeping watch. He shuns the company of lively and warm Christians and, as a result, grows cold to public duty: attending worship, hearing the Word, godly fellowship, and the like.

"At this point, he is emboldened to point out the weaknesses of other believers, subconsciously laying the groundwork to abandon his own religion; for if every pilgrim is to some small degree a hypocrite, how can pilgrimage be a valid pursuit? With this and other seeds of doubt, he devilishly prepares to throw religion off his back.

"The final nail is that he begins to associate with carnal men and women—not to serve as salt and light to them, but through secret discourses and wicked deeds to be dragged back into the dark. If he can find some others who have professed faith in Christ, and yet do and say the same things, all the better. (And, of course, by that I mean all the worse for his soul.) By this point, he has begun to play with little sins openly and it isn't long before he is fully hardened in his heart and inoculated against the Gospel. Thus, he is launched once again into the gulf of misery. And unless some miracle of grace should prevent it, there he will perish eternally in his own deception."

The pilgrims' hearts were heavy at this, and they studied their feet as they walked, observing a moment of sorrowful silence for the lost souls that had deceived themselves.

It was Hopeful who first noticed the difference in the air. He drew in a deep breath and said, "Do you feel that?"

Christian followed suit and answered, "Yes. The air is no longer thin. In fact, it's rather sweet and pleasant. We are through the Enchanted Land." At this, they both looked ahead, only to see the Narrow Way curving to the right, lined on both sides with tall flowering trees (although it was late summer).

The two of them rushed along the lane, which was both smooth and soft underfoot. Rounding the corner, they stumbled to a halt and dropped to their knees. They were looking out over a breathtaking land. Everywhere their eyes fell, they saw flowers and blossoming vines, fruit-bearing trees and crystal clear springs. The sound of cooing doves filled the air.

"Surely, we have reached the land of milk and honey," Christian said, his voice not much more than a whisper. Hopeful could only nod, his mouth hanging wide.

They'd been sitting there for twenty minutes, gazing out over the lushness of the land, when an older woman happened by, gathering peaches in a large basket.

"Christ be with you, my friends," she said. "Are you just arriving?"

Christian and Hopeful nodded, dumbly.

The woman laughed. "I was the same way when I first saw this place."

"Where are we?" Hopeful managed to ask.

"It is called Beulah, which of course means 'married.' Here the sun shines night and day. And so we are well beyond the influence of the Valley of the Shadow of Death and the reach of the Giant Despair. And do you see that hill? The people of Beulah dwell on the far side of it, which is within sight of the Celestial City."

"Please take us there," Hopeful said, rising to his feet.

"It would be my pleasure. My name is Reverence." She offered each of them a peach and led them further along the way, which passed right through this sweet land. Only as they began to eat did it occur to them that the woman appeared to be from some distant land from the North. As they neared the top of the hill, they were surrounded by many people coming and going, who seemed to be from every nation, tribe, and tongue, and yet Christian and Hopeful could understand them all with no difficulty. Cresting the hill, the brightness of the City—no longer a shining point of light in the distance—was at first overwhelming. Over the course of several minutes, their eyes adjusted so that they no longer ached, but still the pilgrims could not see the City clearly when they gazed upon it.

As their vision returned, they saw Shining Ones casually walking here and there, as if they were men going about their business in the market.

"What is the meaning of this?" Christian asked.

"The Shining Ones commonly walk here," Reverence said, "for this land is on the borders of heaven. Come, follow me."

The three of them passed through a massive celebration in progress, and each was handed a piece of warm bread and a goblet of wine. Before they could ask what they were toasting, a loud cry came forth from out of the city beyond: booming voices, calling out, *Say to the Daughter of Zion, "Behold your salvation comes; behold his reward is with him!"*

And the people of the land replied in unison: "To him who sits on the throne and to the Lamb be blessing and honor and glory and power and might, forever and ever!" Only when they looked at each other did Christian and Hopeful realize they too were joyfully shouting the response.

"What kind of a banquet is this?" Hopeful asked.

"A continual celebration," said Reverence, "for here the covenant between the Bride and the Bridegroom is ever renewed. The Bridegroom rejoices over us, his bride, the sought out and redeemed of the Lord. And we rejoice over Him."

Christian and Hopeful stayed in the midst of the celebration for hours, enjoying the food and drink, but all the more enjoying the conversation, which was only about the glory of the city before them and the goodness of their mighty King.

Although the sun was yet shining, Reverence said, "It is time for me to retire for the night. I have enjoyed this time of jubilant praise, and I have loved getting to know you two brothers, but I need to rest for a while and to spend a few hours in solitary prayer. I believe I will be called to the City in the morning. Would you like to see where you two may lay your heads?"

They agreed that some rest would do them well, and followed Reverence to the north end of the slope, which was covered in tents, each one opening toward the shining city. Reverence brought them to the mouth of one, its flap tied open, and said, "Make yourself at home here. You can rest without fear in this place."

Christian and Hopeful bid Reverence farewell and laid down upon two soft bedrolls, already stretched out. They gave thanks to God for bringing them over the Enchanted Ground and into this marvelous place. And then they closed their eyes. And rather than keep them awake, the warmth of the sun on their face and the shining light of the City itself only served to usher them off to a restorative sleep.

When they awoke, they ate again and spoke with more of the land's inhabitants. Christian and Hopeful soon agreed that welcoming new pilgrims into this land was their favorite pastime. With joy, they brought them over the hill, into the midst of the celebration, and in sight of the Shining City, just as Reverence had done for them.

Some of these were surprised to have made it so far and some were so tired as they reached Beulah that they collapsed into the arms of their fellow-saints. Reverence herself was gone now, having crossed over to the City, and it felt good for Christian and Hopeful to carry on her work.

The pilgrims remained in this land for a season, cherishing every day, but also yearning more and more deeply for their ultimate home. Finally, the morning came when Christian and Hopeful arose, and they both knew they would enter the land that day.

- A Clergy Meeting in Fair Speech -

The five parsons sat around a long wooden table at the front of the pleasant chapel, in the town of Fair Speech. They had all traveled a fair distance to be here, save for the Rev. Two-Tongues, whose church it was.

"I believe we are all present and accounted for, Mr. Two-Tongues," said the Reverend Mr. Smoothman, "albeit hungry and parched." He rolled his eyes. "When I've hosted this group, I've always been sure to provide some fine food and drink for my fellows."

Mr. Two-Tongues snuffed. "You are wrong on the first account, sir. And, therefore, your annoyance is misplaced. We will be joined by a sixth man today. A first-timer. And it being his first visit with us, I asked him to bring the refreshments."

The Reverend Whitewash tipped back in his chair and asked, "Who is this mysterious cleric? Anyone we know?"

Just then, the door opened and in walked a simple man, wearing simple clothing, holding a platter of treacle tarts in one hand and lugging a large jug in the other.

"My friends," the host said standing at the head of the table, "allow me to introduce the Reverend Mr. Unswerving, Parson of the Church of the Cross, a rural congregation in the County of Fidelity." They all greeted him and greedily eyed the platter.

"Have a seat, young man," the host said. "And I'll take those from you."

When he'd settled in, Mr. Unswerving gestured at the Rev. Smoothman and said, "I believe we've met once or twice. You're the parson of the First Church of Destruction, are you not?"

"That I am."

"Good to see you again. And of course I crossed paths with the Reverend Two-Tongues a fortnight ago, while traveling the Narrow Way to visit an elderly parishioner—which is how I learned of your wonderful fellowship. And again, sir, thank you for inviting me. Ministry can be lonely work, and I am most encouraged at the prospect of this brotherhood. And so, I look forward to meeting the rest of you."

"I am the Reverend Mr. License of the United Church of Ease in Vain-Glory."

"I am Mr. Whitewash of the First Church of Morality near Carnal Policy. The lovely church up on the perch, where we pray and sing and do the right thing."

"That's quite the . . . slogan."

"We workshopped it."

"And you sir?"

"I am the Most Reverend Mr. Liberty of Affirmation Chapel in the town of Vanity, home of the famous Vanity Fair."

"Oh, that must be quite the mission field. Well, I am pleased to make your acquaintance, gentlemen, and I truly hope it grows beyond mere acquaintance into true friendship. And please, enjoy the tarts. My wife made them, and she sends her greetings and her prayers for your congregations."

Mr. Two-Tongues opened the jug and peered down into it, sniffing disagreeably. "What is—?"

"Oh, I know that you said to bring wine, but it seemed a bit early in the day for such an indulgence, so I brought milk instead. Besides, there's nothing better than a cup of milk with a sweet treat, am I right?"

They all agreed by way of disappointed grunts.

"Before we begin," Mr. Two-Tongues said, "I move that we

formally welcome our new friend into the group, despite this feeble beverage. All in favor?"

There was a chorus of *ayes* and Two-Tongues announced, "It's unanimous."

Mr. Smoothman took a bite of a tart and said, "Tell me, Mr. Unswerving, how many are there in your congregation?"

"On a good Lord's Day, we gather together about thirty saints. And I visit a dozen or so in their homes. It is a rural congregation, after all."

Mr. License choked. "Thirty? Is that all? How do they even pay you?"

"Sacrificially. We lack for nothing. And the Lord has been kind. My fields have been quite fertile and, with very little work, we're able to supplement our own larder and cellar with enough left over to help the needy around us. Of course, we live in a humble parsonage built by strong, skilled men of the church—long since gone to the City—which stands solid to this day, having been built upon the rock, as the King of Princes taught us."

"Yes, yes," said Mr. Whitewash, "but what are the perks? The benefits? With no local tavern in a rural county, you have nowhere to drink for free. With no courthouse or magistrates, there's no schedule of fees and the like, to pad your purse. Why, half the reason I got into the ministry was the perks. Not to mention the seats of honor and many invitations I receive on account of my office."

"Oh, I don't know about that," said Mr. Two-Tongues. "There are indeed certain frills for the clergy, as there should be. But I more appreciate the camaraderie, the fellowship with my fellow men. You may wonder, Mr. Unswerving, why this table is here, where the pews would normally be. It is because I gather together with good men almost every night of the week, breaking bread, having fellowship and the like."

"I enjoy both," said Mr. License. "In Vain-Glory, there are perks aplenty *and* fellowship. I am welcomed in every home without question and often fed fine food, and I continually find myself the recipient of gifts both physical and intangible—those long nights of conversation, drinking, gaming, and amusement. But you know who truly has it all? Mr. Liberty here! He is not only given preferential treatment, but is the most trusted advisor to their judge, Lord Hate-Good. And he sits on the town council to boot. How many terms has it been, Liberty?"

"Oh, I've lost count," Mr. Liberty said.

Unswerving looked down the line of clergymen and addressed Mr. Smoothman. "It can't be this way in a town like Destruction," he said. "I understand the hostility toward the Gospel message and the church itself is at a fever pitch there. In fact, my people pray for you and your congregation weekly."

Mr. Smoothman shrugged. "It hasn't been so bad. The citizens of Destruction may believe what they want privately, but very few are willing to oppose a man of the cloth in public." He gazed out the window and thought for a moment and added, "Lately, though, it has been a bit more of a struggle . . . ever since that horrid day some time ago, when the crowds filled the streets and the people began to weep and wail, rant and rage about the coming of fiery destruction upon our fair city. Foolish myths, of course. But naturally, there were religious charlatans waiting in the wings to pile fuel on the fire. And that has been a bit of a trial for me all around."

Mr. License agreed. "Yes, we've had a bit of that in our neck of the woods too. And I hear the disquiet has even reached the town of Vanity!"

"You have heard correctly," Mr. Liberty said. "There was recently a bit of unrest in our lovely fair. Two *pilgrims*—"he spat the word as if it tasted bitter on his tongue—"were threatening the peace. One of them was found guilty and put to death, while the other slipped away under cover of darkness. And ever since he left, there has been a small but growing upheaval in our midst—disquieting the minds and spirits of our people. And I fear it will get worse before it gets better."

They all nod solemnly. Mr. Whitewash took a contemplative bite and mused, "We've seen this before. It'll pass."

"I don't understand," Mr. Unswerving said. "People fear the coming of judgment, and are looking for the way of escape. Of deliverance. This all sounds to me like the makings of revival—like many men and women are primed to receive the good news of salvation."

Mr. Smoothman looked down his long nose and said, "Perhaps we're not describing it adequately. Many who were otherwise occupied with their vocations and the distractions and diversions of this life are now asking troubling questions, making frightening proclamations, and—worst of all—they seem to think that we, the clergy, ought to be at the center of all this, affirming their delusions and offering some sort of remedy."

Mr. Two-Tongues wrapped his knuckles against the table. "And let's not forget, I've got four men of my congregation on pilgrimage right now! And two left from Vain-Glory not a month ago. It's not as if we are against religious pursuits!"

Mr. Unswerving looked around at these ministers, confused. "But the Gospel is the message of salvation from the wrath to come. That is our calling as ministers! How can this spreading disquiet, as you call it, be seen as anything but an opportunity for Gospel ministry? A wide-open door given by God himself?"

Mr. License looked sternly upon the newcomer and said, "I have better things to do than entertain the hysterical ramblings of religious quacks."

"Agreed," Mr. Whitewash said. "The whole thing is crackers. The best we can do—the best response on our part—would be to gently correct those who are dabbling in such things, and sternly rebuke the ringleaders."

"That is easier said than done," said Mr. Smoothman. "I'm sure you've all heard of this man, Christian, the author of this recent chaos. Well, he originated in my congregation, I'm not so proud to say, and he was not at all the kind of man you'd think.

He was a wallflower. Barely made a peep in the service, filled his pew each and every Sunday. Never once was he fined for missing the service. He'd shake my hand on the way out of the meetinghouse with an absentminded, 'Wonderful sermon, Parson.' Never bothered me during the week, never asked a single vexing question . . . until the day someone infected him with these dangerous ideas. Like a fever passed from one man to the next. And from that day on, rebuke as I might, I could do nothing to shake him of his delusions or stop the spread of the contagion."

"Christian?" Mr. Liberty said, looking more than a little ill. "That's the man who escaped from our prison."

"He's trouble," said Mr. Smoothman. "Troubled, I think."

Mr. Unswerving threw his hands in the air and shouted, "What is it that you men teach? What do you proclaim if not that we are all dead in our sins and trespasses, our only hope resting in Christ himself—in his death and his resurrection on our behalf? Do you not warn your people of the wrath that is surely coming upon the earth?"

They all gaped at him in pure shock, as if he had transformed into a bullfrog and was now hopping up and down, croaking in his chair. Finally, Mr. Two-Tongues shook his head, sadly and said, "Oh, not you too, Mr. Unswerving."

"You men set out to ease the itching ears of your people so that you might reap some meager temporal rewards, the puny perks of this world. But in doing so you are passing up eternal rewards and storing up for yourselves wrath against the Day of Wrath."

Mr. License pushed another pastry into his mouth and spoke around the massive bite. "I move that we expel Mr. Unswerving from our group, post haste." The words emerge in a cloud of powdered sugar.

"Second," said Mr. Smoothman.

"All in favor," prompted Mr. Two-Tongues.

Another chorus of *ayes*.

"Opposed?" He paused a moment and said, "Are you abstaining, Mr. Liberty?" The parson shrugged. "Well, it matters not. The *ayes* have it and the expulsion carries." Mr. Two-Tongues dragged the simple clay dish, still half-full of tarts, to himself. "We will keep the rest of these treats as your dues paid in full. But you, sir, must leave these premises at once. And take your *milk* with you."

Mr. Unswerving hoisted the jug, said goodbye, and made his way out into the churchyard. He was only a dozen steps from the door when a man came rushing out after him.

"Ah, Mr. Liberty. I thought you might join me."

"You did? Why?"

Unswerving smiled. "You tell me."

The Most Reverend Mr. Liberty bit his lip in thought for a moment and, when he opened his mouth, the words came pouring out. "I too have been feeling this sense of unease in my spirit . . . ever since watching that pilgrim, Faithful, perish in the flames. I could have sworn I saw him walk out of that fire, away from his body, and climb aboard a fiery chariot, like that of the prophet in the Holy Book. I have had no peace of mind since then. I haven't been able to sleep! When I close my eyes at night, a question continually echoes through my mind . . . "

Mr. Unswerving nodded. *"What must I do to be saved?"*

"Yes! And I have no answer, even as more of my parishioners are posing this same question, week after week. And the growing weight of all this seems to have somehow manifested itself on my person."

Mr. Unswerving reached out and rested his hand on the man's burden, which had grown larger even since the meeting had begun."

"I saw this the moment I laid eyes on you, sir. Tell me, Mr. Liberty, would you like to know how to be relieved of it? Where you can receive *true* liberty?"

"More than anything."

"Then come with me. I'll walk with you, all the way to the Wicket Gate."

Destination

gnorance spent only a few hours in Beulah land before moving on. Just as he preferred to travel alone, he did not enjoy being in the midst of large groups of people, especially those caught up in a religious fervor. Instead, he made his way south and east, through pleasant grasslands, until he arrived at an imposing river—as far as he could tell, the final obstacle between himself and the Celestial City.

He camped there for two nights, until the food he'd nicked from the big party in Beulah ran out. Then Ignorance followed the river south, downstream and away from Beelzebub's land.

He was expecting to come across a bridge at some point. Perhaps one made of crystal, or maybe a supernatural span of prismatic light. But he came upon nothing of the sort, and soon found himself back at the Narrow Way, which seemed to dead-end at the river, much to his surprise.

Ignorance continued south along the river's edge, the Narrow Way now at his back, hoping to come across some other way to ford it. Soon, though, twilight was upon him. He was just about to give up and bed down for the night when he happened upon a small shack, and a man sitting inside of it, polishing a long wooden oar.

"Excuse me sir," Ignorance said, waving to the man. "I'm looking for a way across this river."

The man glanced up, eyes twinkling. "Are you now?"

"Yes, I'm very near the end of an incredible adventure and now find myself facing this seemingly impassable—I mean, you've got a boat, right? That's why you're waxing that oar?"

The man smirked. "It's a ferry, but folks have been known to call it a boat." He put down the oar and reached out his hand. "Name's Vain Hope and yes, gettin' people across that river is how I make my living. In fact, just twenty years of workin' as a ferryman has paid for *alllll* this." He gestured at the shack around him and chuckled to himself.

"Well, can you get me over safely?" Ignorance asked.

"If you can pay, I'll see you across."

"Have you ever lost anyone?"

Vain Hope snuffed and puffed out his chest. "Do you see me standin' here?"

Ignorance just blinked at him.

"Son, I haven't lost a passenger, a trunk of treasure, or a sack lunch in all my time at the helm. If anyone or anything I was carryin' went over the side, I'd go in over after it. And believe me, I've faced it all. High winds, horizontal rain, lightning and thunder, doesn't matter—I can make landfall and get you disembarked at my dock on the other side without a wasted foot of movement. In fact, I doubt there's any weather or any cargo in the world that could cause me to miss my mark, much less capsize."

Ignorance grinned and nodded. "That's what I like to hear. How much do you charge?"

"How much you got?"

Ignorance dumped his purse into his hand, looked down at the five coins. Then up at Vain Hope.

"Well, what do you know?" the ferryman said. "That's exactly what I charge. And lucky for you, there's no need for money where you're headed."

Ignorance handed over his last coins. "When do we leave?"

"First thing in the morning."

Ignorance was surprised at how well he slept that night. Vain-Hope's confidence and experience seemed to trump even the anxiety of soon standing before the King of Kings. They both rose early the next morning, and shared a hearty breakfast of porridge and salted herring. They then boarded Vain-Hope's simple ferry and began the voyage.

The journey was quite easy with such a skilled oarsman directing the way, and Ignorance felt sorry for the many people he saw struggling to cross the river on foot. He saw men and women disappearing beneath the surface, only to come back up a moment later, sputtering, arms flailing. He thought of offering aid to some of them, but decided this would be foolish. After all, if he let one person aboard, they might soon find themselves overrun and tipping under the weight of many. Besides, Ignorance had paid for this ride and these others had not.

"I knew some men like these," Ignorance said with a sad chuckle. "They thought they were so wise and so righteous as they walked along the path. But look at them all now." Vain-Hope chuckled as well, and winked at his fare.

True to his word, the ferryman docked on the far side of the river, having navigated a perfectly straight line across the rapids. He wished Ignorance well and shoved off once again, reversing course.

Ignorance ran up the hill before him, jostling past men and angels alike, until he was at the enormous City gate, its gold glimmering in the light. He was just a bit offended when it was not thrown wide at his very presence, but he swallowed his pride and knocked three times upon it.

Two men he did not recognize peered down at him from atop the high wall on either side of the gate. "Where do you come from?" one of them asked. "And where are you going?"

Ignorance laughed. "You must be joking! I come from the town of Conceit, and my destination is just the other side of this gate, if you will but open it."

The other man, whose stern face glowed like a lantern, prompted, "And that destination is . . . ?"

"Why, the King himself! He is my destination!" Ignorance laughed again. "If only he could hear you now. I mean, I've only *eaten and drunk in his presence,* and he has taught in our streets. Trust me, fellows, he knows me."

"Do you have a certificate of entry, which we might send on to the holy throne?"

"Oh, ummm . . . " Ignorance fumbled about in his jacket and satchel. "I think I, uh . . . no, I do not have one. Just tell him Ignorance is at the gate. "

The men summoned a Shining One, who stood twice as tall as they did. From his hip hung a massive sword, the sheath of which glowed orange and red from the fiery weapon it contained.

The man with the glowing face gestured down at Ignorance and said, "This one has no certificate, but is trying to invoke some right to enter the King's presence."

"I can hear you down here," Ignorance called up. "And I won't need to enter his presence. When the King hears that I am at his gate, *he* will come down to me! You'll see. . . "

The Shining One departed with the message and Ignorance plopped down on the ground, his back against the gate. He sat and watched the foot traffic of the place and, before long, his own vain hope began to flag, as he saw pilgrim after pilgrim present a rolled document to the attendants at the gate, and gain entry immediately afterward.

He was in the midst of formulating an eloquent case for his own righteousness when two Shining Ones approached him, grabbed him up roughly, and bound him hand and foot. Spreading their mighty wings, they carried him up into the air, away from the gate and the City.

"Where are you taking me?" Ignorance demanded. "Don't you know who I am?"

"We do, indeed," came the answer. "But our King tells us he never knew you, and we have been instructed to take you to the door in the side of the mountain, which opens a byway to hell."

"But I was at the heavenly gates," Ignorance protested. "I was speaking highly of your King to the very last! How can—"

"Not all who speak highly of him belong to our King. And yes, you stood boldly at the City's entrance, but there is a way to hell from the gate of Heaven, just as sure as there is from the City of Destruction."

Christian and Hopeful were beyond joyful as they followed the Narrow Way through the easternmost parts of Beulah. Far from the point of light they once saw in the distance, the gleaming

City now dominated their field of vision, shining with its own brightness, and reflecting the sun upon its many surfaces of pure gold.

As they walked, the two pilgrims took turns looking through the device Sincere had given them. Through it they could make out massive columns of pearl, many domes and spires of gold, and precious stones embedded everywhere. And the beams shining back at them were not only reflected natural light; rather, the majesty of their Great King shone through the whole place.

It was mid-morning, while looking through the darkened glass, that Christian began to feel sick. His vision began to swim and his knees grew weak. It was all he could do to push the glass into Hopeful's hands and lower himself roughly to the earth, lest he fall.

"Are you all right, brother?" Hopeful asked.

"My heart aches," Christian said. "I believe I am lovesick. Overcome with desire. I don't think I can bear it much longer."

"There is only one cure for that," Hopeful said. "We keep on moving, don't we?" He reached down and took Christian's hand, but as he helped his brother to his feet, a wave of the same washed over Hopeful and he doubled over, the two pilgrims holding each other up.

"If you see my beloved—" Hopeful said.

"—tell him I am sick with love," said Christian.

And, leaning on each other, they hobbled on, afraid to look through the glass any more, lest they exacerbate their symptoms. Over the course of several hours, though, they were strengthened, bit by bit, until they were able to bear their sickness well enough to travel once again at full speed, the longing now propelling them forward.

The Narrow Way passed through orchards and vineyards and gardens, all of whose gates opened up to the highway. It was in the midst of these that they happened upon a man, standing in the path with a spade in his hand.

Christian could see that he was the gardener, and tried to pass him by with only the briefest of hellos, but Hopeful came to a stop and asked, "Sir, whose vineyards and gardens are these? They're lovely!"

"They belong to the King," the gardener answered. "They have been planted here for his own pleasure and for the refreshment of his pilgrims." He took a few steps down a row of grapes and beckoned the pilgrims to follow, saying, "Come, see."

At the gardener's invitation, they ate until they were satisfied, marveling at the fulness of the flavor and the crispness of the fruit. The gardener then showed them the King's walkways and the arbor where he delighted to be.

"I have some things to tend to," the Gardener said, as they sat in the midst of soft ground and verdant trees. "But feel free to tarry here and rest for a while. Some pilgrims find that they are still weary from their sleepless days on the Enchanted Ground, and believe me, there is no truer rest to be had this side of the City than right here."

The two of them stretched out and closed their eyes.

Before he knew it, Christian was waking up from a deeply refreshing nap. A few feet away, Hopeful still slept, talking in his sleep, a serene smile on his face. Christian could not make out all that he said, but here and there he picked up words like *Paradise*, *Eternity*, and *Sabbath Rest*.

Christian laughed to himself, and the sound roused Hopeful, who rubbed his eyes and sat up. "What's so funny?"

"You were talking in your sleep," Christian said. "I've never known you to do that the whole time we've traveled together."

"So were you," Hopeful laughed. "In fact, I was kept awake for at least ten minutes at the sound of your sleep-talking."

"It is the nature of the grapes of these vineyards," said the gardener, coming back into the arbor. "They go down so sweetly as to cause sleeping lips to speak. You have been dreaming for hours about untold pleasures and beauty. And you men are in an unusual position. Most awaken from pleasant dreams only be disappointed that they were but dreams. However, you two can rise now, and go live them out."

At this, the pilgrims rose, stretched their limbs, and thanked the gardener profusely, before running back down the walk to the Narrow Way. Again, they took turns peering through the glass at the grandeur of the place they were approaching.

Before long they met two men whose faces and clothes alike shined like gold. These men asked the pilgrims where they had come from and where they were going, where they had lodged, what dangers they had faced and what comforts they had enjoyed.

When they had related the main events of their pilgrimage thus far, the older of the two shining men said, "You are very near your goal, and you will achieve it soon—if you overcome to the end. You have but two more difficulties to meet with, and then you are in the City."

"Would you men go with us?" Hopeful asked.

"We will accompany you," the Shining One answered, "But you must obtain it through your own faith."

The four of them walked together, and soon they crested a small hill and found themselves looking out at a great rushing river, which stood between them and the Celestial City.

Christian and Hopeful stood speechless, standing where the Narrow Way came to an end, and watching the river rage for a few minutes, before Christian asked, "Is there a bridge?"

"There is not. You must go through, or you cannot come to the gate."

Christian shook his head. "No. No, there must be some other way to get there."

"Yes, there is," said the Shining One, "but only two men have ever walked that path since the foundation of the world. And none shall do so again until the last trumpet sounds."

"It's okay," Hopeful said, to himself as much as to Christian. "We can just pass through it. We can do it."

Christian's eyes darted frantically this way and that. "No. It's too deep. It's too fast." His breath was getting away from him. "There must be some other way. You're just waiting to see how we respond, aren't you? This is a test. It's a test! And if we say the right thing or *do* the right thing, you'll show us how we might be whisked up to the King's presence without enduring this terrible trial."

"I assure you," the Shining One said, "it is no trick. You must pass through."

"Then it's not really as deep as it seems. Right? It's an illusion to test our faith. Tell me, how—how deep is it?"

"You will find the water deeper or shallower, depending on the strength of your faith in the King of this place."

Hopeful placed his hand on Christian's shoulder and looked him square in the eye. "Brother, you have been my guide and my rock from the chaotic debauchery of my hometown, all the way to where we now stand, at the cusp of our heavenly home. Your faith in our King has helped me to trust in him when I would have wavered or even fallen away. I have emulated you, as you emulate our Lord. Now let me return the favor and strengthen you. Christian, the same God who brought the Israelites through the Red Sea and the Jordan, who bid Peter walk upon the waves, now calls us to pass through these waters before us. We have nothing to lose and everything to gain. Christian, I am going into that water now, but I do not want to go alone. Come with me."

Christian nodded firmly and embraced his brother.

Together, they walked down to the bank and waded in. Christian immediately began to sink. At first, he thought his armor might be to blame, but he could even now feel that it was buoyant—the only thing pulling him back up. Rather, it was his person that was dragging him down to the bottom, like a rock.

"Hopeful! Help!" he cried out. "The billows go over me! I am undone!" He was sputtering as he spoke, struggling to lift his face above water.

"Take heart," Hopeful said. "I feel the bottom. It is good and solid."

"It is so deep! So—" Christian spat through a lapping wave.

"It is hopeless! The sorrows of death surround me and drag me to the depths! I will never see the City!"

As he spoke those words, a great darkness encompassed Christian, and a frigid horror washed over him. In that moment, the light from the City seemed entirely extinguished. He tried to think back to the comforts and promises of his pilgrimage, but he could only remember his sins—both before he began his journey and those along the way. He saw them passing before him: words of anger at his young sons, a favorable error overlooked on his ledger sheets, jealousy towards both Faithful and Hopeful, a glance of lust at Lady Daring on the road.

Christian's heart felt cold, the lovesickness displaced now by a gripping fear. He knew that if he perished here in this river, he would never enter into that blessed gate. And he knew this was what he deserved.

But that was not the worst of it. Christian felt hands grip him around the ankles and jerk him down into the rushing river. Once beneath the surface, he saw visions of evil spirits, goblins, and phantoms—all reaching for him with outstretched hands and jagged claws. And behind them all, he saw Apollyon, grinning at him triumphantly, once again circling his prey. Lower and lower the pilgrim went, toward the river bottom, his lungs burning, screaming for air.

Then a strong hand grabbed his wrist from above and he felt Hopeful pulling him upward. His face broke the surface just long enough to steal a ragged breath before the undertow and the creatures below drew him back down. Christian disappeared into the murky depths for what seemed like minutes, before his friend managed to pull him once again above the water. By the look on Hopeful's face, Christian knew he must be a frightful sight: half-dead and devoid of all hope.

This continued for some time. Whenever he managed to keep Christian's head above water for a moment, Hopeful did his best to comfort him. "Brother," he said, "I see the gate! It's beautiful! And men standing by to receive us! Do not lose hope!"

"It's all for you," Christian mumbled. "Not for me. As long as I've known you, you've been . . . you've been hopeful."

"So have you!" Hopeful shouted.

"No, brother. If he wanted me to make it, he would come to my aid right now. But instead, he draws me into a snare and leaves me here to perish."

Hopeful hoisted Christian up onto his own back, wrapping his brother's limp arms around his neck. "Christian, the troubles and terrors you undergo in these waters are no sign that God has forsaken you! Remember our Lord promised he would *never* leave you nor forsake you! Rather, he is testing you, to see whether you will call to mind all his goodness, the gifts you have received, and the forgiveness of sins . . . and cling to him in your hour of distress! Christian, cling to him!"

Hopeful took another step and felt something beneath the surface pulling down on Christian so hard that it seemed the poor man might be torn in two. A moment later, he slipped off Hopeful's back, and the younger pilgrim again had to fight to keep his fellow-pilgrim from disappearing.

"Take heart," Hopeful yelled, "for Jesus Christ makes you whole!"

"I see him!" Christian cried. "I see him and I hear him! He is telling me, *When you pass through the waters, I will be with you. And when you pass through rivers, they will not sweep you away!*"

"Oh, thank God," Hopeful whispered.

"Shhh!" Christian hissed. "Do you hear that?"

"Hear what?"

"Exactly. The enemy is still as a stone." Christian stood and found the water rising only to his waist, just as it did on Hopeful. As they neared the far bank, they began to sing again the song he and Faithful had sung in the dungeon at Vanity Fair. And they were singing it still as they emerged from the river on the same side as the City.

There they came face to face with the two Shining Ones who had accompanied them to the river's edge. One of them reached out his hand to help them from the water, and said, "We are ministering spirits, sent forth to aid the heirs of salvation."

Christian felt a flood of relief as he took a step onto dry land. And then he felt his sword fall away from his hip, followed by the shield and greaves. And he smiled at this. There was no need to fight here. No enemies about. One by one, each of these outward things either fell away or was drawn into his inmost being, just as Promise had been.

Glancing at his brother, he saw that Hopeful's mortal garments had likewise come off into the river. They stood, without shame, basking in the warm light emanating from the city, until the Shining Ones instructed them to approach the gate.

Now you should note that the city stood upon a mighty hill, and yet our pilgrims ascended it quickly, with ease, the Shining Ones leading them by their arms. The foundation of the city itself was far above the clouds. As they passed through them, the pilgrims could only think once again of the Israelites passing through the Red Sea, by the power of the Highest King.

Further yet they ascended, through the Region of the Air. Their conversation continued, centered around the comfort they now had, having safely traversed the river, and the glory that lay before them. The Shining Ones spoke sweetly, doing their best to describe the inexpressible glory of Mount Zion, the innumerable company of angels, and the spirits of just men and women, made perfect.

"In the Paradise of God," one of the Shining Ones said, "you will see the Tree of Life and eat of its never-fading fruit. And you will walk and talk with the King for all eternity."

"Yes," said the other, "and there you shall see things you could never have conceived in the lower region, upon the earth. And you will never again see or feel sorrow or sickness or suffering or death. For the former things are passed away."

"What will we do there?" Hopeful asked, his voice quavering with joy and anticipation.

"There you will receive your reward: comfort for all your toil, joy for all your sorrow, the fruit of all your prayers and tears and suffering for the King, along the way. There you will wear crowns of gold, which you will delight to throw at the Savior's feet, for your greatest delight will be to enjoy perpetual vision of the Holy One."

"And there we will serve him still?" Christian asked.

"Yes," said the other Shining One, "continually, and with shouts of praise and thanksgiving. You who desired to serve him in the world, even with great difficulty and infirm flesh, will serve him there with ease and happiness forever, alongside friends and companions who have gone before you! And you will have the honor of welcoming those who come after you."

"I hadn't even thought of that," Hopeful said, looking to Christian. "We both loved welcoming pilgrims into Beulah. How much more joyful to welcome them into Paradise itself?"

The Shining One answered, "And a greater joy yet: when the trumpet sounds, you will accompany the King upon the wings of the wind, and when he sits on the throne of judgment, you shall sit with him, as he passes sentence upon rebellious angels and men—his enemies and yours. And when his holy City swallows up the entire earth, you shall be ever with him."

They were now drawing toward the gate, and a company of the heavenly army came to meet them there.

Their heavenly guide announced, "These have loved our Lord when they were in the world. They left everything for his holy name, and we were sent to fetch them to stand before their Redeemer and receive their reward."

The warriors responded with one voice: "Blessed are those who are invited to the marriage supper of the Lamb!"

The heavenly host parted and four of the King's trumpeters, clothed in gleaming white, came forth, blasting powerful, melodious songs of victory and praise, so loud that the heavens themselves echoed back the joyful noise.

They saluted Christian and Hopeful, saying, "Ten thousand welcomes from the Celestial City, to which we now escort you."

Quickly and silently, the heavenly host encompassed them, bringing them further into the upper regions, all the while praising the King.

And then, in a moment, the clouds all burned away, and the pilgrims were looking straight into heaven itself. Christian felt a moment of panic, as he realized he'd left his darkened glass behind, in the river. But then, he no longer needed it, for he and Hopeful were able to see the brightness of the City without lens or instrument and its light did not make them so much as squint or shield their eyes. Rather, it seemed to open them up all the more to every bit of Truth and Glory and Holiness found in their King, all of which permeated every inch of this place. The pilgrims felt the remnants of their sin natures burned away. The sensation was warm and lovely and ten thousand times more satisfying than any earthly gratification could have ever been.

"Listen to those bells," Hopeful said. Only when he looked at Christian and saw the tears of joy streaming down his face did he realize that he, too, was weeping for happiness and monumental relief.

"I think they're ringing," Christian said, "to welcome us."

"Indeed they are," declared the captain of the host.

"I keep thinking of the Palace Beautiful," Christian said. "The brief moments there when I felt a foretaste of this place. Glimpses and whiffs of the sweetness and the glory and the peace—but always knowing that it was fleeting there, that the Pilgrim Road would bring us back into danger and toil and stretches of darkness. But now . . . "

"But now," the captain said, "you will forever dwell in his company, beyond the reach of all evils."

As they were now less than a bowshot from the gate, the pilgrims could read the inscription above it, in letters of gold: "Blessed are those who wash their robes, that they may have the right to the Tree of Life, and they may enter the city by this gate." For just a moment, Christian thought of Atheist, who had mockingly asked what was written here. If only he could see it, or if Christian could even go back and tell him—

"He still would not believe," said the captain. "He has the Word and the testimony of all creation, and still he believes not. Even if a man were to rise from the dead and warn him, he would only harden his heart all the more. Do not turn your eyes back down to earth, good pilgrims, but up to the top of that gate."

They obeyed, and there they saw Moses and Elijah gazing down at them.

The captain called with a loud voice, "These pilgrims are come from Destruction and Vanity, for the love of our King."

"Do you have certificates?" Elijah asked.

They both provided the scrolls they'd been given at the Place of Deliverance, and these were taken into the City, to be verified by the King Himself. While they waited, Christian and Hopeful felt nothing but anticipation.

"It's odd," Christian said. "The last time I found myself without that scroll, I was beside myself with anxiety. Now, as the all-seeing eye of our King examines it, I feel only comfort and excitement at what is to come."

Hopeful grinned. "As do I, Christian. As do I."

A voice from above announced, "The King has commanded us to open the gate and invite you in."

As the full glory of the place hit the pilgrims, they felt themselves transfigured, and dressed with raiment that shined like gold.

Christian turned to Hopeful and wrapped his arms around his brother's neck. "Thank you," he said. "Thank you for seeing me safely to this place, my friend."

"And the same to you," Hopeful answered, through tears. "But I see another here, whom we both need to thank." Hopeful broke off the embrace and pointed up to a man, smiling down at them from the top of a golden staircase, the water standing in his eyes.

"Faithful!" Christian cried, running with a speed and lightness he had never known, until he practically tackled his friend. A second later, Hopeful collided with them both, laughing.

"We have much catching up to do," Faithful said. "But first, there's someone who wants to see you."

Hopeful's hand went to his mouth. "Is it—?"

"Yes. And he is far greater, far more loving, far more holy, far more powerful than we ever dared to dream. It is even somehow an understatement to say that he infinitely surpasses all of our hopes and expectations."

The three pilgrims entered the City proper, which shone like the sun itself, for the sun was no longer visible. They walked along a wide and easy road, paved with gold, passing many men and women with crowns on their heads and palms in their hands, all singing praises to the King. The two new arrivals and their brother pilgrim joined in the song, the words coming naturally to their lips:

> *Holy, holy, holy is the Lord God Almighty,*
> *Who was and is and is to come!*
> *Heaven and earth are full of his glory!*

Faithful brought them up to a place where fantastical creatures floated in the air, chanting the same blessed words the crowds were singing. *Holy! Holy! Holy!* These creatures were covered with blinking eyes and beating wings and the pilgrims would have gawked at them for ages, save for the fact that these heavenly beings surrounded the throne of the King.

The moment they entered his presence, everything else faded to nothing.

The King looked down at his pilgrims with pure, undefiled love, and said,

"Christian, Hopeful . . . I am so happy to see you."